Bottle Park

Joseph J. Bradley

Black Rose Writing
www.blackrosewriting.com

The final approval for this literary material is granted by the author.

First printing

ISBN: 978-1-61296-272-6
PUBLISHED BY BLACK ROSE WRITING
www.blackrosewriting.com

Printed in the United States of America

Bottle Park is printed in Cambria

For Yvonne:

A kind, intelligent, and thoughtful soul, who inspires me every day.
Since the first fateful day we connected, life has been miraculous.
With matching scars we glide through life together,
as best friends, lovers, and husband and wife.

ACKNOWLEDGEMENTS

I would like to thank my editor Amy Barry.

Also Dr. John Kelsey, and Miriam Gonzalez for their help in editing this story.

Thanks to Kathy Bradley, Mike Bradley, Lynn Lovechio, Kim Connors, Anthony Bradley, Marty Ambrose, Andrew Spiropolous, Dr. Patrick DeFrancesco, Tom Percoski, Eric Carter, Mike Fischer, and Dawn Blood for all the love and support they have given me.

And to my children: Ryan, Taylor, and Sarah Bradley. Finally, a huge thanks my wonderful wife Yvonne.

AUTHOR'S NOTE

It is not my intention to condemn the Catholic Church or imply that the violation of innocent children is commonplace within the church. It is my belief that the vast majority of priests are kind, loving, and God fearing men. I was raised a Catholic, and I believe in God, and that we all must pay for our deeds. However I am a realist, and I do know there are some that have, and continue to use the power of the cloth to commit incomprehensible acts against children. My story is for those children.

This story is based on true events.

Bottle Park

Beware of the false prophets,
who come to you in sheep's clothing,
but inwardly are ravenous wolves.

~Matthew Chapter 7, Verse 15

CHAPTER 1

1972

Stephen and Michael carefully negotiated the bank of the shallow, murky water of Devil's Pond. Once occupied by ducks and Canada geese, the drink, now cluttered with trash and floating debris, had become an eyesore to the community. Michael picked up a piece of broken glass and briefly lost his footing, stumbling and nearly twisting his ankle. He was the taller than Michael, a bit lanky for twelve, which sometimes made him move about awkwardly.

"How about this one?" he displayed a triangle-shaped piece.

"Let me see it." Stephen took it, flirting with the edge. "No good," he said, chucking it into the pond, and they continued their search for the perfect tool. There was no shortage to choose from as the bank was like a sea of broken glass. Stephen dug up a piece from the dirt that was embedded like a tick's head. It was faded green, like an infant emerald, and he surmised it was the remnants of a imported beer bottle.

"This one will work perfectly," he said, running his finger along the sharp, pointed edge. Squatting near the basin, Stephen cleaned it off with his shirt tail, and they briefly looked at each other before proceeding.

"Shouldn't we s-sterilize it first?" Michael asked.

"You got matches?"

Michael scratched his head, "nah."

"That's what I thought. Sterilizin is for pansies anyway."

Michael threw a stone into the pond and watched a small circle magnify until it faded into a smooth pane.

"My Uncle said this is called Devil's Pond because a long time ago four c-catholic boys about eleven fell through the ice as they wuz skatin. He said they wuz pulled to the bottom by the Devil cuz they were followers of Jesus."

Staring into the water, Michael imagined a greenish-black hand with long veiny fingers and rotting nails emerging from the surface of the water.

"All four died, and sometimes at night, you can hear their ghosts cryin out for help."

"Bullshit." Stephen dismissed his story as he toyed with his new tool. "You're uncle is a goddamn drunk."

Michael knew he had a point, remembering the flask of whiskey Uncle Paul carried in his back pocket, but he did enjoy his drunken stories.

"It's called Devils Pond cuz this park has good and evil and both are fightin for power. The north end, where the church is at, is the good part cuz it faces heaven."

Twisting his body, he pointed toward the south holding a perfect pose; attempting to imitate his favorite hero, Achilles, whom he had been reading about the night before, for a school project.

"The evil side of the park is here, at the opposite end. This side faces the south and is closer to hell, and that's why it's called Devils Pond."

Michael thought about what his best friend said, and it made perfect sense. He found Stephen to be right most of the time; he was the smartest friend he ever had, smarter than most grown-ups.

Stretching out from south to north, the long, narrow park sat undisturbed, as the city of Middleborough was built around it in the mid 1700's, and settlers made New England their new home. At the northern point of the landscape, Saint Ann's Cathedral stood erect under a sixteen- foot silver cross that faced north. Devil's Pond was man made and considered by many to be nothing more than a large puddle that flooded the southern base. A five-foot wide path spanned the length of the park from the church to the pond and through the center cut a shorter path as if a concrete cross had been dropped from the sky by a Higher Power. This allowed for quiet strolls and drunken rampages, depending on the time of day. Over the years, the park had fallen dark with neglect and disrespect, only to be supplanted by tall standing silhouettes of oaks, pines, and maples, and two Veteran Memorials built for those who perished during the Second World War and Korea.

It was a season's debut as a battalion of blackbirds and robins mustered along hundreds of wooden tentacles reaching out to the sky, their songs carrying the morning.

Stephen displayed his shiny green tool.

"I'll go first."

Without hesitation, Stephen peeled back his green-and-white flannel shirt sleeve, placed the point against his forearm, and began cutting into his flesh. As the blood began to peek out, he dabbed it with a white handkerchief before continuing on with his artistic mutilation. Once finished, he placed the cloth over the wound, applying direct pressure.

"Your turn now," he said, handing the blood-stained glass to Michael, observing his friends trembling hand as he retrieved the instrument. "It doesn't hurt, really," Stephen lied.

Michael thought about how his mother was going to react when she saw his arm. The last time he did something stupid-she took his guitar away for a month, after he came home displaying his new haircut; a green Mohawk.

He placed the business-edge against his left forearm and slowly began cutting, trying to avoid as much pain as possible. Each cut seemed to last an eternity, and he squinted and clenched his teeth with every stroke.

Stephen handed Michael the handkerchief and he repeated what he watched his mentor do a few minutes earlier. When finished, he applied pressure as Stephen had instructed.

"Hold your arm next to mine." Michael did as he was told.

As they looked down at the crosses carved into their arms, they had very different reactions. Michael thought it was unattractive and much too permanent. Stephen, however, felt like a young warrior during the Crusades. His cross was wider and deeper than Michael's, and would scar much better, yet he didn't boast, because his pride was realized by his ability to convince

Michael to take part in the bloody ritual.

Although the two boys worshiped the symbol, they really didn't understand the true meaning of Christianity. Many of the hard guys in the neighborhood had crosses tattooed on their arms, necks, and chests, and to them, it was a symbol of toughness, not devotion.

"Now it's time to become blood brothers," Stephen said as he took the glass and quickly ran it across his palm, opening up the skin.

He winced at the sting, but held his composure. Michael did the same, but made a painful-sounding grunt and his stomach grew nauseated.

Stephen noticed that his comrade had turned pale and he thought it was probably from seeing his own blood. He reached out to Michael offering his hand, and Michael took it. As they slowly ground their cuts together, mixing blood, Stephen recited his oath.

"I vow that I will be your blood brother until I take my last breath. Our secrets, I will never tell to anyone, or my soul will burn in Hell."

Michael repeated the vow, and they released hands.

"Blood brothers forever," Stephen said as he tossed the spent tool into the water.

A breeze kicked up, cooling their backs as they sat watching the object that bound them together descend below the surface of Devil's Pond.

CHAPTER 2

As parishioners began to enter the cathedral, many stopped in the lobby to dab their fingers into the cool holy water, following with a gesture of the cross. The parish deacon stood at the entrance greeting people with a pasted-on smile, handing out the daily readings. Wearing their Sunday best, people slowly treaded the center aisle, and with the exception of the very young and old, stopped in the aisle, briefly kneeling toward the altar, and once again making the sign of the cross before moving into the pew they selected as their temporary sanctuary.

In his chamber, Father LaPage was draping a teal stole over his white alb. He then laid himself with a large gold cross, resting it in the center of his chest. Gathering his bible and hymn book, he smiled at Robby Anderson as he entered the chamber. A sophomore altar boy, twelve years of age, Robby was donning a black cassock covered with a white surplice. He felt proud on Sundays as he stood at the altar assisting the priest with Mass. Robby was an average boy with red hair and a face doused with freckles. His beaming smile displayed long white teeth that overlapped in the front. Born with DDH (Developmental Dysplasia of the Hip) and an underdeveloped joint, Robby had a slight limp causing him to move about shy of elegance. To compensate for his disability, Robby worked harder than most boys his age on the court and field, and, it paid off.

"Robby, is the altar prepared?"

"Yes, Father, except for the wine."

"Please see to it."

"Yes, Father."

He fetched a heavy gold chalice from the cabinet and covered it with a square pall and draped it with a white corporal that would later be used to wipe the inside of the chalice. Placing it on a gold tray, along with a gold carafe of cheap red wine and a matching plate for the offering of bread, he exited the chamber.

Along with Scott Wray, the apprentice altar boy, Robby stood at the altar waiting as the organist fingered "Der Gerechte Kommt Um," a motet by Bach that was beginning to grow on him. The Mass at ten-thirty was usually standing room only, but this Sunday there were a few seats remaining in the back. The Ionic columns and towering cone-shaped ceiling added to the enormity of the cathedral. Large stained-glass windows told stories of Jesus and his disciples, and flowed into beveled cedar that stretched upward toward the summit. The scent of lavender lingered from candles positioned in perfect order surrounding the pews. It was truly a magnificent place: a place of serenity and forgiveness.

In the third row, seated next to his younger brother, Jonathan, and situated in between his mother and father, Michael McNulty sat with his head down as the Priest stepped up to the altar. Michael's bangs hung down covering his bored expression. Across the aisle, a few rows back, Tim and Betty Anderson sat with their older son, Tommy, watching LaPage as he began reading from the Good Book. Robby was standing to the priest's rear left; fixed and barely moving except to occasionally shift his weight from one foot to the other. He listened to the story of Abraham and Isaac and how God had asked Abraham to sacrifice his only son to prove his love and devotion for Him. Robby wondered if he would ever be tested by God in the days or years to come.

As most members of Saint Anne's, Robby enjoyed a short Mass that only lasted about fifty minutes. After the priest finished his sermon, people began moving out of doors, and Robby followed them to his awaiting family.

"You looked so handsome up there," his mother said as she pulled him in for a hug. He quickly glanced around the room, hoping none of his friends saw him.

"Thanks, Mom. Father LaPage asked if I could help him set up tables for Bingo."

Betty looked at her husband for confirmation.

Tim wondered why he was still wearing his robe.

"Sure you can," his father said "and later on, how about you, me, and Tommy shoot some hoops?"

Robby's eyes lit up and he smiled at his brother. "That would great, Dad."

"So Father LaPage will drive you home?" Betty asked.

"Yeah, Ma. He said it shouldn't take more than a few hours."

Tim patted his son on the back. "All right, we'll see you in while."

They filed out, and Robby turned in the other direction.

It was nearly 3:00 p.m. when LaPage's Buick pulled up in front of the Anderson home. He and Robby entered through the front door of the three-bedroom ranch that was located in the north end of the city.

As the priest entered the house he saw that it was exceptionally neat, moderately decorated, and smelled of baking pie. It was his first visit, and he knew once he got a foothold he would become an extended family member in no time, as he had in so many other homes throughout the community.

"Hello, Father, very nice sermon you gave this morning," Betty announced as she greeted him in the living room.

"Thank you, Betty. Nobody passed out or got sick, so I would call it a successful Mass," he said with a wide grin, showing his perfectly aligned pearly whites encapsulated between thin, dry lips.

Betty laughed. "You're always kidding, Father."

Robby darted past them to his room to change.

"Come in and take a seat," she offered. Would you like a cup of coffee and some homemade blueberry pie?"

"I'd love some. Thanks." LaPage enjoyed the scent of baking pie because it was something he never enjoyed in his kitchen as a child. His mother walked out when he was six years old leaving him to grow up as an only child with an angry and bitter father.

Tim entered the room wearing a black and gray sweat suit that hung loosely off his thin frame.

"Father," he nodded his head.

"Hello, Tim." LaPage smiled and offered his hand and they briefly shook.

"How did Robby do with the set up?" Tim asked, sitting down in his favorite chair facing the couch where LaPage sat.

"It went fine. It was just Robby and me today," he declared. "He's a strong boy."

Tim knew the priest was patronizing him.

"He's coming along for a pre-teen," Tim said.

"How are his grades these days?"

"They could be better. He's about average," Tim answered, crossing his right leg over the left.

"Would you like me to speak with him, give him a pep talk?" LaPage offered.

"I guess it can't hurt, but please do it gently. We've been riding him to study harder."

Betty came in with the coffee and pie. "It smells great," LaPage said, standing to take the cup and dish.

"When I was a missionary in Haiti, I had a hard time picking up the language, so I made a rule that I would study every night between six and eight. It didn't matter if I felt confident that I was doing well for my limited time in country, I continued to study every night until the day I left. Now, I speak fluent French Creole. Maybe I'll share this story with Robby."

"Like I said, Father, it can't hurt," Tim replied.

Tommy came into the room followed by Robby, who was spinning a basketball off the tip of his index finger.

"Are you ready, Dad?"

Tim nodded and turned to the priest. "Are you up for some basketball?"

"Some other time, I have some rounds to make this afternoon."

They stood and shook hands again.

"See you on Sunday, Father."

"See you Sunday, Tim."

LaPage sat back down with Betty while Tim and his two sons dribbled to the driveway.

CHAPTER 3

Stephen always felt more comfortable sitting in the back of the class, so he wouldn't be watched as closely by the teachers. He often tried to persuade his teachers to change his seat after being assigned to a front row, and he was usually unsuccessful. Having been assigned to the second to last seat in the first row of his History class, Stephen thought he was well positioned in the room.

Mr. McCartney, the history teacher, sat on the edge of his desk with his weight trying his arms. His brown sports jacket nearly matched the color of his well kept beard and his blue oxford shirt was a tad lighter than his eyes. A legend in his own mind, McCartney was always right about everything, and there was little chance of persuading him differently.

"There was a famous duel in July of 1804. Who can tell me the names of the participants?"

Stephen quickly scribbled on a piece of paper and handed it to Wendy, the girl sitting to his left, and she promptly raised her hand.

Gesturing toward her with an open hand facing the ceiling, like the Pope, McCartney looked to Wendy for an answer.

"Yes, Miss. Carlson."

"It was Burr and Hamilton."

"That is correct. And who was the victor?" Wendy quickly shifted her eyes toward Stephen's paper, trying to avoid detection.

"Burr won the duel," she confidently answered, after watching Stephen quickly circle the name.

"Yes. Burr was the challenger, and the man left standing," he said as he began to slowly pace with his hands lodged behind his back. "This seemed to be commonplace in the history of duels.

Why do you think that is?"

There was a moment of pause as he looked around the class waiting for a champion. Shifting his head to the right, he examined Stephen, as he slouched lower in his chair avoiding eye contact.

"Mr. Haney, any thoughts on this?"

Sliding back up, Stephen straightened out his posture, realizing all eyes were fixed on him.

"When a guy challenges another to a gunfight, he has more confidence and is less nervous. His hand would probably shake less, giving him a steadier aim."

"Well stated, Mr. Haney. Also, if he's the challenger wouldn't he feel passionate about his cause?" The teacher moved over by the window not expecting an answer, just some deep thought.

"I have the results of your tests and I must say I was less than pleased with the results as a group."

He walked back to his desk and picked up a pile of blue notebooks and began to scale the room, dropping them onto desktops. Stephen didn't look up as he walked past his desk and carefully placed the booklet down. He wouldn't look at it until he was alone. Once his hands were empty, McCartney went back to the front of the class.

"I expect the results of your next exam will be much more promising." Noticing the time on his gold wrist watch, he knew the bell was about to ring. "You can go now."

As the classroom began to empty, he called out, "Mr. Haney. Please allow me a minute of your time."

Stephen reluctantly shifted course and headed toward the teachers desk. After the last student was out of sight, McCartney began. "Would you agree that it's in Ms. Carlson's best interest to answer questions without your help?"

Surprised he was caught, Stephen pinched the tip of his nose before responding. "Yes."

"Why do you hold back?" he asked, "only providing answers when confronted?"

"I don't know," Stephen shrugged, avoiding eye contact.

"Yes you do. Did you look at the results of your exam?"

"No."

"Well, as usual, you aced it. You are the only student that got a 100 percent correct on the test. There is no reason to be ashamed of being bright. You probably work much harder than most of your classmates and it pays off."

Stephen didn't feel the need to reveal the truth that he hardly ever studied. Once he heard or read something it usually remained stored in his mind for easy access.

"Yeah, I guess it pays off," he said shifting his eyes toward the light shining through the window.

"All right, Mr. Haney, please keep the cards close to your chest going forward."

Not wasting any time, Stephen headed toward the door.

"Mr. Haney."

Stephen stopped and turned around.

"Be proud of your special abilities. You are a gifted student. Try to embrace it."

Stephen thought about what his teacher said and abruptly dismissed it.

"Thanks," his voice echoed as he vanished into the hallway.

On the court, Robby was unstoppable with his outside shot. Even with his disability, he performed fairly well in all sports, but basketball was his game. This was primarily due to his endless one-on-one driveway battles with his brother and father. Gym class was split up into two teams, and Michael and Stephen were facing Robby from the opposing side. The game was intense, as both teams were pushing hard for victory.

Stephen was extremely strong and agile and wasn't deprived of muscle in his v-shaped frame. Not caring for team sports, his triumphs usually came when he had only himself to depend on.

Michael, the second tallest in his class, enjoyed slapping back the ball when his opponent attempted to make a lay-up, and he was a terror under the boards while snatching up the re-bounds.

Unlike most of his opponents, Michael wasn't very confident covering Robby. Although he was much taller, he couldn't stop the smaller boy's outside shot. Trying his best, he stuck to Robby like glue; not allowing any space for him to bring the ball up for a shot. The pressure Michael applied didn't seem to make a difference, and his frustration was growing with every swishing sound of the threads. Robby couldn't miss. Dribbling forward, he would come to an abrupt stop, throwing the ball up without effort and watching as it passed through the hoop.

"Son of a bitch!" Michael blurted out, as Robby trotted away with his head held high.

"Mr. McNulty, watch your language," Mr. Hastings warned.

When the opportunity arrived, Michael moved in closer to Robby, packing a threat. "Make another shot, and after school, your ass is mine."

Robby heard him, but quickly dismissed it. As they moved down the court, the ball was passed to Robby and he moved to the right with a quick dribble, stopped, and threw the ball up. It was a three pointer from outside the key.

"Bang!" Robby sounded out as the ball slipped though the basket just prior to the whistle blowing.

Michael's team took a staggering defeat and the look on his face was obvious to everyone. He was humiliated and he couldn't let it slide.

"Your ass is mine," he muttered to Robby as he passed by, shoving him aside.

Robby wasn't a fighter and he was feeling a bit nervous as they headed for the locker room, listening to one of Michael's teammates heckling him.

"Beat by a gimp," the boy said, laughing.

"Sh-Shut the fuck up, B-Barry," Michael stuttered as they moved into the long rows of lockers.

Robby went directly to his locker and began undressing, feeling nausea growing in his stomach. A few seconds later, Michael came strutting over with a look that could kill as Stephen circled around from the rear and out of Robby's view.

"So you think you're a hotshot on the court," Michael said with a raised fist. "Bang." He faked a punch and Robby flinched, raising his hands up in a protective manner. "You're not such a hot shot now. Are you punk?"

Robby began to feel lightheaded and his legs followed.

"It was just a game, Mike," Robby minimized. "I don't want any trouble," he said turning toward his locker.

Frustrated and angry, Michael pushed Robby hard with both hands sending him flying backwards, and before Robby realized it, he was airborne and heading toward the floor. Just prior to the shove, Stephen had gotten down on all fours behind Robby, causing him to trip over Stephen, fall backward and crack his head on the tile floor.

"Oh shit!" Michael cursed as he heard Robby's head collide with the floor.

Several other boys started reacting on Robby's behalf, calling for Michael and Stephen to back off.

"He's okay," Stephen reassured them as Robby lay on the floor rolling side to side and groaning.

"What's going on in here?" Hastings roared. His six-foot-two frame barreled into the locker room, swiftly coming to Robby's aid and helping him onto his feet. "What happened, Robby?" His question went unanswered.

Stephen blended in with the lockers as Mr. Hastings looked toward Michael. "Did you do this?"

"I don't know what you're talking about," Michael lied.

Robby was holding his head as a splitting headache was born.

"Let me take a look," Hastings said. "You have a nasty bump and a small cut, but you'll be all right."

Hastings reached out and grabbed Michael by the neck. "You, Mister, are to go directly to the principal's office and wait for me." He tightened his grip on Michael's neck and the pain set in. "Understood?" Michael nodded in agreement as he watched the large man's face grow red.

Mr. Hastings escorted Robby to the nurse's station where she cleaned and sterilized the cut, administered an ice pack and had him lay down on the infirmary cot.

Michael was sitting outside the principal's office when Hastings and Robby arrived a half hour later. The closet-sized hall seemed isolated and bland, like a prison cell. There were four chairs lined up in perfect order and the walls were bare except for a Norman Rockwell print of a runaway boy sitting with a state trooper in a diner. Michael thought it a fitting picture for the location.

"Robby, have a seat out here and I'll be right back," Hasting said, and Robby took a seat two chairs apart from Michael, not daring to look at him. Once Mr. Hastings closed the door, Michael leaned toward Robby. "You better not say a word about what happened or your dead."

Robby didn't acknowledge him. He was both scared and angry and he tried hard to conceal his trembling fingers.

A few had minutes passed when the door to Principal Darter's office swung open and Hastings gestured for the boys to come in.

Sitting behind his desk like a judge, Darter spoke. "Sit down boys."

They took seats directly in front of his desk and the trembling shifted from Robby to Michael. Hastings stood behind them, like the Leaning Tower of Pisa.

"Tell me what happened, and don't lie because I'll know if you are," Darter glared at Michael. He was a tall figure with a pot belly that once boasted rippling abdominal muscles that along with his hair had disappeared over the past two decades.

"I don't know, I guess he fell," Michael said, his eyes glued to his knees.

"Mr. Anderson, is this true?"

After a short pause, Robby spoke. "No." He looked at Michael and tears began to fall. "He pushed me and Steve helped him."

"I take it you mean, Stephen Haney?" the Principal asked.

"Yes," Robby mumbled under his breath.

"Is this true, Mr. McNulty?"

"Yes, but he started it."

"How?" Robby shouted. "By beating you in basketball? That's

all I did."

Michael didn't respond, he just kept his head down.

"Okay Robby, you can go to class," Darter said.

Robby walked out with Mr. Hastings, leaving Michael behind, alone with the Principal and his fate.

CHAPTER 4

A crowd of seventeen had gathered in Bottle Park for an event people had been talking about for weeks. Some lit up cigarettes, and others marijuana, as they anticipated the action that was about to commence. Sitting on fine trimmed grass, they argued the merits of their champion, and why they thought he would prevail. The oldest of the spectators was Kevin Garber and he was fifteen. Adamant that his boy, Brock, would take the prize, he boasted about the size and strength of his warrior.

Michael helped Stephen strap on the old catcher's chest guard he wore when he played in the Little League. In one hand Stephen held a baseball catcher's mask, and with the other, he balanced his unicycle.

His opponent was much larger and cockier, but Stephen had an edge: he invented the sport and he was the challenger. It was a dangerous undertaking and very few boys dared to participate in the revived primitive sport.

Wren Brock had been pushing Stephen for months, calling him a monkey and attempting to embarrass him in front of the neighborhood girls. Being small and agile, Stephen spent much of his time running, jumping, turning cartwheels, and balancing handstands. Eventually, he worked his way up to handsprings and back flips. This ability earned him many names including Brocks favorite: monkey, which Stephen resented more than any other. In Stephen's mind, Brock was implying that he was mentally challenged, and this was the worst of insults.

Garber came strolling over carrying a long wooden crutch. "Is there enough padding on that one?" He pointed to a crutch on the ground.

Michael picked up the crutch and handed it to him, "Check it out."

In turn, he handed his crutch to Michael and they both examined the point.

"Let me see that." Stephen took the crutch from Michael and

began to squeeze the foam rubber that was duct taped onto the end. "It looks okay," he acknowledged like a professional.

"So is yours," Garber said, handing Stephen his crutch. "Can I ask you something?"

"What?" Stephen responded as he slipped the catcher's mask over his head.

"Where did you ever come up with the idea of jousting on unicycles?" Garber asked.

"It came to me in a dream," Stephen answered through his mask.

"A dream," the older boy paused as he thought "That was one crazy dream," he said before returning to Brock who was wrapped in battle garb. Also wearing a baseball chest guard, kneepads and a catcher's mask, Brock didn't look as sharp as his opponent, appearing too large for his protective gear.

"The best out of three," Michael called out. "If a combatant can't continue, he loses. The first warrior that knocks the other off his saddle two times is victorious. The winner must remain in his seat or on his feet after the impact, in order to be deemed Jousting King."

Stephen mounted his unicycle. His long brown hair was squeezed tight against his face by the mask straps and was tapering down his neck, stopping short of his collar bone. Pulling his crutch in tight to his shoulder, Stephen raised it to a horizontal position.

Both knights were clad in armor, and preparing to attack, with each coach keeping them balanced on their bikes. As spectators quieted in anticipation of the duel, Stephen could hear his heartbeat. For the past few weeks, in his mind's eye, he had seen this moment over and over. First, he would get his one-wheeled machine to go as fast as he could to cover the hundred-foot battleground, and just prior to the moment of impact, he would tuck his chin down and aim for his enemy's center. In his fantastic visions, he was always victorious.

The designated starter appeared, wearing a tall hat like the one the cat wore in the Dr. Seuss picture books. Standing at the halfway point, he raised his right hand high.

"On your mark, get set, go!" He dropped his hand, like an axe chopping off the head of a condemned prisoner.

Each coach immediately gave their champion a strong push, followed by a word of encouragement. Michael's words were precise and vindictive. "Go for the throat."

Stephen peddled as hard as he could without losing his balance. His eyes were fixed on Brock as they closed the gap quicker than he remembered in his previous match against Samuel Carter. As they were about to engage, Stephen tightened his grip on the crutch handle, pulling it tight to his shoulder and leveling it while he simultaneously tucked in his chin. Just prior to impact, he remembered what Michael had instructed and he brought his weapon up six inches, aiming for Brock's throat.

Brock quickly shifted his upper body to the left, avoiding the point of Stephen's lance. However, his crutch landed directly in Stephen's breadbasket. The impact was sudden and painful, causing Stephen to instantly jolt backwards; landing on the back of his neck, causing an uncomfortable crunching sound as he clashed with the earth. The ground was much harder than he remembered. A direct blow to the abdomen took away his wind and any air that might have been left behind was expelled when he landed.

Michael came rushing over in a panic. "Stevie, are you all right?" Kneeling down on one knee, he removed the mask as Stephen was wheezing in an attempt to regain his breath. Thirty seconds later he started to breathe normally and the defeat began to settle in. "Are you okay, man?"

"Yeah," he whispered. Michael helped him to his feet and they both looked over at Brock, who was smirking. The bitter taste of revenge consumed Stephen's palate. Rolling his head around a few times in a circular motion, Stephen felt his neck stiffen and a sharp pain invade the base of his skull. "Let's go," he said, as he slipped the mask back over his head.

Once again, Stephen mounted his bike and got into position, and Brock did the same. The starter resumed his position, as the spectator's maintained complete stillness. Only the wind was defiant, as it rustled the leaves on the trees.

Standing with an open hand in the air, the starter sharply brought it down like a karate chop and the jousters were off. Peddling as hard as possible and quickly closing the gap, Stephen decided to keep to his original plan. Once he was within striking distance, he steadied his weapon, locating the center of Brock's chest. The impact knocked Stephen off his bike, but he managed to regain his balance, and he was still standing. His opponent, however, was not so fortunate. Brock was knocked to the ground with a severe twisting contortion to his right side.

He immediately got up cursing. "Son of a bitch!" He scooped up his unicycle and gave Stephen a look that could kill. Through his mask, Stephen smiled back, and they both turned and began walking back to their starting points.

Once in place, the starter began his recital. "Gentlemen, it's now a tie breaker. The last warrior remaining in his saddle, or on his feet, will be the winner."

The match continued and both contestants were in place with their coaches balancing them in preparation for the starters signal. With both hands, the boy in the funny looking hat thrashed downward, cutting through the air. "Go!"

Stephen had a new strategy this time as he peddled furiously toward the large boy that was breaking ground in his direction. His heart rate, along with his breathing, had increased to a rapid pace as he pushed onward. Not only did Stephen want to win, he wanted to hurt Brock and claim his revenge. As they approached, in the last second before making contact, Stephen lowered his lance just above Brock's saddle. The point of his weapon skimmed the top of Brock's seat, catching Brock directly in the groin. The crushing blow pushed Brock's lower body backward causing him to fall face first into the ground. During the moment of impact, the fallen boy let out an eerie sound that could only be described as excruciating pain. While Brock lay flat on his belly moaning and rolling side to side, Stephen raised both hands in the air in a gesture of victory. As he strutted over to Brock, Stephen felt like a victorious gladiator in the arena, and Brock was nothing more than his whimpering prey.

"Who's the fucking monkey now, Brock?" he gloated as he walked away, collecting pats on the back and handshakes.

Brock had suffered a severe rupture which nearly caused him to lose a testicle. Somehow, Stephen still didn't feel that he was quite even. Not yet.

CHAPTER 5

The sun had fallen and was replaced by an infant moon that ascended over the northeast skyline. Betty Anderson was gripping a towel and pacing the kitchen floor when her husband entered the room.

"I called all his friends and no one has seen him since school," she said in a quivering tone.

The horizontal lines on her husband's forehead appeared to deepen. "Did you call Father LaPage?"

Betty stopped pacing, like a marcher at the end of a parade. "Yes, he hasn't seen him either. He's on his way over now." Her eyes filled up like an overflowing well. "Where could he be?"

"I'm sure he's fine, honey." He wasn't so sure, he thought, as he gently caressed his wife's back.

"I'm calling the police." Betty darted toward the phone and Tim didn't argue. He went for a glass of water and found a chair.

Father LaPage arrived a few minutes later. He brought along a comforting and optimistic demeanor that temporarily calmed Betty's nerves. Tim decided to drive around the neighborhood and look for Robby while Tommy searched the neighborhood on foot for his little brother. LaPage stayed with Betty and waited for the police to arrive, consoling her to the best of his ability.

The police officers came and logged a report, reassuring Betty that this kind of thing happened all too frequently. The senior officer seemed sure that Robby was probably out playing with a friend and would soon walk in through the back door.

As the night slowly dragged on, Betty was less than convinced they were right. She knew her son, and she could sense something was wrong. Once the clock struck twelve, she called the police again and a new pair came over. They advised her that they had all the information that was passed on to them by the last shift and that Robby was their top priority.

The morning came without sleep and without Robby. Betty had been crying most of the night and Tim comforted her as best he could under the circumstances. When he needed a break, Father LaPage picked up the slack. Tim was strong and tried to remain optimistic about his missing son by pushing any negative thoughts out of his head. Tommy popped in and out of his room throughout the night to check on his mother and glance at Robby's tightly made bed. In the morning he planned to hit the streets and resume his search. He had a bad feeling in the pit of his stomach that wouldn't subside, and he knew something was wrong, very wrong.

Roll call was at 7:45 am sharp. Four rows of officers dressed in blue stood waiting for their names to be called out by a sergeant who always seemed to be miserable and on edge. The smell of spent coffee and hangover filled the room. It was another day and another paycheck for most of the patrolmen, although there were a few in the ranks who thought they were going to change the world.

Jake Waterfield had been on the job for three weeks. His boots were spit shined and his uniform crisply pressed. His hat was worn a bit lower than the others and his eyes were nearly hidden as he stood in the first row feeling a bit taller than usual. Remembering the look on his parents faces on graduation day from the academy, he was never prouder and it showed as he took the line.

The first shift was preparing to hit the streets and Jake was glad to be able to work the day shift and sleep at night, at least for a short while. His training period would last six months before he was pushed back to the dog watch shift. Until then, his job was to keep his ears and eyes open, and his mouth shut. That's what the sergeant had told him on his first day, and he had taken the advice to heart.

"Crowley. Waterfield," Sergeant Manley called out.

"Here, Sergeant," Jake answered.

"Present," Dennis Crowley responded in a less than

enthusiastic tone as a stabbing pain cut from his forehead to his left eye. He knew he should have declined that last Wild Turkey double at last call.

"You'll be Bravo 6." Manley assigned their district as he shot a nasty look at Crowley.

Jake snuck a quick glance to see who he would be working with. Crowley, his partner for the day was a tall and raggedy looking character with straight brown hair and a protruding forehead, the wrinkled uniform hanging off him looked as if it hadn't been washed in a week. He appeared to be in his early forties, but he was only thirty-six. *Great, I have to spend the day with Sad Sack. Good thing it's only for a day.*

All cruisers were rolling to their assigned areas and another day of fighting crime was underway. Jake was a rookie and he was getting used to the fact that he wasn't going to be behind the wheel for quite a while, unless he was paired up with a guy who didn't like to drive. However, that was unusual, because it was all about control with the senior officers.

"Don't take that gun out of your holster unless I tell you to." Crowley nodded his head up and down as he spoke as if he were convincing himself while giving orders. Jake didn't respond, thinking Crowley's comment didn't justify an answer. He gazed out the window, appreciating the spring morning. The sun beamed through the cruiser at a slant, painting a shadow across his older partner's frame. Jake cracked the window and inhaled deeply, a pleasant aroma found his nose and he thought it smelled like home fries cooking on a hot grill.

"You follow boxing?" Crowley asked without turning his head.

"Only what I read in the newspaper." Jake continued looking out the window as the city came alive and folks hustled to make it to work on time.

"One of my favorite fighters was Joe Lewis, The Brown Bomber. That boy could throw a punch." Jake turned briefly to look at the guy sitting next to him, and then he turned back to the world outside the car. "Too bad he got screwed in the end by the

IRS, though. They chased that boy to the edges of the earth. Took nearly every nickel he ever made and didn't care that he helped sell all those war bonds either."

"That sounds about right with our government," Jake said.

"How about that Hank Aaron; wasn't he something?" Crowley belched out. "755 home runs. Hammering Hank, Number 44, left Babe Ruth in the dust. That boy was the best there ever was."

"Yeah, they both did pretty well for a couple of colored boys," Jake responded.

Jake could tell that his sarcasm hit Crowley like a sudden and uncomfortable cramp. Jake was one of a few black officers in the department and he knew he was going to have to work hard to earn respect from his peers, but he didn't like the way Crowley used the word "boy" while speaking of great men. He also didn't like that his partner for the day only saw the accomplishments of black men inclusive to sporting events.

Crowley took one hand off the wheel making an open hand gesture. "Hey, I was just trying to make conversation."

"I think it's best if we just keep it to police work." Jake looked at his watch, realizing it was only 8:23 am. *It's going to be a long day.*

About a minute later, the radio dispatcher sounded. "Bravo 6."

Jake picked up the hand set. "Bravo 6."

"Go to Bottle Park, near the Korean War monument. See a Mr. Julian Rankin. Subject states he found the body of a juvenile male while walking his dog. The DB has been notified."

"Bravo 6, acknowledged." Jake replaced the mike and looked at Crowley. "Do you know the place?"

"Yeah, I know the place," he said in an exasperated tone. "It's probably just a doll or something, don't get too excited."

Jake looked through the glass as the car took a quick left turn. He had a very different feeling about the call than his colleague, yet he was hoping Crowley was right.

They drove into the park as far as they could, and then got out on foot and began walking toward the monument. It was a cool sunny morning with a light breeze staggering the young leaves through the trees. Jake tried to avoid walking in the shady areas, keeping in the warmth of the sun. He took in the beauty of the white and gold wild flowers and it reminded him of his high school colors. His football jacket still hung in his closet displaying the same colors he had been so proud of several years ago. As they approached the monument Jake observed two middle-aged people talking. One was a man holding a leash with a small dog that wasn't much larger than a sewer rat, and the other a woman wearing a pink and white sweatsuit. After noticing the police, they opened ranks, facing the officers as they closed the gap.

"I'll do the talking," Crowley demanded. Jake's jaw tightened, which was beginning to happen nearly every time Crowley opened his mouth. He hoped this would be the last time he would be assigned as Crowley's partner.

"Mr. Rankin?" Crowley addressed the man with the dog.

"Yes," he responded with a nervous and apprehensive look.

"We got a call that you found a body."

"It's over there," Rankin said pointing toward the wood line. "I was walking my dog and she pulled me over here." He started toward the wood line. "I thought she had to take care of business, and then I saw the boy. He's over there." Rankin stopped in his tracks and pointed once again.

The woman in pink stayed near the monument. She had been taking her morning walk when she happened upon Rankin, and when he showed her the body, she nearly lost her breakfast. She had no intention of taking a second look.

As they moved closer, Jake could see the silhouette stretched out on the ground. His heart began to beat faster, and he had a strange feeling invade his mind and body that could only be described as pity. "It doesn't look like a doll to me," Jake said.

"No. He can't be much older than fifteen," Crowley said.

Jake noticed that Crowley didn't seem as upset. It was obvious this wasn't the first time he'd seen a dead body, and Jake wondered if he would become as calloused as Crowley one day.

"I'd say he's younger than that," Jake said.

The boy was lying on his stomach with his face positioned to the right. His jacket and blue jeans were soiled from the damp ground. A small puddle of dried blood surrounded his head, and an opened wound defined the top left side of his skull. One of his sneakers had disengaged from his right heel and his white sock was soiled with dirt.

"Looks like someone bashed him over the head," Crowley said, kneeling down to get a closer look.

Slowly pacing the crime scene, Jake scanned the area and observed something a few feet from the body. Stooping down, he reached into his pocket retrieving his pen. A black button leaned against the grass at a slant. Using his pen Jake turned it so he could see the face of the button.

Crowley came over. "What have you got?"

"It looks like a button with an anchor of some sort on it."

"Well, don't touch it. Let the detective bureau handle it." Crowley took out his hand set and pushed the button activating the transmitter. "Bravo 6."

"Bravo 6," the radio sounded.

"We have located the body of a young boy that fits the description of the missing juvenile we got at roll call."

"Anderson," Jake reminded him.

Crowley stopped and looked at Jake, thinking what a good memory he had. "Anderson is the name of the missing kid. You better dispatch the photo and print squad."

There was a brief hesitation on the other end. "Received."

"The detectives are here," Rankin informed the officers.

Jake walked over to Rankin. "Thanks for calling this in. Give me a few minutes with the detectives and then I'll need to ask you a few questions. You've been a big help."

A smile blossomed on Rankin's face. "Sure thing, officer," he said, reeling his dog in closer.

As the two detectives approached, Jake noticed they each wore a jacket and tie. One of them was in his late forties and the other was about thirty. Jake had seen the younger guy around the stationhouse, but the older detective was unfamiliar. A couple inches shorter than Jake, the elder detective was well built and had kept himself in good shape. The top of his head was exposed to the sunlight and he had a slight salt and pepper mustache that was kept short to his upper lip. His small brown eyes were set deep in his face and appeared intense, yet compassionate.

The younger detective was a short, pudgy, Irish-looking guy with a smile that appeared fixed to his face. He was clearly the junior detective. "Bob Finn." He reached out and Jake shook his hand.

"Jake Waterfield." He let go and turned to face the older detective.

"How long have you been on the job?" the older detective asked, as he offered his hand to Jake.

"Less than a month." Jake wasn't sure why he felt embarrassed revealing this.

"Well, don't fret. In the blink of an eye it will be twenty-five years. I'm Sergeant Fitch. Call me Tom." He smiled and Jake experienced a slight relief.

Crowley slithered in to greet the detectives. "Good morning, gentlemen."

It was apparent by their limited responses that they didn't care much for Crowley, but that didn't prevent him from sucking up and attempting to convey how bright he was.

"Tom, I want to show you what I found over here," Crowley said with his chin up.

They moved toward the body. "See the button, right there," he pointed.

Detective Fitch produced a clear plastic bag from his jacket, followed by a pair of tweezers.

"This might be trace evidence," Fitch said. Like a surgeon he carefully extracted the button and placed it in the bag. Slowly sealing it; he placed it back into his pocket. "I wouldn't want to be the parents of this kid," he said to Jake.

"I called for photos and fingerprints," Crowley bragged.

"That's great, Officer Crowley. Now I'd like you to get a statement from the two witnesses that found the body, and don't leave a stone unturned."

Crowley was irritated that Fitch didn't ask Jake to take the statement, after all he was the rookie, but then he rationalized that Jake wasn't qualified. "No problem," he said as he headed toward the monument.

Bob Finn was busy searching the vicinity for evidence, and that left Fitch and Jake alone by the body.

"You found the button, didn't you?" Fitch asked.

Jake looked at the seasoned detective, appreciating his perception. "Yes, I did."

Fitch frowned and nodded his head back and forth "Most of the squad tries to avoid getting paired up with Crowley, and I don't blame them." He took in a deep breath and scanned the treetops. "This used to be a clean and safe park," he said with a hint of despair. "Do you know why they call this place Bottle Park?"

"No, I don't." Jake never really thought about it having grown up on the opposite side of the city.

"Many people think it's because of all the broken bottles scattered everywhere. Some even believe it's because of the traffic jams that bottleneck the northern point of the park." Fitch knelt down and pulled the victim's jacket aside, exposing his stomach area. "The park adopted its name is simply because it's shaped like a bottle. If you observe it from the air, you'll notice it looks like a whiskey bottle."

Jake was intrigued by the detective. He had a serious and thoughtful way about him that made Jake feel that he would enjoy spending time in his company. There was much to learn from this man, he thought.

"It looks like the boy may have been sexually assaulted," Fitch observed. "See the belt? It had been undone and then refastened, probably after he was killed. It was pulled way too tight," he said as he tugged on it with his pen. "The victim wouldn't have done that. It would have been too uncomfortable." He looked over to his partner. "Bobby, has the coroner been notified?"

"I just called him. Photos should be here in a few minutes.

"Keep your eyes peeled for a weapon. It could be a large rock or a pipe or something with a very solid surface," Fitch said thoughtfully. "It doesn't look like a wooden stick could do this kind of damage." With his gloved hand, he rotated the boys head a notch in order to gain a better view. "Based on the Livor Mortis, I would say he's been dead less than twelve hours," Fitch ascertained.

Jake moved away from the body, figuring he had spent enough time with a dead person for a day. He tried to imagine what kind of person would do this to a child, and he felt anger building up inside like an itch he couldn't reach. "Tom, I'm going to help Crowley interview the witnesses."

Fitch looked up from his kneeling position. "I have a feeling you're going to do just fine here, Jake. Thanks for your help."

A smile sprouted across Jake's face. "Anytime, Detective." Jake walked toward Crowley thinking that one day he wanted to wear a tie and jacket to work.

CHAPTER 6

Maple Grove cemetery was nearly five acres of manicured green lawn, flowers, trees, and stone, with hundreds of gravesites planted into the majestic landscape. The first coffin was lowered into its earth nearly two hundred years earlier, and it was filling up faster than anticipated.

Father LaPage stood near the small casket with his Bible and was reading a passage from Lamentations 3:32-33: *"Though he brings grief, he will show compassion, so great is his unfailing love. For he does not willingly bring affliction or grief to the children of men."*

The Anderson family sat a few feet away under a lean tarp that was blocking out the morning sun. A bagpipes player dressed in a plaid kilt stood in the distance under a huge maple with his instrument in the ready position. The crowd in attendance was magnificently broad and unusually somber. Many people not known to the Andersons had come to pay their respects to a family stricken with unbearable grief.

The murder in Bottle Park was front page news every day since the body of Robby Anderson was discovered. It was a tragedy that cut deep into the heart of the community. Every news station was covering the crime and Robby's picture had been on display on the front page of all local newspapers. Many people in the community were staying clear of the park, afraid that it may not have been a random crime: that it could possibly occur again.

Tim held Betty's hand as she dabbed tears away with the other. He hoped that with each tear drop that fell from his wife's eyes, a bit of anguish was falling along with it. She hadn't stopped crying since the day Tim came back from the morgue bearing the worst news she could have ever imagined.

The remorse Tim felt was only outmatched by his anger for the perpetrator. The death of his son was determined a homicide, and he wanted justice. He couldn't fathom why anyone would want to hurt such a young and innocent boy, his boy. If he could only find the person responsible, he would choke him to death with his bare hands. His older son, Tommy, felt the same as he did, and like his father, he kept it hidden. Tommy hadn't spoken much since he received the news of his younger brother's death. It hadn't sunk in, and he hadn't come to terms with the tragedy. He hadn't shed his first tear.

The Andersons were grateful that they had such a caring and supportive priest to help them through their unbearable time of loss. Father LaPage accompanied Tim when he went to identify the body, and he had continued to comfort the family every day since.

Jake stood alone behind the gathering of mourners, listening as the bagpipes player slowly erupted into "Amazing Grace." His peripheral vision alerted him that someone was moving close to him. The blurred vision cleared, as he turned to see who was approaching, and he nodded his head in a welcoming motion as Detective Fitch approached.

"Good morning," Fitch said in a whisper, extending his hand.

"I'm not sure how good it is, but its morning." Jake shook with a firm grip.

"You have a point there."

"Yes sir."

"It's Tom," Fitch said, gazing out at the piper. "Every time I hear bagpipes someone has died. Well, for the exception of the St. Patrick's Day Parade."

"They do have a haunting effect, don't they?" Jake said.

"I'm a little surprised to see you here today."

"Why is that?"

"You're new to the job, and its Saturday. I figure you'd be laid up with a young girl, nursing a hangover." A smile developed on Fitch's face.

"I don't drink." Jake smiled back. "This murder has buried itself into my craw and I can't get it out." His smile faded to a frown.

"I know the feeling," Fitch said. "We'll find whoever did this. I promise you that."

Jake looked deep into Fitch's eyes and his determination was apparent. "I was going to come and see you," Jake said as the pipes faded. "I ran a check on the guy that found the body."

Fitch listened carefully. "Go on."

"Rankin is a convicted felon."

Fitch was impressed with the rookie. "I know," he said, "I ran him, too."

"Six years ago he was arrested for molesting a ten-year-old boy. Do you think there's a chance he may have killed him?" Jake asked. "Maybe he tried to have his way with the boy and it wasn't working out and during the struggle he hit him over the head."

"I was wondering the same thing. It's a possibility, but it doesn't make sense that he would call in the discovery and wait until we arrived if he was the perpetrator."

Jake nodded in agreement. "Do you think he found the body and decided to mess with the boy after he was dead?" Jake asked, remembering how the belt was fastened too tight.

"The coroner's examination determined he hadn't been raped, but he did say there were signs of possible molestation."

"Are there any other suspects?" Jake asked.

"I'm looking into a schoolmate that threatened him about a week ago. I'll be adding Rankin to my short list for interrogation as well."

"Would you mind if I check in once in a while to see how it's going?"

"Sure. Anytime you like."

Fitch gave him a light punch on the arm and he walked away with the sun reflecting off his summit. Unlike Jake, who wore a black suit, Fitch had on his daily detective uniform. Jake wondered how many funerals he had attended of homicide victims he was investigating, and how many of them he found closure.

The casket was being lowered into the ground and the decibel of sobbing increased, so Jake decided it was time to leave, and started toward his car. As the cries of the mourners dissipated, he thought about how quiet and peaceful it was in the cemetery, and he wondered if Robby Anderson was truly at peace, or would he not rest until his murderer was found and brought to justice. Jake pondered how long it would take before he would find peace himself, because he couldn't get the picture of the boy, lying lifeless in Bottle Park, out of his head. What he needed was a long hard run; that usually helped to take the edge off. As he drove out of the cemetery, in the distance he could see that nearly everyone had left the gravesite except for Tommy Anderson, who remained standing over the hole in the ground where his brother was laid to rest. Tommy's tears had finally found him.

After changing into his sweatsuit, Jake drove to a convenience store to purchase a bottle of water and some chewing gum. As he entered the store, the pale and unfriendly face of the clerk greeted him with a blank stare. He started down the aisles looking for the rack that held the gum. At the gum and mint rack, Jake scanned through the different flavors searching for his brand. He passed by a large jar of Bazooka Joe's bubblegum on the end of the shelf, and he continued past the cigar and cigarette bubblegum, stopping near the assortment of Wrigley's gum lined up with blue and green colors. His favorite brand was located at the top of the shelf just passed the Wrigley's spearmint gum, so he grabbed two packs of Dentine and moved on.

Over his shoulder, Jake noticed a young man watching him as he walked toward the cooler for his water. The chubby man in the blue shirt was following along from a short distance, like a poorly coordinated dance partner. Jake retrieved a bottle of water and closed the door. As he started down the aisle, the man in the blue shirt approached and grabbed onto his arm. "How many packs of gum do you have?" he asked in a sharp tone.

Quickly pulling his arm away, Jake thought the man lives dangerously. "Who the hell are you and what's your problem?" Jake asked.

"I work here," was his boast. "Just makin sure you pay for everythin you took off the shelf. We got a lotta shoplifters comin in here and stealin stuff," he said with apprehension.

"And I look like a shoplifter, right?" Jake could see that he overstepped his boundary and decidedly took a step back. He reached into his pocket and the young man took another step away from him, thinking he might end up with a knife in his belly. Pulling out his badge-wallet, Jake flipped it open, displaying his shiny silver badge.

"I'm a police officer, and if I ever see you approach a customer like you just did, I'll make your life very unpleasant. Are we clear?"

The man in the blue shirt was lost for words. He just nodded up and down with a gaping mouth. Jake tucked his badge-wallet back in his pocket and went to the counter to pay for his items. The clerk rang him up without making eye contact.

Once inside his car, Jake headed toward Bottle Park. Driving past the big cathedral at the Northern Point, he squinted up at the large cross, and then pulled into the park and parked his car. He got out, took in a deep breath of air and opened his pack of gum; he popped a piece into his mouth, then he started out in a slow, even pace.

CHAPTER 7

Fitch sat behind his desk thumbing through a book he had checked out of the city library. He had marked off a chapter on sailing insignias. The button Jake had uncovered at the crime scene was positioned on his desk to his right. It had been dusted, and was determined clean of any legible prints. As he turned the pages, he looked for anchors that might resemble the one on the button. His partner carefully strolled over with two cups of coffee; he handed one to Fitch. They were oversized blue ceramic cups with white MPD letters inscribed in the center.

"Any luck yet?" Finn asked.

"No. It doesn't look like I'm going to find anything in this book." Fitch took a sip of his coffee and it bit him. "Thanks," he said. It was too hot to drink.

"The McNulty kid is here with his mother. Should I bring them in?"

Fitch swept the button into the evidence bag. "Yeah, room two." Fitch brought the button back to the evidence room and signed it back in. When he returned to the detective bureau office, he put on his jacket and grabbed his coffee. He motioned to Finn and they both headed into the small room where Michael McNulty sat with his mother.

"Good morning," Fitch greeted the pair as he entered the small room. Finn did the same and closed the door behind him. Fitch squeezed in behind the desk and Finn sat in the corner next to him. Michael and his mother sat in two metal chairs a few feet away from the desk, facing the detectives. She was an attractive woman with a thin face and long light brown hair pulled back with barrettes and resting on her shoulders. Michael sat slouched in his chair, looking at the floor.

"Michael, we asked you to come down here because we're investigating the murder of your classmate, Robert Anderson. I have witnesses that observed you assaulting him in the boy's locker room a couple days prior to his death. Can you tell us what happened?"

"Sit up," his mother demanded and Michael immediately did so.

"We were j-just messin around, that's all," he answered without looking up.

"The witnesses said you pushed him while your friend Stephen Haney got down on his hands and knees to help you knock him down. Is this right?"

"Yeah," he said in a low monotone.

"Why did you do it?"

"Like I s-said, we were just g-goofin on him."

Michael's mother knew he was nervous because his stuttering increases when he was upset.

"Goofing on him," Fitch repeated. "Did anything happen between you and Robert prior to you goofing on him?"

Michael shrugged his shoulders.

"Look at me when I speak to you!" Fitch demanded. "This is not a joke. We have a boy your age buried under six feet of dirt."

Michael raised his head, making brief eye contact with Fitch. "We had a d-disagreement on the basketball court."

"I have a witness that states you threatened to kill him and that he feared for his safety. Is this true?"

"No." Once again he made eye contact.

"So they are all liars, is that it?"

"I guess so."

Fitch was puzzled by the kid's lack of emotion or remorse for the dead boy.

"You're telling us that you never threatened to kill Robert Anderson?"

Michael glanced at the tape recorder on the desk with the tape rolling. "Yeah, t- that's right."

"Where were you on the afternoon of April fifteenth?"

"At school."

"And where did you go after school?"

"Home."

"He was home," Mrs. McNulty quickly corroborated. Fitch noticed her eyes were blinking rapidly as she spoke. He knew that was a possible sign that she was lying.

"It didn't take you long to remember that day. Why is that particular day fresh in your head?" he asked while resuming his focus on Michael.

"Because when I heard b-bout what happened to him, I figured I would be questioned because of the fight we had."

"So, you weren't just goofing around. It was a fight?" Fitch shot a quick glance at his partner.

"No, I m-meant-"

"I know what you meant," Fitch abruptly cut him off. "To you it was a fight, not just a couple of kids horsing around. You were mad at him, right?"

Michael didn't answer.

"You wanted to hurt him because he humiliated you on the basketball court, and after school you followed him into the park and you hit him over the head. You may not have intended to kill him, but you wanted revenge for your humiliation.

"That's not t-true." Michael raised his voice for the first time.

"Mr. Fitch, we both told you Michael came home right after school that day," Mrs. McNulty spoke up. "Is there anything else you need today, or can we go now?" She looked at Fitch and then to Finn with very determined dark brown eyes. With one hand she tightened her grip on her black purse and with the other she reached out squeezing her son's hand.

Fitch hit the button on the tape recorder and it came to a sudden halt. "That's all for now. Thank you for bringing Michael in. We will be in touch if we have any more questions."

Fitch opened the door and they filed out.

"Oh, one more thing," Fitch said.

Michael turned around displaying an impatient look.

"You say you went directly home after school. Did you walk or take the bus?"

Michael hesitated and looked at his mother before answering.

"I walked."

"Was Stephen Haney with you?" Fitch added.

He thought for a moment as he rubbed the corner of his eye. "Yeah, he was w-with me."

Fitch examined the boy as he spoke and he came to the conclusion that he had classic body language that would indicate he was not telling the truth. "Alright then, you can go."

"Mr. Fitch." Michael's mother spoke up; her chin elevated a bit higher than normal. "If you ask us to come down here again, we'll be bringing our lawyer."

"Mrs. McNulty, if I ask you to come here again, I would highly recommend that you do."

A slight frown appeared on her face as she escorted her son out of the office.

For nearly the entire ride home she scolded Michael. She had born two boys, and with Michael being the oldest, she was concerned that his troubled ways might rub off onto her youngest son. Jonathan was her baby and he looked up to Michael and was highly influenced by him, and this was very concerning to her. She decided to ask Father LaPage if he would consider Jonathan as an altar boy. After all, she knew there was an opening.

Fitch went back to his desk and Finn followed. "That didn't prove to be very fruitful," Finn muttered.

"No, it didn't. There's something about that kid that bothers me. He's definitely got some social issues. It's as though he's detached from the rest of the world."

"Well, we have Rankin coming in this afternoon. Let's see how that goes," Finn said.

Fitch began tapping his pen on the desk. "I'm not very optimistic that Rankin will have anything to add to this investigation. I think the answer lies in the button."

"Well, we can't get a warrant for every suspect and go through their closets in search of a lost button," Finn said. "Now can we?"

"No, we can't. And we can't ask any suspects if they are missing a button, either. They would most certainly destroy the jacket it came from in record time. We need to find out who makes the damned button. " Fitch stopped tapping his pen by tossing it on the desk. "We don't even have a murder weapon," he said. "We have a dozen large rocks that may have been used but none of them have any DNA on them. No skin, no hair, no prints, and no blood," he sighed.

"Shall we bring in the Haney kid?" Finn asked. "Maybe we can sweat him."

"Yes. I doubt it will help, but we need to cover all the bases. We also need to head over to the school and see if we can locate any witnesses that saw Robbie leaving school the day of the murder."

That afternoon Rankin came in and sat in the same seat Michael had occupied earlier in the day. He stuck to his story that he was walking his dog and was pulled to the body after his dog caught a scent. When asked about the condition of the victim's pants, Rankin shrugged it off as if he didn't have any indication of what they were talking about.

Finn took the wheel and brought up Rankin's past conviction for child molestation, and he threatened to lawyer up.

The interview with Rankin didn't add anything concrete to their investigation. They didn't rule out that he may have tampered with the corpse, but it would be nearly impossible to prove. They had no prints or witnesses that would indicate otherwise.

Both detectives agreed that he had probably not committed the murder. It wouldn't make any sense for him to kill Robby and then stay to call it in, unless he was insane, and his demeanor didn't indicate that. They decided to rule Rankin out as a suspect.

After interviewing Rankin, the detectives drudged across the campus looking for leads, but they were unable to find anyone that saw Robby leaving the school on the day he was murdered.

The interview with Stephen Haney was brief. He came to the police station with his mother, an attitude, and a far-fetched story that he was tying his shoe when Robby tripped over him. Stephen also stated that he and Michael walked home from school together the day of the murder, and that he never saw Robby Anderson.

Fitch had a disturbing gut feeling about Stephen because of the way he answered his questions in a carefree, yet clever manner. And he looked Fitch right in the eye. Most juveniles were uneasy when they were called to the police station for an interview, but he saw no fear in Stephen, just a confident and condescending facade.

At this point their investigation lacked any real momentum. Their prime suspect was Michael McNulty, but the condition of Robby's pants, and the fact that Michael had an alibi, caused some concern. They also considered Rankin, but he was a distant and unlikely possibility. Fitch was not one to give up. He knew that like a great lover, a solid clue appeared when one least expected it.

Three days had passed and they were still at the pole position. Fitch was typing a report on a stabbing that occurred over the weekend when his phone rang. He picked up the receiver without taking his attention off the awaiting keys.

"Detective Fitch."

"Detective, my name is Charlene Balsom. I understand you are the investigator in the case of the Anderson boy?"

Fitch straightened up in his chair, ignoring the machine in front of him. "Yes, that's right."

"My daughter is in one of his classes," she paused. "Well, *was* in one of his classes."

"Go on." Fitch was trying not to indicate impatience.

"My daughter, Sandy, saw Robby Anderson the day he was killed."

Fitch snatched up a pen and notebook while holding the phone in place with his right shoulder.

"Please continue."

"Sandy was leaving school through the side door after she had stopped to visit her math teacher for a moment. She had taken the closest exit to her math class and that's when she saw him."

"Please go on," he abruptly responded.

"She said she saw him get into a car with..." once again she hesitated.

"Please, Mrs. Balsom, tell me who he was with?"

"Well," she cleared her throat, "she saw him get into a car with Father LaPage."

CHAPTER 8

It appeared like an ambush on Saint Anne's Cathedral as the pair of investigators dealt with the cluster of traffic merging around the long great neck of the park. Finn was behind the wheel impatiently pounding his fist on the wheel like a flailing jack hammer.

"Who the hell ever came up with the idea to design a road this way?"

"Take it easy," Fitch calmly responded. "We're almost there,"

"Probably an overpaid civil engineer," Finn came back.

Fitch pointed through his window. "Pull in to the side lot and we'll walk from there."

They got out and proceeded to the rectory located on the west wing of the complex. It was 5:15 p.m. and they were hoping LaPage wasn't out extorting a meal from one of his parishioners with the threat of staying too long.

"Let me do most of the talking on this one," Fitch requested as he rang the doorbell.

Less than a minute later the door crept open and a short, older woman dressed like an Amish maiden stood at their service. "May I help you?" she wisped.

"Good afternoon. We're here to see Father LaPage."

The woman had a puzzled look about her. "Father didn't mention anything about having visitors. Do you have an appointment?"

Fitch wondered if the volunteer went through some sort of gatekeeper training. "No, we don't." He produced his badge and she carefully examined the shiny gold shield.

"I see," she said with a curious grin. "Come in and I'll see if he can see you." She escorted them to a small waiting area off the foyer with three antique chairs and a small oval table. The tall ceilings breached the stained glass windows and oak door frames. A large picture of Jesus with his arms stretched out, and his palms open to world, hung on the tallest wall.

The silence was broken by a strong and confident voice. "Gentlemen, please come into my study."

The priest was dressed in all black, except for a bright white collar. He led the way to a door off the hallway and opened it and the detectives walked in with LaPage following.

"Please have a seat," he said gesturing to a pair of chairs in front of a large mahogany desk. The men sat down and watched their host maneuver around the desk to take his chair. His tall leather chair included a rocker and swivel that creaked when turned to the left.

The room was elegantly decorated with an oak bookshelf that sprawled out along the rear quarter, and Fitch noticed the leather-bound books as he entered the room. He recognized at least three classics and was pretty sure the rest followed suit. Probably first editions, he thought.

"I assume you're here to discuss the death of Robby Anderson," he said, looking Fitch in the eye. "It's not very often we get visitors carrying guns." An arrogant smirk defined his face. Fitch got the impression LaPage thought he was superior to them.

A black framed diploma hung on the wall behind the desk, and it was hard to read from where he sat, but Fitch deciphered that the priest had earned a Master's Degree in Archeology. A matching diploma that was more readable hung next to it. The priest had been awarded a Master's Degree in Theology from Notre Dame.

"Yes. That's why we're here. I understand you were very close to the boy?" Fitch said with eyes that pierced like daggers.

"Yes, I am very close with the entire family." LaPage straight back without flinching. Finn was attending to his pen and pad.

"You and Robby spent a lot of time together, right?"

"No more than I do with any other altar boy," he answered with confidence. "He helps us around the church and rectory from time to time, and I stop by his parents' house on occasion and we see each other then. Is there a point to all this?" His tone was unwavering and finite.

"Yes, we'll get to that," Fitch said, maintaining control. "When was the last time you saw Robby Anderson?"

LaPage noticed that Finn lifted his head from his pad to focus on his answer to the question. Both men were intently watching him and awaiting an answer, and LaPage knew the whole line of questioning had narrowed to this particular inquiry. He knew he had to think carefully before answering.

Fitch observed every motion made by the priest as he was studying him for signs of deceit.

"I saw him the day before he was found," LaPage said.

"You did?" Fitch was surprised by the answer.

"Yes. I picked him up from school and took him out for ice cream. After that, he came here to help me sort out canned goods for a food drive for the needy."

Finn had a picture in his mind of LaPage clobbering Robby over the head with a can of B&M baked beans.

"What time did you drop him off?"

"It was around five o'clock when he left."

"So you didn't drive him anywhere?"

"No, he wanted to walk home." LaPage was completely still as he spoke.

Fitch examined the priest carefully. He was quick with his answers and seemed very intelligent. "Were Robby's parents aware that you were picking him up from school?"

LaPage paused before answering, placing his index finger on his left cheek. "Robby told me he asked his mother and she said it was okay." LaPage stood up, ambling around his desk. "If that is all gentlemen, I have a meeting to attend."

Both men sat still for a moment, watching the six-foot tall priest standing over them. Fitch thought he was in very good shape for a priest. He had light blue eyes and a strong jaw that met with a razor at least once a day. His hairline was declining, which made his forehead appear longer. He was well polished.

Fitch stood up and Finn followed his lead.

"Where did you go after Robby left?" Fitch asked, as they stood facing each other like two determined debaters.

LaPage thought it was a trick question because Fitch was speculating that he went somewhere. "I didn't go anywhere that night. I stayed here and read a book."

The detectives slowly moved toward the door and Fitch quickly turned around. "Is there anyone that can verify that?"

LaPage was trapped in thought. "I don't think so. I was alone."

Finn opened the door and held it as a servant would.

"We'll be in touch," Fitch said before exiting.

"Goodbye, Father." Finn nodded and walked out behind his partner.

LaPage didn't say anything. He watched the men leave, and then took a seat in one of the antique chairs near the window and thought about what had transpired. There wasn't any meeting for him to attend.

Working late had become commonplace for the detectives, and this was one of those nights. They had stopped for a quick burger before heading to the Andersons' house. Fitch was determined to find out what the parents of the murdered boy had to say. As the detectives walked to the front door it opened before they reached the stairs. Betty stood in wait, wearing a kitchen apron with a big, yellow, smiley-faced sun on the front.

Fitch knew it would take much more than that to brighten up their kitchen. "Mrs. Anderson," Fitch said as he took her hand into both of his and squeezed tight. She felt his warmth, and the compelling compassion in his eyes.

"Come in," she said through a forced smile and they followed her into the kitchen. "Would you like some coffee?"

"Sure," they both answered at the same time, like an old married couple. Betty went for the cups as Tim walked into the room.

"Hello Detectives." He shook both of their hands. "Please have a seat." Unlike his wife, who had never shed the pounds childbirth had put on her, he was a thin and wiry man who wore his hair short and slicked back, and the thick black glasses resting on the bridge of his long nose were in concert with his hair. He wore a plaid' collared shirt wrapped with a maroon sweater vest. "Is there any news on the investigation?" His voice crumbled. Fitch wondered why LaPage had never asked *that* question.

"We're following some leads." Fitch's words sounded distant.

"Is there anything concrete?" Tim asked through a face void of emotion, as he took a chair across from the investigators.

"I'm afraid not quite yet," Fitch responded. "These things can take time, but I assure you we are on this. No stone will go unturned."

"We won't rest until we find and apprehend whoever did this," Finn added.

Betty brought the coffee over on a silver tray and placed it on the center of the table. She had been carefully listening in silence as the men spoke. There were three cups with a matching silver sugar bowl and pitcher of cream. The detectives helped themselves with Tim following suit.

"We just came from a visit with Father LaPage." Fitch elevated his voice a bit. "Did he ever mention to you when he last saw Robby?"

Tim looked at his wife and she walked over and took a seat. "No, why?" she asked.

Fitch continued. "On the day Robby went missing, did he ask you if he could help Father LaPage at the church after school?"

A curious look found both their faces. "No," she answered. "Why?"

"We have a witness that saw Father LaPage pick Robby up from school the day he didn't come home. When we asked Father LaPage, he said that Robby had informed him that he had your permission to help him sort canned goods after school. You're telling me you knew nothing about this?"

"No, I didn't." She stirred in her chair.

"Wait a minute." Tim stood up. "He never told us that he saw Robby the day he was killed." His anger was brewing.

“Timothy.” Betty stood up along with him. “Father would never hurt Robby. I’m sure there’s an explanation why he didn’t mention it. Maybe he just forgot,” she suggested, before taking her husband’s hand and guiding him back down to his seat.

“We can look further into this,” Finn said as he placed his coffee cup down.

Fitch wasn’t surprised by the Anderson’s confidence and trust in the priest. He looked at Tim admiring his initial intuition. “How often did Father LaPage see Robby alone?”

Tim thought for a few seconds. “Quite a bit, he’s an altar boy, so he helps him out at the church.

“How often?” Finn asked again.

Betty jumped in. “About once a week, sometimes twice, lately.”

Finn looked at his partner and they both knew what the other was thinking. That it was a lot of time to spend with one boy. Fitch dabbed his mouth with his napkin, cleared his throat, and stood up. “I think that will be all for now.” He nodded to Finn and he got up as well. They both thanked the Andersons and were escorted out.

“I think we need to pay another visit to LaPage,” Finn said as they walked back to the car.

“I think you’re right, but this time we’ll have him come to the station.”

They got into the car and drove back to the station, where Fitch called LaPage and requested that he come down in the morning for questioning. He could tell by the apprehension in LaPage’s voice that he was not very pleased with the idea and he expected that LaPage wouldn’t come alone.

District Attorney Mark Corbin was having coffee at his kitchen table when his wife handed him the phone. “It’s Bishop Reardon.” Corbin’s eyes squinted and an odd expression born his face. Although he and the Bishop had a close relationship, Reardon had never called him at home, so he knew it must be very important.

"Good morning, Evan." Corbin always called Reardon by his fist name, unless they were in mixed company.

"Good morning, Mark. We have a bit of a problem," Reardon said in an agitated tone. "Can you come over this morning to discuss it?"

Corbin paused to think how he would have to cancel a breakfast meeting with the clerk of courts. "Is this something that can wait until later today? I have a meeting scheduled this morning."

"I think not, Mark. This is very urgent."

"All right, I'll be there in half an hour."

"See you then."

A buzz took the line and Corbin pushed the receiver button and called the clerk of courts.

The Bishop's house was less than a mile from Saint Ann's Cathedral in an older section of the city. The surrounding homes were mostly Victorians with immaculately landscaped grounds. Many doctors, lawyers, and local politicians occupied the large dwellings, and they enjoyed calling Bishop Reardon their neighbor. On the east wing of the Bishop's home was nun's quarters of the Middleborough diocese. Two nuns lived on the end of the estate that overlooked the flower garden.

Sister Louise was eighty-six years old and wheelchair bound and was seldom seen out of doors. The second of the pair was Sister Hathaway. She was a fraction of Sister Louise's age and quite the opposite; spending much of her time outside the rectory.

District attorney Corbin walked along the sidewalk dressed in a dark blue pinstriped suit with a yellow tie. As he peered through the black, iron, gate that surrounded the estate, he observed a young nun pruning flowers in the garden, a stealing wind trying her scarf. She was dressed in gray and white, and Corbin noticed the fine silhouette of her face. She was a beautiful woman, and he wondered why she had chosen the life of a nun. The Sister stopped for a brief moment and watched Corbin as he walked past, and then turned back to her work, as he opened the gate that led to the Bishop's residence. Corbin rang the bell and waited less than a minute before Bishop Reardon answered the door. He was dressed casually with black pants and a white oxford shirt that concealed a small gold cross his mother had given him when he was fifteen. A few inches taller than Corbin, Reardon stood five-eleven, carrying a small pot belly over a medium build. His graying hair was premature and full to his scalp with sideburns that closely mimicked Elvis's.

"Come in Mark. Thanks for coming on such short notice." He stretched open the door and Corbin entered the hardwood foyer. "Would you like some coffee or tea?"

"I'm fine, Evan, thanks."

Corbin wanted to get to the point of the urgent visit that had cut into his morning meeting. He followed the Bishop to a den where he was seated in a black leather chair. The room was large with cherry paneled walls flowing to a cathedral ceiling. There was a hand crafted sixteenth- century galleon pirate ship model on display in the center of the room. Pictures of many of the great saints hung on the walls, well-preserved behind antique frames. Corbin perused the room looking for his favorite Saint. He spotted Christopher near the entrance, and thought it was a good place for him to hang. A small television was on with the Star Worlds Championships playing. Reardon turned off the TV and took a seat in a matching leather chair next to Corbin, examining him before starting, looking for the right words to begin the discussion.

"This is about the investigation into the Anderson boy," Reardon began.

Corbin was totally caught off guard thinking it may have been about a fundraiser or some vandals desecrating a diocese property.

"The Anderson investigation," Corbin said, "I don't understand." He crossed one leg over the other and folded his hands together as if he were about to pray.

"I appreciate what your office is doing to catch the perpetrator of this tragic offense," Reardon twisted in his seat to position himself in a more direct line to Corbin. "The issue is, the investigating officer on this case seems to be harassing one of my priests, Father LaPage. I received a disturbing call from Father LaPage last night stating that a Detective Fitch came to see him and had some very accusatory questions regarding the death of the Anderson boy." Reardon glanced at his watch as if he was anxious to get the matter off his plate. "My priest answered all of his questions in an attempt to cooperate in the investigation. My Lord, he loved the boy like his own son, and is determined to see justice served as much as anyone," Reardon said. "However, we don't appreciate the insinuating line of questioning from the police department."

Corbin thought about Fitch's style and was surprised to hear that he conducted himself in this manner. "That doesn't sound like Detective Fitch to me. He is one of the best investigators in the department, and he has a high regard for the church and its clergy."

"Well, that may be true, but he called Father LaPage again last night, asking him to come to the station this morning for more questioning." Reardon tapped his fingertips on the end table between them. "I advised him not to comply; that I would address this with you first thing this morning. And here we are," he said. "Your detective is looking in the wrong direction, and making one of my best and highly regarded Priests uncomfortable."

"I understand, Evan." Corbin uncrossed his legs and placed both palms down on his thighs. "I'll have a talk with the chief and see that this matter is taken care of immediately."

Reardon stood up. "Thanks, Mark."

Corbin slapped his palms on his thighs and got up and took the Bishop's hand. After a quick and firm shake they started toward the door. "Have you convinced your wife to allow you to come golfing with us at Myrtle Beach this fall?" Reardon asked.

"I think I'll be all set to go," Corbin responded, not really caring one way or the other.

"Good. You won't need to bring anything except your clubs and a suitcase. This trip is on the Church." He smiled and touched Corbin's shoulder.

"I look forward to it, Evan," he lied. Corbin cringed at the thought of spending that much time with a narcissistic control freak, but Reardon was a man who could provide a huge payday for him.

Reardon opened the door, letting in the sunshine. "Thanks for your understanding and cooperation on this, Mark."

"You're welcome. See you at church." Corbin walked out the same way he came in, glancing into the garden as he walked by. The nun he saw earlier was gone; only the breeze and flowers remained.

"Any luck getting a hold of him yet?" Finn asked as he pulled open the file cabinet drawer.

"Nope." Fitch closed the drawer slightly harder than normal. "He never showed up and he's not answering his phone. Let's give him another hour, and if he doesn't come in, we'll head over to the rectory."

"That sounds good," Finn replied.

Fitch went back to his desk and flopped into his chair. He thought hard about LaPage, and his gut told him that something wasn't right with the character. *Why was he not fully cooperating with the investigation? What was it that he was hiding?* Fitch was determined to find out what made LaPage tick, but for now he decided to look into Rankin, so he reached for his file and began reading. As he turned to the second page, the phone rang, and he picked it up on the second ring.

"Sergeant Fitch," he answered.

"Tom, can you and Bob come to my office, right now?"

"Sure Chief. We'll be there in a few minutes."

"Good." The line died and Fitch placed the receiver down. He sat for moment thinking about the Chief's tone of voice. It didn't sound good. After collecting Finn, they scrambled to the office of the Chief of Police. As they entered his secretary's office, Fitch noticed the frown on her face. It read like she knew what was happening and it wasn't good news for them. She rolled her eyes to the right toward the chief's office door. "Go ahead in, he's expecting you."

"Thanks Marla." Fitch followed her direction with Finn holding up the rear. He knocked twice and went in.

Chief Kevin Kearney sat behind his large desk. His white shirt was pressed to perfection and his black snap-on tie barely reached his belt buckle when standing. Tall and lean, Kearney hadn't gained many pounds since the days he wore his Army officer's uniform. He was clean shaven with a crew-cut hairstyle that was starting to turn color. "Take a seat." The detectives did as he ordered. "I just got a call from the DA. He had a meeting this morning with the Bishop, who informed him that you two have been harassing Father LaPage. What the hell is going on?"

Fitch jumped right in. "Chief, I have a bad feeling about this Priest."

"Why is that?"

"He was the last known person seen with Robert Anderson. He picked the boy up from school the day he was murdered and he never bothered to mention it to the family, with whom he is very close, I might add."

"What did he say when you asked him about it?"

"He admitted that he picked the boy up from school, took him for ice cream, and then back to the church to help him with a chore. LaPage said Robby walked home around supper time, and that was the last time he saw him."

"It doesn't sound like you have much to go on, *here*." He looked back and forth at the detectives sitting in front of him, like he was watching a tennis match.

"LaPage told us that Robby told him he had gotten permission from his mother to help him after school. When we asked her she said she knew of no such thing. LaPage was supposed to come here this morning to answer a few more questions and he never showed up."

"Of course he didn't, the Bishop told him not to. Guys, do you really think a Priest had something to do with the murder of this boy?" His voice elevated a notch.

"I'm not sure, Chief, but something smells funny here." Fitch stirred in his chair.

The Chief got up and walked to the picture that had all former police chiefs' photographs lined up in sequential order. He stood in front of a particular photograph of a rugged looking officer. "Do you see this man?" He pointed. "This was Chief Shawn Blakely, the longest sitting chief of police this city has every employed, and do you know why?"

Both detectives sat looking up, not knowing where this was going or what it had to do with the issue at hand.

"Because he didn't buck the system, and he didn't create waves when the sea was calm. Gentlemen, the Bishop is a very powerful man and the District Attorney assures me that Father LaPage is a man of high moral character and integrity." He turned around and looked directly at them. "A man of God."

Fitch stood up. "Chief, you can't pull us off this. This priest could have something to do with this boy's murder." Now Fitch's tone was elevated. Finn sat quietly, avoiding the crossfire.

"I'm afraid I have no choice. You are not to contact Father LaPage again, unless you're in a confessional at Saint Ann's."

"Chief-"

Fitch was cut off. "That will be all!" Kearney yelled. "Now get out of my office," he said, pointing toward the door. "You should be investigating the boys that beat him up at school. That's your best lead," he insisted. "The Priest had nothing to do with this."

The beaten detectives were out the door and walking past his secretary. "I don't want to hear anymore about Father LaPage." Kearney's rough voice resonated through the doorway.

Fitch went to the coat rack, pulled his jacket off the hook, and walked out of the building without saying a word, feeling discouraged and powerless, like a young boy that had just been scolded for something he didn't do.

Fitch got in his car and drove to Bottle Park where he walked off his anger for well over an hour before stopping at the site where Robby's body had been found. Sitting on the ground in the same spot the murder had occurred, he thought about how scared and alone the young boy must have been in the seconds leading up to his death. The anger came back.

CHAPTER 9

1989

Friday night brought out the city boppers with hundreds of young people drinking and drugging to remember or to forget the past. Some were just living for the thrill of the moment, and many ended up at Carrigans pub resigned to emptying as many glasses as possible. The back room at Carrigans was a large, dark wood-paneled rectangular hall with a gray concrete floor. The pictures that once hung on the walls were replaced by old stains from drinks tossed against it, dried blood, and vomit that had not been completely cleaned off.

Stephen cursed at the pinball machine as he rocked it back and forth with care, just short of a tilt. A short young woman with brown hair and oversized breasts appeared beside him, holding a beer in one hand and a cigarette in the other. She swayed to the tune of Jim Morrison's "Light My Fire" pouring out of a beaten-up juke box.

"Ya kinda look like um, ya know," she slurred.

Stephen glanced at her for a second, trying not to lose his concentration. "Like who?"

"Like Jim Morrison." She hid a belch and tipped back her glass eliminating three ounces.

"Cept your nose is a lill longer."

Stephen took another quick glance at her, and this time, she could sense he was a little irritated.

"Not in a bad way or anythin," she back peddled. "You're cuter than he is, was."

"Shit!" Stephen growled, shaking the machine one last time and slamming it against the wall as the ball rolled out of sight. Slowly turning to face her with an agitated look, he began speaking in a low monotone voice. "You come over here with your bad breath and sour my game with insults about my long nose, and I don't even know you."

She didn't know how to react, so she reached out her hand, "I'm Mandy."

Stephen looked down at her hand without any physical or emotional reaction. "Yes, you are," he said, and he walked away, leaving her alone with her defeat and bad breath.

At the bar, Stephen found Michael sitting with his brother, Jonathan. The long bar was a solid mahogany landing-strip with bottles lined up behind it in three tiers in front of a large mirror. A wooden sign centered above the bottles read, "If you're drinking to forget, please pay in advance." A neon Schlitz sign winked at the patrons only to be challenged by a bright Budweiser sign, a smug-looking leprechaun with his dukes in the ready staring down the toughest of customers. The bartender came over with his usual attitude in tow, "Yeah" he greeted, nodding in an upward motion, as if he had a hook in his mouth and a fishing line tugging from the ceiling.

Stephen wanted to cuff him, but smiled instead. "Bud." The large bartender went to the cooler, scooped out a bottle, and slammed it down with authority. "Buck twenty," he barked.

"Take it out of here," Michael said, pointing to his small stack of bills stacked neatly on the bar. The bartender snatched the money off the bar and moved to the register. "What an asshole," Michael said, loud enough for the bartender to hear. Instantly turning around, the bartender reached under the bar picking up a miniature bat with a Boston Red Sox logo stamped on it. "Are you talking to me?" he gushed.

Stephen looked at the irate guy fuming behind the bar, and then turned to Michael, and they both busted out in laughter. The bartender stood gripping his club, as they both got up and walked away, continuing to chuckle at him.

Jonathan, in his normal state of drunkenness, sat hovering over his beer in silence.

Richard Stack was a former city worker who retired on a bad back that wasn't as bad as he led everyone to believe. A barrel-chested lad with a rough beard and a missing front tooth that was seldom obvious, he earned the reputation of being a tough guy who didn't take any crap from anyone. On his first night working at Carrigans, a drunken customer was out of line, so Stack tossed him out, cracking the guy's head against the wall, leaving a trail of blood along the way. Stephen and Michael watched from a distance and their hatred for him grew stronger every day since. Stack was not liked by anyone, including himself. The complaints to the owner of the pub went unheard, because he needed someone that could keep the place in order on the weekends. Too many bartenders in the past had failed, but Stack wasn't one of them, so he kept him on. After beating several customers to a pulp, the word was out that it was in your best interest to not act up when Stack was working. He was the epitome of bullying.

Stephen and Michael stood in the corner watching a couple of guys playing pool, a glass of Bushmills whiskey cooling in Stephen's hand and a Miller beer in Michael's. The eight ball sat just as it had before the break, and the rest of the colorful balls surrounding it were on one half of the table, indicating a loose rack or a weak break.

"I'd like ta shove that club up Stack's ass," Michael said in a low raspy voice.

Stephen looked at him without responding and then glanced across the room at Mandy, who was talking with a strange looking guy near the juke box. The lean built guy wore a black-leather Harley Davidson jacket with the arms cut off, and he had a shabby haircut, with silver earrings dangling from both ears.

"Do you see the girl talking with sleazy rider?" Stephen asked.

"Yeah, what about her?"

"She told me I look like Jim Morrison." A half smile erupted and Stephen raised his chin a notch.

Michael examined his friend for a few seconds. "You kinda look like Morrison, but your nose is bigger than his."

"Shut the fuck up! That's exactly what she said."

A commotion began in the bar, which they couldn't see from their location. The music had died once the last quarter was spent, and the loud chatter carried into the pool room, indicating a fight was irrupting. Quickly, Stephen and Michael moved toward the bar to see what was happening. Michael, being tall, had a better view over the crowd than Stephen. What he saw nearly brought his blood to a boil. Stack had Michael's brother Jonathan by the throat and was choking and dragging him toward the door. As they frantically worked their way through the jeering crowd, Michael watched as Stack threw a series of right hand punches, which caused blood to immediately pour from his brother's nose. When they finally made it through the mob, Jonathan had already been tossed to the curb, and Stack hopped back behind the bar to retrieve his club. He had noticed Michael and Stephen moving through the thick cluster of people and he wanted to be armed for any kind of retaliation.

"You mother fucker!" Michael shot his index finger out at Stack like a spear in flight. Stack stood behind the comfort of his bar tapping his weapon in his palm as if he wanted Michael to try and make a move against him. Stephen didn't speak, and he didn't need to, because the way he looked at Stack told it all. It was a look of hatred and pending revenge.

When they made it out the front door, Jonathan had picked himself up and was holding his nose in an unsuccessful attempt to stop the bleeding. Michael yelled toward the crowd of people gathered by the door. "Get me a towel or something." Several seconds later a young girl came over with a handkerchief and handed it to him. "Let me see," Michael demanded, and his brother lowered his hands. "It's broken. That son of a bitch broke your nose," he said glancing toward the bar and then back to his drunken brother. "Let's go, I'll take you to the hospital."

"I'll go with you," Stephen offered. They began heading towards Michael's car in a slow, even pace, holding the cloth to Jonathan's tilted back and beaten face.

"I'm going to get that..." Stephen tugged on Michael's arm, cutting short his sentence. Michael looked at his friend and knew what he was thinking. Soon, they were going to get even with Stack.

CHAPTER 10

Friday afternoon arrived and the streets were busy as people were hoping start their weekend early. Jake and his long-time partner, Rick Mosko, had been planted in their olive-green unmarked Ford for three days watching an apartment building on the corner of East Main and Dover Streets. The sun was fading in and out as the clouds moved along in a hurry, pushed by the western wind.

The five story brick building was a nightmare for the police and fire department, and had been for the past decade. Once it became low income housing with many section-eight tenants, the crime rate increased tenfold. The calls received were mainly for domestic disturbances, loud noise complaints, and drug dealers. Occasionally the wagon would come and take away a corpse with a hole or two in it. Dealers behind the building stood in wait from noon until four in the morning, greeting walkers and cars for a quick exchange of crack cocaine for cash. Every few months the narcotics bureau would hit the dealers, but they usually tossed the drugs as they fled, or swallowed them. Most dealers kept the small rocks wrapped in cellophane hidden in their mouths, making it easier to swallow as the cops approached. The beat cops would occasionally surprise them, choking the rocks out before they could swallow them. Most of the pushers only carried small amounts of crack while selling on the street, and this made it difficult for the officers to make a case for anything other than possession, even after they observed the dealers making transactions.

Jake sat in the passenger seat in a semi-slouching position. Reaching into his pocket, he retrieved a piece of sugarless gum and unwrapped it. Once out of the wrapper, he took the spent piece out of his mouth and carefully folded it in the gum wrapper and popped the new piece into his mouth.

"When I worked this district on the dogwatch, I used to park behind that building and study for my undergrad," Jake said while staring at the tall brick building.

Rick glanced at his partner of four years. "If you tried that today, they might find you in the morning with a bullet in your head."

"Yeah, you're probably right." Jake chewed a bit faster. "Now, those were busy times. I had just gotten married to Charlotte and I was going to school full time during the day and working nights. What an angel that woman was to put up with all that," he said as he thought about his young bride.

It was apparent to Rick that Jake missed his wife, but he never talked about it.

"There he goes," Jake said. "See him in the white hat leaning into the Toyota?"

"I see him. It's hard to watch this and not make a move."

Jake shifted his weight to alleviate a tingling sensation in his left leg. "Let the narcotics guys handle it."

Rick changed the channel on the radio. "Do you think he's in there or what? It's been three days and this is getting pretty goddam old."

Jake examined his partner. He was also tired of waiting and his aching back was a constant reminder. "Well, he grew up with this guy and they did time together. If I had to guess where he might be hiding out, I'd say it's here."

Rick thought about what his friend and superior officer said. "If I shot and killed my girlfriend, I wouldn't hang around, hiding out in some ratty apartment block. I'd get the hell out of Dodge," Rick argued.

"He might have skipped town," Jake said, "or maybe, he's just waiting for things to cool down. It's also possible he's short on cash and is waiting for a score before he leaves town."

"Maybe both," Rick added.

"I hope so," Jake said focusing on the building. He was committed to remaining on the stakeout for five days before switching to plan B. "Wait a minute!" Jack sat up a bit. "See the guy in the blue knit hat? I think that may be him."

Rick pulled down his sunglasses for a clearer view. "Who wears a knit hat on a day like this?"

"Someone who's hiding something," Jake said. "That's him."

Jerome Baker walked out of the front door of the building, took a left, and started heading up the street. He was wearing an army jacket, blue jeans, a dark blue ski hat, and dark sunglasses.

"Let's roll." The excitement in Jake's voice was apparent. Rick reached for the door handle. "Hold on." Jake said. They both stopped and watched as Baker turned into a liquor store located right next to the building. "He's going in for some booze. Let's bag him when he comes out. I'll wait in the doorway of the building and you go to the other side of the store near the parking lot." Jake looked at his partner. "Be careful."

"Okay," Rick acknowledged, and they quickly exited the vehicle, moving into position.

Baker was a tall, lean, and muscular career criminal with a daily crack habit. His girlfriend had been sleeping with Baker's best friend, and when he found out about it, he felt like a fool because everyone knew, except him. Angry, and mentally distorted from excessive liquor and drugs, Baker shot her in the head. Fearing for his life, his former best friend fled to Georgia after hearing about the murder. Baker was going after him next, but first, he needed time to think and figure things out, so he decided to look up his old pal for a place to hide out. They were both cop haters and were always attempting to out-smart the police, so his friend agreed to take him in.

Baker was alone in the apartment, and out of vodka, so he decided to run next door, quickly purchase a couple bottles, and head right back to his place of refuge. He wasn't counting on the building being watched by the police.

The door opened and Baker exited the store, glancing both ways, like a child crossing a busy street. When he thought it was safe, he started back toward his building. With a brown paper bag in his left hand, he started down the sidewalk on full alert. His instinct told him to look to his rear, and he quickly turned his head around, instantly noticing something out of the ordinary. A white guy wearing a jacket and tie was approaching from behind. With his free hand, Baker discretely reached into his belt line, taking a hold of a Smith & Wesson 9mm automatic handgun.

Jake saw him reach for his gun, and yelled out, attempting to warn his partner, who couldn't see what was happening from his angle, but it was too late. Baker heard Jake's warning and quickly determined that it was a sting. He dropped the paper bag, turned and fired, hitting Rick in the left shoulder. The impact knocked Rick back a step, but he continued to draw his gun even though the impact was traumatic. Baker took another shot as he dashed across the street, and the bullet passed by Rick's head. The pain started to take residence, and Rick became dizzy, as Jake sprinted over to assist him. People on the street were ducking and quickly moving out of harm's way as the shots rang out.

"Rick, are you all right?" Jake took a quick look at the wound and saw that it wasn't life threatening.

"Just get the bastard!" Rick shuffled to the base of a streetlight post and sat down.

Several people began to creep out from their hiding places. An attractive young woman handed Rick a clean handkerchief to apply pressure on his wound, and Jake figured he was in good hands, so he took off like a rocket. Jake spotted Baker ducking behind a building across the street and he followed with his gun in one hand, and a radio in the other, calling for an ambulance and back-up. He put out a description of the suspect, and as Baker changed direction, he yelled it into his handset without breaking stride. Jake was gaining on Baker as he ran down the busy street, trying to focus on Baker's gun hand to avoid any surprises. All the jogging and exercising Jake had been doing was paying off, as he closed the gap on his subject.

As Jake approached, Baker turned and fired a shot, before ducking into an alley. Carefully, Jake approached the alleyway, and when he reached the edge of the building, he quickly turned his head around the corner anticipating an ambush. The alley looked clear, so he slowed down, scanning the area with his .357 revolver in the ready.

Baker was out of breath and had stooped down behind a dumpster. Wiping the rolling sweat off his forehead with his sleeve, he listened as the approaching sirens in the distance became louder. He knew he didn't have much time. Once his heart rate slowed, he sprinted out from behind the large green container and began to take flight. Jake was scaling the graffiti-smeared wall of the building and wasn't noticed by Baker as he popped out to continue his escape. Jake stood with his weapon in position with one hand under the other and his left leg forward in a balanced Weaver stance.

"Jerome!" Jake yelled. "Give it up."

Baker turned, pointing his gun, and Jake instantly reacted by taking a shot at his center mass, just as he had been trained, hitting Baker in the middle of the chest. The bullet pierced his heart and exited through the back, knocking him to his knees. Baker's gun dropped to the ground, and he knelt glassy-eyed looking at Jake as he slowly approached with his weapon in a locked in position. As he got closer, Jake could see the lost and confused eyes of a dying man. Baker never said a word, and his eyes never closed, even when he fell forward expelling his final breath.

It was the first person Jake had ever shot, and the look on Baker's face as he knelt dying in the alley would stay with him forever. Even though he was justified in the shooting, and Baker had shot his partner, there was something dark about taking the life of another human being. It was something one got used to, or never wanted to experience again. It all depended on the character of the individual. Jake being a man of compassion and pity he was hoping this would be the last time he took a life.

CHAPTER 11

Last call was given fifteen minutes earlier than usual, because Stack had a pounding headache and he wanted to clear out the bar and get home. He had dragged out a customer an hour earlier and that's when his head began to throb. Three aspirins later, he still hadn't gotten any noticeable relief. Once the last person was out, he locked the door and began his closing routine. After cleaning off the bar and back room, he cashed out the register and placed the day's receipts in a small blue leather pouch. Prior to setting the alarm, he made sure all the lights were off and he shut down the video recorder.

As always, Stack exited through the rear door that opened up to the alleyway. Turning the deadbolt until he heard a metallic clicking sound, he extracted the key and shook the door vigorously making sure it was secure. As Stack turned around, he realized he wasn't alone. Swiftly drawing a double-edged blade from his belt buckle, he confronted the two men that had crept up on him. In a split second, before the pain set in, he saw the faces of Michael and Stephen. As Stack extended his blade, Stephen administered the first blow to his right wrist with a three-inch steel pipe wrapped in duct tape. The pain was excruciating and Stack howled in the morning air as his knife immediately fell to the ground. It was instantly apparent to Stack that he was in serious trouble, as he clutched his fractured wrist, contemplating an escape.

The second blow came from Michael at full swing and landed across Stack's left ear and upper jaw. Michael's pipe was the same width as Stephen's, but a few inches longer. Stack felt a sudden surge of pain and a flash of light, before falling into a state of darkness. As he lay bleeding in the parking lot with a broken jaw and ruptured eardrum, Stephen came down with a final blow to the top of Stack's head, fracturing his skull. Both assailants pulled their ski masks down, covering their faces. They had rolled them up just before the attack, so Stack would recognize who was taking him out and why. Despite Stephen's reluctance, Michael had convinced him to expose their identities for just a few seconds. Michael wanted his face to be the last thing Stack would ever see, and he wanted him to take it to the grave.

The masked pair stood over the body for a brief moment looking down as the blood swamped Stack.

"He's not so tough now is he?" Michael concluded.

"Get the car," Stephen commanded.

Michael ran to his car and quickly pulled it up. Swooping around to the back, he opened the trunk, pulling out a large green tarp, and then quickly spread it out next to the body. The blood was spreading, so they knew they had to move fast. Together they picked Stack up and dropped him in the center of the tarp and folded it over him. Stephen wrapped a plastic kitchen bag over Stack's bloody head and drew the strings tight across his neck, and then went to work with the duct tape. Michael wiped up the blood and then poured oil and then gasoline over the stains remaining on the ground. Once Stack was wrapped tight, they picked him up and threw him into the trunk that was laced with thick clear plastic.

"Get the money," Stephen hissed, and Michael moved abruptly, scooping up the pouch that was lying on the ground before darting to his car and settling behind the wheel.

Stephen lit a match and dropped it on the ground and they watched the flame explode, illuminating the night air, before it subsided as the oil took control. Stephen darted to the car, hopped in, and they sped off with the flame behind them glowing in the night. Michael's license plate was covered with a small dark-green garbage bag. Once they were out of the immediate area they would remove it, but they would use it again at Stack's gravesite in Vermont.

Stephen had staked out the rear exit of the bar for three Thursdays in a row at closing time. He sat on the main street in his car watching Stack appear from the alley after his shift was over. Stack was usually like clockwork, walking across the quiet street to his car and driving to the bank deposit box around 2:50 a.m.

The rear door of Carrigan's pub faced a large brick building that was an old meat packing plant; and there weren't any apartments or open businesses with a view of the rear exit. The alley was a dead end on the opposite end of the main street. There was only one way in and out of the alleyway, and the back door of Carrigan's was hidden, like the inside of a horseshoe. It was the perfect place to take Stack out. Stephen knew the beat cops and he was pretty confident they would be tucked in behind some building sound asleep.

Stephen and Michael arrived in Vermont less than two hours later. Stephen remembered the secluded area from an affair he had nine years earlier with a college student whose parents owned a cottage a couple miles up the main road. Parked on a dirt road, they got out on foot and made their way through the dark woods. A half moon shone in the sky and was beginning to fall, but it offered some visibility to help them carefully maneuver through the brush. A couple minutes later, they arrived at the destination Stephen had chosen. He didn't want to have to drag the body too far, so he had picked a spot close to where the car was to be parked, and with two lengths of rope it would be less cumbersome to drag the body to the hole. Stephen tied one rope under Stacks arms, and the other around Stack's neck, indicating it would act as a tourniquet and prevent the blood from exiting the head. Heaving the heavy body in synchronized tugs, they were both out of breath when they arrived at their destination. The five-foot long, four-feet deep hole had two shovels and a rake lying on the ground beside it, where they had left them six hours earlier.

Stephen had carefully planned the murder from start to finish. His strategy was to take his car and locate the perfect site and dig the hole in advance. They would take Michael's car later that night when it was time to dump the body, being less conspicuous using two different vehicles. Time was going to be very tight, so he planned the entire night to the minute. Stephen planned to arrive at the location around 8:30 p.m. because there would be fewer people out and it would be harder for anyone to identify his vehicle in the dark. He calculated that would leave them two hours to dig the hole before heading back to Middleborough. Stephen thought about going earlier in the day, so they wouldn't have to rush, but he didn't want to take the chance that a hunter or hiker would happen upon the hole and draw attention to it. Even though the ground was rocky, he was confident that the two of them could dig a large enough hole in two hours. When they returned to bury the body, they would be done in short order because he knew it would be much faster to fill in the hole than it was to dig it. Stephen figured they would be back in the city around 12:45 p.m. That would give them an hour to clean up, switch cars, and get to the bar before closing. Michael's trunk was already sealed and loaded with bags of lime, a tarp, oil, and gasoline.

"We need to move fast, you know what to do," Stephen said as they pulled the body from the trunk. Michael let go and Stack hit the ground with a hard thud.

"Why do I have to do the shitty work?" Michael complained.

"Because I'm helping you get revenge for your brother, remember?"

"What am I, a f-fuckin dentist?" Michael snarled.

They dragged the body over to the hole and Michael took out a pair of pliers and began pulling out Stack's teeth, one at a time, placing them in a plastic zip lock bag. Stephen filled two gallon size baggies with lime and taped them over each of Stack's hands leaving his finger tips submerged in the quick-lime. His research indicated it would take about six months for decomposition to take effect. After completing the tasks that would eliminate any identification, they dropped the body in the hole. Stephen tore open and poured five fifty-pound bags of lime over the entire body, and then they went to work filling in the hole. Once the hole was filled and even with the ground, Stephen raked leaves, sticks, and branches over the site to make it blend in. The sun would be coming up soon and they wanted to be out of the area before compromising themselves, so they quickly moved out of the woods and back to the car.

As they drove off the dirt road and turned onto the pavement, Stephen glanced over at Michael as he let out a huge yawn.

"Make sure you show up for work today," Stephen said. "We can't have anything out of the ordinary, *today*." Michael nodded. "As far as our alibis are concerned, I was home all night, and my mother will attest to that. After dinner I told her I'd be in my room and was not to be disturbed. I left the TV on and snuck out the window. She's been sick lately and goes to bed early, so I should be all set. What about you?"

Michael was nearly nodding out from exhaustion. "I live alone, so I'd just say I was home all night watching TV." He let out a lingering yawn, like a sleepy giant.

"Okay, hopefully it won't come to that, but just in case, we need to be prepared." Stephen glanced at his failing friend with hard eyes. He knew Michael had big balls and would do anything he asked, but he also knew he wasn't very smart, and that's what bothered him.

Michael was fast asleep as Stephen, wide awake, accelerated down the highway heading south. His adrenalin had not completely decreased, and his mind was racing. *Stack got what he deserved. The world is better off without him in it. Actually, I helped mankind and should be considered a humanitarian. The world is better off now.* Reaching out, he switched on the radio and immediately recognized the song playing: "Another One Bites The Dust." He smiled, thinking what a fitting song it was for the moment.

CHAPTER 12

Captain Farris opened his door and called out to Jake, who was at his desk catching up on paperwork. Farris, a sixty-five year old family man, poorly dressed and overweight and with a large head, was often the subject of many station-house jokes, such as "Would you rather have a million dollars or Farris's head filled with quarters?" It was only said in a whisper because Farris didn't tolerate unprofessionalism on the job, especially at his expense.

"Close the door and take a seat." Farris pointed toward a chair in front of his metal desk. Jake did as he was told. "I just got off the phone with the city doctor and he said he had a conversation with Rick's neurosurgeon. It doesn't look very promising that he'll be back on duty for quite a while." Farris straightened out a folder on his desk. "Hell, he may never come back."

"Yeah, I know. I spoke to his doctor a couple days ago when I went to pay him a visit." Jake let out a sigh as he spoke. "The nerve damage in his shoulder may cause partial paralysis in his left arm."

Farris noticed Jake clenching his right fist.

"And Rick is left-handed," they both said simultaneously.

Farris displayed a moderate grin thinking they were on the same page.

"If his gun hand isn't one hundred percent, he can't return to duty," Farris shrugged.

"There are worse things in life than early retirement," Jake said.

"You have a point there." Farris picked up the folder he had been diddling with. "Well, you've been cleared in the shooting investigation by internal affairs, and the feds also agree that you had reasonable cause to pull the trigger." Farris reached into his desk and took out Jake's service revolver and Jake began to feel a sense of relief. "It was a good shoot." He handed the weapon to Jake. "I got to tell you, if it were me, I might not have gotten my piece back so quickly," Farris said earnestly.

Jake knew he was indicating that a white officer shooting a black suspect would be scrutinized harder by the public.

"Even though you have your gun back, the Chief wants you to stay under the radar. There are still some people in the black community that want your ass tied to the whipping post."

Jake didn't stir. He could sense there was more by the way Farris clutched on to the manila folder.

"I want you to investigate this case," Farris said as he handed over the folder.

Jake opened it and began browsing. "Come on Captain, a missing person case. I'm a homicide detective. Give it to David."

"No! This one comes directly from the Chief. You're a one man show, Jake. Rick is out and I'm short on manpower," Farris said in an exasperated tone. "I don't have anyone to partner you up with. This should keep you out of trouble for a while."

Jake sat tilted, motioning his head back and forth.

"When the dust settles, I'll get you a new partner and back working on stiffs again."

Looking into Farris's eyes, Jake knew there was no point in arguing, so he flipped open the file again. "Richard Stack, a bartender that went missing two weeks ago. This guy is forty-one-years-old, Captain. He's probably somewhere in Mexico, drunk as an Apache on furlough."

"It doesn't fit the profile," Farris responded. "He never misses work, and he hasn't withdrawn any money from his bank account or used any credit cards. The last time he was seen was three weeks ago, this Thursday, after closing up. The night receipts are missing along with him." Farris leaned back in his chair and folded his hands across his chest.

"Don't you have a missing child or something else I can look in to?

"No I don't, Jake." It was apparent his boss was becoming agitated.

"Eight hundred and twenty-two dollars," Jake said as he took to his feet. "I doubt he would skip town for that amount."

"That's why I'm putting my best investigator on it. Something smells funny here; see what you can find out." Farris stood up, which was another way of telling Jake to get the hell out of his office.

Jake walked out with his gun and folder feeling as though *he* had just been molested.

Happy to be back on the street, Jake hurried past his pile of paperwork and right out the back door. He decided to head to the bar and talk to some people.

The visit to Carrigan's didn't turn out to be very fruitful because it was early in the day and not many people were available to speak with. A different crowd occupied the bar stools during the day: mostly older drunks and retirees that considered the bar their second home. Jake decided to come back in the evening and see what he could learn about the missing bartender.

After dinner, Jake returned to the bar wearing jeans and a tee shirt in an effort to blend in and not look like a cop. As he slipped into the bar, Jake drew many stares from the locals sitting behind their half empty glasses. Scanning the bar, he selected a stool next to a young woman sitting alone, cuddling her White Russian. The bartender came over with a stale look and took Jake's order. A couple minutes later, Jake sat with a glass of beer contemplating who he might buddy up with. His choices were not very plentiful, so Jake decided to go with the closest person to him. He took a sip of beer and quickly placed it back down, remembering why he didn't drink.

"Is it going to pick up in here later? It's kind of dead," Jake said.

The young woman had given him a nod of approval when he took a seat next to her and he hoped she would open up.

"Usually around nine o'clock." She drew hard from her glass.

Jake figured she was around thirty-five, but she was seasoned and looked nearly ten years older. Her nails were chewed to the quick and her clothes smelled like a hamper in August. Her brown hair was pinned up, with stragglers hanging down along her rough cheeks. Jake thought she may have once been an attractive young girl before the bottle took hold of her.

"Do you come in this place a lot?" He wasn't good at small talk and he didn't want to talk with her longer than necessary.

She looked at him longer than usual. "You're a cop, aren't you?"

He hesitated, contemplating if a lie was in order. "Is it that obvious?"

"Hell yes," she smiled.

"What are you drinking?" Jake asked, aware that his plan of blending in was a failure.

"A White Russian." She tapped her glass and Jake signaled the bartender. "You're here about Stack, right?"

Jake thought she was pretty intuitive for a lounge lizard. *The vodka hasn't completely destroyed her brain.* "Do you know him?"

"I used to." Her expression became more serious and the way she was talking in the past tense interested him.

"Why do you say, *used to*?"

She took a long sip from her new drink. "Do you play pool?" she asked. And without waiting for a response, she picked up her drink and bag and moved toward the back room. Jake followed with his full glass of beer to the pool table.

"Do you have any quarters?" she asked, as she picked up the rack.

Jake reached into his pocket and produced two coins.

After racking up the balls, she carefully removed the rack and Jake noticed her shaky fingers as she tried to maintain the integrity of the triangle. Jake broke the rack with a hard stroke of the cue, but nothing found a hole. She quickly chalked the tip of her stick and took a shot and the three-ball fell into a pocket. Moving around the table short of grace, she sank four balls before turning the game over to Jake.

Jake took a shot, cutting in the nine-ball, and then he continued to the next shot where he wasn't so lucky. "Damn," he cursed as he stepped away from the banged up table.

"You like music? she asked.

"Sure I do."

"Got any quarters for the juke box?"

Jake reached into his pocket and handed her two coins and she went over to the music machine, put in the money, and began selecting songs. A few seconds later, Earth Wind & Fire sounded out, filling the back room with harmony.

Jake liked the song "Fantasy" and hoped she was breaking the silence to open up and talk. *She doesn't look like a rhythm-and-blues type; a rock and roller for sure.*

They were alone, so Jake figured it was a good time to dig for information.

"What kind of guy is Stack?" he asked, chalking his cue.

"Not too many people liked Stack," she said. "But he wasn't so bad once you got to know him. He had a tough life and couldn't brush that big chip off his shoulder." She moved to take her next shot. "He had beaten up a shitload of people since he started bartending here." She motioned like she was throwing a jab. "He was one bad-ass dude."

Jake handed her the chalk. "Were there any altercations that stand out in your memory; someone that may have wanted revenge?"

She stopped playing and looked at him without speaking. He figured she had something to give up and was contemplating if she should. Picking up her drink, she drew a long sip through the straw.

"About a month ago, I was sitting at the bar and Stack had words with a guy before tossing him out on his ass. Broke his nose," she said, banging the cue once on the floor. "Man, the blood poured out of his face like a hose."

"Really, what was his name?"

"Jon McNulty." She moved into position for a bank shot. "His older brother Mike and his friend Steve were here, and they were pretty pissed off."

"So, why was this scuffle different than any other?" Jake asked.

"I don't know. I hear those guys really hated Stack." She chalked her cue and then blew the remaining dust off the end. "If looks could kill, you know?" She took careful aim and sank the eight ball into the side pocket.

"Nice shot." Jake gestured toward a small table and they sat down. "What started the fight?"

"Mike and Stack had words at the bar, and after he and Steve came back in here, it started up again with his brother, Jon," she said. "Jon is usually pretty quiet. He doesn't bother anyone, so I was kind surprised when Stack thumped him up." She took a hard drink. "Jon really pissed Stack off."

"Do you know what he said?" Jake felt like he was gaining traction as she rambled on.

"I didn't hear them, but the rumor is that Stack called Jon a fag, and Jon spit at him."

"That could have done it," Jake said. "Did any of them threaten Stack?" he asked, straightening up in his chair.

"Not that I heard." She let out a short yawn, and Jake felt his window closing.

"What's the word on the street?"

"The word is that those two maniacs made Stack disappear. Those are two crazy bastards." She pushed back a strand of hair that was testing her glass. "I heard they even killed some kid in the park when they were like ten-years-old."

Jake's antenna went up as he remembered Robby Anderson lying lifeless in the park. "Are you talking about the boy killed in Bottle Park in 1972?

"Yeah, I think that's the one." She pulled out a cigarette from her bag and Jake lit it for her.

"His name was Robert Anderson," Jake said thoughtfully.

She caught his stare and was briefly locked in as his eyes told her that he was connected to the murdered boy in some way.

The stare was broken as two people entered the room and walked over to the juke box.

"Yeah, that sounds like him," she said, facing Jake once again.

Jake handed her his card. "I didn't even get your name."

She reached out, gently shaking his hand. "It's Karen Huff," she said with a slanted smile.

"Well, thank you for your help, Karen. If you can think of anything else, please call me."

She glanced at his card, "I will, Sergeant Waterfield."

Jake returned the smile and walked away, and she sat watching as he moved out the back door. Karen found him very attractive with a nice build. She briefly fantasized about Jake on top of her, pressing his ebony skin hard against hers, and then she looked down, realizing her glass was empty.

Early the next morning, Jake went back to Carrigan's and examined the premises for any clues that might help him determine what occurred the night Stack went missing. The initial report from the uniformed officers indicated there were no signs of a struggle inside the bar, and that Stack's car was found across the street from the bar where he always parked it before heading into work. The search of his apartment showed no signs of foul play, and his neighbors hadn't seen him since the night he went missing. Jake came to the conclusion that Stack had most likely been abducted somewhere between the rear of the bar and where his automobile was parked.

It was gravely quiet in the alleyway except for the quick retreat of a feral cat that was spooked as Jake rounded the corner. Carefully pacing toward the rear exit of the bar, he examined his surroundings for windows on buildings or a vantage point where a witness could have noticed Stack leaving the bar at the end of his shift. Jake quickly determined that was not a possibility because their view would have been blocked by the large building adjacent to the back door of Carrigan's.

As he made his way closer to the bar entrance, Jake noticed a large dark stain in the alley just outside the back door and out of view from the street. He walked over, knelt down, and dabbed his finger in the center of the stain and brought it up to his nose. It smelled like motor oil, but it was not consistent with a normal oil leak. The stain was erratically shaped and had a burnt smell. Also, Jake thought it wasn't located where a car would normally be parked, unless someone was moving something from the bar and backed a vehicle up for that purpose. He took out a swab, extracted a sample, and placed it in a clear bag.

Moving toward the door, Jake observed that it was metal and painted dark brown with a long metal handle. It was secured with a dead bolt that locked from the outside with a key. Closely examining the door, Jake noticed something about three feet up from the ground on the doorframe that abutted the brick wall. *It looks like a tiny spatter of blood.* With a pocket knife, he scraped a specimen off the door and dropped it into a small bag.

The case was becoming more interesting because the evidence was beginning to indicate foul play, and the possible connection to the Anderson case inspired Jake to learn more about Stephen Haney and Michael McNulty.

CHAPTER 13

Lines extended outside the stadium gates for nearly a quarter mile as scalpers discretely haggled with people who were trying to get a deal on tickets. The sun was sliced nearly in half by the horizons edge. Stephen and Michael hid behind their dark shades as they cut into the beer line.

"Hey, get in the back of the line like everyone else." A heavy blond girl said as she stood in line along with her two of her girlfriends, agitated by the arrogant and disrespectful pair.

Stephen turned around and looked at her awkwardly. "Everyone else," he mimicked. "All I see is you and your two friends."

Her face turned a shade paler and her lips thinned. "That's right and we were here first, asshole!" She placed her hands on her hips, like a referee.

Stephen turned his back and ordered a beer. Michael had already bought his while they were quarreling, and he moved out of the line.

The three girls were agitated and began cursing them under their breath. A smile found Stephen's face, and he turned around with his cold beer in hand, directly facing the girls.

"I fart in your general direction," he said, prior to shifting his hips to one side and letting out gas with a loud bang.

Michael uncontrollably spit out his beer before he was able to swallow, spraying one of the girl's shoes. Roaring in laughter, Michael wiped off his face as Stephen marched away, void of any emotion and standing tall, like a palace guard.

The girls began yelling at them, and one of them threatened that her boyfriend would kick Stephen's ass for his disgusting behavior.

Michael caught up to Stephen and patted him on the shoulder. "That was awesome, man."

Stephen stopped and turned back, looking at the girls who were still watching them from a distance. One of them gestured with her middle finger and Stephen grabbed his crotch and shifted his hips forward. He looked at Michael, and once again, they erupted in laughter, before heading toward the building.

Stephen pulled a small piece of aluminum foil from his pants pocket and extracted two pills. He handed one to Michael, and popped the other into his mouth, and chased it down with his beer.

"What's this?" Michael asked with a delighted grin.

"Mescaline," Stephen responded with protruding eyes making a peculiar face.

"Mescaline," Michael repeated. "Nobody does this shit anymore. Where did you get this?"

With a crooked smile, Stephen answered. "I have a connection."

Inside the stadium, people were being ushered to their seats. Michael had the tickets and motioned toward the nose bleed section.

"We're way up there?" Stephen asked. "Let me see those." He quickly glanced at them. "No, our seats are down there," he said, pointing toward the floor. "Follow me."

Michael chuckled and did as Stephen said.

A section up from the floor, Stephen found two seats and they seized them.

"You know somebody is going to claim these seats."

Stephen shrugged. "If they do, then we'll move. There are always open seats at concerts. Would you rather see Jethro Tull from up there, or down here?"

"These seats are fifty bucks more, each," Michael replied. "I'll take these."

A young dirty-blond haired girl caught Stephen's attention as she and her friend edged their way into their seats.

"Not for us, they aren't," Stephen said.

She looked over to Stephen and their eyes connected. Her teeth were perfect, he thought, as she smiled at him.

"Wait here." Springing from his seat, Stephen dashed over and took an empty seat behind her. Michael watched as he began whispering in her ear, and she responded with a giggle, softly touching his arm. A couple minutes later he came back, picked up his beer, took a long slug and sat back down.

Michael glared at Stephen, expecting him to say something, but he didn't. "Well, what the hell?" Michael hissed.

"What?" Stephen acted as if he'd never left.

"What did you say to her?"

After another sip of beer, he belched. "I told her I wanted to take her golfing."

"Golfing," Michael said with a curious look. "You don't golf."

Stephen displayed a full set of glowing teeth. "Well, I do now." He tipped back his beer.

"You're a crazy bastard, you know that?"

"Yes, I do," Stephen said, thinking of how his father had walked out on him and his mother when he was four years old, and how the label "crazy bastard" was fitting for him.

Peering across the rows, Michael examined the girl with the short brown hair. "I'm not going with the fat one."

"Yes you are," Stephen said.

Michael reasoned that he might be able to accommodate with a few more beers in his belly.

"Alright, but you're going to owe me big time." He turned to his beer.

As the show started, the drug was beginning to take effect. They had to move after a middle-aged couple appeared to claim their seats, so they found two others in the next row that offered Stephen a better view of the girl. Stephen spent much of the concert going back and forth to visit her, and by the end of the show, they were engaging in short talk and long kisses. Michael sat taking in the concert, and occasionally, glancing over to watch his friend making time with the attractive girl. He had become accustomed to Stephen always getting the hot ones; leaving him with second choice.

The stars were on full display and a half moon shone

unblemished in the clear night sky. Stephen and Jane lay naked on the third green of Bunker Hill Country Club. Side by side and breathing heavy, their hearts were beating fast after engaging in vigorous sex on the fine green grass.

Stephen sat up, guzzling from his pint of Southern Comfort and handing it to Jane. She took a quick sip and returned it.

"This is your idea of golfing?" she asked.

He screwed the top onto the bottle. "Yes. Can you think of a better way to play?"

She paused for a moment. "I think you got a hole in one tonight."

Stephen laughed and she followed.

"Have you ever done it on a green?" he asked.

"No, I can't say I have." She thought about the time she had sex while lying in the grass next to her picnic basket. And there was the time under the high school bleachers, but it wasn't the same. "How about you?"

"First time for me too." He took another drink and lay back down, gazing up at the stars, wondering if there were any golf courses out there. The green felt nice against his skin, like he was stretched out on a floating cloud. The drug was wearing off. His stomach ached and his laugh-lines felt deeper. She lay back down next to him, keeping her legs crossed while thinking about bugs. A distant light shining from the club house reflected off her skin, defining the contour of her smooth curves like an oasis at dusk.

Stephen admired her body as he ran his fingers along her hip and down her long slender leg.

"Did you like the concert?" he asked.

"Yeah, that dude can play the flute, and he does it standing on one leg."

"Ian Anderson is the best. One of my favorite bands."

"The lyrics are different than most bands," she concluded. "A little odd."

"Poetry," he said as he rolled to his side and kissed her breast. "That shit is poetry." He glanced toward the parking lot. "Do you think they're getting it on in the car?"

"No. Mary thinks he's too tall."

At six feet four inches tall, Stephen thought she may be right. Especially because Mary couldn't be more than five foot one. "Well, he thinks she's too fat," he countered.

"She's not fat; a little chubby, maybe."

Stephen began to get aroused again. "You're not chubby." He reached for her lower abdomen, softly rubbing. "Ready for round two?"

She moved in to kiss him and their lips collided.

"Roll over on your knees and grab onto the pin," he commanded, and she complied. Moving in behind her with pint in hand and holding her hip with the other. "Life is good," he said, as he plunged forward.

CHAPTER 14

The street was quiet as Jake pulled to a stop in front of a yellow ranch nestled in a moderate neighborhood in the suburbs. The yard was well kept with a green lawn cut and trimmed to near perfection. It was a fairly large yard-about an acre in size-more than he would want to keep up, he thought. Leaving his car parked on the street, Jake walked up the driveway toward the back of the house. The windows and doors were open, allowing a fresh breeze in, as the sun was cooking the asphalt under his feet. When he made it to the backyard, Jake saw Tom Fitch on his knees planting a bush in the garden.

"The yard looks great," Jake hollered as he approached.

Fitch turned to see who was there and was pleased to see Jake coming his way. Standing up, he took off his gloves and firmly shook Jake's hand.

"Jake, how are you?"

"I'm fine. How's retirement treating you?" Jake noticed Fitch appeared physically fit and looked well.

"One day falls into the next month and the next year, but it's peaceful. Can I get you something to drink? I'm ready for some ice tea."

"Ice tea sounds good." Jake followed him toward the house.

Fitch motioned to the patio set on the back deck. "Have a seat. I'll be right out."

"Thanks." Jake found a chair in the shade and he sat listening to the birds chirping and the occasional breeze sweeping through the leaves of the tenured sugar maple. He was beginning to understand what Fitch meant by peaceful.

A few minutes later the door opened and Fitch came out with two large glasses with wedges of lemon impaled on them, and he took a seat across from Jake.

"How are things in the department?"

Squeezing the lemon and then dropping it onto the glass, Jake examined his old mentor.

"It's not the same with you gone."

Fitch felt a sense of pride overcome him and he sprouted a smile of appreciation. "Thanks, Jake."

"The Commission is running the department now and the chief bows to their every command," Jake said. "When you were chief, you ran the show. You didn't let a bunch of civilians tell you how to run the department. Mearald has no backbone."

"That's what you get when you promote a paper-pusher to the job," Fitch said. "The best person to run any department is a cop who worked the streets." Fitch took a drink and placed his glass down.

"How's Barbara doing?" Jake changed the subject.

"She's doing well. I'm a lucky man to have her. If I can continue to keep her shopping under control, I think we'll stay strong through the final stretch."

Jake laughed.

"How are you doing, Jake?"

Jake figured Fitch was referring to the death of his wife and how he hadn't moved on to find another steady woman. "I'm fine." He picked up his glass thinking the tea needed some sugar, remembering the sweet tea he used to drink as a child in South Carolina.

"Are there any special ladies in your life?"

"No, just dating here and there." Jake shifted in his chair and looked up at blue sky doused with blotches of white.

"I read about the shooting in the paper. I put a word in for you, you know?"

"I appreciate that, Tom."

"I'm glad you were cleared. How's your partner making out?"

"He's recovering, and probably going to retire on this one." Jake sipped his cool drink.

"What brings you here, Jake?"

Pulling on his tie knot, Jake felt relief as his neck became less constricted. "Remember the Anderson case?"

Fitch's eyes widened. "How could I forget? It still haunts me."

"Me too," Jake said. "You liked a couple kids in that case, didn't you?"

"There were two kids I was investigating, but they were cleared. To this day I still think the priest, LaPage, had something to do with it. He was the last one seen with Robert Anderson, Fitch said.

"Yeah, I remember that. It was squashed by the Chief, wasn't it?" Jake asked.

"Yes. Corbin ordered the chief to pull me off the priest and I'm sure it all came down from the Bishop." Fitch tugged on his ear. "Bishop Reardon and Corbin are thick as thieves."

Jake thought he could actually see the man age with discontent. "I know the priest was your main suspect," Jake said, "but do you think the two boys could have possibly been involved?"

Fitch was curious why Jake was asking about them, *now*. "Possibly, why do you ask?"

"I'm working on a missing person case and I think those two may have something to do with it. Their names are Michael McNulty..." Fitch cut in interrupting him, "and Stephen Haney," he finished.

Jake watched his old friend closely. "That's right, Stephen Haney."

Gazing out into the yard, Fitch appeared mesmerized by the past. After a short pause he snapped out of it and returned to Jake. "I'll tell you this. There was something about the Haney kid that bothered me. He had a cold and calculating way about him, and he was definitely the leader of that pair. I spoke with a couple of his teachers and they said he was an academic prodigy." Producing a pocket knife, Fitch began cleaning embedded dirt from under his finger nails. He hesitated briefly, staring back into Jakes eyes. "A genius," he said.

"Do you think he's capable of murder?" Jake emptied his glass of tea and wiped off his mouth with the back of his hand.

"Isn't everyone?" Fitch said, slowly motioning his blade up and down.

Jake thought he had a point, under the right circumstance anyone was capable of taking a life. He scanned the yard one last time and rose to his feet. "Tom, it was good to see you again. The place looks great, and thanks for the tea."

Fitch shook his hand and led the way to the front yard. "If you have a missing person and Haney's name is on your list of suspects, I would move it to the top."

"Thanks again, Tom. You've been helpful. Say hello to the bride."

Jake walked back to the car feeling good about what he had learned. The blood taken off the bar door had come back as a positive match for Stack's blood type. Jake was inclined to conclude Stack was surprised as he closed the bar and was taken from the scene. His missing person case was becoming very interesting.

Jake sat in his car outside Michael's apartment waiting for him to show up. A couple hours earlier, Michael's elderly neighbor had opened up and told Jake everything she knew about him. She went on to reveal what time he usually came home from work and how late he stayed up on the weekends. Her life was spent collecting her monthly social security check and watching what her neighbors were up to on a day-to-day basis, a monotonous existence, Jake thought.

Another day of driving was completed without incident, and Michael was hot and tired. His boss didn't like him, and made sure Michael was assigned the truck with the broken air conditioner. As Michael made his way toward his apartment building, Jake caught up to him before the front door closed behind him.

Surprised, Michael turned around quickly. "Hey, do you live here?"

"Michael McNulty?" Jake asked.

Michael looked at the way the man was dressed and quickly

concluded that he was the police. "Yeah, what do you want?"

Jake displayed his badge. "I'm Sergeant Waterfield, Middleborough homicide. I'd like to speak with you for a few minutes. Can we do this inside?"

"For what?" Michael asked contemptuously. "I ain't done nothin wrong. I'm tired and I don't got time right now."

"Would you prefer we do this at the police station?"

Hesitating for a moment, Michael realized the officer was serious. "Alright, but just for a few minutes."

Michael started toward his apartment with Jake behind him. Once inside, he led the way to the kitchen where they both took a seat. Jake was curious why Michael hadn't asked what the inquiry was about. Was it because he already knew?

Stirring in his chair and avoiding direct eye contact for any substantial duration, Jake thought Michael was hiding something.

"You seem a bit uneasy, Michael. Is there something bothering you?"

Jumping out of his chair, Michael went to the fridge and extracted a beer. Jake wasn't expecting Michael to offer him a beverage.

"What do you want?" Michael popped open the can and stood leaning on the sink; raising the can to his lips more often than normal.

"Relax and have a seat, Michael. I just have a few questions about your brother, Jonathan."

Feeling a bit of relief that this was about something relating to Jon, he took a seat, now curious what his brother had done.

"Your brother was beaten up a couple months ago by the bartender at Carrigan's Pub, right?"

Michael raised his beer and drank. His relief was short-lived. "Yeah, that's right."

Jake hadn't questioned Michael's brother yet, but was planning on doing that soon. "I haven't spoken to him. Is he alright?"

"Yeah, he's fine, but his nose has a bump on it."

"How did you feel about Richard Stack after he beat up your younger brother?"

Michael had to think for a few seconds. He couldn't say that he hated Stack and wanted to kill him, yet he also couldn't act like it didn't bother him.

"It was a fight and my brother lost."

Watching his eyes shift toward the ceiling when he spoke, Jake knew it was classic body language for a person who was hiding something.

"You were there when it happened, right?"

"I was in the back room," he said, before lassoing his ear with a strand of hair.

"So you didn't see what happened?"

"No, I came in after Stack bounced him, and then I took him to the hospital."

"Were you alone or with someone else?"

Michael didn't want to implicate Stephen, but figured he already knew they were together. "I was with a friend."

Jake crossed his left leg over his right. "Who was that?" He appeared relaxed.

"S-Steve Haney," he stuttered.

"If that was my brother bleeding all over the place with a busted nose, I'd want to beat the shit out of Stack. Didn't you want revenge?" Jake coyly asked.

Michael didn't like the way Jake's stare burned into his eyes and the way he remained completely still as he spoke. He felt like he was sitting with a shrink, as he had as a child when his mother used to drag him to the dark office with the uncomfortable chair.

"Well, maybe at first, but then I figured Jon probably deserved it."

"Do you think Jon may have wanted revenge?

Michael turned his head to a right angle and Jake followed in an attempt to keep eye contact. "No. Jon didn't have anything to do with Stack disappearing." His tall frame seemed to shrink in his chair.

"I didn't say anything about a disappearance."

"It's common knowledge. Everyone knows he's missing," Michael said with confidence.

"I suppose it is. Where do you think he is?"

Michael took a long drink nearly emptying his can. "How

should I know?"

"Where were you on the night of May 21st? The Thursday night Richard Stack went missing."

"I was here," he quickly answered without recollecting.

Jake was surprised by his fast response. "Were you alone?"

"Yes."

"What time did you go to bed?"

Michael finished his beer and got up and dropped it in the trash can. "I don't know, the usual time, around eleven."

Jake stood up and moved by the sink, attempting to preserve eye contact. "Did you have to work the next morning?"

Michael opened the fridge for another beer. "Yeah, I had to work the next day.

Moving closer to stay connected, it was apparent to Jake that Michael was becoming more nervous. "So you went to work the next morning?"

"I just said I did," he responded in an elevated tone.

"Okay, Michael. I think that's all I need for now."

Without wasting any time, Michael darted to the door and opened it wide.

"If you hear anything, or have anything you want to add, give me a call." Jake handed him his card and walked out.

"I will." Michael closed the door, glanced at the card with the police department logo centered on it, and threw it into the trashcan. He thought about the interrogation and how he answered the pointy questions and he wondered if Stephen would be proud.

As Jake walked back to his car, he wondered why Michael had lied about going to work the Friday after Stack went missing. Earlier that day while Michael was on his route, Jake went to see his boss, and the log book indicated that Michael had called in sick on May 22nd.

CHAPTER 15

The humidity inside the court was almost unbearable. Mark Corbin didn't mind because he figured it was to his advantage. He was thinner than his opponent and in better shape. Big Al Zingarelli had many more years experience playing handball, but he couldn't move around the court as quickly or with the same level of vigor.

"So how do it a feel to be re-lected asa DA for da fourta time?" Al asked as he got into position to serve the ball.

"It gets less exciting every time, but I do appreciate all your help," Corbin quickly raced to the oncoming ball and slapped it hard against the wall, and Al back-pedaled into place and gave it a whack of his own. The volley went on a few more times until Corbin was defeated by his determined older friend.

"No big," Al said, as he wiped the sweat from his forehead with a small white towel. "Salvatore is a very happy widda di outcome of his acase and we offa our gratituda."

"I'm glad I could help out," Corbin said.

Al moved into position. "If he hadda go backa to the joint, he saida hisa wife woulda divorce him."

Corbin smiled. "Maybe he would have been better off with a conviction."

"Youa pretty fuckin funny for an Irish guy," Al said. "Prepare for a beatin." He served the ball.

At the completion of the match, both men were drenched in sweat. Al looked at his defeated opponent with a smug and victorious glare.

"The drinks are on me," Corbin said. "I have something to talk to you about."

Al examined Corbin. They had been playing handball together for eight years, and he knew by the look on Corbin's face it was serious. "Sure, no problemo," Al said.

They climbed the stairs to the bar and Corbin bought two drinks, a bottle of light beer for him and a vodka and tonic with a slice of lime for Al. Sitting at a small table in the corner overlooking a court where a husband and wife team battled out their frustrations, Al raised his glass. "Salute," he said dryly.

"Cheers," Corbin toasted.

After a long slug of beer, Corbin started. "My daughter, Ellen, has been seeing this creep for about two years. I've talked to her about dumping him, but she is crazy about this guy. Ever since she started dating him, she's not the same person." His voice was cracking. "We noticed that her personality has become erratic and she has a very short temper with her mother and me. She's always broke and asking us for money and we're getting concerned about her weight loss. I have a bad feeling she's on drugs and that piece of shit is responsible." His eyes squinted and his lower lip quivered. "I did some checking around and found out that he's a coke head." He let out a rumbling cough. "About six months ago, I had one of my cops pay him a serious visit to convince him to stay away from Ellen." He picked up his glass. "It didn't work and she confronted me about it." He took a drink. "Now she says they're getting married."

Al dabbed his forehead with his white towel. "There's ano reasonin wida her?"

"I'm afraid not." Corbin took another drink and placed his glass on the table. "Last weekend she was over the house, and when I had the opportunity, I went through her purse." He frowned and cleared his throat. "I found a bag of crack."

Al broke eye contact and looked down at the couple swatting on the court. "So you thinka disa punk hasa your daughter hooked ona crack and now she'sa goin to a marry him?"

Corbin squeaked out a sigh, feeling like a weakling. "That about sums it up." He scratched his head. "Not only is this guy a crack head, he's a loser. He hustles for a buck and has no job or sense of responsibility."

Corbin thought about what he had just said and realized he should be careful because he had just described Al's way of life. Al had never worked an honest day in his life and one could conclude that he hustled for a living.

Slowly swirling his straw around the glass creating a mini-whirlpool, Al stopped and looked up at Corbin. "So, youa askina for mya help ona dis?"

Pausing for a moment, Corbin thought about what this would mean. He knew he would be in debt to a man who was the boss of the mafia throughout New England. "Yes, I need this taken care of, once and for all."

"What's hisa name?" Al asked.

"Ben Fitzgerald. He lives at 123 Withers Avenue." Corbin needed another beer.

A stern look overcame Al's face, like a judge handing down a sentence. "We never hada dis conversation. You are never toa speak of Ben Fitzgerald again, capisci?"

"Yes, understood."

Corbin sat across from Al, looking into his dark eyes. There was something missing, something detached. His hand reached across the table and Corbin took it without a shake, just a moderate squeeze.

"Ila see you here nexta Tuesday, right?" Al asked.

"Of course, same as always," Corbin said guiltily.

Al got up, glaring at him. "Good," he wisped as he turned and walked away.

Corbin ordered another beer, wondering if he had made the right choice, or the biggest mistake of his life.

The smoke and booze in Kristie's Tavern was flowing heavy, and where Ben Fitzgerald sat, the bullshit was just as consistent. He sat next to a droopy looking woman who couldn't see past her next drink, and she ignored anything that wouldn't benefit her.

"Yeah, it won't be long now." Ben swiveled in his stool with false optimism. "I have a big score coming into town and when it gets on the train to leave, it's taking me along for the ride."

The woman wasn't impressed, but she played along in an

effort to secure a free drink. “That sounds like a plan. Where ya goin?”

Snatching his shot glass off the bar like a professional, Ben took a snort. “I’m going to a remote beach in Mexico with my wife and we’re going to party till we puke.” Ben roared out in laughter and she joined in with an awkward cackle.

Motioning to the bartender, a frail wrinkled man in his sixties ambled over with a bar rag in one hand and a cigarette in the other.

“Get us both another drink.”

Ben looked to his old amiga, assuring her, “I’ll be right back,” and he shot up and shuffled out the door.

The parking lot was full as he walked to his car that was parked in the rear corner of the lot. Ben strategically parked where it was less illuminated and more discrete, which made him more comfortable when he snuck out to hit the pipe. Quickly checking out the lot as he opened his car door, the coast was clear, so he slid in behind the wheel. Reaching into the glove box, he pulled out a crack pipe and plastic bag containing three small rocks. Placing a rock into his pipe, he retrieved a lighter from his shirt pocket, and with a flick of his thumb, he was in take-off mode, accelerating into the clouds. A sudden rush overtook his mind and body, and in that exact moment in time, he was invincible. When the rock was ash, he put his works back into the glove box and crawled out of his car. As the car door closed, he realized he had company, and they weren’t there to party with him.

“What do you want?” Ben’s voice was shaky and his mind scrambling; trying to figure a way out. A tall man held a gun to the back of his head and the other heavyset guy pushed him into the back seat of the car. Ben had never seen these guys before and he didn’t have any idea what they wanted from him.

The heavy guy stuck a gun into his ribcage. “If you don’t cooperate, I’ll blow your fucking kidneys all over the back seat.”

One look at him and Ben knew he meant business. He resigned

himself to going along peacefully and doing whatever they asked.

The clouds rolled in bringing along a steady rain, pounding on a 1979 gray Chrysler that was parked behind a boarded up Bonanza Restaurant in the south end of the city. The district patrolmen were dispatched after a neighbor called in the abandoned automobile, stating it had been there for two days. Ben Fitzgerald's body was found in the trunk with two thirty-two caliper bullet holes in his head. The preliminary investigation concluded it was a drug deal gone array, but Ellen Corbin knew better.

The following week, Corbin, slightly bent at the waist, prepared to serve as Big Al readied himself in the back of the court. "Afta the gama let us sit adown for a drink," Al said, looking through Corbin. "I needa favor to aska you."

With legs growing lighter, the room seemed to be growing smaller and closing in on Corbin. He looked at the man with the dead eyes; acknowledging him with a faint nod.

CHAPTER 16

The decision to conduct Stephen Haney's interview at the police station was determined after Jake's conversation with Fitch over a cool drink in his backyard. Jake's inquiry into Haney confirmed that he was dealing with a highly intelligent and elusive character. He wanted to have an edge by holding the interrogation in a controlled and authoritative environment. After checking out most of the leads in the case, Jake wasn't able to locate any other suspects he felt could have been responsible for Stack's disappearance. The list of people that hated Stack was long, and although many had threatened him in the past, Jake didn't think any of them would have the courage to take action to that degree. In his experience, it was the individual that kept silent and didn't threaten that would be more likely to take revenge. Jake had thought hard about robbery being a motive, but he had pretty much ruled that out. He figured if robbery was the motive, why would the perpetrators take Stack along with them? Wouldn't they simply take the money and run, and if Stack fought with them, wouldn't they take Stack down on the spot? Jake concluded this crime was well planned and executed, and with a lack of traceable evidence, it was perpetrated by someone very calculated and smart. He also determined that the crime was most likely perpetrated by more than one person.

Interrogation room number two was a square hall painted a dull gray and equipped with a camera, three chairs, and a table in the middle. Stephen had been sitting idle for fifteen minutes before the door finally opened and Jake walked in. Circling round him like a shark preparing for a kill, Jake took notice of his attire and a gassy stench that filled air, both which immediately confirmed Haney's lack of respect for authority. He was wearing camouflage shorts, purple flip-flops, a bright yellow tank-top, and dark sun glasses. On the front of his t- shirt it read "IF?" in large black print. The back of his shirt read, "IF WORMS HAD MACHINE GUNS, BIRDS WOULDN'T FUCK WITH THEM." There was a picture of a worm mounting a fifty caliper machine gun and shooting birds out of the sky. Jake knew Stephen was purposely mocking him and the establishment by how he had dressed for the interview.

"Take off the sunglasses," Jake demanded as he pulled up a chair.

Stephen paused for a few seconds and then did as he was told. He gently folded them and placed them on the table.

"Do you make it a habit of wearing obscene shirts or is this just for our little visit?"

A smile immediately defined Stephens's face. "It's one of my favorite shirts. It displays a revolutionary concept, don't you agree?"

"No, I don't," Jake said with a straight face.

Stephen's smile faded. "I've been watching your career from a distance. You've done well for yourself, considering," Stephen said smugly.

Jake dismissed the comment, figuring it was in reference to his race. What troubled him was Haney's lack of nervousness. He seemed comfortable in the interrogation room, which was unusual, even for the innocent.

"I've looked into your background as well." Resting his hands on the table, Jake continued. "You work construction and seldom miss a day, and your boss says you're a good worker, but your co-workers don't have many good things to say about you. You live alone with your mother and you don't have a steady girlfriend. Your father left when you were a small child, and you haven't seen him since, and you have an older sister that lives in California. You have an IQ of 169, but you never went to college or took advantage of your intellectual ability. You were arrested twice as an adult, once when you were seventeen for indecent exposure and trespassing, and the other just three years ago for assault and battery." Jakes eyes burned deep. "The fight I understand, but the charge when you were seventeen puzzles me."

Stephen knew where he was going with this.

"It was in the month of August, I believe, when some people in your neighborhood were complaining about someone jumping in their pool at night while they were sleeping. At least two witnesses said they heard the sound of bare feet pounding against the pavement, and when they looked out the window, a naked man was running away from their property."

A smile came alive on Stephen's face.

"The streaking pool hopper often left something behind floating in the water."

The look on Stephen's face told a story of pride and accomplishment.

"Don't you think seventeen is a bit old for that kind of behavior?"

"It was great exercise," he sarcastically responded.

"And defecating in your neighbor's pool; was that great exercise as well?"

"No, that was payback," he said with wide, bulging eyes.

Jake knew Stephen was attempting to play a mind game.

"Did you ask me down here to talk about why I shit in my neighbor's pool eleven years ago, or is there something else more pressing?"

"Why didn't you attend college? It's apparent you're very bright, and to me, a waste of a very capable mind."

"Why would I want to sit listening to some liberal professor who spends his days dictating his opinions and tainted knowledge to young naive minds, and his nights working on a novel that will never be published?" He folded his hands, cracking his knuckles. "What do they know about the real world; about the streets? What do they know about survival and despair?" What do they really know about young naive minds?"

"That's quite an observation, Stephen. You seemed to have summed it up for me, thank you for that."

Stephen didn't appreciate Jake's sarcasm, but he didn't reveal it.

"I asked you down here because I'm curious about a couple of things."

Stephen thought of a story book when he was a child about a curious monkey named George.

"And that would be?" He gestured with his hands opening up toward the ceiling.

"I'm wondering why you went as far as planning and killing Richard Stack for something as trivial as a broken nose." Jake examined Stephen's demeanor for any unusual signs, only to be disappointed. "Why not just beat him down, maybe break a bone or two, but to actually take his life seems a bit extreme to me," Jake slouched back in his chair anticipating an answer.

"What is trivial to one man may be extreme to another," Stephen said as his eyes did a short dance from Jake's eyes to his gun holster and back. "However, I didn't kill him. What was your other question?"

Jake thought if Stephen tried to go for his gun, he would pivot, grab a hold of his chair, and smash it down on Stephen's upper torso.

"The other question is: How did you manage to show up for work the next day, but Michael called in sick? I figure you probably drove quite a distance to dump the body. Did you weigh it down and drop it into the drink, or bury it deep in some secluded wooded area?" Jake leaned in closer. "Either way it would have been a very late night."

Stephen shifted his weight and bit his lower lip and Jake took a mental note of it. By Stephen's reaction, Jake thought he may have hit a sore spot.

"Michael has always been weaker than you, right?"

Stephen showed no reaction.

"Maybe after all the hard work moving around Stack's heavy body he was too tired to get up for work."

"Like I said, I didn't kill him," Stephen said. "If Mike called out sick the day after Stack went missing, it was just a coincidence. You'll have to take that up with him. I'm not his keeper."

"Where were you the night Stack was killed?"

Stephen was concerned by the way Jake kept referring to Stack's disappearance as a murder.

"I was home, sleeping."

Jake moved the small recorder on the table a few inches closer to Stephen, as an intimidation factor. "Can anyone collaborate that?"

Glancing at the recorder, Stephen knew the game that was being played and he was resigned not to show any external emotion. "My mother was home."

Jake chuckled. "You live with your mother? How old are you, twenty-eight and you still live with your mother?"

Stephen wanted to lunge forward and take out an eyeball. "She's been sick, so I take care of her."

Jake realized he hit a nerve. He got up and walked toward the wall and continued with his back facing the table. "Do you want to know why I have such a problem with you, Stephen?"

"Do tell." The voice behind him echoed.

Jake turned around and walked back toward Stephen; their eyes fixed on each other. "When I first started as a police officer, I found a young boy in the park who had been beaten to death, and guess what?"

Stephen didn't retract eye contact, and sat motionless.

"Your name was at the top of the list of suspects. *Now*, sixteen years later, your name is once again at the top of my list for another case."

Jake sat back down searching for any emotion Stephen might display, but there wasn't any.

"A missing person case that is probably a murder. Why do you think that is?"

"Poor police work."

"You have an answer for everything, don't you?"

They both sat motionless, just staring into each other's eyes, like two rams preparing to charge. The sound of the recorder clicking off as Jake pushed the button broke the silence.

"I'll be watching you, and we will talk again. You can go." Jake got up and opened the door and Stephen proceeded through with a rebellious attitude.

Outside, Stephen sat in his car thinking about what had occurred in the police station. His mind drifted back to the time when Robby Anderson was discovered with his head bashed in. He hadn't thought about that for quite some time, and he was confident that the detective was on a fishing expedition. Pounding the steering wheel with the palm of his hand, he had a bone to pick with Michael for calling in sick. He could kill him for that.

CHAPTER 17

Edward Gallagher sat in the waiting area of the district attorney's office with his briefcase open, browsing through a file. Still single, he was open to every opportunity that came his way, but very few did. He smiled at the administrative assistant who poked her head up from the computer screen, and she smiled back, sensing he was attracted by her appearance. His quick wit and charm sometimes overcame his physical appearance, but not this time. She continued typing and he licked his thumb and turned a page. Borderline anorexic, his dark gray suite fit him well and he didn't have to worry about adjusting his white shirt tucked in around his waistline. While standing erect, the tip of his yellow silk tie was centered on his belt buckle. His light brown hair was short and neatly trimmed just above his ears, and his thick glasses were nearly the same shade of color.

Ed had recently celebrated his thirty-second birthday with friends from the courthouse. He had taken a new stenographer on a first date that inevitably turned into a last, which seemed to be typical of Ed's dating life.

Glancing up over the top of his file, Ed noticed the assistant reaching for the phone, but he didn't hear it ringing. After a quick conversation, she replaced the receiver and looked at him with a short smile.

"Mr. Corbin will see you now, just go ahead in." She gestured toward the door.

"Thank you," he said as he dropped the file into his briefcase and moved to the door without hesitation. Ed was focused on what might prove to be the biggest case of his career, and he was determined to prevail at any cost. Entering and closing the door behind him, Ed found Corbin standing by the window looking out as if he were king of the city, and he wondered if Corbin greeted all newcomers in this manner. Rumor had it that Corbin had an intimidating demeanor and was a very serious man. Ed never had the opportunity to meet Corbin in person, as he worked in Bolton and only ventured to Middleborough on occasion. But he was looking forward to meeting Corbin regarding the case at hand. Ed was *not* an intimidating man; however, he was not one with whom to match wits, unless you did your homework.

Corbin turned and walked over without breaking eye contact. "Attorney Gallagher is it?" He reached out and they shook hands. His grip was strong for a man with small hands, Ed observed.

"Yes, that's correct. Thanks for taking the time to see me this morning."

Corbin motioned to the chair in front of his desk. "Have a seat."

Ed noticed the matching chair a few feet away against the wall, thinking he may have moved it away from the desk before he came in. Unlike Ed's suit, the District Attorney wore a flawless custom-tailored dark blue silk suit with subtle pinstripes, a blood red tie with a gold tie clip of Lady Justice tipping the scale. Ed admired the man's attire, thinking he needed to beef up his own wardrobe; this case may afford him to do just that.

Corbin took a seat behind his desk, maintaining eye contact with his left hand covering his right fist, like a kung fu bow. "I've heard you rattled a few cages in Bolton Superior Court. What brings you to our zoo?" A rubber smile defined his face.

Ed was glad to hear he was building a reputation that carried outside the Bolton Courthouse walls. "Please, call me Ed."

"All right, Ed. How can I assist you today?"

"I have a client named Alan Brick who has lived here in Middleborough all his life and he has retained me as his lawyer in a case against the diocese of this city."

"What kind of case are you referring to?"

"I'm talking about the sexual molestation and rape of a ten-year-old boy by a priest in the diocese of Middleborough."

Corbin shifted to a more comfortable position in his chair. "What priest?"

Ed noticed that the man hardly ever blinked. "Father Robert LaPage."

The silence was deafening as Corbin sat across from the puny messenger aware that he was going to be a big problem, a very big problem. "When did this molestation allegedly occur?"

"Nineteen years ago, and for over a period of a year, give or take a month or two."

Corbin folded his hands and shifted his eyes to Ed's shoes. Ed looked down, wondering what Corbin was thinking. Was he overdue for a shine? Bringing his eyes back in line with Ed's, Corbin responded without pity or concern over the tragedy that was just disclosed.

"Counselor, I'm sure you are aware there is a statute of limitations on a case such as this," Corbin said. He stood up and walked around his desk and sat on the edge directly in front of Ed. "Even if we had solid evidence against this priest, which I'd venture to say we don't, it has been nineteen years and the statute is limited to seven. I couldn't prosecute this case if I wanted to."

"Mr. Corbin, I'm aware of the law regarding the statute of limitations in a sexual assault case. I'm here as more of a courtesy than anything. I've done a little browsing around and I have learned a few things about this priest, LaPage." Ed cleared his throat. "I understand he was a suspect in 1972 in the murder of twelve-year-old altar boy, Robert Anderson, who may have also been sexually assaulted."

Corbin was beginning to feel uneasy in his comfortable chair.

"I have filed a civil suit against the diocese of Middleborough just prior to coming here this morning. When the media catches wind that the same priest may have murdered a boy seventeen years ago and is still on the loose, and possibly molesting other children, you may have a problem in this cage of yours."

It was apparent that Corbin was drowning in deep thought as he paced toward the window and peering out. He was putting together a huge real estate deal between the city and the diocese and couldn't have something of this magnitude unfolded, *now*. As Corbin turned and faced Ed, he could see that he had the wind taken from his sail.

"The city can't afford a major scandal involving the church

right now. I'm asking you for a professional courtesy not to open this can of worms up to the press," Corbin roughly pleaded. He wanted to drive his letter opener through Ed's tongue.

Ed fumbled with his folder, scratched his neck, and took in a deep breath. "I don't intend on saying anything about the murder case; however, I will make a statement to the press regarding the sexual assault of my client. I need to expose this creep and put pressure on the church to defrock him. We may not be able to prosecute, but we can certainly disrobe him and try to keep him away from children."

The DA was steaming inside. In his head he could hear Bishop Reardon threatening to pull the plug on the East Bottle Park real estate deal. "You had better be very careful what you say to the media, Mister." With a reddening face, he gestured to Ed with an open hand, like Pope John Paul addressing a crowd. "The church has a lot of power in this community and a lot of friends, including yours truly," he pointed out. "A young attorney, like you, could find yourself having some major career problems if you piss off the wrong people."

Ed sprung out of his chair. He didn't like being threatened, or told what he should do regarding a case so important to the security of children everywhere. He also figured this case would resonate throughout the country and possibly expose other pedophiles wearing white collars.

"Let's be clear on this issue, so there are no misconceptions," Ed barked. "I despise any man that preys on young children for his own sick, deviant, sexual cravings, especially one who has gained a child's trust by supposedly being a man of God. As far as I'm concerned, they are worse than your average pedophile on the street for that very reason. Make no mistake, I would jeopardize my career to expose and ruin any one of these dirty bastards."

Corbin was surprised by Ed's aggressive tone of voice. He wasn't use to that. Most people quivered like a beaten dog when Corbin confronted them in his office.

Ed reached into his folder, took out a report, and dropped it on

Corbin's desk. "I made you a copy of the statement I took from my client Mr. Brick. You read this and then tell me how important your diocese is. The things that son-of-a-bitch did to my client when he was a young boy nearly made me vomit. Understand this, I'm gunning for his ass and I'm going to get it."

Turning his back on the DA, Ed marched toward the door stopping just short of the exit, and then he swiftly turned around.

"To me, nothing is more important than the preservation of the innocence of a child."

Ed walked out with his shoulders back and his head high. He didn't have any children of his own, but he had two young nieces and a nephew, and he loved them dearly.

The phone only rang twice before Bishop Reardon released it from the hook. "Good afternoon." His voice was low and steady, lacking its normal vigor.

"Evan, this is Mark. We may have a small problem."

"A small problem, you say."

Corbin could sense Reardon's sarcasm and he started to worry.

"Yes, I was just paid a visit by an attorney representing a man who alleges he was molested by Father LaPage nineteen years ago."

After a brief silence, the Bishop responded. "I know. I just received a call from our attorney. Martin informed me of the action that was filed against us this morning."

Corbin was surprised how fast they learned of the suit.

"I can't tell you how badly this will reflect upon the church if it gets released to the press. What can be done to help this attorney understand our situation?"

"I'm afraid there is nothing we can do. He has taken this thing personally, like some sort of crusader."

"Every man has a price, Mark," Reardon said. "Does he have any ground to stand on here?"

"It sounds as though he may. I have a copy of his client's

statement and it isn't very pretty. Is this priest capable of such vile things?"

"This is my very best priest, and I am confident he would never do anything to harm a child."

"Then maybe we should respond to the allegation as a fabrication and blackmail against the church for plaintiff's financial gain."

"No!" the Bishop shouted. "If this get's out to the public, people will begin to make their own judgments and the media will have a field day. It will look like we operate some sort of freak house, instead of God's house. We have to stop this from getting out, and we need to do it now."

Corbin could hear someone in the background on the other end of the line speaking to the Bishop. There was a silence and then he returned to the phone.

"It's too late," Reardon roared. "You're damned attorney is on TV making a statement as we speak."

Corbin didn't appreciate the way he said "your attorney."

"Don't worry Evan, we'll figure this thing out."

"You better, Mark," he hissed. "I can't see a land sale going through *now* with this hanging over our heads."

A knot was forming in the pit of Corbin's stomach. "Let's not be rash here. Let me see what we can figure out to discredit this man's allegations and make the church look like its being black mailed. I'll contact Martin and we can put together a counter-statement for the press."

"It better be a good one, or we are both up shit's creek without a paddle," Reardon sighed.

Corbin never heard the Bishop used foul language before. This was a clear indication that he was stressing out over the situation. "You may want to speak to the priest and find out what he has to say about all this."

"I intend to," Reardon fired back.

"I have to go. I want to watch his statement on television. I'll be in touch."

"You do that, Mark." The line went dead and Corbin stood alone holding the buzzing handset.

The restaurant was picking up as the clock struck seven. Corbin glanced at his watch as his comrade Terrence Perkins, slid through the room as if on wheels, showing up on time just as Corbin had demanded.

"Mark," Perkins said, reaching out to shake while he was still in motion, heading toward the table Corbin had selected in the far corner of the room.

"Hello, Terry."

A handshake ensued and the heavy set man took a seat across the table. As Commissioner of the City of Middleborough's Real Property Division, Perkins spent much of his day meeting with various people regarding city real estate and private properties for sale. He was a jolly sort of man and this played to his advantage because he was well liked and most people were happy to conduct business with him. Perkins had earned the nickname Jiggles from those closest to him because of the way his jowls shook when he laughed. Even though he resented the label, he never mentioned it.

Perkins and Corbin had two real estate deals with the diocese over the past several years and both were very fruitful for the pair, but nowhere near the magnitude of the East Bottle Park deal.

"We have a situation. Have you seen the news today?" Corbin asked, as he gestured to the waiter to capture his attention.

"No, I've been out of town all day. What's up?"

The waiter strolled over and took their drink order and handed them menus. Corbin continued talking as he walked away.

"A suit was filed against the diocese today and Evan is running scared. He's putting pressure on me to deal with it and he is threatening to put a kibosh on the East Park deal."

Perkins smile faded, and was replaced with a frown. "What kind of suit?"

"Some guy claims he was molested by a priest seventeen years ago."

"What priest?" Perkins jowls jiggled as he shook his head side to side.

"Father LaPage."

He straightened up in his chair and leaned forward. "That son of a bitch is guilty. I always knew there was something wrong with that guy."

"Whatever the case, we are screwed if he puts this deal on hold. I've invested way too much effort into pulling this deal together to jeopardize it now."

"That can't happen," Perkins said. "Fontaine is counting on breaking ground in 90 days."

"Yeah, I know."

The waiter came over with a beer and a glass of scotch for Corbin.

"I have a check ready to go out the door in the amount of 4.6 million bucks for a piece of land that we will sell to Fontaine for 5.7 million. This will be a huge payday for both of us."

Corbin sipped his drink, and then, crushing the ice between his teeth, he began talking with a slight slur. "Yeah, 400 grand for each of us off the books and the city will make 300 grand."

"Mark, we can't lose this deal. The bishop is giving this property to us for short money." Perkins guzzled his beer and wiped the remains from the corner of his mouth. "Fontaine is on board with making us whole on the side, so there won't be any trace of foul play. This is the perfect deal."

"I know the deal," Corbin said. "The city, through you, purchases 214 acres of prime real estate from the Church and sells it to Fontaine Construction Company for a 1.1 million dollar profit. They build 142 custom homes and slip us our taste over the next five years on the side, in cash. Everybody is a winner."

"You have the relationship with the Bishop. How can you get him to change his mind and continue forward with the process?"

"Keep Fontaine warm. I'm working on a plan to smooth things

over with Evan."

The waiter came over to take their order. Ironically, he was dressed in a black jacket and pants with a white shirt peeking through at the collar.

CHAPTER 18

The news of the suit filed against the Catholic Church spread like a vicious cancer, and the Pope was briefed on the situation shortly after Gallagher appeared on television. Many international networks and newspapers carried the story, and some included a twist of their own to meet their individual agendas. Some people didn't believe the allegations made by Mr. Brick, offering support to Father LaPage, while others called for his head on a platter.

Jake sat at his kitchen table with a glass of orange juice, reading the article that started on the front page and continued on page six. After carefully reading the article, he placed the paper on the table and sat motionless, consumed in thought. Having been fairly confident that Haney and McNulty were responsible for the murder of Robby Anderson, he now began to think he may have been wrong. The priest had been a main suspect, but he had set him aside after Stack's disappearance and his focus was now on the pair of friends. *How could a priest be capable of murdering a young boy?*

Jake was not a regular at church, and since the death of his wife, he had drifted even further away from religion. Raised a Lutheran, he used to attend service every Sunday when his mother dragged him out the door with a suffocating necktie compromising his throat, wearing crushing shoes that often left blisters. It was very different from New England in the South because going to church on Sunday was routine, and missing the weekly ritual was highly frowned upon. If a member of the community didn't attend service, people noticed, and treated the person accordingly, as if he or she was possessed by the Devil. Jake's mother used to say: "A Sunday without church, is like breakfast without a biscuit; you just went through the day feeling unfulfilled." To make ends meet, Jake's father worked most Sundays, and was not able to join them on the half-mile walk to church. Watching his father work his life away, Jake resolved himself to pursue an education, so he could ultimately enjoy a better quality of life. Jake's father was a good man who was defined by his ability to support his family. His pleasures in life were limited to the love he received from his wife and his son. Out the door as the sun was rising, he often didn't return until it was dark. His father worked at a local pig farm and he had eventually moved into a lead role, proud that he supervised four men. Jake missed his father terribly and he cherished the limited time they had together. His dad often reminded him that he was the man of the household and that he counted on him to protect his mother and their property while he was away. Jake took it as a challenge and he vowed to never let his father down, and he never did.

As Jake sat thinking about his days in the pews, a noise broke his train of thought, startling him. Shooting a quick glance to the kitchen window, he saw a cardinal as it crashed into the glass and quickly flew away. Was it a testament to how clean his window was, or was it a sign? The cardinal was his favorite bird, especially the male, proudly displaying his bright red crest. Jake looked at the clock on the wall; it was nearly ten o'clock on Sunday morning. Picking up his glass, he downed the remainder of his juice.

Father LaPage was escorted to the Bishop's study, where Reardon was sitting behind his desk. Father Loftus, a young priest Reardon had been mentoring, sat in a chair a few feet away. The look on Reardon's face was less than welcoming.

"Sit down, Robert."

Moving like a monk dressed in black, LaPage slowly paced to the empty chair facing the large desk. He took his place next to Loftus, who was sitting upright with his knees together and his hands folded as if he was praying.

"I'm going to get right to the point, and I want direct answers. Am I clear?" Reardon asked.

"Yes." LaPage looked like an adolescent being questioned by a parent for change missing from a purse.

"Did you commit the offense that Mr. Brick is accusing you of?"

"No, I did not."

"Have you ever touched him inappropriately?"

"Never." With the exception of blinking eyes, LaPage was completely still.

"Did you ever indicate to him that you wanted to have inappropriate relations with him?"

"No, you're Excellency." LaPage glanced at the young priest to his left wondering if the conversation would be different if he wasn't present.

"This morning I spoke with Cardinal Lacoski. The Vatican is not taking this very well. I have been told to advise you to be very careful in your day-to-day activities. I would suggest that you stay indoors unless it's necessary to do otherwise."

"Yes, you're Excellency."

"Do not speak to anyone about this, especially the media, understood?"

"Yes," LaPage said through a drying mouth.

"That's all for now. Everyone is watching this, and you, Robert." Reardon got up and started toward the end of the room and swiveled on his feet. "Why do you think Mr. Brick is making these allegations?"

After a brief silence, LaPage responded. "Money."

"Yes. Money," Reardon mimicked. "You're walking on egg shells. Tread lightly." He looked toward the door, clearly indicating he wanted LaPage out.

The Cardinal had made it clear that this was a very serious matter and it reflected very poorly on Reardon. It was his territory, and he was directly responsible for anything that occurred in one of his parishes. He went on to say that the 2.5-million-dollar lawsuit that Gallagher filed was not an unbearable amount of money for the church to pay out in the event of an unfavorable outcome at the trial. However, the embarrassment and negative perception it would unleash upon the church would be immeasurable.

The following Sunday morning, Jake returned to Saint Luke's to attend the 10:30 service. It was a combination of the sermon and an attractive lady that offered him a soft handshake and a warm smile that brought him back. He liked the fact that the pastor was married and was allowed the comfort of a woman. It was a comfort all men should have the privilege to enjoy, he thought, and he had a hard time understanding men who gave up that privilege.

After the service, Jake joined the others for coffee and refreshments. He didn't drink coffee, so settled for orange juice that consisted of watered-down sugar. As he made his way through the serving line, he immediately spotted the attractive lady he had met the week before as she stood behind the counter. She caught his eye and began glancing over at him every several seconds as he closed the gap. Jake thought that she was in her early thirties, but could pass for twenty-nine. Her golden hair was tied back and flowed down between her shoulders, ending just below the center of her back. A few inches shorter than Jake, she looked like a runner or someone that participated in regular cardiovascular exercise. Her dark-green eyes could be mistaken for light brown in a dim light, and she wore a smile that seldom went unnoticed. As Jake approached, he noticed the light freckles spread out just below her neck surrounding a gold cross. This time when he reached out to take her hand, the engagement lasted longer than the previous one.

"You came back," she said with a smile larger than life. "Was it the sermon or the refreshments that did it?"

"I'd have to say it's the breakfast server that brought me back, but the rest came in a close second."

He let go of her hand and she let out a subtle giggle. Moving through the line, he knew he had to continue the conversation without seeming too overwhelming. Jake was a firm believer in good things come to those who wait, and also to those that pursued them.

Toting a wheat bagel doused with cream cheese and a cup of

orange liquid, he moved away from the crowd and found refuge in the corner. Watching the kids run around expending the energy that was pent up from sitting still for an hour inside the chapel, he remembered what it was like to sit through service as a child. Wearing their Sunday best, people were gathered in small huddles, conversing with half full mouths; some still clutching the weekly readings and bulletins. Watching the gathering crowd of people, Jake stood alone and accepted that no one would come over to engage him in conversation and welcome him to the parish. There was only the beautiful lady behind the refreshment counter, and he was hungry for her company.

Once finished with his food and drink, Jake started toward the exit. People moved out of his way, looking at him like a stranger or an untrusting citizen of the community. Before he left the building, the woman trotted over, and stopped him in his tracks with a gentle nudge of the elbow.

"Hi," she gushed. "I wanted to introduce myself before you left this morning."

She had an air of excitement combined with a look of embarrassment, and Jake found that comforting. He noticed a certain sense of innocence in her that made her appear pure and untainted.

"I'm Colleen Kelly." She extended her hand, and Jake reached out absorbing her warmth.

"It's my pleasure Colleen. My name is Jake Waterfield."

"I know. I've read about you in the paper."

"So you know that I'm a police detective?"

"Yes," she said admiringly.

"Do you think that's why I'm getting the cold shoulder from the people here?"

She hesitated before answering. "No, I don't think that's the reason. My shoulder is pretty warm, right?"

He knew what she meant, and thought she was clever to change the subject with a swift and positive twist.

"This may be a little direct, but would you like to have lunch with me today?"

The anticipation was torture. She could see how nervous he was, and it made her feel at ease with him.

"I'm sorry, I can't," she answered.

"I understand." Turning his head away he glanced at a family of four that was closely watching them.

"But, I'd love to have dinner with you tonight," she added.

Her acceptance made his heart jump a beat. It had been a long time since he was this excited about a woman. The last time was when he proposed to his wife and she accepted.

"Do you have a card?"

Jake quickly fumbled through his wallet and extracted a business card and handed it to her. She looked at it with a pleasant curiosity.

"Alright, Sergeant Waterfield, I'll call you this afternoon for the details."

"I'll be waiting for your call, Colleen." He smiled and started toward the door.

She walked by several people gathered in the hallway that were spying and mumbling under their breaths. She moved past them with her head held high and without acknowledgment

CHAPTER 19

Chick's Diner, on the east side of the city, had been in business for over thirty years. It had earned a reputation as a greasy spoon not long after opening its doors. The booths were wrapped with orange leather and many had holes mended with duct tape. Small plastic-covered menus and metal napkin holders, usually empty on one side, were placed on tattered tables. On the wall behind the counter hung a chalk board with the daily special scribbled across it, with a misspelled word: *omilet.*

Stephen sat across from the two brothers, as he always did when they went out to eat. They ordered coffee and juice; Michael and Jon browsed through the menu.

"You clowns have eaten here for fifteen years and you still don't know what's on the menu. Michael, you'll get the number four and Jon will either get the number two or seven," Stephen said, having memorized the menu by the second time he sat down in the diner.

The waitress came moseying over wearing more stains than smiles. She smelled of stale cigarettes and looked like she was two days behind in sleep.

"What can I get you?" she asked through a wedge of bubble gum.

She looked at Michael first, so he ordered. "I'll take the number four with white toast."

He glanced at Stephen who was nodding and displaying an "I told you so" grin.

Jon ordered next, and he went with the number seven. Stephen followed with his order and the brothers knew what was coming.

"Bring me a three-egg omelet with mushrooms and a mix of American and cheddar cheese and have the cook grill the mushrooms first. I'll have a side of bacon. I like it crispy. Home fries well done and crispy as well, and rye toast, dark."

"My pen just ran out of ink," the waitress sarcastically muttered. Michael started laughing and a grin pushed up Jon's cheeks.

"Go ahead, laugh it up boys," Stephen said.

Jon reached into his pocket and pulled out a pint of Wild Turkey whiskey and began topping off his coffee.

"What the hell are you doing?" Stephen asked.

"A hair of the dog, Steve. Just a hair of the dog."

"A hair of the dog my ass," Stephen said. "Didn't you drink enough last night?"

"Apparently not." Jon said, before taking a drink from his spiked java.

"You have a problem, man," Stephen said.

"Hey, take it easy, alright?" Michael said in his brother's defense. "Give me that." Jon handed Michael the bottle. He poured some into his coffee.

"How about that LaPage," Stephen said changing the subject. "Do you really think he's a chicken hawk?"

Michael glanced at his brother and then back at Stephen. "That son of a bitch used to have tea in our living room with my parents. Christ, Jon used to be an altar boy under him."

"Hopefully not under him," Stephen responded, with a smile and bulging eyes.

"Watch it," Michael warned.

"What do you think, Jon. Is this priest guilty?" Stephen asked.

"I don't know," Jon said expressionless, taking his bottle back out and pouring.

"If he did do it, he should be taken out. Priest or no priest," Stephen said.

Jon looked up from his cup. "Just like Stack, right?"

Stephen resented the insinuation. "What do you mean by that?" he asked, his eyes quickly shifting to Michael and then back to Jon.

"Nothing, just that I heard Stack is dead, that's all," Jon said.

Who told you Stack is dead?" Michael asked.

"Hey, rumor has it that Stack was wasted after his shift." He shot a quick glance at them before dropping his head back down.

"I heard he took the cash receipts and skipped town," Michael said. "He's not dead."

"That's not what people are saying. Everyone hated that piece of shit, anyway, and nobody's talking to the cops.

"Who are *they* saying killed him?" Stephen asked.

Jon didn't respond, he drank from his cup until it was nearly empty. "What does a guy have to do to get a cup of coffee in this place?" he complained.

"Don't change the subject, Jon. What's the rumor about who killed Stack?" Stephen pressed on.

"I heard that you guys did it," he said without making eye contact with either of them.

"Us? What are you crazy?" Michael asked, between clenched teeth.

He looked up at his brother. "Hey, I'm not saying you did it." Jon back peddled. "That's just the whisper in the neighborhood."

Michael sat peering at his younger brother, wondering when it was that he changed and became so meek. He was like a sheep, he thought, always looking down and talking in a low and subdued tone. The drinking was out of control and Jon was getting worse as time passed by. Michael was tired of having to watch over him like a parent with a child.

The waitress came over with their breakfast. Michael had lost his appetite, but Stephen was hungrier than ever.

Later that day, Jake sat in a booth at the Pizza Palace waiting for Colleen to arrive. She had called him and suggested they have dinner at her favorite pizza parlor. Jake arrived early and found a booth in the corner. He sat with his back to the wall, looking out over the entire place. His drifting mind found its way back to his case. Stack had fallen off the face of the earth and not a single soul had been in contact with him, nor had there been any trace of his existence.

The endless interviews had turned up nothing, except rumors.

The most common was that Stephen and Michael had killed Stack for beating up Jon. Jake had interviewed Jon. He came to the conclusion that even though Jon had issues, he didn't know anything about the disappearance of Stack. There was something about him that troubled Jake; it was as though Jon kept a hidden sadness buried deep within his core. He seemed lost.

Jake figured whoever was responsible for Stack's disappearance was very clever. When he thought about the type of person who would be capable of such a perfect crime, he always came back to Stephen Haney. His frustration increased with every dead end. The captain suggested they bring Stephen back in, tag team him, and try and get him to reveal something that would prove incriminating. Jake agreed, but he was not very optimistic. Stephen was smart enough to know they had nothing on him. He would be as cool as a housecat. They didn't have a body or murder weapon, and they couldn't produce one witness that put Stephen or Michael at the scene the night Stack disappeared. On top of all that, Stephen had an alibi.

Jake concluded that Michael was the weak link in the pair. He didn't have a solid alibi, and the morning after Stack's disappearance he called in sick. Even though Michel was slippery in his own way, he wasn't nearly as bright as Stephen. Jake decided to bring him in again, and see if he could squeeze something tangible out of him.

Colleen looked more beautiful every time he saw her, Jake thought, as she walked toward his booth. Standing up to greet her, Jake took her by the hand and escorted her to her seat. She wore a tight short-sleeve white blouse that flattered her round breasts. Her legs were solid as those attached to the hips of a professional dancer. The light gold shorts were it concert with her shiny hair.

"You look stunning," Jake said, beaming.

Colleen blushed. "Wait until you see me in the morning."

Jake laughed. "I'll bet you look just as good when you roll out of bed first thing in the morning as you do now." He knew he was pushing it.

"You keep talking like that and you may soon find out." She winked.

Now it was his turn to blush, but nobody could tell. "So tell me, what you do when you're not at church."

"I'm a social worker for the city of Middleborough."

A slight wrinkle occupied the space above the bridge of his nose. "How come we've never crossed paths? I've dealt with most of the social workers in this town at one time or another during my career."

"Probably because you deal with the Department of Family Services. I work for the school system. You wouldn't run into me unless I killed someone."

"Well, it's probably better that we met in church." He grinned and she offered a subtle giggle.

"Tell me Detective Waterfield, how come a handsome man of the world like you isn't married?"

Colleen noticed discomfort in Jakes demeanor. She thought she may have hit a sore spot.

"I was married, but I lost my wife to a drunk driver."

The waiter came over and took their order. Jake briefly went back to a time of agonizing internal suffering as he remembered being dispatched to the accident scene on the off-ramp of the northbound highway that ran adjacent to Middleborough. His wife Charlotte had taken the ramp onto the highway when a young man in a pickup truck ascended the ramp going the wrong way and hit her head on. His blood alcohol count was 2.7 at the hospital where he was treated and released. Jake's young wife was killed on impact. Part of him had died along with her. When Jake arrived at the scene, Charlotte was being carried into the ambulance. The sight of his one true love covered in blood was too much to bear. His legs had given out and he fell to his knees. As he now looked at Colleen, he felt like he was finally getting back up.

"I'm sorry, Jake." He could see the compassion in her eyes, and Jake thought that she was a good soul. She reached out and took his hand, holding it soft and firm.

"It was a senseless and tragic accident. She was an extraordinary woman and I loved her with all my heart and soul." His voice crumbled.

"What was her name?"

"Her name was Charlotte. What about you, ever get married?"

She let go of his hand. "I was married once. Everyone loved John except me. He was a big, strong fireman." She puffed out her chest. "When I divorced him, my family and friends were angry with me for quite a while. I think my father is still mad, but he doesn't talk about it anymore."

Jake wondered if he was dead because she spoke of him in the past tense.

"Is he still a firefighter?"

"Oh yeah, he'll always be a firefighter. It's in his blood."

"What happened?"

"We were going in different directions, and he had a spending problem. He was a quick draw with the credit card, if you catch my drift."

A synchronized laugh formed as they gazed into each other's eyes.

Colleen wondered if they would make it, or if this was going to be another short story. Jake's thoughts were elsewhere. He was thinking about how much he wanted to make love to her.

The waitress appeared with their drinks and set them down. Colleen could smell the oaky aroma of her wine, and Jake slowly stirred his lemonade.

Jerry Laconia had arrived at District Attorney Corbin's office a half hour early. He wanted to make sure he and Corbin were on the same page before Ed Gallagher arrived. Bishop Reardon had briefed Laconia earlier that day. He made it very clear that he wanted this ordeal settled immediately.

Ed was escorted in by the attractive assistant, this time, she was all business. Laconia was seated in one of two chairs in front of the Corbin throne. Behind his desk, Corbin sat gnawing on an unlit Cuban cigar.

"Attorney Gallagher, please come in and have a seat. Corbin pointed to the chair with the wet end of his cigar. Ed took his seat, wishing he'd been a spider on the wall five minutes earlier, listening to their conversation.

"Good afternoon, gentlemen," Ed belted out.

"As you are aware, I invited you here on neutral ground, because Mr. Gallagher had brought this issue to me. The Bishop also agreed that this is a good place to hold this meeting,"

Corbin said, slowly swiveling in his chair, back and forth, like a restless child. "I assure you I will not interfere with any of the proceedings, unless it involves a criminal element." He gestured to the awaiting attorney. "Mr. Laconia."

"Let me get straight to the point," Laconia started. "We feel that these allegations by your client are not only extremely belated, but also outrageous. We are talking about a well-liked and respected community clergyman." He slapped the back of his right hand on his palm as he spoke.

Ed wondered why Italians could never keep their hands still while making a point.

"This is a priest who has done so much good for the poor and needy," Laconia continued. "You will have a very difficult time convincing a jury that this honorable and kind man of God has committed such immoral acts."

This guy is good. "Well, Mr. Laconia, I think we'll have a very good chance in front of a jury, Ed disagreed. "Have you read the statement provided by Mr. Brick?"

"Yes," Laconia said, with a slight shrug of the shoulders.

"Do you honestly think a man that wasn't the victim of such disgusting and vile acts could make something like this up, something so detailed and humiliating? My client's reputation is at stake here. He has a hard time looking in the mirror, and Lord only knows how his friends and family look at him *now*." Ed crossed his right leg over his left and folded his hands with a relaxed confidence. "We are prepared to take this all the way to the Supreme Court, if necessary."

Laconia stood and walked away, facing Corbin's array of awards and plaques hung so orderly on the wall. "The diocese can't afford a scandal; the media will have field day with this story." Laconia's voice bounced off the wall as Ed sat surveying his back. He twirled and looked at Corbin briefly before facing Ed. "We are prepared to settle this case in the amount of $250,000 dollars.

It was funereally quiet. Ed studied Corbin, believing he didn't look surprised one bit. He figured Corbin was part of the rehearsal and knew exactly what was going to transpire.

"So, you're offering ten percent of the initial suit?" Ed asked.

"Reluctantly. Yes."

"You need to understand something here. This priest is a low life pedophile that should be locked up. My client wants this guy exposed and defrocked."

"That is not an option," Laconia returned without hesitation.

Ed looked to Corbin. "The reason I agreed to have this meeting *here* at the district attorney's office, is that I want to get this whole mess out in the open." Quickly shifting his eyes and focusing on Laconia, he continued. "LaPage is a prime suspect in the murder of Robert Anderson. The boy was twelve years old when he was sexually assaulted and beat over the head in Bottle Park."

Laconia's face tightened. "Wait a minute. That was a long time ago and there was no evidence proving him responsible," he barked. "That case is long closed and has no bearing on this issue."

"He's right, let's not bring that up again," Corbin sided.

Now on his feet and pacing, Ed continued. "Here is our offer. The amount will be 1.2 million, LaPage is defrocked and the Anderson case is re-opened."

"You can pound sand up your ass!" Laconia jumped to his feet shouting with a reddened face."

"Gentlemen, sit down. Let's be reasonable here." Corbin was looking at Ed as he spoke and it was clear where his loyalties lied.

"You have nothing, except some gold digger looking for a quick handout." Laconia was pointing his finger at Ed, like a Turkish prosecutor. "There is no evidence, no witness, and no medical verification. All you have is a client with a good imagination and the balls to make false accusations. It's his word against a Catholic Priest who is highly regarded in this community. We'll see you in court."

Ed picked up his case and started toward the door, stopped short and turned around. "That's not all we have, counselor. Yesterday, a man came into my office claiming he had been raped by Father LaPage in 1975. I took a full statement and will be filing suit in short order."

Laconia's jaw nearly hit the floor and Corbin looked like a man that had lost his life savings. Ed turned and walked out the door leaving his last words lingering behind. "Good day, gentlemen."

CHAPTER 20

The waterbed was state-of-the-art sleeping technology. At least that's what, Carrie, the girl lying next to Stephen said. Shifting to his right in order to avoid a vacuum between the long tubes that ran the length of the bed, Stephen grunted.

"This bed sucks."

"What are you talking about? It's almost brand new."

"I don't like waterbeds, especially ones that have separate cylinders."

"This is the newest and most expensive waterbed on the market," she said, as if she were the manufacturer.

"Yeah, well whoever came up with this idea is a moron, and the concept won't last very long."

"What are you talking about?" Carrie snapped.

"There are voids created between the cylinders that displace your weight. It's not consistently smooth."

"Well, I love it." She thought about the day her boyfriend had it delivered to her apartment as a birthday gift. In his mind, it was just as much as a gift for him as it was for her. She was a sexual goddess and the bed would make for many pleasurable nights.

Carrie lit up a cigarette and thought about how good Stephen had just performed.

"Why do you still live with your mother?"

He turned his head, examining her. "She's all I have left and she's getting older. I'm keeping her out of trouble." Stephen's wide smile reminded her of The Joker. There was something devious about him that intrigued her, but she wasn't sure exactly what it was.

She took a long drag and let out a perfect stream of smoke that ascended toward the high ceiling and lingered without escape. "What happened to your father?"

Not wanting to answer, Stephen thought about how good she was in bed and he wanted more, so he caved in. "He left us when I was a kid." He reached out, running his hand along the soft skin of her naked breast.

"You have a sister, right?"

"What are you, a cop?"

"Just making conversation," she said while raking her fingers through his hair.

"She lives in California with some movie editor. We don't talk much anymore. She was sixteen when my father split and she had a hard time with it. My mother and sister weren't getting along, so she packed her bags and headed west. I've only seen her once since then."

"Have you heard from your Dad?"

Looking up at the clouded ceiling Stephen fell into a trance. He thought about his father and how much he missed him. It was strange to him that he could still love a man that was cruel most of the time and absent the rest. It was the few good times that he remembered. A void existed somewhere deep inside his body. He couldn't pinpoint exactly where, but it was there-a faint, lingering, dull pain.

"No," he said, as he snapped free and began sliding his hand from her breast down to the dark triangle between her legs. She opened up, letting him explore and they merged for another episode.

As he walked down the steps leading out of Carrie's apartment, Stephen wondered if he had made a mistake by not agreeing to spend the night. He had only known her for three weeks, but there was something about her he liked. They had engaged in intercourse four times. Each time seemed more exciting than the last. She was somewhat intelligent, he thought. If she didn't ask so many questions, he wouldn't have many complaints.

It was dead quiet at 3:40 in the morning as the streetlights illuminated the cars parked along the street. Stephen gazed up at the tall brick building to his right as he walked down the sidewalk and turned the corner to the place his car was parked. As he got closer to his car, he felt his jaw tightened and his fists balled up.

He stopped near the driver-side door then walked around the car until he was back where he started. Stephen stood furiously glaring at the damage. All four tires had been slashed and the windows were shattered. The entire car was riddled with dents and his front seat was torn open. It was apparent to him that a crowbar and a knife were most likely the tools used. He started up the street looking at other cars parked near his and they were all intact. It was obvious that his car was targeted. This was not a random act of vandalism.

Carrie was surprised as she heard her front door buzzer going off.

"Who is it?"

"It's Steve. Can you quickly get dressed and come down here?"

She could tell by his tone that something was wrong. "I'll be right down."

A few minutes later the door opened and she came out wearing a sweatshirt and jeans.

"What's wrong?"

"Someone trashed my car," he responded, anxiously.

"Where is it?"

"Come on, I'll show you."

They started up the street in silence. Once they arrived at his car he turned to her. "Carrie, I want you to be straight with me. Is there anyone you know who would do this?"

Without looking at him, her eyes were fixed on the pile of junk in the street. "I don't think so."

"That's bullshit! My car was targeted, and nobody around here knows me, except you. Is there an old boyfriend or someone who might have a score to settle with you?"

Carrie's eyes began to fill up. "It might be Tom," she admitted.

"Tom! Who the hell is Tom?" Stephen stomped his right foot hard on the pavement in synchronization with the name.

"He was my boyfriend," whined.

"He *was* your boyfriend. When did you split up?"

"We had a fight the other day and I told him I didn't want to see him anymore."

Stephen put his hand over his mouth, causing ripples up his cheeks as he thought for a moment.

"How long have you two been going out?"

"Over two years." Her weeping increased.

"So you were banging me while you were still with him?"

She didn't answer.

"Alright," he said, taking her in his arms. "Calm down, it's not your fault. What's his last name?"

"Please, don't hurt him," she pleaded.

"I won't. I just want to get reimbursed for the damage, that's all."

"It's Tom Downey."

"Where does he live?" Stephen had a vision of Downey with a crowbar shoved up his ass.

Carrie was reluctant to tell him and he pulled her in closer. "Look, I can't get any money from him if I don't know how to find him, right?" He smiled at her and she forced out a slight giggle.

"I guess so. He lives at 44 Dayton Drive, in Bolton."

"Okay, let's go back to your place, so I can figure this thing out." Taking her by the arm they headed back up the street. The car had more damage than it was worth, and he was calculating

what was owed to him, including the cost of his aggravation.

By the time the bartender finally convinced Tom Downey to leave it was after 2 a.m. Drunk and depressed by the realization that he had lost his girlfriend, he staggered out of the tavern reeking of whiskey and cigarettes. In the past two years he had tumbled head over heels in love with Carrie, and in his mind, he had concocted a lifetime spent with her.

The bartender followed Tom out and secured the door behind them. He asked Tom if he was alright to drive and Tom assured him he would be fine because he lived less than a mile away. Satisfied with the response, the bartender got in his car and drove away.

Tom lit a cigarette and fumbled with his car keys, attempting to unlock his door. After turning the key, he pulled open the door and immediately sensed that someone was behind him. As he casually turned around, he was clocked below the right eye with a quick punch delivered by Stephen. The flash and instant pain caused him to take two steps back, but it didn't knock him off his feet. Charging at his attacker, Tom was swinging wildly in desperation. It all ended with a blackjack blow across the side of his neck and it was lights out as the blood supply to his brain was instantly cut off.

"Help me throw him in the back seat," Stephen ordered, as he slid the seven inch long leather weapon into his back pocket. Michael helped him drag the unconscious man into the back seat, and they went to work duct taping his hands behind his back and taping his mouth and eyes shut.

"Follow me to the warehouse," Stephen said.

Sitting in a metal folding chair with a pounding headache, Tom was beginning to sober up. As the duct tape was quickly ripped off his eyes, it took part of his eyebrow along with it. He let out a grunt that was muffled by the tape over his mouth. When the initial blur had cleared, he was looking at two men standing over him wearing potato sacks over their heads with three holes cut out in the front. Tom immediately began to tremble uncontrollably not knowing who they were or what they were going to do. It reminded him of a horror movie he had seen years earlier and it didn't end well for the victims. Sitting in the middle of a large warehouse with graffiti covered walls; coupled with the unpleasant smell of urine and feces, led him to believe he was in an abandoned building.

"Two nights ago, as you were punching holes in tires and smashing out car windows, I bet you never thought you'd be sitting in a shithole like this awaiting a painful death." Stephen began circling the chair, like a tiger his prey. Tom was rambling on behind the tape and they both had a good idea that he was attempting to deny his involvement.

"Shut up! I don't want to hear your bullshit," Stephen yelled. If you had a problem with me fucking your girlfriend, or should I say ex-girlfriend, you should have come to me like a man and discussed it with me. Instead, you decided to destroy my car."

Continuing to circle the chair, Stephen walked around the five gallon gas jug that sat directly behind the quivering man. Stopping directly in front of Tom, Stephen reached out and tore the tape off his mouth. Following a short grunt, Tom immediately began his blundering denial.

"Shut up!"

Stephen walked around him and leaned over, picking up a tire iron off the floor, and then moved back in front of Tom, holding the tool.

"Do you see this tire iron? Does it look familiar to you?"

He placed the edge of the cold metal against his eyelid. Tom moved his head back to avoid the possible loss of an eye and Stephen pushed it in closer. There was no refuge for Tom.

"It should, because it's yours," Stephen yelled. "We found it in the trunk of your car, and guess what, Tommy boy. There's red paint on it that matches my car."

With a sudden thundering blow, Stephen came down on Tom's thigh with the heavy, metal weapon. Screaming out in pain, Tom continued to deny that it was him that vandalized the car.

"You still won't admit that you are the culprit, you defiant bastard." Stephen clutched the iron in both hands and wound up swinging the weapon directly at Tom's head, and just before he made contact, he stopped, like a check swing from a baseball player. Tom closed his eyes as he flinched in anticipation of a deadly blow.

"Alright, I guess maybe you didn't do it."

Once again, Stephen walked behind his chair. Tom tried to turn to see where he was going and Michael quickly shuffled in and slapped him across the face.

"Sit still!" Michael warned.

Fearing the worst, Tom did as he was told. The next thing he sensed was the smell of gasoline and he began to get extremely frightened. As he sat paralyzed, his mouth became dry and bullets of sweat crept down the sides of his face until they plunged to their end. His polyester shirt clung to his body, like a wet leaf on a car windshield. Stephen reappeared holding a gas jug, and he started pouring gas over Tom's feet and lower legs. Screaming out in a panic, Tom desperately pleaded for Stephen to stop, until Michael returned with duct tape, re-covering his mouth. Tom's widening eyes looked as though they were going to pop out of his face as his muffled cries for help went unheard. Once Stephen saturated Tom's lower extremities, he took out a cigarette and produced a lighter.

"Do you know why the Indians used to burn their enemies from the feet up?"

Tom shook his head back and forth. It was more of a plea for Stephen to not ignite the lighter than it was that he didn't know the Indian answer.

"Because it took much longer to die and the pain was excruciating as the flames slowly moved from the feet, crawling up the body, until it engulfed their entire head."

Stephen lit the cigarette and Tom's tears began to mix with his sweat.

"I'm going to ask you one last time if it were you that trashed my car."

He ripped the tape off Tom's mouth, but he didn't feel the sting this time.

"Yes!" I did it. I'm sorry. I just love her so much," he testified in a whiny and crumbling voice.

Stephen stood examining his prey without speaking and Tom was wondering if he had just made the biggest mistake of his life.

"How much money do you have in the bank?" Stephen asked.

"About $3,600" he answered without hesitation.

Pacing back in forth, Stephen began his calculation.

"Well, I figure to replace my car, and the aggravation you cost me, and the gas I just wasted, comes to about $3,500. Does that sound fair to you?"

"Yes! No problem. I'll bring you the money this afternoon."

"No, I'm going to tell you how this is going to go down."

Stephen extracted a hand-held recorder out of his pocket.

"First you are going to state your full name, and then, you're going to describe in detail where my car was parked and what exactly what you did to it, and why. I'm going to tape your confession, and keep it, just in case you decide to go to the police. Am I clear?

Tom sat still looking at his captor, offering no response.

Stephen lit the lighter and the flame came to life and he began moving it towards Tom's feet.

"If I light your feet on fire, we won't be able to put it out in time."

"Okay, whatever you want," Tom cried.

"Good. The bank will be open in a few hours and my friend here will drive you, so you can make your cash withdrawal. You will be blind-folded when you leave here, because this place is sacred to us," Stephen said with a smile. "There are two things I want you to remember."

Tom was relieved that he wasn't going to go up in flames, yet he was still scared.

"The first one is that you are never to contact Carrie again, and secondly, if you go to the police, I will find you. When I do, I swear I'll set your sorry ass on fire. Are we clear?"

"Yes, very clear."

"Good and remember, I will have a copy of your confession." Stephen pushed the button, activating the recorder.

CHAPTER 21

The leaves had fallen and were covered by the winter's first snow shower. Ed Gallagher snapped on his rubber shoe covers, slid into his insolated London Fog overcoat, and headed to the office.

Sitting behind the wheel of his Audi, he sometimes did his best thinking as the traffic clustered around him in a mad frenzy. He dreaded the ride to work whenever it snowed or rained because it would nearly double his commute. People just can't seem to drive in precipitation, he thought.

Thirty-four minutes later, he arrived at his office building. He stopped at the cafeteria on the first floor to buy his usual black coffee and morning paper. His secretary was late again and his tolerance was wearing thin. The forty-three warnings apparently hadn't sunk in yet. Ed doubted they ever would. After hanging up his coat, Ed retired to his high-back chair, hot coffee, and cool paper.

The front page had caught his attention as he approached the news stand, and he was anxious to dive right in. The article read "Catholic Church Sued Again." To Ed's surprise, this was the eleventh law suit filed against the diocese for alleged sexual abuse at the hands of Father LaPage. Nearly all of Ed's clients had decided to settle out of court except for Mr. Brick. He was holding out for more than a payoff. Brick wanted to see LaPage pay himself. Not just the church that was protecting him. His wounds had sliced to the bone and forgiveness was not an option.

Ed could hear a stir in the reception area; he instantly recognized the normal sound his secretary brought along with her tardiness. He took a sip from his drink and turned the page.

Attorney Laconia sat admiring the silverware and china in Bishop Reardon's dining room. The bone china had to be at least 150 years old, he estimated. The room was elegantly decorated with original paintings and antique furniture, including a ten-foot long inlaid Italian walnut dining room table and a five-foot tall wine rack that was once used as a boot drying rack during the Civil War.

Reardon stormed into the room, wielding his newspaper like a broken sword. "Did you see this?" He slammed the paper on the table with the bad news facing up.

"Good morning, Evan."

"Don't act cheerful with me! The Vatican has just chewed off the left side of my ass. If you notice me sitting awkwardly, you'll understand why."

"Yes, I read the article and I'm preparing a response."

"Yes, well, by the time you respond there may be another suit brought against us. When does this end?"

Pushing the paper aside, Laconia moved his chair into a direct position of the Bishop.

"That is a question for your Priest."

Pondering his response, Reardon began rubbing his forehead in anguish. "Make sure your statement is a good one. I don't want the community thinking we are condoning this kind of behavior, yet I also don't want them to think this is a widespread problem within the Catholic Church."

"It is a fine line," Laconia agreed.

"Get a hold of this guy's attorney and see what they want. All of them have settled, except..."

"Except Mr. Brick," Laconia cut him off.

The Bishop rose to his feet and wandered over to the window that faced the garden.

"Yes, Mr. Brick. Money does not seem to be his concern. He wants more than that. He wants revenge, and he is relentless in his quest."

"We offered him the highest settlement *ever* in the history of the church. He's holding out on principal," Laconia said.

"Yes, I know. I have decided to accommodate Mr. Brick and move Father LaPage to another church."

"Where?" Laconia asked. He was hoping it wasn't close to where he lived.

Reardon looked out the window, admiring the powdery snow perched on the tree branches. Such a beautiful landscape, he thought.

"Swift River. That's as far out as I can possibly send him."

Laconia was relieved. His house was located in the other direction.

"Yup, that's in the boonies alright. Have you told him?"

Reardon turned around and walked back to his chair and sat down. "Not yet."

Laconia polished a scuff mark off the face of his watch with the remote side of his tie. "He's not going to like it."

"Now that's too damned bad, isn't it? Our Mass has diminished nearly a third because of this mess. Do you have any idea how this has affected our cash flow?" Reardon asked.

"Evan, let me ask you a direct question." Laconia rose to his feet and moved to the desk, scaling the edge with his pant seat. Focusing on the Bishop, he asked with caution. "Do you think Father LaPage might be guilty of these terrible allegations?"

Reardon looked at Laconia as though he was an imbecile. "Of course he's guilty," he barked. "To what extent, the Lord only knows." He shifted in his chair. "There are many in our community that support him and believe he's innocent, and he has done quite a bit of good, you know."

Laconia watched the performance, unconvinced.

"Do you realize how hard it is to locate and recruit priests these days? Sixty-five percent of Catholic priests are over the age of forty-five. Very few young men are joining the seminary."

"Maybe the Church should allow priests to marry," Laconia said.

"That will never happen. The union of two turns into a family of five and it multiplies out of control. It would be too costly for the Vatican to absorb."

Reardon's sciatica alarmed him and he needed to stand. On his feet, he walked to the south side of the room and opened the door, indicating that Laconia should leave.

"Hopefully, Mr. Brick will be pleased with our decision to relocate Father LaPage."

Laconia straightened out his stance and brushed off the lint from the lapel of his Brooks Brothers suit. "I doubt that will be enough to make him change his mind."

Reaching down and securing his brief case, Laconia started toward the exit.

"Offer him another 150 grand. Maybe that coupled with the relocation of LaPage will convince him to reconsider," Reardon said.

Laconia was amazed at the amount of money the church had to throw around in order to avoid a scandal, yet they wouldn't consider supporting a priest's family should he be allowed to marry.

"I'll run it by Gallagher. Have a nice day, Evan."

"You do the same," Reardon said to Laconia's back as he walked out of the room.

The diner was nearly empty and Jake came to the conclusion that his eggs were always cooked better when it wasn't busy. An hour earlier, he was stretched out in bed with a heavy mind. His thoughts were scattered shifting from Colleen, to Stack, and then back to the Anderson case. It was beginning to look more and more like the Priest may have been involved with the murder of Robert Anderson, yet he was still convinced that Haney and McNulty were the culprits. He drifted back to Colleen and the anticipation of meeting her family at her Uncle's retirement party. Jake's attempt to convince Colleen that it was too soon for him to meet her family fell to deaf ears. She was a hard-headed woman.

Unable to fall back to sleep, he got up, took a shower, and drove to Megan's Diner. As Jake ate his breakfast alone, he thought about how much better the food tasted when Colleen sat across from him. He could almost smell her light citrus perfume that reminded him of a tropical beach he once explored as a child. His thoughts drifted as he fantasized about caressing her soft pale skin and shiny hair. As the sun breached the window pane; he thought of her sparkling eyes and smile that illuminated a room. He was ecstatic to have found her, yet petrified by a potential loss. This one he had to hold on to and never let go.

The gathering was moderate and growing by the minute. Jake and Colleen sat in a corner of an open hall with high ceilings supported by light gold walls. Red and yellow streamers were draped overhead and a six-foot handmade sign spanned a portion of the windowless wall.

Jake thought about what retirement might feel like. He still had quite a long road ahead and couldn't imagine not having police work in his life. What would he do, spend his days waiting to die? He thought about retired Police Chief Fitch working in his garden, and how he didn't look very happy. The way he moved around lacked enthusiasm and the bounce he once had in his step had resigned to an effortless shuffle. Jake hoped his retirement would be more fulfilling.

Colleen nudged Jake, and she gestured toward Uncle Smitty, who was downing a shot at the bar. He didn't seem to have a loss of spirit, not on this night. Who knows what tomorrow would bring? Jake thought.

A thin graying woman wearing a light green dress came walking toward Colleen and Jake.

"That's my mother," Colleen said with a smile. "She's the rock of the family."

"You must be the detective I've heard so much about," her mother said as she approached.

Jake stood up and they found each other's hands. He could see where Colleen inherited her beauty.

"I'm Jake," he said with a full smile.

"Hello Jake, I'm Mary. It's nice to meet you."

Mary had a pleasant way about her that made Jake feel at ease.

He hadn't met anyone since the party started, and he wasn't sure what the night would bring. Strange looks from across the room and a couple faint nods were the extent of his interactions with the crowd of new faces.

"Honey, can you help your mother in the kitchen for a few minutes?"

Colleen looked at Jake. "Would you mind?"

"Of course not." He hoped it wouldn't be too long.

"You'll be okay here by yourself."

Jake pondered whether it was a question or a statement. "I'll be fine, go ahead."

Mary took her daughter's hand, and they headed across the room behind the buffet and into the hidden kitchen. Jake sat alone with a glass of soda water laced with lemon, watching a room of people talking, drinking and gesturing as they spoke. He felt like he was alone outside a building peering in through a glass window, unable to get in.

A gathering of four men stood in a circle by the buffet talking. Occasionally they looked in Jake's direction and he wasn't sure if it was a coincidence or on purpose. One of the men wore a long apron with a skeleton holding an assault weapon in one hand and a spatula in the other. Jake had noticed him bringing food out from the kitchen just after he and Colleen arrived.

"Chow time, let's eat," the man wearing the apron called out.

As people began to rise and form a line, the man in the apron came walking toward Jake. He stopped short of Jake's table and looked back at his friends by the buffet before turning back to Jake. "I'm Kevin, Colleen's brother." He didn't offer to shake. "Come on up and I'll make you a plate," he said, forcing a half smile.

"Thank you," Jake responded, standing up and followed Kevin to the line. Taking his place behind a couple with a combined weight of at least 500 pounds, he thought he might get a large salad. As the line crawled along, Jake watched Colleen's brother serving the food and commenting to each person as they move through the buffet. Appearing to be in his early thirties, Kevin was in as good physical condition as a dedicated weightlifter. His short cropped hair over a chiseled face gave him a military look. As Jake approached the first table where the plates, utensils, and napkins were neatly sorted out, Kevin darted over, standing across from Jake on the serving side of the table.

"Let me make you a plate," Kevin said as he reached over the table snatching up a plate. Kevin quickly went to work with a set of tongs and when Jake made it to the end of the serving line, Kevin offered him his plate. The grin on Kevin's face was slanted and sinister.

"Here you go," Kevin said holding out a plate.

Jake looked down to see a chicken leg and a slice of watermelon sitting alone on the plate.

As reality set in, Jake's thoughts were thwarted by a group of Kevin's friends that began roaring in laughter, and Kevin followed suit. Jake felt a wave of humiliation, starting in the pit of his stomach and spreading throughout his entire body, surging to his right arm. Jake suddenly slung his arm forward, flipping the plate back up at Kevin. The food bounced off Kevin's face and chest area. With this act of retaliation, the laughter immediately died.

"You goddamn nigger!" Kevin hissed, leaping over the table, attempting to get a punch in on Jake. Desperately trying to push through the men that had jumped in between them, Jake charged forward at Kevin with flailing arms. Both men struggled in a rage to get to each other, but several people had moved in between them and were holding them back.

"You stay the fuck away from my sister," Kevin yelled, as Jake was pulled away and ushered toward the door by two large men.

Colleen's father watched from the bar, grimaced, and then turned his back to order another beer. Colleen heard the commotion from the kitchen and rushed out to watch in surprise as her new boyfriend was being pushed out the door, her brother yelling at him in a fit of anger. Colleen quickly darted toward the door, cursing at Kevin as she passed by. Jake was in the parking lot walking toward his car when Colleen caught up to him. As he reached to open the car door, Colleen approached, softly touching his shoulder.

"Jake, I'm sorry."

As he turned around, she could see the disturbed look on his face. It appeared to be a combination of humiliation, anger, and sadness.

"It's never going to work." The muster of words came hard for him as though they were buried somewhere deep in his core and had to be dug out. Jake felt as though he had left something behind in the reception hall. No one could see it, or sense it, but it was there, lingering somewhere in the building. He gently removed Colleen's hand from his shoulder, got in his car, and drove away.

CHAPTER 22

Father LaPage sat in his new quarters with a glass of scotch whiskey attached to his right hand, sipping in short intervals. The new living space was a third the size of his place in Middleborough, and he was frustrated with indecision about what items he would be able to keep and which would be stored in the damp basement below.

Tormented by a less than friendly reception by his new congregation, he placed all blame on the media that relentlessly attempted to destroy him. Feeling sorry for himself, LaPage thought of ways he might be able to redeem himself in the eyes of the church and community. Maybe he would initiate a fundraiser for terminally ill children, or go on a mission to fight hunger in Africa.

With an uneasy mind and a determination to regain respect, he wasn't able to sleep more than three hours at a time. A nagging urge to be with young boys consumed his thoughts and weighed on his libido. *Why has everyone gotten so bent out of shape over my relationships with the boys? It's like a religious fraternity that's been accepted in many places throughout history. Why is it so different now? he thought. Alexander the Great is regarded as one of the greatest generals in the history of the world and he kept young boys as lovers. Why isn't he seen as a tyrant, but I am, by so many? I've never mistreated my boys and they've learned so much from me. I should charge their parents a teaching fee.*

LaPage's first Mass had less than a hundred people in attendance and most of the people that turned up were over the age of fifty. The priest LaPage replaced had decided to retire at the age of seventy-one. His health had been compromised in the past year and he was no longer up to the task. Reardon thought LaPage would be the best option for the time being.

While speaking to the old priest, LaPage listened to him brag that his Mass had been standing room only on Sundays with more than 300 people in attendance. LaPage fretted over the loss of participants and refused to take any blame. He poured another glass to the brim and consumed a substantial fill. *Why can't they see how brilliant I am and how much good I've done in the past? How could they not know that I'm truly a man of the Lord and that my faith is unquestionable?* Consuming one last hit from his drink, he emptied the glass, snatched the car keys off the table, and made his way to the door with a jacket draped over his arm.

On the first day LaPage arrived in Swift River, he had located the largest playground in town, and that's where he was headed.

With each step onto Bottle Park's wet asphalt, tiny drops of tainted rain splashed back up onto Tim Anderson's black wingtip shoes. A light gray mist ascended from the earth with a smoky-clouded defiance of the distant sun kneading through the trees. A still morning shuddered as an intruder dared to invade its solitude; calling out into the open void.

As Tim scaled the edge of the grass line; nothing moved except his legs and swaying arms. The paralyzing calmness of the morning reflected his echo back to him with a faint lingering drawl. Bringing his hands up and cupping the corners of his mouth, like a man-made bullhorn, he called out. There was no one there, nobody could hear him, yet he continued calling out in desperation. In the distance he spied a foggy pond and thought he heard a faint cry echoing from the stagnant water. Moving closer, and in slow motion, the voice became louder and more familiar. Tim tried to run to the pond, but his legs were weak and without traction. His heart fell to his center, just below his abdomen, and his lips trembled as he watched his son slowly slipping under the water. "Robby!" Tim cried out, running as hard as he could, but going nowhere. "Robby!" He watched in horror as his boy slipped deeper into the water, his arms stretched out for help. "Daddy, help me." Feeling helpless and panicked, Tim tried to save his drowning son, but he couldn't get to him. "Robby," he cried out as he watched in pure agony as his child disappeared into Devils

Pond; the water finally covering his head. He was gone.

"Tim, wake up." Betty said, shaking him. "You're having a bad dream." Tim quickly sat up, relieved it was a dream and not reality. Tears beaded his on cheeks and his heart tried to regain a normal pace. He fell back down feeling the soft, dry, comfort of his pillow.

"Are you alright?" Betty asked.

He began sobbing and she closed in to embrace him. Betty rarely saw Tim cry and she knew it could only be for one reason.

"It was Robby," he moaned. "He was drowning and I couldn't save him."

"It's alright honey. Robby is at peace now. It's not your fault," she said pulling him closer.

"I couldn't save him," he cried. "I couldn't save him."

The Swift River High School gym was hustling with young men shooting hoops and playing mock games of two-on-two. It was open gym, which meant anyone could come and work up a sweat without being expelled by a structured full-court game. LaPage had been invited by Henry Carpenter, a parishioner with a Napoleon complex. Even wearing his thick-healed sneakers, he barely measured in at five-foot four inches.

On the first Sunday LaPage gave his sermon, Henry sat alone in the second row, intently listening. He found LaPage charismatic and interesting, and he felt a need to be in his company. Henry saw something in the priest that he himself lacked, and in his mind's eye, he figured if he spent significant time with LaPage, he might be able to adopt his ways. If he could only learn to have more confidence and become more articulate, he might be able to talk to women without stumbling over his words. Maybe it would even help Henry in his career at the post office and he could catapult himself into a supervisor position, instead of loading packages onto trucks all day.

"Pass it here." LaPage zipped the ball underhand to Henry and he missed the catch, fumbling before he went for a layup.

Scanning the room for the youngest of boys, LaPage trotted to the basket making a quick hook shot. He kept in fairly good shape by occasional jogging and exercising in his quarters.

Henry had heard rumors about LaPage and his alleged improprieties with young boys, but after hearing the priest speak during Mass, he completely ruled it out as a possibility. A devout Catholic, Henry savored every word that spilled out of LaPage's mouth.

After being destroyed in a couple games of two-on-two and countless apologies by Henry, his teammate, LaPage decided to wrap it up. The courts were thinning as they walked toward the exit with Henry continuing to dribble on the way out.

"Are you going to hit the showers?" LaPage asked.

Henry couldn't imagine being naked in front of a priest. "No, I always shower at home."

"I guess we part here, then." LaPage reached out and they shook hands. "Thanks for the invitation. We'll have to do it again," LaPage said.

"How about next Wednesday?" Henry fired back.

"I'll have to let you know about that. See you at church."

"Okay, I'll see you at church," he mimicked.

In the locker room, LaPage's antenna went up as he discretely watched from the corner of his eye as sweaty young men retreated to the shower room. His mind began to drift back to his days as a young boy at his Uncle Ray's house. Ray, his father's only brother, used to sit for him after his parents divorced, while his father roamed the bars in a desperate hunt for women. When LaPage was eight-years-old his mother walked out, leaving only a note and bad karma behind. Uncle Ray was more than happy to watch his young nephew when his older brother went out on the weekends. On occasion, when he got lucky, his brother didn't come home until the next day. LaPage remembered the long nights spent with his uncle and he began to feel a stir. This is when it all began and when it all ended.

CHAPTER 23

Pastor Steven Mead was in his office sitting behind his desk when Colleen arrived. She was fifteen minutes early, and she hoped she wasn't interrupting him. Happy that he was able to see her on such short notice, she left the house early to make sure she was on time. Colleen had called her Pastor the day before, asking for a meeting to discuss her relationship with her boyfriend and her family situation. Pastor Mead could sense by the way her voice was cracking up that she was hurting, so he agreed to meet with her the following afternoon.

Standing up when she appeared in the doorway, the Pastor never completely straightened out his posture. Colleen thought he looked like an old man bent forward at the waist, needing his walker.

"Close the door and come in and have a seat, Colleen." He sat back down. Wearing a cranberry sweater vest over a white, long-sleeved oxford shirt and dark trousers, he looked more like a college professor than a Pastor.

"From our brief conversation, I can tell you are very upset about the situation with your family. Tell me what has happened and I'll try to comfort you with some advice, or at least some objective insight."

"Thank you, Pastor, for seeing me so soon. I really appreciate it." She stirred in her seat as if there was a spring protruding through the leather. "You've met my boyfriend, Jake?"

"Yes, he seems like a fine gentleman."

"Yes, he's a good man and I'm very fond of him. The problem is that my family, well, I should say, everyone except my mother, doesn't approve of me seeing him. They haven't even gotten to know him and they won't even try."

"Do you love this man, Jake?"

Looking at the cross on the wall, she thought for a moment. "I think I do."

"Colleen, you're a grown woman and you have to make your

own choices in life. Whether they're good or bad, they are your choices to make, no one else's. I have known you since you were a child and I've watched you grow into a fine lady. I'm very proud of whom you have become and your family should also be proud of you."

Colleen's eyes became glossy. "Thanks, Pastor. The truth is they aren't proud of me. My brother looks at me with contempt and my father hardly looks at me at all. Last week at a party for my Uncle my brother humiliated Jake in front of a hundred people, and now Jake won't return my calls. I'm afraid I may have lost him over this." Her left eye pushed out a tear that gravitated to her chin and hung a few seconds before falling to her lap.

The Pastor snapped a tissue out of a box and handed it to her. "If he cares for you as much as you do for him, he'll come around. He may just need some time to process what has happened."

Pastor Mead's words were already comforting her and she felt lighter around her shoulders.

"What about my family? Will they ever come around? What should I do?"

Bringing his hand up and covering his mouth, Mead thought for a brief period. "That is a decision you have to make for yourself, my dear. If your family really cares about you and your happiness, they will come around. If they don't, then you'll know you made the right decision." He adjusted the picture of his wife and daughter that rested on his desk. "But, if you have any inclination that this affair may be nothing more than trains passing in the night, you may want to think hard about the effect it will have on your future relationship with your father and brother."

Carefully absorbing his advice, Colleen knew what she had to do.

"I understand, and as always, you have given me sound and comforting advice. Thank you."

Rising to her feet, Colleen moved in to embrace him.

"If there is anything else I can do, please call."

"I will, Pastor. Thanks again."

"God bless you, Colleen."

"And you as well," she said before leaving.

Pastor Mead watched her walk out, before sitting back down and removing his shoes for relief. His left foot had been bothering him more than usual. It must be the damp weather that's causing it, he thought. As he sat rubbing his foot, his mind began to drift back in time.

The year was 1951 and the snow had been falling for two days, accumulating on ground that was as solid as a never ending sheet of diamonds. Somewhere north of Seoul, he sat alone preparing for battle. Even though he didn't carry a weapon, he had to mentally prepare himself for a visit to hell. This wasn't his first battle, and it wasn't going to be his last.

The time for battle had come and the company commander came hustling over to where he was sitting. "Chaplin Mead, top of the morning to you."

Captain Flannigan was a tall, lean, rugged man that greeted everyone in the same manner, even if it weren't morning. Mead wondered if he had been tipping the whiskey bottle more than condoned. Kneeling down next to Mead, he reached into his fatigue shirt pocket and pulled out a silver cross attached to a long silver chain. Wrapping the chain around his hand and holding the cross between his fore finger and thumb, he looked at the Chaplin. Mead knew the drill because it was always the same. He began with a prayer to the Virgin Mary to expedite the battle, and to give the soldiers the courage and honor to fight hard and be victorious. Mead finished by asking the Lord to bless the men with the compassion to be merciful and to treat the enemy with dignity.

Flannigan ended with a short prayer of his own, asking that they take few casualties, and that the war come to an end so they could all go home.

"Keep your head down, Chaplin, and God be with you."

Mead watched him double time toward his awaiting troops and then he gathered the rest of his gear to join them in the march.

The Chaplin's job was simple, but not easy. On the battlefield he ran from soldier to soldier, offering the fatally wounded their last rights, and when he wasn't doing that, he prayed for the wounded and young warriors as they fought for their lives.

The battle went on for days and the casualties piled up. Mead was glad the temperature was below zero because the cold helped preserve the corpses. But the cold was taking a toll on his feet as the pain gave way to a stinging numbness. His selflessness and love for the soldiers had prevailed as the battle subsided and victory was eminent.

Carefully removing his left boot and then peeling off his cold, damp sock, what he saw was worse than he imagined. All four toes had turned black from frostbite, leaving only his big toe intact.

The doctors were able to save two of the dying digits, but the smallest two had to be removed. His right foot had frostbite on the smallest two toes and he was relieved to hear the prognosis was good.

Mead glanced at his watch and then to the picture of his family. Dinner would be ready soon. He carefully placed his shoe back on and then slipped into his jacket before turning off the lights and closing his office door.

The sound of the doorbell intruded on Jake's serenity, and he pondered if he should just ignore it. After the second ring, he quickly finished drying off, wrapping himself in a long white robe. Peeking though the small hole in his door, he watched Colleen patiently standing on the other side. Thinking for a moment, he almost walked away, but something pulled his hand to the door knob. As the door slowly swung open, Jake's heart sank as he was in awe of her beauty. Deep down inside, he was thrilled she was there. She was wearing a beautiful red dress and black high heels and her lightly saturated blue eyes sparkled.

"I'm sorry, Jake."

"Please don't," he said.

"These are for you." She handed him a dozen black roses that she had special ordered.

Hesitating, his heart began to soften; he accepted the flowers and moved in to embrace her.

"No one ever bought me roses before. Hell, I didn't even know they came in black."

They both laughed and he pulled her in, pushing the door shut with his foot. She took his hand and led him to the sofa where they sat.

"I don't care what my father or brother thinks. I love you," Colleen said in a whisper. "And if they can't accept that, then I guess I won't be seeing much of them. My brother was so out of line at the party. Words alone can't describe my disappointment and frustration with him. He was totally wrong and acted like an insensitive asshole and I have made my feelings very clear to him." Colleen squeezed Jake's hand tighter. "I promise I'll never put you in a situation like that again."

"I love you, Colleen," Jake said. "I'm sorry I doubted you and it won't ever happen again."

A tear of joy snuck out and he dabbed it off her cheek with the point of his knuckle. A short kiss became a long passionate one that ended when she pulled his robe off and threw it on the floor. Standing naked before her, Jake slowly removed Colleen's dress and began gently kissing her entire body with his full lips. A quick flash of light invaded the window, followed by a loud crack that captured their attention, and they both turned to the window.

"A nasty storm is coming," Jake whispered. She pulled him into her arms. "I know," she said.

CHAPTER 24

It took several months of nagging and belittling before Stephen actually convinced Michael to agree to take the long jump. They had gone bungee cord jumping two years earlier and that was a first and last time for Michael. As he plummeted toward the water, all he could think about was that the cord was going to break and his neck would follow. Now, he sat in a small airport with an upset stomach that was growing worse by the minute.

"Why can't you get your kicks on a roller coaster or something?" Michael asked.

"Roller coasters are for wimps and little girls," Stephen replied.

"I can't believe I let you talk me into this shit."

"Take it easy," Stephen said. "There's going to be a guy attached to your back. He does this all day long."

"Yeah, well I don't."

"Take a drink of water or something and quit your crying," Stephen scolded.

A stubby looking guy that appeared about ten years older came over holding a clipboard. "McNulty, Haney?" He looked at Stephen and Michael.

By his tone and demeanor, Stephen figured he was ex-military. "That's right," Stephen countered in a confident voice.

"I'm Dan, your instructor." They shook hands. "You guys are with me and Chuck. He's getting the gear ready. You both took the class. Are there any questions?"

"Just one." Michael cleared his throat. "Who packed my parachute?"

"How the hell should I know?" Dan replied with a smirk. Michael, not entertained, just sat looking at him with a dead stare.

"Don't worry, you'll be fine. I've been doing this for ten years and I haven't lost anyone, yet," Dan reassured him.

"Come on you fag. It will be a hoot," Stephen insisted.

"I need a John Hancock from you guys." Dan handed the clipboard to Stephen.

Five thousand feet above the ground, Stephen stood with Chuck attached to his back, tolerating his bad breath with every bit of instruction spilling out of his mouth. Michael was behind them with Dan snuggled up to him. He wasn't feeling up to the upcoming jump.

"Let's go!" Chuck yelled, as he shuffled toward the hatch. Michael watched as his friend teetered on the edge before vanishing from the plane. He could hear Stephen's fading voice as he yelled out in delight; falling into the thin air. Michael was not so enthusiastic, he was trembling and felt like he might piss himself. Wanting to call it off, he couldn't, knowing he would never live it down with Stephen. He would rather plunge to his death than withstand that abuse for the rest of his life, so he shuffled to the edge, held his breath, and jumped.

Safely sitting in a bar with a shot and beer in arm's reach, Stephen raised his small glass of whiskey. "Here's to skydiving."

Picking up his glass with much less enthusiasm, Michael clashed glasses with Stephen and they swallowed them down in one quick swoop.

"Let me ask you something." Michael hit his friend on the forearm as he spoke. "Why is it that you have to do everything to the extreme?"

"Is there any other way?" Stephen grinned and motioned to the bartender for two more shots.

"Yeah, there is."

Stephen's face changed. He looked at Michael as though he were an infant. "A life spent in fear, is not a life worth living."

"Don't hand me that bullshit," Michael said. "You have serious issues, man." Tightening up his fist and releasing it as though he had a stress ball in it. "I suggested that you slap around a guy that trashed your car, and what do you do? You nearly set him on fire."

The bartender placed two shots down and Michael snatched his up, shot it back in defiance and motioned for another.

"Then there's Stack," he continued. "I wanted to break a bone or two for thumping up my little brother, and you convince me to off him."

"Keep your voice down," Stephen said in a rough whisper.

Another whiskey landed on the bar in front of Michael.

"Now, you won't settle for a rollercoaster, or bungee cord jumping. You have to go skydiving."

"Stop whining like a pansy." Stephen picked up his shot and held it high, waiting for his comrade to join him. Hesitating at first, Michael, once again, caved in to Stephen's manipulation.

LaPage was the last one to leave the gym. It had crossed his mind to call Henry and ask him to meet him for a few games of basketball, but he quickly ruled it out after recalling how poorly he had played. Besides, he didn't want anyone catching on to his real motive for being at the gym, and Henry was getting a little too close. During his shower, LaPage was drowning in disappointment, because the young man with the injured knee rejected his advance when he offered to help him apply ice and a bandage. Once he was dressed, LaPage took one last glance around the room. He was alone and appreciating the smell of a boy's locker room. Zipping up his gym bag, he walked out less than victorious, but knowing his day would come soon.

Entering the cool, fresh air, LaPage noticed that the parking lot had cleared out as he walked along the brick building, turning the corner to the adjoining lot where he had parked his car. As he negotiated the corner his car came into view, but only for a split second. A painful spark lit up his face and he fell backward into a sitting position. The sting of the hammer, just above his left eye caused a gash two inches long and blood poured out covering his face. Everything was a blur and he did all he could to remain conscious. The swelling above his eye grew with every breath. Through all the chaos, LaPage determined that there were two attackers. As they began kicking him in the ribs and head, he covered himself up in order to minimize the extent of injury.

"So you like little boys?"

A foot collided with his groin and the pain took his breath away.

"You better get the hell out of our town, you fucking Chester the molester!" The second attacker yelled out.

There was a brief pause, and as he lay moaning, it was over. The final blow arrived and everything went black.

In the window of the school a shadow watched from the second floor as LaPage was beaten half to death. He was about to open the window and yell at the attackers when it all ended with the final kick. The two assailants ran off, vanishing behind the building, and he quickly shuffled to the phone in the teacher's conference room, where he dialed the emergency number, requesting the police and an ambulance.

Bob Carol had been a custodian for nineteen years and he had never witnessed anything this violent. Kids had gotten into fights and he had to clean the blood off the gym floor, but this was different. This was a deliberate and vicious attack on an adult, and when he ran outside to aid the victim, he realized just how vicious it had been. The worst part was Bob knew the two young men that committed the attack. They had both graduated from the high school a couple years earlier. He knew this was going to put him in a difficult position.

On the front steps of his large brick colonial house, the pumpkins had been replaced with poinsettias, and the wind blew fiercely, forcing the plants to bend sideways. Corbin stood looking out his front window; sipping a glass of Johnny Walker Blue Label Scotch on the rocks. The house was empty for the weekend, and he figured it would be a discrete place to meet with Bishop Reardon.

Thinking about where his life had taken him, Corbin was proud of many of his accomplishments, yet not so proud of others. What would his father say to him *right now* if he were alive? Would his father be proud of what he had done with his life? How he advanced his career, rising from a young assistant district attorney to the highest law enforcement position in the city? Would his father be proud of the way he raised his children as Christians, with sound values and a formal education? Would his father be impressed with his son's thirteen-room house with a new Lincoln Continental parked in the garage and enjoying several bank accounts and a hefty portfolio? With everything Corbin owned and had done, would his father truly be proud of him?

Corbin took a long hit from his glass until the ice rolled down crashing against his lips. He thought about his childhood home in the Irish section of the city. Occasionally he would drive by just to see how it was holding up. Every time he went by, it looked smaller than the last. When he was a young boy terrorizing the neighborhood, it seemed so vast. How could it have been so puny and he didn't recognize that until now? Was it because he was so small back then, or was it that he was now accustomed to a huge house? The neighborhood he remembered was his whole world when he was growing up, yet he had abandoned it years ago, watching it deteriorate year after year. The house he shared with his four brothers and sister had one bathroom, and he had to pair up with his older brother in a small bedroom that looked down over the street. Most of his childhood was spent fighting over a saltine cracker and a baseball glove, and now he ate fine steaks, and sat in box seats at Redsox games.

His father Daniel Corbin was a man of principal and integrity. A master printer at a large toy and game manufacturer, he was seldom at home during the week and worked most Saturdays. If there was overtime to be had, he was the first to raise his hand. In order to keep up with the needs of a large family, and being the only employed parent, he had no choice. It often saddened him that he missed out on most of his children's youth, but it was a tradeoff he had to accept.

Corbin remembered what his father had told him when he was caught stealing a candy bar from the corner store. Just before he laid leather on his son's back-side, his father scolded between clenched teeth, "When you steal from a man, you're stealing from his entire family and their right to exist in a safe and just world."

Corbin thought about the innocent boys that had been molested at the hands of Father LaPage and how he aided in the protection of the church, therefore, allowing the crimes to go unpunished. Thinking about his actions, he grappled with his involvement in depriving children the right to live in a safe and just world.

Car lights shone at the start of his long driveway and became brighter as a shiny black Mercedes Benz slowly crept toward Corbin's house. Coming to a stop in his driveway, he watched as Reardon held onto his hat and scrambled toward the front door to avoid the stinging wind.

"Hello, Evan. Come in." Corbin held the door open and shut it behind him.

"Good evening, Mark. The winds from hell are blowing tonight," he shuddered.

"Let me take your coat and hat," Corbin offered. Reardon peeled off his hat and slipped out of his coat, handing them to Corbin who hung them on the brass coat rack in the foyer.

"Why don't we go to the library for a drink to help warm your bones?"

"That sounds delightful." Reardon was hoping for a taste of the good stuff.

Corbin led the way directly to the bar and poured two glasses of Johnny Walker Black. He wasn't about to offer Blue Label Scotch for Reardon at a cost of nearly a 150 dollars a bottle. Maybe he would when the Bottle Park deal went through. They both took a chair by the fireplace, and with a remote control, Corbin ignited his gas fireplace.

"The wife's not here?" Reardon asked.

"No, she went to her sister's house in New Hampshire for the weekend. She's probably complaining about me as we speak."

Reardon let out a phony laugh, quickly drowning it with his drink.

"We have a situation that I need to discuss with you." Reardon cleared his throat and crossed his right leg over the left. "As you are aware, two men were arrested in the assault on Father LaPage."

"Yes." Corbin had a strong feeling this was the reason for the visit.

"We need to set an example of these two guys. We can't have people going around beating our priests to a pulp."

"My office will be prosecuting this case. What are you suggesting?" Corbin asked.

"Those two should not be on the street. What is the maximum penalty you can impose for this?"

Corbin swirled the ice around his glass, "Realistically, a year or two."

"What, a year?" Reardon straightened out his posture, pushing his chest forward like a sprinter waiting for the pop of a pistol. "That's all you can give these maniacs?"

"Evan, both these guys have clean records. This is a first offense, and to be frank here, LaPage isn't regarded as a Saint around here. If this goes to a jury, they might even walk. A year or two behind bars would be the result of a plea bargain."

Reardon abruptly stood up and moved away from the faint heat of the flame. "Father LaPage took fourteen stitches above his eye, a broken jaw, a concussion, and two cracked ribs, and these two lunatics may only do a year?"

Corbin stood and moved closer to the Bishop. "Look, I'll do the best I can to assure these guys get as stringent a sentence as I can impose without going to trial."

"Maybe we should go to trial."

"Evan, I don't think that's a good idea."

Reardon walked to the bar and poured himself another drink. "Alright Mark, I'll leave this in your hands, but I expect a firm outcome."

"Understood. Now, what about the construction project? Fontaine is ready to roll and everything with the city is all set.

We're just waiting on the land sale. What's the hold up here?"

"I'm working on that." His answer was less than convincing.

"We need to get going on this, Evan."

"Look, with all these allegations of abuse and law suits, I've been told to hold off on any deals with the city, right now. I'm hopeful we'll be able to get moving on this very soon, don't worry. I do have someone that I answer to, you know?"

"I understand," Corbin acknowledged. "Is it fair to say we'll be breaking ground by spring?"

Reardon didn't like the way Corbin was pushing him for a concrete timeframe. "Yes." He started toward the door that led to the foyer.

"Please help me with my coat." Reardon held out his left arm like a king being dressed by his personal peasant. "I have a fundraiser to attend for the Make a Wish Foundation. Such a great cause."

"Yes, it is." Corbin held the coat as he pushed an arm through, followed by the other. "Don't forget your hat." He handed him the black wide brim hat.

"Remember, I want you to nail these bastards to the wall," Reardon demanded.

Corbin didn't respond, he just nodded, opened the door and watched as Reardon went back out to meet the dark night and angry wind.

CHAPTER 25

Thomas Archer sat with his son Matt patiently waiting for instruction from the secretary to enter the adjoining office. Matt sat erect, looking straight ahead at nothing in particular. His father thumbed through a *Sports Illustrated* magazine, mostly looking at the photographs. On this particular morning, concentration was a challenge, as his only son's fate hung in the balance.

The door opened and Ed sprang to life. "Good morning." Both men stood up and Ed shook their hands, starting with the father. "Can I offer you some coffee or water?"

"No thank you," Mr. Archer replied.

"I'll have water, please." Matt's throat was dry and his palms wet.

Ed looked at his secretary without speaking. She knew the drill. "Come in and take a seat."

Moving behind his desk, Ed watched as the father and son sat down in the two chairs in front of his desk. There was no mistaking that Matt was his father's son, the resemblance was remarkable. Take away some wrinkles and weight, add some hair, and you had a near perfect match, Ed thought.

"We spoke briefly on the phone and you asked that I consider taking this case. Why me? There are much better trial lawyers out there."

Mr. Archer seemed uncomfortable in his skin. He scanned the office, observing the framed law school diploma on the wall behind his desk. He noticed the only other picture was that of Albert Einstein. "I thought you would offer a better chance of preventing my son from going to jail."

"How so?"

"You represent several men that were molested by LaPage, and are more familiar with his past and his tormented victims than anyone I can think of."

The secretary came in with a cup of coffee and water, placed them down, and swiftly walked out. Every time she had to do this task she felt more demeaned. One day when she ran her own company, she wouldn't fetch beverages for anyone.

"I see your point." Ed picked up his pen and began tapping it on the pad on his desk. After several seconds, he stopped and placed it down, staring into Matt's eyes. "Did you do it?"

Matt looked at his father as if he had the answer.

"Answer him," his father demanded.

"Yes."

"Why?"

"We - I was disgusted that this guy molested so many young boys and was allowed to move into our community. After what he's done, shouldn't he be in jail? Everyone is afraid of him." His lower lip was quivering. "He watches the boys in the gym like they're his prey. I guess I just lost it."

"Apparently you aren't very afraid of him," Ed countered. "The extent of his injuries was very severe."

Matt didn't immediately respond and Ed noticed that his father seemed to tighten up around the temple area.

"I guess we got a little carried away," he downplayed.

"Yes, you did," Ed responded. There are some people out there that will demand your head on a platter, and there will be some that will rally for your acquittal. The question is: What will a jury decide?"

Mr. Archer let out a sigh that only a father in this situation could relate to. "We have to keep the faith that his punishment won't be too harsh," Mr. Archer said.

"Yes. The only evidence the prosecution has is a custodian that witnessed the incident from a second floor window in the school. LaPage is not able to identify any of his attackers because it all happened so fast. With your clean record, and LaPage's history, there is a good chance you may get off with probation and a suspended sentence, but there are no guarantees."

"I understand," Matt acknowledged in a low tone of voice. He looked over at the fourteen- inch tall brass statue of Lady Justice balancing a scale. She stood erect on a cherry pedestal facing directly where he sat. It was one of Ed's most cherished belongings, a gift from his father the day he passed the bar. Matt wondered if she would tip the scale in his favor this time.

"Will you take the case?" Mr. Archer asked.

"A case like this will take a lot of time and work, not to mention traveling up to Northfield district court. My fee will probably be around $25,000 depending on the man hours. I'll need a retainer of $10,000. It may be less, or more, depending on how long this goes on. I charge a $125.00 an hour."

Archer glanced at his son in an irritated manner and then shifted back to the lawyer. "I'll agree to that." This was going to deplete his savings and then he would need to ask his sister for a loan to cover the rest, his younger sister.

"I'll need to begin with a full statement of what happened the night of the incident and we can do that later this week. Please see my assistant on your way out and she will schedule you to come back in. She'll also answer any questions you may have regarding payment of services."

Ed walked his new clients to the door and shook their hands, patting Matt on the back as he passed by. After thanking Ed, they walked to the reception desk to speak with his assistant.

Two days later, Richard Coby, along with his mother, came to see Ed. He was LaPage's second attacker and he also asked Ed to represent him. Ed agreed, after Mrs. Coby began sobbing uncontrollably, pleading with him to help save her son from a potentially ruined future.

The district attorney's office pushed hard to have the defendants tried separately. But as a cost-saving measure, as well as limiting court hours spent on the case, the judge decided it was in the best interest of all involved to try both Archer and Coby together. Ed was pleased with the decision because he knew it would be harder for a jury to convict while looking at both young men sitting in front of them, instead of individually.

As Ed was escorted into the DA's office, Corbin and his assistant district attorney Raymond Courtier were already seated and awaiting his arrival. Courtier was a heavy-set man with short black hair and a round, pudgy nose. He had small indentations along his cheeks that traveled to his jaw like a small scale map of the Rocky Mountains. Ed thought he must have had a serious acne problem in his youth. He had seen him on occasion waddling around the courthouse, but was never introduced, until now. After the fast and cold greeting, Ed took a seat in front of Corbin's desk.

"Ed, it doesn't make sense to prolong this case and tie up the court if we can come to an agreement on a plea bargain." Pushing back his shoulders, Corbin studied Ed from behind the comfort of his prosecution thrown.

"I agree," Ed responded. "Why don't we come to an agreement of two years probation and a one year suspended sentence?" Ed wasn't comfortable having Corbin call him by his first name.

"That is not acceptable. These boys beat a Catholic priest with a dangerous weapon. They have to do some time," Corbin argued.

Turning his head to one side and feeling the crack of relief in his neck, Ed refocused on Corbin. "What kind of time are you suggesting?"

"Two years."

"I'll see you at trial." Ed stood up and reached for his case.

"Wait a minute, Ed. Let's not jump so fast. How about fifteen months and a three year suspended sentence with time served?"

Still standing, Ed rested his case on the chair he had just occupied. "Both my clients are very adamant that any time behind bars in not an option. If you change your mind, you know where to reach me. Good day gentlemen."

Both prosecutors watched Ed walk out without an exchange. It was going to be battle and there was no way around it. Bishop Reardon was clear that he wanted the defendants to do time, yet that was not an option for Ed and his clients.

Spring had arrived and the trial was beginning to peek out its ugly head. The pending trial was front page news and the main topic in most coffee shops and taverns. For a small town, this was big news. It was clear to the public that Corbin's office was pushing for the maximum penalty allowed by law. In order to appease Reardon, Corbin had made a public statement to that affect. The jury selection process had taken weeks, as both sides excused any prospective juror they thought was leaning toward the other side. The county was divided with those that were hardnosed Catholics refusing to accept that a priest would commit such horrible atrocities and those that believed he was guilty and thought a beating was an acceptable penalty. The majority of the community seemed to be leaning against LaPage.

On the first day of trial, the naked sun was warm in the sky. Hundreds of people were gathered along the courthouse common, bearing signs like swords and shields held high for a pending battle. Protesters were calling for the acquittal of the defendants and their numbers were rapidly increasing throughout the morning. The police department had called for assistance from several outside agencies in order to form a unified riot squad.

Corbin was livid as he watched a mob chanting on the television set he kept tucked away in his office. His eyes were like daggers in search of a target as he attempted to recognize protesters gathered at the scene. Corbin was worried that his real estate development deal would never happen if the defendants walked away from the trial unscathed. He had put Courtier, his best assistant prosecutor, on the case, and he was coaching him throughout the process from the beginning. Failure was an outcome he was determined to avoid.

The prosecution's only witness and primary evidence against Archer and Coby was the eye witness testimony of custodian Bob Carol. Unable to capture a good night sleep in weeks, Carol had been undergoing an internal battle on the concept of right and wrong and the administering of justice. His initial statement to the police was a clear account of his witnessing the assault on LaPage by Archer and Coby and he had identified both assailants in a line-up without question. It wasn't until he started to hear about LaPage's history from people in the community and from what he read in the paper, that he began to do research at the library searching for articles that might give him a clearer perspective on the man for whom he was going to testify.

As he studied the biography on LaPage, Carol began to note down the names of the victims that had allegedly been molested by the priest. In the end, his list had twenty-three names of men that had come forth seeking justice against LaPage and the Catholic Church. At the top of his list was the case that bothered him the most, the murder of Robert Anderson.

On the day he was to testify, Carol told Courtier that he wasn't sure he could say for certain that the two defendants were the perpetrators he had witnessed assaulting LaPage, and that if forced to testify, he would say just that.

When Corbin learned of this he jumped in his car and headed to Northfield, cursing Carol the entire way. When he arrived, he swooped into the prosecutor's office, ignoring the staff that straightened up in their chairs, greeting him as he quickly swept past. Pushing open the door and marching in, he immediately confronted the two men sitting in the office.

"What do you mean, you can't be sure the two men you witnessed attacking LaPage weren't Coby and Archer?" Corbin stood over Carol yelling at him with a beet red face. Courtier thought the tremors from Carol would measure a 4.7 on the Richter Scale.

"Now that I look back, I can't be sure it was them. I think I might have been wrong," Carol said in a subdued tone.

"Wrong!" Corbin shot a glance at his assistant DA who was hiding behind his desk and focused on Carol. "I have an affidavit signed by you, Mister. You were very sure five months ago that it was Coby and Archer you saw assaulting the priest. Now, all of a sudden you have amnesia."

Coughing several times, Carol was hoping Corbin might back up and give him more space, but he was wrong. "The more I've had a chance to think about it, the less certain I am that it was them," he bumbled.

"You're pathetic," Corbin shouted. "Why did you wait until the day of the trial to come forward with this?"

"I don't know. I guess it all just set in today."

"Bullshit!" Corbin turned and walked toward the bookcase that contained the shiny red and green leather bound law books perfectly lined up in uniform. Twisting his upper torso without completely facing him, he stared down Carol from eleven feet away.

"You will go into that courtroom and get on the stand, and then, you'll swear on the Holy Bible and you'll testify that you saw, without a doubt, Archer and Coby beat the shit out of Father LaPage. Am I clear?"

"I can't do that," Carol murmured through shaky lips.

"Then I'll charge you with obstruction!"

"Do what you must do." His whispered response was deafening.

Corbin squinted at Courtier. "Get this piece of shit out of here. I can't stand the sight of him."

Jumping to his feet, Courtier ushered the shaken man out in a hurry.

As he was escorted out by the arm, Carol took one last look over his shoulder at Corbin before he was pushed through the doorway. The district attorney had a look that could kill, and he was aiming it directly at Carol. He knew right then, he had made an enemy for life, and it wasn't an enemy that anyone would want. Corbin had a reputation of being a powerful and vindictive man. There had been rumors that he had been involved in murder, but it was never proven.

CHAPTER 26

The case against Archer and Coby was dismissed due to a lack of evidence. The media had run rabid with the story of the acquittal, and in turn, the Catholic Church's cover-up of the sexual abuse of many young boys. The church was settling cases against LaPage at a record number and other sexual abuse cases around the country were beginning to surface. One local news station had started running stories on the unsolved murder of Robby Anderson and how it was linked to the infamous priest.

With all the negative press on the diocese and the public outcry against LaPage, Corbin decided not to go after Carol. The timing wasn't right for him to make his move on the janitor, but he would take him down when the time was right.

The real estate deal with Bishop Reardon was a vision that was moving further and further from his sight with each story that unfolded against the diocese. In the past, when Corbin called Reardon, his call was answered or returned promptly. Now, Reardon seldom took his calls and didn't return messages.

Ed was thrilled that both his clients were acquitted and the media was running daily stories on the pedophile priest. All of his cases against the diocese had been settled out of court, except three. Brick was still holding out for his taste of sweet revenge, and two new cases had come up within the past six months. Ed thought either Brick must have really been abused traumatically, or maybe he was more sensitive than the rest. With Brick it wasn't about money, he wanted to see LaPage suffer and he was patient to this end. With every case that surfaced against LaPage, Ed became more vindictive and understanding of Brick's relentless pursuit of justice.

Soon after Jake arrived at work, he was summoned to Chief Merald's office. He figured it had to be important because nearly all of his conversations with the Chief occurred passing in the hallway or inside the snack room. The few times he had been summoned to the Chief's office, it usually wasn't a pleasant conversation. Jake wasn't too concerned because he had a clear conscience and he quickly reminded himself of this after he got the message.

As he entered the Chief's assistant's office, he immediately observed it was empty. A voice belted out from the other side of the wall. "Jake?"

"Yes Sir."

"Come on in."

Tucked in behind his big desk, wearing a crisp white shirt and a black clip-on tie, the Chief motioned to a single chair in front of his desk. Jake took the seat without speaking or taking his eyes off his boss. An uncomfortable silence deadened the air, like a space in a vacuum.

Jake moved his head to one side, attempting to break the spell that mesmerized the man. "Chief," Jake said.

Regaining his thought process and refocusing on his detective, the Chief snapped out of wherever his mind had drifted and he was back to his usual self. "I'll get right to the point, Jake. I'm putting you on a cold case, effective immediately. I spoke with Captain Farris and he has agreed to spread out your caseload to other detectives so you can focus on this case."

"It must be pretty important," Jake concluded.

"No, it's a political bee's nest, but I have no choice on this one. We are re-opening the 1972 murder case of Robert Anderson."

Jake felt a chill run from the back of his neck down his spine and settle in his toes.

"Really?" Hardly containing his excitement, Jake bit the inside of his lip.

"That's right." The Chief flipped open a folder that had been tainted with time. The pages had lost their crispness and faded to a dull yellow. "The media and the public are putting pressure on the state attorney's office to begin investigating this child molester, Father LaPage. I understand you're familiar with the case." He tossed the folder onto his desk within Jake's reach.

A vision of Robby's body lying in the park swept through his mind. "Yes, I was a rookie on patrol when he was killed. My partner and I found his body in Bottle Park," Jake said, as he scooped up the jacket, opening it up to the first page and briefly scanning it.

"Fitch is retired and probably bored out of his mind. He was the lead investigator on this case and knows more about it than anyone," the Chief said.

"With the exception of the killer," Jake added.

The chief glared at him. He didn't like being out smarted. "That's right, except the killer. You may want to start with Fitch, seeing that we don't know who the killer is."

"Good idea, Chief." Jake didn't tell him that he and Fitch were tight. The Chief didn't need to know about his relationship with Fitch or that they had discussed the case many times over the years.

"This is not going to be an easy case to solve." Chief Mearald leaned back in his chair, examining the detective. "It's been a long time since the murder. Memories are blurred and evidence is stale."

"I'll do my best, Chief."

"Yes." A brief silence followed. "Jake, a lot of people are watching this. Make sure you cross all your T's and dot your I's. You better walk a straight line on this case." He stood up and moved across the small room over to a tall mahogany stand with a cedar humidor lying on top. "The church has a lot of power, you know." He opened the lid, took out a cigar and raised it to his nose, inhaling the sweet aroma.

"Yes, I know," Jake said.

"Whoever murdered that young boy should hang," the Chief said. "I have a kid not much older than the victim when he was killed. You need to make sure you have solid evidence before you make any accusations about who did this. Hell, I doubt if this case will ever be solved." He carefully placed the cigar back into its place in the case. "Just be careful, that's all."

"I will, Chief." Jake stood up with his folder and walked toward the door.

"Jake, one more thing. I've decided to put Applebee on this case with you."

"Chief, come on. Applebee is loose cannon." Mearald's words came like a kick in the nuts.

"Some might say that about you, Jake." Jake knew he was talking about the Baker shooting.

"He's a narcotics guy, Chief."

"Not anymore. He's on the case," the Chief said as he walked toward the door. "Applebee is a solid investigator. I'll admit, a little unorthodox, but he's good."

Jake was not about to argue. The last thing he wanted to do was piss off the Chief and take a gamble that he might change his mind about giving him the case.

"Alright, Chief." Jake forced a smile and walked out.

When Jake got back to his office, Randy Applebee was sitting in his chair resting his feet on Jake's desktop. He had a toothpick lodged in his teeth and he was reading a *National Inquirer* magazine. His face was sandy with a three-day old beard and he wore blue jeans and a black sport jacket. Jake didn't think his red Converse All Star sneakers were in concert with the rest of his attire.

It wasn't that Jake didn't like him; he just thought he was dangerous. Regarded as a worker, Applebee had three kills in his sixteen year career. If there was trouble to be found, he was the first in line.

"Get out of my chair! And don't ever put your nasty feet on my desk again," Jake warned. "Let's get something straight, right now. Do you see this badge?" He pulled his jacket aside displaying his gold badge.

Applebee smiled and slightly nodded his head.

"It reads Sergeant. That means you answer to me while we work this case."

Applebee was now standing.

"Am I clear, Detective Applebee?"

"Sure, I'll agree to that on one condition."

"What's that?" Jake barked.

"Don't call me Detective Applebee. The name is Randy."

"Fine." Jake dropped the file onto his desk. "Have you studied this file yet?"

"Yes I have."

"One more thing," Jake said. "You're not in narcotics anymore. This is homicide, and you are to act like it. That means when you come in tomorrow, you'll be clean shaven and you'll wear shoes. Understood?"

"Sure, Boss."

"I know you're used to running around with your gun drawn, yelling at people. Things are done differently here. We are investigators trying to find out who murdered a little boy a long time ago. One of our main suspects is a Catholic priest. Most of the people we'll interview won't be drug dealers or pimps.

"Back up," Randy said. "You just said one of our suspects is a priest. Does that mean there is more than one suspect?" he asked as he pulled up a chair.

"I was working patrol when the kid was killed," Jake said. "I found him in the park and I've been following this case for years. There were two boys that went to school with him and they had been pushing him around and threatening him just prior to his death. These two boys are now men, and they are both suspects in a case I was recently assigned to.

He had Randy's full attention. "What kind of case?"

"It's a missing person case with all the evidence of a homicide."

"Let me get this straight. Nearly twenty years ago, two kids that may have killed the Anderson boy are still running around and possibly killing people as adults?"

"It's a very real possibility," Jake said.

"What are their names?"

"Stephen Haney and Michael McNulty."

Randy's eyebrows elevated. "I know those two guys. They're a couple of whack jobs."

"Yes, they are," Jake agreed. "The other possibility is that the priest did it. Look, either way this is not going to be easy. This is an old case and it will be very tedious. Are you sure you're cut out for this?

Randy flipped open the file, stopping at the page that contained the photographs of the dead boy. He sat peering down at the pictures and then he raised his head and looked into Jake's eyes. Randy was not known as a serious person, but Jake now observed a side of him that most had not.

"I love kids, and I want to nail the bastard that did this." A unifying moment of clarity settled in as two very different men found common ground.

"Alright, we're both on the same page then." Jake reached over and shook Randy's hand. "Let's get to work."

Jake decided to start with the case evidence, so he and Randy headed down to the evidence room. As they approached, Jake could see Elliot through the thick bullet proof glass that separated the evidence from the rest of the people in the building. The door to the evidence room was locked from the inside at all times when it was open for business, and when it wasn't, it was locked from the outside. Three people had keys to the room: the Chief, Elliot David and Frank Saber. Frank was the evidence room Sergeant and had been there the longest. He wasn't afraid to let anyone know that twenty-six years had earned him the right to claim head of household.

"Good morning, Elliot." Jake leaned on the window ledge watching as Frank came out from the back room.

"Gentlemen," Elliot responded with little enthusiasm. Randy watched in disgust as Elliot cleaned the sleep out of his eyes. "What can I do for you guys?"

"We're going to need all evidence on the Robert Anderson case."

After overhearing what Jake had requested, Frank came

walking over to the reception area.

"They put you guys on that case?"

That's right," Randy said.

Frank looked at Randy with noticeable contempt. He had been dealing with Randy for many more years than he would like to admit. Having been in narcotics and holding the department record for drug and weapons arrests, Randy was always interrupting Frank to dig out evidence for court cases. Over the years Frank learned to despise him. Elliot didn't care one way or the other.

Several minutes later Frank came back carrying two large plastic bags. He unlocked the sliding glass window, pushed it to the side, and handed the evidence log book to Jake. After Jake signed for the evidence, Frank handed the bags to Jake, and the two detectives moved along.

Back in their office, they took the evidence to an open interrogation room and placed the bags on the table. One of the bags contained the clothing Robby was wearing the day he was found, and the other had an assortment of items that were collected at the scene. Jake started with that bag; taking one piece of evidence out at a time and placing it on the table.

First, he retrieved several photos of the body and crime scene, neatly lining them up, like a portfolio of death. As he continued, he became anxious, pulling out a couple of small plastic bags that contained a gum wrapper and a cigarette butt. Randy could see the concerned look on his face as he stared into an empty bag.

"What's the matter?" Randy asked.

"Something is not right." Jake snatched up the bag that contained the clothing, and began taking out the evidence one piece at a time until the second bag's contents were spread out on the table.

"Son of a bitch!" Jake cursed.

"What is it?" Randy asked again.

"The button is missing. It's not here."

A curious look defined Randy's face. "What button?"

The day we discovered the boy, I found a button near the body. It was about the size of a nickel and it had an anchor on it." Jake stopped and thought for a moment. "Photos," he said. "We had photos taken of the button."

Quickly Jake began to shuffle through the array of crime scene pictures, looking for the shots taken of the button, but they weren't there.

"The pictures of the button are also missing."

"Did you log it into evidence?"

"No, I gave it to Fitch, the lead investigator on the case."

"What are the chances that the button and the photos of it are both missing? I think we need to pay Fitch a visit," Randy suggested.

"Yeah, but first we need to make sure these are the only bags of case evidence, and we need to go over the log books and find out who else logged out this evidence."

"It sounds like we'll be here for a while," Randy complained.

"Yeah, it looks that way," Jake said, with an undeniable look of disappointment.

Prior to making the drive, Jake called to make sure Fitch was at home. Fitch's wife noticed the car as it pulled up in front of their house, and she opened the door and greeted the two men with a warm smile.

"He's in here." She escorted them to the den where Fitch was wrapped around a thick book that must have been a thousand pages. Jake noticed it was a Civil War book, and that didn't surprise him. Fitch was a Civil War buff and he had read just about every notable book on the war.

"What do we have here, an ambush?" Fitch asked as he stood up to greet them.

"Spoken like a true marine," Randy said, and they shared a limited chuckle.

Randy was glad to see his old Chief of Police. On many occasions, Fitch had covered Randy's ass when others wanted to see him fall for allegations of police brutality and various civil rights violations. Fitch had always liked Randy because he was a hard worker who got results. There were too many cops in the department that rarely did any proactive police work, and Fitch had little use for them. He saw a lot of himself in Randy in that way, even though he knew Randy was a bit more of a cowboy than he was.

"Don't tell me you two are paired up?"

All three took a seat. "Yeah, what the hell were they thinking, right?" Randy said.

Jake engaged Fitch with a look of apprehension. "We just started the first inning. Let's wait and see how the game plays out," Jake said.

"Well, I hope you two get a grand slam. What brings you here?"

"Like I said on the phone, the Anderson case has been resurrected and we're on the case. We started going through case evidence, and the button with the anchor is missing." Jake made a tight fist with his right hand. "The damned button is gone."

"What?" Fitch jumped out of his chair, as if he was shot up with a huge spring. "What do you mean it's missing?"

"I mean it's not there. It's gone."

"Did you have those two jokers in the evidence room re-check to make sure they didn't miss it?"

"Yes we did and they were positive that the two bags of evidence is all there is. And get this; all the photos of the button are also gone. It's like the button never existed."

"The photos are missing, too?" Fitch began pacing the floor back and forth from one wall to another. It reminded Jake of the movie, *Papillon*, where Steve McQueen paced his cell for exercise and preservation of sanity.

"There were only two bags as I recall. Has anyone signed out the evidence since I was on the case?" Fitch asked.

"No, you were the last one," Jake said.

"The button was there when I signed the evidence back in. It had to vanish between then and now. Someone doesn't want that button or any trace of it to be found. Who has had access to the evidence room since then?"

Jake started tapping the arm on the chair with his knuckles. He did this when he was absorbed in deep thought. "Just the Chief, and the two evidence room guys, right?" Jake asked.

"Saber had been assigned to evidence long before the Anderson case came about, but David has only been there for around ten or twelve years," Fitch proclaimed.

"What officer was replaced by David?" Jake asked.

"Jim Jacobson," Fitch said. "And Jacobson is now the court criminal liaison."

There was a brief pause, and simultaneously, Jake and Fitch finished the sentence together: "liaison to the District Attorney's office."

Randy felt left out, as he watched the two men have a meeting of their minds. "Guys, what does this all mean?"

Jake glared at Randy. "It means that Jacobson may have tampered with evidence," Jake said.

Fitch pounded his fist against the door jam and it aroused the attention of the two investigators. Both men looked at Fitch as he began. "When Jacobson was transferred to the DA's office, everyone was curious why, and I never told anyone that Corbin had lobbied with the Mayor to push the transfer. It was a political move and I was reluctant to agree, but I really had no choice. Hell, there were plenty of guys that deserved to finish their careers in that cake walk before Jacobson. He never did shit as a street cop, and then a few years later, he was transferred to the evidence room where he put his feet up until he was transferred to the court."

"You know the DA and Jacobson are pals, right?" Randy spoke up, feeling good that he had something to contribute. "They are members of the Elks Club and are known to tip a few back while playing poker in the back room."

"It looks like they may be involved a lot more than poker," Jake added.

"And Corbin and the Bishop are joined at the hip," Fitch said.

Randy was confused and didn't want to appear naive, but had to clear the air. "Do you think the Bishop would be involved in the cover up of a murdered child?"

Fitch didn't hesitate to speak up. "The Bishop would do whatever is necessary to preserve the reputation of the church."

"That son of a bitch Corbin is in cahoots with him," Jake said.

"Was there any other evidence missing?" Fitch asked.

"Not that I'm aware of. The victim's clothes were there along with the crime scene photos, a gum wrapper, and a dead cigarette stub. Only the button and the pictures of the button are missing." Jake looked to Fitch for answers. "Is there any other evidence lifted from the crime scene that I didn't mention that you can recall?"

Fitch thought hard. "It was a long time ago, but this case has festered mind for almost twenty years. The most important piece of evidence was the button. I can't think of anything else that stood out. I think you mentioned all of the evidence taken from the scene."

"If the button was the only piece taken, it must have been pretty significant," Jake concluded.

"Hell yeah it was," Randy jumped in. "It probably fell off the jacket of the killer."

"I think we need to pay a visit to Jacobson," Jake suggested.

Fitch walked over and patted Jake on the shoulder. "Be careful. Corbin has a lot of power in this town, and if he feels threatened, he might try and have you taken off this case. I suggest that you tread lightly when you interview Jacobson."

Jake looked at his old Chief, offering a slight nod. "I understand."

"If there's anything else I can do, just give me a call."

"Thanks, Chief. I appreciate it."

Jake shook hands with Fitch and Randy did the same.

"You take care of this crazy bastard." Fitch said, motioning to Randy.

"I'll try my best," Jake responded.

"Jake, do me a favor."

Jake stopped in his tracks before reaching the exit. "Anything, Chief."

"Find the son of a bitch that killed Robert Anderson."

Jake didn't make any promises, he just nodded in acknowledgment

CHAPTER 27

As Jake and Randy strolled through the courthouse, they were greeted with respect by most people in passing. Having tried hundreds of cases, both men had spent countless hours in the courthouse in a vigorous attempt to prosecute and lock up criminals, and they both had very solid reputations in the criminal justice arena.

Officer Jacobson was sitting behind his desk in the corner of a room filled with courthouse clerks. He had just returned from his first morning break and he wasn't far away from the next.

As the two men approached, his first thought was what are these two very different men from different bureaus doing together?

"Hello Jim." Jake greeted Jacobson by offering his hand and Randy followed suit. They stood over him like the twin towers, and Jacobson's mind began to scramble, wondering what they wanted with him.

"What's up guys?" He twisted in his chair to face the men, but his belly prevented a full frontal engagement.

"Jim, we need to talk. Can we find someplace a little more quiet?"

"Sure." Jacobson pushed himself up and started through the room, waddling past the rows of people talking on the phone and punching keys at their stations. Popping his head inside a small room, he moved in, after confirming that it was unoccupied. The detectives followed him through the threshold and closed the door.

"Have a seat Jim." Jake pushed a chair in his direction. After a brief hesitation, he sat down and they took two chairs across from him. "How are things going in the courthouse?"

"What can I say, it's like a picnic that never ends," he boasted, followed by a short fake cackle. His hair was dusty brown and barely covered his symmetrically-shaped head, and his second chin jiggled as he laughed. Randy thought he would make a great

Santa Claus at the police Christmas party.

"Good for you," Jake responded, glancing at his partner. "Jim, we're investigating the murder of Robert Anderson. You remember that case, right?"

He looked at the two detectives, wondering what they had on him. "Yeah, it's all over the news," he said looking at Randy curiously. "You're in narcotics, what are you doing investigating a murder?"

"They needed the cleverest investigator in the department, so they called me," Randy said in monotone, like a bad high school teacher. Jacobson played along with a short laugh that resembled the sound of a donkey.

"The thing is, Jim, when we pulled the case evidence, we noticed there's an item missing and we're speaking with everyone that had access to the evidence room."

Jacobson shifted his weight to one side, looking up at the ceiling and back down.

"You and Frank Saber were the only officers with access to the evidence at the time, other than Chief Fitch."

Jacobson wondered if they had cleared this interview with Chief Mearald, which they had earlier that morning. "Elliot also had access, right?" Jacobson asked.

"No, he was your replacement and the evidence was missing well before he was transferred to the evidence room," Jake said. "We spoke to him as well," he lied.

Randy was curious why Jacobson didn't ask what evidence was missing. It had crossed Jake's mind as well.

"There was a button removed from the crime scene that mysteriously disappeared from the evidence room, along with all photographs of it. What do you think may have happened to them?"

Tapping his fingers on the arm of the chair and avoiding eye contact, Jacobson appeared nervous. "How the hell would I know?" The pitch of his voice had gone up an octave and he cleared his throat to regulate it.

"Do you ever remember going through the Anderson case evidence for any reason *or* was there someone that may have pulled the evidence without signing it out?"

Jacobson's face had changed to a paler shade. "Do you think I would allow that to happen? What do I look like, an asshole? I was very good at my job as a property room officer and I had no reason to tamper with evidence. I can't help you guys and I have a lot of work to do." He stood up and moved toward the door.

Jake and Randy stayed in their seats, watching the show.

"Okay, Jim, thanks for your help," Jake said.

"No problem," he sniggered as he walked out.

They watched his wide frame slither through the doorway. "He's lying," Randy said.

"Yes he is," Jake agreed. "He showed classic signs of lying: avoiding eye contact when I mentioned the button, and then becoming defensive and sarcastic. Did you notice how the pitch of his voice changed?"

"Yeah and did you see how his face turned white?" Randy asked.

"Yup, he's our button culprit alright," Jake concluded.

Randy stood up and leaned over his chair. "The problem is, we'll never be able to prove it, and he knows it."

"Right, but now we know what happened to the button and who is behind it. The question is: where is the jacket with a missing button?"

"What next?" Randy asked.

"Interviews, my man, we are going to be balls to the walls with interviews."

"My favorite thing to do," Randy whined. He was beginning to think that he'd rather be chasing drug dealers where there would be some excitement stuffed into his day. He thought about the pictures of the dead boy, and once again, it became clear to him why he was there.

The two detectives started by speaking with Sandy Balsom, the girl that observed LaPage picking Robby up from school. Other than the LaPage and the killer, she was the last person to see Robby alive. Now, a beautiful woman with two children of her own, Sandy's recollection of that day was a faded memory. She had never forgotten the tragedy that had consumed her thoughts for a short period during her youth, but there wasn't anything concrete she could add to the resurrected investigation.

Jake decided the next step would be to dig into the tragic and disgusting accounts of what the victims of Father LaPage had gone through as children. He wanted to see if there was a pattern or anything that might tie LaPage to the murder. Their initial interview was with Mark Trombley, a complete zombie with anti-social behavioral patterns. Every time Jake asked a question, he responded by repeating the question back in a sarcastic manner. He completely shut down when they got to the point of the actual physical encounters with LaPage. Nothing was to be gained from the interview.

The second victim on their list was Alan Brick. Randy had contacted him by phone and was happy to hear Brick's willingness to cooperate in the investigation. The next afternoon they arrived at Brick's apartment in a complex that sprawled across a two block area. The old buildings rolled on one after the next, and the graffiti was the easiest way to distinguish one unit from another. Once they were in the general location of the apartment, Brick called out to them as he waited on the stoop with a beer in hand. The detectives followed him to his one bedroom studio on the fourth floor. Inside the building it smelled like a sewer with loud music and televisions blaring from behind the thick bolted doors.

"Do you guys want a beer?" Brick held his can of Bud up, so they could see it was a reputable brand. After declining, they all found a seat.

"I read in the paper that you declined all settlements offered by the diocese," Jake said.

Before answering, Brick took a long drink of beer, and once it was empty, he crushed the can in his hand and tossed it across the room, landing it in the trash can like a pro.

"That's right."

"Why wouldn't you just settle and take the money? Randy asked. "Think of the place you'd be living in then."

Examining Randy for a few seconds, Brick thought he and Randy might be a lot alike. A detective wearing jeans was pretty cool, he thought. "The money will come eventually. They keep raising the amount, but I want to see that bastard pay. If I settle, it will only be the church that pays, not him."

Jake could see the hatred in his eyes when he spoke of LaPage. "We want to thank you for taking the time to speak with us," Jake said. "As you are aware, we are investigating the murder of a twelve-year-old boy found in Bottle Park in 1972. LaPage was the last person seen with him while he was alive. What can you tell us about LaPage's behavior when he committed the crimes against you? Where did he take you?"

Jumping to his feet, Brick went to the fridge and pulled out another beer. After resuming his place at the table, he popped it open and took a hard sip. Jake brought out a small tape recorder and held it up. Brick nodded in approval and Jake pushed the button and placed it on the kitchen table.

"LaPage was a cool cat and it was so easy to relate to him. It was as though he was going through adolescence himself. When I spoke to him about what was going on with my parents and friends, or the trouble I was having in school, he was an understanding guy." Brick looked at the rolling tape recorder and then to Randy. "I thought he was okay for a priest. Sometimes I would forget that he was a priest; he was more like a friend. LaPage used to let me drink wine with him, and he would tell stories about the fights he got into as a kid and how he was in trouble all the time." Brick took out a pack of cigarettes, lit one up and drew in a heavy load of smoke. "It was all bullshit and part of a larger scheme he had been planning for me."

"Go on," Jake said.

"After I really began to trust him, he started with the touching.

He used to like to wrestle and he would play grab ass while we rolled around on the floor."

"Where did these incidences take place?" Jake asked.

"Mostly at the rectory, but as things got worse, he used to take me to his brother's house while his brother was away on business trips. The bastard told me that what we were doing was normal and part of a boys' club." The detectives listened as Brick's eyes began to fill up. He downed his entire beer and his eyes seemed to dry as though he drank the tears away.

"Did he ever become violent with you?" Randy asked.

"Not really, but he wasn't one to take no for an answer. He is one controlling and manipulative son of a bitch."

Jake reached across the table and embraced his forearm. "I know this is hard for you, but we need to hear what happened on those nights at his brother's house." Brick nodded and put out his cigarette butt, crushing it until the smoke failed.

As Brick started telling his story, Jake's fist tightened up and his right foot began to shake. Randy was disgusted, feeling like he needed to take a shower. It was a long interview for a short period of time. Once the interview was finished, they thanked Brick and wished him well. They walked back to their car in silence and remained quiet for the entire drive back to the police station.

All of LaPage's victims of shared a similar story. Most of the abuse occurred on weekends at his brother's house in a neighboring town. With the exception of Brick, the other victims were apprehensive regarding the amount of detail they provided in their interviews with the detectives. In two instances, the victims stated that LaPage had forced himself on them on at least one occasion. In all cases, LaPage had gained their trust and friendship before moving in for the hunt. With each testimony, Jake and Randy's determination to nail LaPage got stronger, like a burning fire in the pit of their stomachs.

They decided it was time to bring LaPage in for questioning. Jake's call for an interview was returned by Tanner Hagen, LaPage's criminal attorney, and he agreed to accompany LaPage to the police department for a meeting two days later.

The phone rang twice before Jake shuffled over to his desk to pick it. The front desk officer in the lobby called to inform Jake that two men were asking for him and one was a priest. Jake thanked him and advised that he would be down in a little while. Randy came walking over clutching a doughnut and a cup of coffee.

"Those things will kill you." Jake gestured toward the doughnut.

"Breakfast of champions," Randy smiled through a semi-full mouth.

"I don't know how you do it. You eat like shit and you manage to look fit."

"I work out four days a week for two hours at the gym," Randy said. "That's the only thing that keeps me sane."

It was apparent by his physical condition that he worked out, but they had never discussed it until now. "Do you ever run?" Jake asked.

"Only when I'm chasing bad guys. I hate running." He shoved the rest of the doughnut into his mouth. "For cardio, I punch the heavy bag and walk the stair climber. Have you ever tried that?"

"Nope, I don't go to the gym, I'm strictly a callisthenic guy."

"Well, you look good for a man of your years," Randy said convincingly.

"Thanks, I think," Jake said as he opened his desk drawer retrieving his recorder.

"LaPage is downstairs with his lawyer," Jake said.

Randy placed his coffee on the desk. "How long have they been waiting?"

"About five minutes. I figure we'll make them wait twenty minutes and then we'll get them."

A smiled formed on Randy's face. "Yeah, let's let them stew in their own anxiety for a while."

Fifteen minutes later, Jake had the office assistant fetch LaPage and his lawyer and bring them to the interrogation room. When

Jake and Randy entered the room, they were sitting just as they were a few minutes earlier as the detectives watched them through the two-way glass. They hadn't said anything regarding the case as they waited because Hagen knew they were on display.

"Good morning gentlemen." Jake said. Randy didn't say anything. He didn't like either of them and it was clear by the way he looked right through them as though they were merely images of men.

The attorney reached out to shake Randy's hand. "I'm Tanner Hagen, Father LaPage's lawyer." Randy looked at his hand as if he had leprosy, declining to engage. At that very moment, Hagen knew where he stood.

"I'll be taping our conversation for the record," Jake said, placing the recorder on the table and sliding a chair over and taking a seat; Randy followed suit. A short silence followed as Jake stared directly into LaPage's eyes. Without taking his eyes off LaPage, he reached over and activated the recorder. Uncomfortable with the device, LaPage knew he had to think before he opened his mouth and everything he said had to be calculated and precise.

Jake thought he was wise to wear his collar to the interview, but it didn't make a difference to either of them because they had both listened to what his victims had said about what he had done to them as young boys. He wasn't a real priest; he was an imposter that preyed on innocent children. Randy wanted to reach over and rip off his collar, taking a piece of his esophagus along with it.

"We don't have a lot of time this morning, so if you'll get to the point, we can wrap this up and get going," Hagen said.

"Shut up!" Randy barked out. Hagen quieted and straightened up in his chair.

"We're here to interview Mr. LaPage," Jake said. "If you want to whisper sweet nothings in his ear, then be my guest. Other than that, you keep quiet and don't interrupt our line of questioning."

"My client is a respectable priest and he will be treated accordingly, as I will as his attorney."

Jake looked at the average-looking man with glasses and balding hair. He figured he was around fifty years old, but looked nearly sixty.

"Your client is a suspect in the murder of a twelve-year-old boy who was sexually assaulted and then beaten to death, and he is being treated accordingly. Now, I suggest you remember why he's here and that you don't interfere with our investigation. Do I make myself clear?" Jake leaned forward awaiting a response.

Hagen nodded, indicating he understood. It wasn't only that he was intimidated by the police, he had two young children of his own and he knew LaPage was guilty of molesting children, and possibly even murder.

"Up until the time of his death, how long had you been in contact with Robert Anderson?" As he stared down LaPage, Jake's eyes were like daggers slicing through the air.

"It was a long time ago, I don't really remember," LaPage responded in a dismissive way.

His smug demeanor rubbed Randy the wrong way and he wished his attorney wasn't present.

"Then take an educated guess," Randy suggested in a condescending tone. LaPage could see the hate in both detectives and he knew they could taste prosecution, but he knew he was smarter than they were, and in the end that would be proven.

"I would guess about a year or maybe a year and a half."

"In that time, how often did you take him to your brother, Bryan's house?"

LaPage crossed his right leg over the left and entangled his fingers as if he was praying. He looked too relaxed, Jake thought. "I don't know, maybe once or twice."

Randy jumped in. "Remind me why you were taking young boys for overnight adventures to your brother's house?"

LaPage didn't like where the line of questioning was heading. "Many of the boys in my parish had troubles at home and in school, and were acting out as a result, so I counseled them as a good priest should. It was often better to take them out of a traditional religious setting in order to relate to them."

Jake could sense that LaPage was proud of his answer and his narcissism was apparent. Randy wanted to back hand him across his snickering face.

Jake stood up, spun his chair around, and sat back down, so he could lean over the back of it. "How many times did you have sexual relations with Robert Anderson?"

"Objection!" Hagen yelled out as he jumped up from his seat.

"Objection, we're not in a court of law, you moron," Randy ridiculed.

"Sit down, Mr. Hagen," Jake ordered.

Hagen sat back down in defiance. "This investigation is about the murder of a boy and how this case relates to my client, or doesn't, it's not about attacking his character," he said.

Randy began to slowly clap. "Good one."

"Councilor, we are looking at motive, and this type of behavior with a young boy can certainly lead to motive. Let's not be coy here. Your client," he pointed at LaPage, "is being sued in a civil court, and has settled in many cases in the sexual abuse of young boys." He glared at LaPage, and in a louder and more demanding tone, he addressed him once again. "Now answer the question!"

"I never had relations of the sort," LaPage said looking Jake in the eye.

He was very clever Jake thought because when he answered there were no body signals or classic indications that he was lying.

"You were the last person seen with Robert the day you picked him up from school. Where did you take him?"

"I took him for ice cream."

"And where was that, what place?" Jake asked.

"We went to Sparky's Ice Cream Parlor.

"What did he have to eat at Sparky's?"

"Ice cream," LaPage responded condescendingly.

"That's strange, the autopsy report didn't reveal any ice cream in his stomach," he lied.

"Then I guess it had been digested," LaPage pushed back.

Jake sat staring him down, thinking their conversation should be between iron bars. "Where did you take him afterwards?"

"Nowhere. I dropped him off." Only the priest's lips moved when he answered and the rest of his body was calm as his eyes darted from one detective to the other without moving his head. Just his eyeballs were in motion, like a dummy sitting on a ventriloquist's lap.

Jake wasn't getting anywhere and he was becoming anxious. "Where did you drop him off?"

"At the park."

"Bottle Park?" Jake asked.

"Yes, near the west entrance."

"Why didn't you drive him home?"

"He wanted to walk, so I respected his request."

Randy jumped to his feet and pointed his finger a few inches from LaPage's face. "You've never respected anyone, you piece of shit!"

Hagen snatch up his case. "I think we're done here, gentlemen. Father LaPage has cooperated in this inquiry and he has told you everything he knows about the victim."

LaPage slowly rose to his feet with a smug look on his facade. "May the Lord walk alongside you." He smiled at the detectives and moved out of the room with Hagen picking up the rear.

Jake refocused on Randy. "Nice job. You chased him out of here before we had a chance to get anything concrete out of him."

"We're not getting anything incriminating out of him, he is one smart maggot," Randy insisted.

"Maybe so, but you better get your emotions in check. I don't want to see that type of unprofessionalism again. Am I clear?"

Randy got up and moved toward the door. "Crystal," he said before exiting.

CHAPTER 28

Saturday morning found Michael a few minutes before noon, as he cleaned the sleep out of his bloodshot eyes. He sat up in bed, turned on the TV, and watched a clip of George H.W. Bush speaking on the liberation of Kuwait and the success of Desert Storm. His mouth was cotton dry and he had a headache that was unique to dehydration. Rolling out of bed, Michael stumbled to the kitchen and downed a tall glass of water. The liquid ran down his throat like an incoming tide over dry, sandy rocks. It was going to be a long weekend with a Saint Patrick's Day celebration that started the night before and would continue through the parade Sunday evening. Looking at the clock, he realized that he was late picking up his brother for breakfast, so he grabbed the phone and dialed his number. The line rang until the machine kicked in and he left a message apologizing to Jon, assuring him that he was on his way over.

Their parents had left the day before on an annual trip to Ireland, and Jon was home alone, as he was every year on Saint Patrick's Day. The brotherly ritual was to get together the day before the parade and hoot and howl as they bounced from one pub to the next. This year wouldn't be any different, except they were a year older.

When he arrived at his parent's house the door was locked. After knocking a few times he went around to the back and tipped the small lion statue to find the hidden key. His parents had taken away his key a month after he moved out after noticing a depletion of their whiskey stock.

"Jon," he called out as he opened the back door, entering through the kitchen. There was no answer, but Michael figured Jon was home because his car was parked out front. He knew Jon must still be sleeping after what would have been a long night of heavy drinking, so he headed to his room.

The house was still as he moved down the hallway leading to the bedroom, except for the grandfather clock that ticked with each passing second. The door was closed, so he turned the knob and pushed it open and it cried from the hinges. As he suspected, Jon was still sleeping. "Wake up you lazy bum," Michael said. Noticing an empty bottle of Crown Royal on the bed stand, he had figured right. His little brother had tied one on and he was surprised to see that it was with top shelf liquor. Michael thought that he couldn't afford to drink that brand, and he made more money than Jon.

"Jon, get up." Michael reached out and pulled the covers off his brother. Right away he realized something was wrong, Jon's color was off. Reaching out, he put his hand on Jon's face only to feel the coldness of his skin. It was as though it wasn't really Jon; it was like a replica of his brother.

"Jon!" he cried out, immediately stripping the blankets off his brother. Placing his fingers on Jon's neck, he looked for a pulse, but there was none. "No, God, please don't take my brother." Pulling him off the bed and onto the hard floor, Michael started to perform CPR. Leaning over the body, he rhythmically pushed against his chest, and with every push, his tears spilled onto his brother's face and neck. "Jon, please wake up!" Michael didn't know how long he was blowing air into Jon and pumping his chest, he just continued on, and with every unsuccessful attempt, he was losing a piece of himself. When he started to get tired, he finally came to the realization that it was too late. Pushing himself onto his feet, he stumbled to the phone on Jon's desk. Reaching out for the phone, he noticed a yellow note pad with Jon's handwriting on it. Slowly picking it up, he began to read.

Writing this letter is the hardest thing I've ever done because I know it will cause all of you unbearable pain. The torment you will go through will only be a fraction of what I've endured for the last sixteen years. I'm sorry to put you all through this, but I can't live with myself anymore.

I thought that I could drink away the guilt and shame, and for a long time it was working, but with all the recent media coverage it has all risen back to the surface. When I was an altar boy, Father LaPage had sexually abused me on many occasions. I knew it was wrong, but he was so convincing and I was so young and naïve. I have spent my entire adult life trying to forget, but now I have been reliving it through the victims that have come forward. I feel filthy and depleted of all my self esteem. The pain I feel inside is immeasurable. Try not to mourn my passing for I have been dead for a long time.

I love you all, forever.

Jon

Michael felt his legs grow weak and his stomach sour. He tore the sheet of paper off the pad and folded it and tucked it into his pants pocket. Picking up the phone, he dialed the emergency number, softly spoke into the receiver, and hung up. As he moved to his brother lying on the floor, he couldn't feel his legs in motion. He dropped to the floor, pulling Jon in close and holding him tight. Gently rocking back and forth with his kid brother's head against his chest, he was unaware that he was sobbing. His mind began to drift back to their childhood together and a mixture of sadness and anger began to consume him from the depth of his soul.

The park was damp and cold and gray. Stephen sat on rusty metal bleachers that ran along a baseball diamond. The small field was scattered with puddles and the infield was overgrown with weeds. Flipping over one card at a time, he rolled through the blue Bicycle playing cards as if each one was a new unexpected turn in the draw of life. A hawk screamed, and he paused to take notice as it circled above the gray skyline blotching out the sun.

Listening to the footsteps closing in, he watched his friend approaching with his head down. Spitting on the ground with nothing less than contempt, Jon looked up to Stephen, as if he was the only person that would understand. Without speaking, he reached into his pocket and handed the note to Stephen, and then he climbed up to take a seat on the cold, ridged bench. Stephen carefully read the note, and when he was finished, he handed it back to Michael as if it were poisonous.

Michael took a cigarette out of his near-empty pack and

ignited it with a butane lighter. Taking in a hard drag, he raised the note and lit the bottom and held it until a hint of pain singed his fingertips. The pain was good, as it eased his interior suffering, if only for a brief moment. Letting the small remains fall to the ground, he watched as it transformed into a dark gray ash and scattering away in the misty breeze.

"I'm sorry man." Stephen placed his hand on Michael's shoulder, tightening the squeeze before removing it. He could see that his friend had changed in a day's time and he wondered if it was permanent. Would he allow this to consume his existence and wander through life void of spirit? "What now?" Stephen asked.

"Now." He looked at Stephen through sleepless eyes. "Now we bury my little brother."

"How did he do it?" Stephen almost didn't ask, but he had to know.

"I don't know. He killed a bottle of Crown Royal and I'm guessing he took some pills, a lot of pills." Michael's eyes began to well up and he took a drag off his cigarette, offering some drying time.

"That cocksucker LaPage is still out there preaching behind his altar," Stephen said.

"Yeah, he's still out there and he probably doesn't know about Jon, and no one will ever know about the note." The butt fell out of his grasp and bounced off the bleachers to die in a puddle below. "Once everything is settled, I will find LaPage and turn him into dust," Michael said, "For I am my brother's keeper."

"It will be fun to kill that son of a bitch," Stephen said.

"When the time is right, we'll rid the world of that maggot, once and for all." Michael pulled back his sweatshirt sleeve exposing the scar on his forearm. Stephen took off his jacket, displaying his cross as well. With arms raised, once again, they made a silent pact.

CHAPTER 29

April Fool's Day had arrived with a trick of its own. The weather was unseasonably warm and dry as if the clock had fast forwarded to mid June. Jake decided to take walk on his day off and he found himself turning the block adjacent to the Bishop's compound. As he approached, he saw a woman in the yard tying rose bushes to the black iron fence that surrounded the property. Closing in, it became apparent by her attire that she was a nun. Opening the gate with care, he slowly walked toward her, hoping he wasn't disturbing her to the point of annoyance.

"Good afternoon," Jake said as she turned to face him. He immediately noticed her beautiful features. He thought she must have been a knockout when she was young, and he wondered why she had chosen a life of celibacy. By his estimation she appeared to be around his age, or maybe a few years older.

"It is a wonderful day, isn't it?" Her head was covered with a light scarf and her dress only left her hands and ankles exposed. The high cheekbones displayed a hint of European decent and as she spoke her dark blue eyes sparkled, like a slanted sun off an autumn lake.

"I hope I'm not disturbing you. My name is Jake Waterfield and I'm a detective with the Middleborough Police Department." He didn't offer his hand; instead, he bowed his head slightly, showing a sign of respect one might encounter in Japan.

"You're not on duty today, are you?" she asked.

His running shoes and jeans were a dead give-away, he thought. "Well, I'm told I'm always on duty, but I'm not on the clock, right now."

"I'm Sister Patricia Hathaway. Are you here to see the Bishop?"

"I was just taking a walk and I saw you, so I thought I'd stop and have a chat. If the Bishop is free, I'd like to meet him."

"He's not here this afternoon. I'm sorry Mr. Waterfield."

"Please, call me Jake. May I?" he asked, and with her slight nod of approval, he reached out avoiding the thorns and held the rose shrub. With a piece of twine she secured the rose branch to the fence. "Is this a Hybrid Rugosa?" he asked.

Surprised by his knowledge of roses, she examined him for a moment. "You know something about roses?"

"Not really. An old friend of mine is retired and he spends a lot of time in the garden."

"Yes, they are Hybrid Rugosa's. They tend to adapt to the northern climates better than most." He held another branch and she tied it down. "You're not here to talk about flowers, are you?"

"No, Sister Hathaway, I'm not."

She smiled. "Please call me Patricia."

He returned a smile. "Alright, Patricia, how long have you been living here?"

"I've been here since 1969, right out of the convent."

"Do you remember a boy that was found murdered in Bottle Park? His name was Robert Anderson."

She stopped what she was doing and looked Jake in the eye. "I remember." She had figured this was his reason for being there. "I read the newspaper from time to time."

"Then you know Father LaPage is a suspect in the case?"

"Yes. That should do it for now." She gathered the twine and scissors from a small table and began walking toward the entrance to the gate.

"How well do you know Father LaPage?"

Studying him, she was thoughtful in her response. "How well do you know your Chief of Police?"

Jake saw her point. It's hard to know someone that you work with from a distance. What did he really know about Chief Mearald, other than the policies he set forth? Who was he when he was out of uniform? Jake really couldn't say.

"Have you ever seen him act out of line with any of the altar boys, or children in general?"

"No." She stopped at the gate entrance and Jake got the hint.

"Patricia, is there anything you can tell me about the murder of the Anderson boy? I'll even take a rumor." He smiled.

"I'm sorry, Jake. Thanks for assisting me with the roses."

"You're quite welcome. If you think of anything, please call me." He handed her a card, un-hatched the gate, and started out under the tall rounded archway displaying figures of angels in flight. After closing the gate behind him, Jake smiled at the nun once again and briefly paused to study the figures of angel's above him. He thought about all the lost children of the world, and if there truly were a God, why wasn't He protecting them? Taking a deep breath of fresh air, he looked up toward the blue sky and began back up the street.

Monday morning arrived faster than usual and Jake thought it was because of his inability to sleep through the night. His eyes stung and he felt hung over, even though he didn't drink.

He had taken Colleen to the movies the day before, but he wasn't able to relax and she took notice of it. His case was stagnant and he was weary from all the dead ends and a lack of solid leads. Someone had killed Robby Anderson, and they had to pay. Justice had to be served, and he was the only person who could deliver. The case had consumed all his thoughts, and his lack of enthusiasm in his relationship with Colleen was apparent to both of them. She did all she could to understand and support him, and he loved her for it. Knowing that one day he would be off the case and he would come back around to his usual self, she decided to be patient, hoping it would be sooner than later.

Sitting behind his desk with a pencil and a plain white sheet of typing paper, Jake drew and erased and repeated again, taking his time to get it right.

Randy came gliding over, full of energy after a weekend of hiking and meditation in the mountains. "How was your weekend, Jake?"

"Fine." He kept working the pencil.

"What's that?" Randy asked, moving behind Jake for a better look.

"It's a button."

"Looks like an anchor in the center," Randy observed.

"Yes, it's an anchor," he responded with his head down.

"Is it the infamous missing button?" Randy asked.

After making one last scribble, he tossed it on the desk. "It's about the best I can do from memory, but that's it. That's what it looked like."

Randy picked up the sheet of paper and studied the drawing. "I'll make a couple photocopies." He walked over to the machine in the corner of the room and ran off three copies and returned, placing the original and two copies on the desk.

Jake picked up the original, studying it as if it were the secret to the universe. "We need to find out where this button came from. Who manufactured it, where it was sold, and what type of clothing it was attached to."

"And more importantly, who was wearing it when it fell off in the park," Randy added.

"Yes." Jake looked up, examining his partner. We need to search the phone book for button manufacturers and check out the Army and Navy stores, and also do some research at the library. It will be a tedious effort, but we need to find out where this button comes from."

"Where do we start?" Jake liked Randy's optimism, but he knew the tediousness would be draining on him. He wondered if he would be able to last or weather the boredom would eventually get to him. Jake was beginning to really like Randy and he hoped he would be able stick it out.

"Why don't you start with the phone book, and I'll hit the library," Jake suggested.

"Fair enough." Randy headed toward his desk with the drawing in hand.

Two weeks later, Jake and Randy sat in a local diner with breakfast cooling in front of them.

"So this is where we are?" Randy asked.

"Looks like a stalemate," Jake said, snatching up a slice of wheat toast, spreading grape jelly on it. "Out of hundreds of button manufacturers, we came up with three that make buttons similar to our missing button. The amazing thing is that none of the three companies are American." Jake pulled out his notebook and flipped a few pages. "Lilly Corporation, Taiwan, Tin Hung, Hong Kong, and Zhejiang Weixing, from China. These three companies produce millions of buttons with anchors like ours and they're spread out all over the world. They're on windbreakers, jackets, sweaters, and even some hats." Jake took a large bite from his toast and washed it down with fresh-squeezed orange juice.

Filling his mouth with scrambled eggs, and speaking with a semi-full mouth, Randy had an idea. "What are the chances that the person who lost the button didn't know it was lost at the crime scene, and he still has the jacket hanging in his closet?"

"First of all, you're assuming that the button came from the perpetrator's clothing. If it did, then chances are he would have gotten rid of it, or, he would have been tipped off by the person that had it removed from the evidence room, and again, he would have gotten rid of it."

"District Attorney Mark Corbin," Randy declared.

"Yes. Even if we wanted to take a shot and see if a garment with a missing button existed, what judge would give us a warrant based on my memory of a missing button that was found at a crime scene in 1972?"

"My guess, none," Randy said.

"Exactly."

"So what do we do now?"

Jake rubbed his eyes and yawned. "I think it's time we went to see District Attorney Corbin."

"What do you expect to get out of that?"

"A reaction," Jake said.

"A reaction, what does that mean?" Randy frowned, imagining himself handing over his gun and badge to Chief Mearald.

"It means that when confronted about the missing evidence, he will react. How he reacts will hopefully determine if he was in on it, or not."

"I can tell you the Chief's reaction," Randy said. "It will have something to do with you walking the beat in uniform for the rest of your career."

Jake finished his juice, and wiped off his mouth. "If that's the way it goes down, then so be it. I was put on this case to find a killer and I'm running out of options."

Randy picked up his last piece of bacon and folded it into his mouth. "There is one other option."

"Yeah, what's that?"

"What if the priest were to vanish?"

"Vanish?" Jake repeated with a puzzled look.

"One day he's here and the next he's gone, forever."

"Are you crazy or something?"

"Look, were talking about a predator that has diddled and raped little boys for the past twenty years. It's what you want, right?"

"It's what I want? What do I want?" Jake's voice was getting coarse.

"Justice," Randy said.

Shaking his head, Jake got up and pointed his finger at his partner. "This conversation never happened." He threw a ten dollar bill on the table and walked out.

CHAPTER 30

Jake was growing inpatient by the minute. He began questioning why he bothered to make an appointment to see Corbin in the first place. He had been waiting for twenty-six minutes in the outer office, and he decided to wait ten more minutes before leaving. Corbin's secretary did her best to avoid eye contact with the frustrated looking detective as he sat thumbing through a Readers Digest magazine. Randy decided against attending the meeting because he had thought it was a bad idea from the start and he didn't want to deal with the possible repercussions. Jake understood and respected his feelings, and thought he might do the same if he were standing in his shoes. The difference between how the two detectives thought about this approach was significant. Jake was the officer that found the dead boy in the park nineteen years earlier.

Thirty-four minutes had passed before the door opened and Corbin appeared, looking agitated.

"Detective Waterfield," Corbin said as he waved him in. "Have a seat." He motioned to a chair in front of his desk and marched to his comfortable leather chair. "What can we do for you today?"

Jake was upset that Corbin didn't even bother to apologize for making him wait for over half an hour. "I've been waiting so long that I almost forgot," Jake said with a serious look on his face.

Corbin let out a grunt. "I was engaged in an important phone call." The truth is that he knew Jake was heading up the case against LaPage and it was against his interest to be involved, so he was hoping Jake would simply grow tired of waiting and leave.

"A phone call," Jake said.

Corbin didn't like Jake's tone of voice and he was bothered that Jake was not intimidated by him.

"How's my friend Chief Mearald doing these days?"

Jake knew the game he was playing by bringing up his boss from the start. "He's fine, and as you know, he put me on the Anderson case."

"Yes, I'm aware of that," Corbin followed unenthusiastically.

"Are you aware that I found the boy's body when I was a rookie on patrol back in 1972?"

"I had heard that somewhere. That must have been disturbing for you, so early in your career." Corbin picked up his gold pen and began twirling it between his fingers, as if he was already bored with the conversation.

Jake studied the expensive pen being manipulated before decisively returning his attention back to Corbin. "Yes, it still disturbs me today, as it would disturb any rational human being, especially one that has a child of his own." Corbin figured Jake was referring to him and his children and he resented the comparison.

"It is tragic," Corbin said roughly. "Can we get to the point?"

Jake straightened up, detached his back from the chair. "My first point is that case evidence has been taken from the police evidence room and it's now missing."

"That sounds like something Chief Mearald should be looking in to." He gently placed the pen back down as if it were a precious artifact. "What evidence is missing?"

"A button." Jake noticed that his left eye ticked as he registered the word. Producing a copy of the drawing, he handed it to Corbin. "This is a drawing of it."

After a quick glance, he handed it back to Jake without expression. "A small button was lost in the evidence shuffle, so what?"

"I believe this button may have been worn by the killer and possibly fell off during a struggle." He folded the paper and placed it back in his inside jacket pocket. "Also, all associated photographs of the button have mysteriously vanished. So, do you think they got lost in the shuffle as well?"

Corbin didn't respond.

"Here's what bothers me. There are only a few people who have had access to the evidence, and after speaking with those few officers, I have reason to believe that Officer Jacobson may have been involved."

Corbin's jaw shrunk as he clenched his hidden teeth. "I still don't see how this has anything to do with my office. This is an internal police matter."

"Yes. It is an internal matter, except that the prime suspect in this case is a Catholic Priest that works for Bishop Reardon, and we all know how tight you are with Reardon."

Corbin's face was turning pink and darkening by the second as if his brain was roasting. "Are you accusing me of involvement in this?"

"Let's just say I have a lot of unanswered questions and you seem to be a common denominator."

"Get the fuck out of my office!" Corbin shot to his feet and pointed at the door.

Jake sprung up from his chair. "Everyone knows you and Jacobson are close and that you got him the cushy job as court liaison. What price did he pay for the job, Mr. Corbin?"

"You son of a bitch!" Corbin yelled. "Do you know who you're taking to? I'll have your ass for this, you snot-nosed punk!"

"Mr. Corbin. What do you stand to gain from this from the church?" Jake's voice was now elevated and the two men faced off like gladiators.

"You get the hell out of here, now," Corbin said in a firm and lower voice.

Jake didn't respond with words, he just offered his back as he left the room. He had accomplished what he had come for. If Corbin were innocent, the conversation would have gone in a different direction, Jake thought. He would not have been quite so defensive from the start and maybe even offered support in finding the killer. After observing the way he reacted to the word "button," Jake knew he was onto something. He hit a sensitive spot, and he played on it until Corbin had nothing to contribute except angry threats and rage. *Why would he stoop so low as to cover up evidence that may have implicated a child killer? What was in it for Corbin?* This was the million dollar question. Jake was determined to find out Corbin's motive.

Having two people screaming at him in the same day was very unusual for Jake. He sat in Chief Mearald's office with the tall man leaning over him, like a furious drill sergeant in boot camp. "What the hell were you thinking by going into the District Attorney's office and accusing him of tampering with evidence in a murder investigation?"

"Chief."

"Shut up!" he cut him off. "The first thing you should have done was to come and see me, Jake."

"You're absolutely right, Chief." Jake couldn't refute the point.

"Then why didn't you?"

"First of all, I didn't know the conversation was going to sour until I saw the way he reacted to the inquiry." He stood up and faced his boss. "When I mentioned the button, you should have seen his reaction. He became extremely agitated and eventually blew up, barking threats at me. He's hiding something, Chief."

"What?" Mearald roared.

"I don't know yet, but I do know that he and Bishop Reardon are friends, and Reardon will do anything in his power to help LaPage and save face for the church."

"What has that got to do with a button?"

"I found a button at the crime scene and I believe it may have fallen off the perpetrator during a struggle with the boy."

Not amused, the Chief leaned back against the corner of his desk and folded his arms. "Go on."

"Well, ironically the button has since vanished from the evidence room. There are only a few people that have had access to the evidence, and I've interviewed all of them, except you."

"Hold on a second. Evidence is missing from my evidence room and I'm the last person to find out about it?"

"I didn't want to bother you until I had something solid."

"No, bother me, please." Mearald's tone was condescending and arrogant, but Jake preferred it to the alternative.

"Everyone I spoke with seemed on the up and up, except Jacobson. He had guilt written all over his face, and we all know the relationship between him and the DA."

"Hence, your conspiracy theory," Mearald concluded.

"I know it sounds a little farfetched, but it's a real possibility when you think about it."

"You know what I think?" He slapped his palms against his thighs, straightened out and walked around his desk, leaning over it, like a chess player waiting for his turn to move. "I think you're on a wild goose chase, and this is the only thing you can come up with. The DA wants me to yank your ass off this case, and I'm inclined to do so."

"Chief, can't you see that this guy is dirty?"

"I know all about the DA and the cloud that surrounds him, but that doesn't excuse what you did at his office today. This case has a super-high profile. Hell, every time I turn on the TV or pick up the paper there's a story about this case. Frankly, I'm sick and tired of this damned case and I want it over with. If I pull you off the case, it will open up a whole new can of worms and reporters will be asking all kinds of questions about why you were yanked of the case. There are more leaks in this department than a sinking Titanic." Jake was enthused by the way the conversation was heading. "I'm not going to pull you off the case, but another stunt like this and you'll be working with the parking matrons. Are we clear?"

"Yes sir." Jake was overcome with a sense of relief and his shoulders felt lighter.

"Stay away from Corbin and Jacobson. Find another path to explore and find the son of a bitch that killed that kid. Now get out of here!"

"Thanks Chief." Jake didn't waste any time scrabbling out of the room. In a blink of an eye, he was gone.

CHAPTER 31

The pressure from the media and the community was becoming too heavy to bear on the Church as it stretched all the way across the Atlantic to the Vatican. New lawsuits were popping up, including a few more levied against LaPage. Finally, the word came down from the Pope, himself. It was clear that Father LaPage was guilty of abusing children, behavior the Catholic Church could not tolerate from one of its clergy. The Pope's top cardinal held a press conference condemning this type of behavior and confirmed that the Church did not condone these violations against children. The Cardinal went on to say that any violations in this regard would be dealt with swiftly and justly by the Vatican.

LaPage sat in his quarters, watching the Cardinal's statement on TV and a bad feeling came over him. Every word spoken was like a long, rusty nail being driven into his flesh. His head began spinning. He started to contemplate all the things that might go wrong in his life, and how he would overcome them. He was a survivor. It would take a lot more than bad press and a speech to take him down. *Maybe I'll move to another country and open an orphanage.*

The Cardinal concluded his statement and LaPage turned off the television and darted for the liquor cabinet. Not bothering to find a glass, he pulled the bottle to his mouth and started guzzling. The scotch flowed down burning in his throat, and soon, the tingling knot near his shoulder blade began to subside.

The sudden ring of the phone startled him. Wiping his mouth with the back of his hand, LaPage reached for the receiver and put it to his ear.

"Hello."

"Hello Robert. Did you see the Vatican's press conference?" He knew right away it was Bishop Reardon because he always greeted him the same way.

"Hello Evan. Yes, I saw it."

"Robert, I'm here with Mr. Hagen and we are on a speaker

phone. Robert, this is a hard conversation for me. I have always supported you and your efforts. Hell, I fought tooth and nail for you on this, but my words fell on deaf ears."

LaPage didn't like the way the conversation was heading; he took a seat.

"I just received a call from the Vatican," Reardon said. "Cardinal Verossa called, and it was a vigorous debate to say the least."

"Evan, I'm innocent. It all started with one person making up a story, and now, all the rest have jumped on the cart for financial gain. Can't you see what's happening here? The church continues to settle, giving away millions, and anyone with a story and a lawyer is capitalizing on it."

"I'm not judging you, Robert. That is left up to God. However, the Vatican cannot withstand the negative impact this has brought upon the Church. I'm sorry Robert, you have been ordered to be defrocked."

"Defrocked?" LaPage felt a nasty tingling birthing in his core and it quickly spread to the ends of his extremities, rendering his body numb. "What will I do *now*?"

"I don't know, Robert. It is effective immediately. You are not to preside over another Mass, and all Church related activities are suspended. Father Dember will be taking over starting tomorrow and you are to report here in the morning to begin the exit process."

LaPage was speechless and his mind was racing to no end.

"Cardinal Verossa wanted you out in two weeks, but I convinced him to allow you a month to find a place to go."

"One month," a whimpering response came from the other end.

"I'm sorry, Robert. I'll see you tomorrow."

After hanging up the phone, Reardon felt an unexpected immediate feeling of relief. He had endured the comments and apprehensive looks far too long, and the pressure from the Vatican was becoming tiresome. Hoping that things could finally get back on track, and in time, forgotten, like a poorly written tragic novel.

The next morning the headlines read, "Priest Defrocked." A photograph of LaPage didn't show him in the best light. His collar was fixed and straight, but his expression was that of a criminal in a line up. LaPage remembered the day it was taken, while being questioned at a civil hearing on the suit brought by Alan Brick. He thought about Brick and he hated him for starting the whole ordeal. *Brick enjoyed the times we had spend together, he even welcomed them. I should have killed that little weasel when I had the chance and maybe none of this would have happened.* Now, he had less than a month to find a place and decide what he was going to do with the rest of his life. He thought he would move out of the country for a while, until things cooled down. *I'm an intelligent and educated man. I shouldn't have a problem finding a good job in the private sector. Maybe I'll look into being a guidance counselor for children.* Scooping up a magazine, LaPage opened it to a section on Brazil and he began reading about the street children in Rio de janeiro. How he could help them... Maybe this was his calling in life. He started feeling better about his situation and his prospects for moving on. Things might even turn out better than he contemplated. Now smiling, he licked his finger and flipped the page.

Ed Gallagher hung up the phone, experiencing an inner joy that came seldom in his line of work. After calling Alan Brick to congratulate him on LaPage's termination, he learned Brick had decided to move forward with a cash settlement, hoping to put the tragic episode behind him.

Ed advised Brick to hold out for more money than the previous offer, and Brick agreed, only if he could make it happen sooner than later. Ed was optimistic that they would settle fast and be done with it, so he advised Brick to go for another $200,000.

Brick knew the money would never be able to compensate him for the abuse he endured as a child, but he wouldn't need to worry about his next meal or a roof over his head. He thought about all the broken children in the world and how he might help one of them to heal, and maybe in turn, it would help in his own healing efforts. Brick decided he would look into becoming a Big Brother.

CHAPTER 32

It was 4:36 p.m. when Stephen glanced at his watch, as he sat in an old abandoned warehouse that was once a thriving and lucrative appliance manufacturer. The room he and Michael occupied was a storage area off the main floor that was once used to house appliances that were piled up for repair, or would be discarded if determined unsalvageable. A single metal chair was in the center of the room, where they had placed it, and that's where Stephen was sitting. Michael found his place on top of an old dryer.

"So this is it. I think we have everything we need," Stephen said.

"Hopefully he will stick to his normal schedule, so we don't have to wait all night. Are you sure the stun gun works okay?" Michael asked. "The last thing we need is a dead battery or something."

Stephen looked at his friend who, like him, was dressed in all black. "What do you say we try it out on you and make sure?"

"I'll pass," Michael said.

"I checked it out and everything is fine with the stun gun." Stephen pulled out a .38 Caliber handgun from his lower back waistline. Opening up the cylinder, he spun it, and it turned round and round, sounding like a wheel of chance at a carnival. "I have this as a backup, just in case something goes wrong."

Michael sniffled, rubbed his nose, and hopped off the dryer. "Well, let's go and g-get this over with."

They drove to the rectory, parked, and sat slumped down in Michael's car a distance from the building, yet close enough to see the door that LaPage would exit from.

"When he comes out we'll follow him until the time is right." Stephen said, taking out a Snickers bar and peeling the wrapper off. "Taking him here is too risky, there are too many eyeballs and its way too lit up." He bit off a large chunk of the candy bar and began chewing loud enough that Michael was becoming annoyed.

"Where's the duct tape?"

"In the glove box with the tape recorder," Michael said. "How long have we been waiting? What time is it?"

Pulling back the sleeve of his black sweatshirt, Stephen looked at his watch with the camouflage wristband. "Almost 1900 hours," he said, pushing the remainder of the chocolate bar into his mouth and stuffing the wrapper into the ashtray.

"What?" Michael looked at him like he was insane. "How about the normal time?"

"Don't you know military time? It's seven o'clock."

"I hope this bastard doesn't decide to stay in tonight," Michael said.

"If he does, then we come back tomorrow night," Stephen said in a patient tone that bothered him. Michael just wanted it over with, so he could finally let go and put his brother to rest.

"There he is," Michael alerted.

Stephen turned his focus to LaPage as he walked out of the building and quickly shuffled toward the detached garage, avoiding a biting wind. With a remote control, LaPage activated the automatic garage door opener and entered the dimly lit garage. A minute later his sedan drove out and the garage door closed behind him.

The drive lasted about twelve minutes, until LaPage parked his car at the side entrance to a movie theater. Stephen and Michael watched from across the street as LaPage got out and entered the theater. Locating a spot across the street, they hunkered down in anticipation of a two hour wait.

"So, you haven't been going out that much lately," Stephen said. "What the hell have you been doing?"

Michael was biting his fingernails and stopped to spit a piece out which landed on his dashboard, sticking to the vinyl. "Not much, I've been staying in more, that's all."

"Look, I know losing Jon has been hard, but eventually you have to move on with your life and start having some fun again," he said, playfully back-fisting Michael in the shoulder.

"Like what, skydiving?"

"Exactly." They both shared a laugh.

"This has been stuck in my mind and I can't seem to think about anything else."

"What, what's been on your mind?" Stephen asked.

"Wasting LaPage." Michael tightened his fists.

Stephen understood what he meant. "It will be over tonight," Stephen assured him.

When LaPage finally walked out of the theater it was a few minutes past nine. They followed him to a bar on the city line. It was a secluded and quiet bar that had a reputation for an older crowd and the big weekly event was karaoke on Saturday night. They were glad it was Thursday night because it was much less crowded. Stephen had stopped in the lounge seven years earlier for a quick drink and he never cared to return. It was one of those places that made you feel better about your life after observing the walking dead in action.

Once LaPage was inside, Michael parked his car about forty feet away, close to the wood line. The small cedar-shingled building was nestled in a wooded area with a dirt parking lot on both sides and the main road was mostly hidden by thick brush and trees. The right side of the tavern, where they parked, had one small window seven feet high that acted as a kitchen vent. Both men got out and moved to the rear of the building to wait. Keeping their backs pressed up against the building, Stephen was peeked around the corner, as Michael reached for a butt.

"Do you want one?" Michael held the pack toward his comrade.

"No," he whispered as he fondled the stun gun in his sweatshirt pocket.

Michael tucked the roll of duct tape under his arm, wedging it against his ribcage while he lit up. His heart was beating faster than usual, as he thought about the man they were hunting. He had read the news that LaPage was defrocked and was no longer a priest; he was just your average Joe, *now*. Three months ago, he never would have even considered taking out a Catholic priest because he believed there was such a thing as hell, but he wasn't sure what that meant. No one did, he thought. Maybe he would come back as a sheep stuck in a crowded pen waiting to be slaughtered, or a maggot crawling on a dead carcass. Whatever Hell was, he figured it wouldn't be a pleasant existence.

Stephen was calm and focused on the task ahead, not wanting any mistakes or traces that they had been there. In his mind, LaPage was just a child predator that didn't deserve to breathe the same air as decent human beings. He didn't think about going to Hell. He figured if there was such a place, he surely would find out once his time on earth expired.

The door opened and LaPage surfaced. Stephen figured he had consumed one drink and decided to move on.

"Here he comes," Stephen said. Quickly scrambling to the pre-determined designation, they moved into place, hidden in the night shadows. LaPage negotiated the corner of the building and pulled the car keys out from his jacket pocket. They listened as he approached, hearing the beep of his car alarm being deactivated.

"Get ready," Stephen whispered as the car door was opened. "Let's move."

Like two Special Forces soldiers, they quickly ran to LaPage's car as he was getting in.

Hearing the commotion, LaPage turned to see who was approaching. Before he could close the car door, Stephen jammed the stun gun into his neck, administering 350,000 thousand volts. LaPage was instantly incapacitated, shaking and mumbling incoherently. In a flash, Michael was on top of LaPage wrapping duct tape around his head, covering his mouth. Still twitching, they dragged LaPage out of his car and hoisted him into the trunk of Michael's car. Once inside the trunk, Michael went to work taping his hands behind his back and his ankles together. Stephen jumped into LaPage's car, where the keys were dangling from the ignition. He noticed a smooth silver cross hanging from the key chain. He started the car and watched as Michael closed the trunk and dashed behind the wheel of his car. Surveying the area to see if anyone had witnessed the abduction, Stephen thought the coast was clear. He pushed down on the accelerator and drove out to the main street with Michael following behind.

LaPage sat in the chair under a spot light in the center of the storage room in the abandoned appliance factory building. The light was hooked up to a small generator that Stephen had stolen many years earlier. A combination of his nerves and the heat from the light caused beads of sweat to form on LaPage's forehead like raindrops on a freshly waxed car. The musty smell of fermenting mold mixed with stale urine lingered throughout the stagnant air. Duct tape tightly secured his wrists and ankles to the chair and his mouth was taped shut. Alone in the room, his mind was scrambling in many different directions. *Who did this to me and why? Are they coming back, or am I left to die a slow death of starvation. Will anyone come to my rescue, or is this place too remote and desolate a location?* Struggling to free himself, LaPage tried standing up, but fell back in failure. His hands were wrapped with thick silver tape many times over and he felt his circulation being depleted the more he struggled. *Don't they know I'm a priest, a man of God?* He sat totally helpless, praying to an unforgiving God.

LaPage heard movement to his rear and tried to turn and see who was approaching, but he was limited in his motion and could only see to his flank. An arm clutched onto his throat and jerked his head back. His breathing increased and his pleading was unheard, muffled by the duct tape. Michael stood holding him as Stephen watched quietly from the rear corner of the room. With his other hand, Michael pinched the priest's nose shut, cutting off all avenues of air. After thirty seconds, LaPage began violently shaking and he thought he was going to suffocate right there in the metal chair he was bound to. Michael finally let go and moved around to face the predator, who was frantically trying to catch his breath through his nose, like an angry bull in the arena.

"How does it feel to be helpless?" Michael asked, knowing his answer wouldn't be heard. "It might feel something like what a young boy felt when you held him down and raped him." He slapped LaPage across the face. "Pay attention!"

Stephen walked over and stood next to Michael, his right hand grasping a pistol. LaPage's eyes expanded when he noticed the gun. LaPage was thinking it was a bad sign that his captors didn't bother to hide their identities, especially because Michael was familiar to him.

"To me you are less than snot," Stephen calmly professed. Sticking his finger in his nose, he extracted a lump of soiled mucus and held it up. "I have more respect for this than I do you." Leaning forward he wiped it on the point of LaPage's nose, so that it was always in his vision. "I bet you're wondering why you're here and why we are treating you so poorly." Stephen wedged the gun in his waistline and began pacing back and forth in front of LaPage. The gun was in plain sight, and his hands were clutched behind his back, as he slowly took four steps before pivoting and continuing in the other direction. "The main reason is that you are responsible for the suicide of Jon McNulty. Do you remember him?"

LaPage began rapidly shaking his head. Thinking back, LaPage remembered the young altar boy and the sexual encounters he had with him.

"It so happens that Jon McNulty was the brother of my best friend." Stephen turned and gestured toward Michael.

"You son of a bitch!" In an instant, Michael lunged forward with a straight right punch hitting LaPage in the abdomen, knocking the wind out of him. With a tear rolling down his face, he yelled out in rage. "How could you do that to a child? That was my little brother," Michael cried.

Stephen closed in and patted his friend on the back and Michael took a step back. "The second reason you're here is for all the young boys you molested and raped over the years," Stephen said. "How many lives do you estimate you have destroyed?" Stephen resumed his pacing as LaPage was beginning to breath normally again. "From what I've read in the paper, I estimate at least forty, maybe more." Pulling the pistol out from his waist, he walked over and placed the barrel against LaPage's forehead. Tears were rolling down LaPage's face as he mumbled behind the duct tape. "This is what's going to happen here. We're going to remove the tape from your mouth and you are going to confess to raping all those kids. Then you're going to confess to murdering Robby Anderson in Bottle Park."

Opening the cylinder, Stephen removed all of the bullets and put them in his pocket, except one. Holding up a single bullet so LaPage could clearly see it, he pushed it into the cylinder and quickly spun the chamber before closing it shut. The sound of the cylinder snapping into place, made LaPage twitch in his chair.

"As you can see, there is one bullet loaded in the gun and none of us knows where it lies. It could be the next one to be capped off, or maybe not. It's a one in six chance, not bad odds, right?" He took a step closer to LaPage and pointed the gun at his groin. "How bad do you think it would hurt if I blew your nuts off? How long would it take for you to bleed to death?" LaPage was breathing heavily and mumbling at a rapid pace. Stephen slowly squeezed the trigger until the hammer extended all the way back before dropping forward and making a clicking sound. They watched as a puddle began forming on the floor under LaPage's chair.

"If you had to use the restroom, all you had to do was say so," Stephen said, chuckling.

Michael just stood watching without emotion. He wasn't appreciating the humor they usually shared.

"Here's how it's going to go down." Stephen walked over to an old washing machine and picked up a tape recorder that sat in wait. "You're going to speak and I'm going to tape your confession. You are not to address us in any way. Just start out by confessing to raping the altar boys and children in your parish, and then the murder of the Anderson kid. Do not mention Jon McNulty's name. You will finish by declaring you have confessed because your conscience is tormenting you and you realize you need to be taken off the streets. If you do this, you are finished here. Understood? LaPage nodded his head and Stephen activated the recorder.

Michael walked over and abruptly tore the tape from his mouth, taking dead skin along with it and LaPage let out a painful grunt.

"Wait! I didn't kill the Anderson boy."

Angry that he didn't follow his instructions, Stephen moved in, placing the gun against LaPage's right temple and he pulled the trigger. The relief of hearing a clicking sound shuttered LaPage, deeming him silent with fear and gratitude at the same time. "Alright," he cried. "Please don't."

Stephen pushed the button, deactivating the recorder. "Next time you probably won't be so lucky. You've used up two cylinders already."

Erasing the tape, Stephen held it in front of LaPage, and once again, he pushed the button and the green light illuminated. Through a crumbling voice, LaPage began confessing about his sexual crimes against the children of his parish. Once he finished, Stephen stopped the recorder. "Very good, now you'll confess to murdering Robby Anderson in Bottle Park," Stephen demanded as he pointed the gun at the priest.

Briefly hesitating, LaPage looked at the gun thinking the next cylinder was probably not empty. "Okay, I'll do it."

"Okay," Stephen said as he pushed the record button and the tape started rolling. Once LaPage was finished confessing to the murder, Stephen stopped the recorder and looked at Michael who had been quietly listening with hate-filled eyes.

"Please, can I go now? I did what you asked," LaPage pleaded.

"Sure." Stephen walked over to Michael and handed him the gun before starting to undo LaPage's left wrist. Michael strolled in behind LaPage and out of his sight. He opened the cylinder of the gun and moved the lone bullet into position. Before LaPage's left hand was free, Stephen let go and walked away. Michael moved in, placing the barrel of the gun against LaPage's right temple. "This is for Jon," he said just prior to pulling the trigger, and this time, the gun sounded off with a loud, jolting bang.

For a few seconds they both stood watching as LaPage's body went limp in the chair and he expelled his last breath.

"Let's move!" Stephen barked out, snapping Michael out of his trance of revenge.

Stephen began undressing LaPage, avoiding the blood flow as best he could. Once undressed, he replaced his clothing with a pair of blue jeans, a sweatshirt and a pair of sneakers. They had watched LaPage on several occasions and determined his approximate size. With a damp cloth, Michael went to work, cleaning off his face in an effort to wipe off the glue from the tape. The careful way they had secured his wrists and ankles left the glue remnants only on his clothes, and his clothes would never be found. Stephen removed the chair LaPage had occupied and replaced it with another. Because he was sitting when he was shot, they had to have a clean chair to replace it with, again, avoiding the traces of tape glue. Situating the chair and body to make it appear as a legitimate suicide, Stephen thoroughly cleaned the gun with a rag and placed it in LaPage's right hand. He firmly pushed LaPage's index finger on the trigger and his remaining fingers on the pistol grip, before allowing the gun to fall naturally to the floor.

The last order of business was to plant the tape with his confession. Stephen and Michael knew they were suspects in the murder of Robby Anderson, and this would exonerate them once and for all. Stephen had used latex gloves when he put the tape into the recorder, and he did the same to extract it and place it in LaPage's pocket. Before he planted the tape, he pressed two of the dead man's fingers against the cassette, leaving behind only the body, the tape, the chair, and the gun. They cleared everything else out, providing no traces that could link them to the crime.

Driving away from the scene, Stephen took one last look at LaPage's car that was thoroughly wiped clean and left behind. "Don't ever think that we killed a priest," Stephen said. "He was nothing more than an evil child rapist and he deserved what he got. The world is a better place without that piece of shit."

Michael fixed his eyes on his friend. "The world is a better place now," he agreed.

CHAPTER 33

After eating a late lunch, Jake and Randy discussed the interview they conducted with LaPage's older brother that morning. He stated that he traveled most of the time and was unaware that LaPage was bringing young boys to his house on the weekends he was away. He also said that he had broken all contact with his brother after allegations of sexual abuse had surfaced. The detectives showed him a drawing of the button and he assured them that he didn't remember seeing his brother wearing anything with that type of button on it. They both believed he was sincere and concluded the interview, reserving the right to question him in the future if needed.

Jake and Randy cruised around the neighborhood surrounding Bottle Park, to kill a half an hour before their appointment with the Andersons. They had spoken to the parents at the start of the investigation and that conversation added no leads or anything that would help in their efforts. This time they had a drawing and some additional information they had gathered since their last meeting.

While stopped at a red light, Jake's pager went off, indicating his office was calling him. They pulled up to a pay phone and Jake called in. Detective Andrew Polopoulos answered the phone. Cupping one ear to avoid the traffic noise, Jake stood outside a liquor store on a main artery in the center of the city and spoke louder than usual. "Andy, this is Jake. What's going on?"

"Jake, you're not going to believe this. The District Twelve patrol car was investigating an abandoned automobile at the old appliance warehouse on Jensen Avenue."

"I know where that is," Jake said.

"Yeah, well they ran the plate and it came back to one, Robert LaPage."

"You have my attention," Jake said.

"Good because it gets better."

Jake looked over at Randy and saw him flipping through a

newspaper as he waited in the car.

"Go on Andy."

"They went into the building, and guess what they found?"

"I'm listening." Jake was growing inpatient.

Andy cleared his throat, delaying his response even longer. "They found Father Robert LaPage with his head blown half off."

The line went silent as Jake began to process the news.

"Jake, are you there?"

"Yes, Jake said. "Are you sure it's him?"

"His license was in his pocket, it's him. They said it looks like a suicide."

"We're on the way. Thanks, Andy." Paralyzed in thought, Jake hung up the phone and stood in the street glaring at his partner as the traffic moved past him at fifty miles an hour. *How will I ever find out who was responsible for killing Robby Anderson?*

As they pulled in behind the factory building, three cruisers were parked near LaPage's car; two were empty and one was occupied by two patrolmen. When the patrol officers saw Jake and Randy pulling up, they got out to greet them. Jake recognized the taller of the two as Freddie Bugge, alias Bugger. Labeling cops with nicknames was similar to how the Mafia did it, and in many cases, the cops were crueler.

"Hello Freddie." Jake declined to call him Bugger and he appreciated it. "Do you know Randy Applebee?" Jake shook hands with Freddie.

"Sure, we've run into each other a few times," Freddie said. He extended his hand and Randy engaged him.

"This is my partner, Tom Ferklin." Jake and Randy greeted the young rookie.

"What's going on?" Jake asked.

"We're out here watching LaPage's vehicle. District Twelve is inside with a supervisor. It's pretty messy in there, Jake."

"Have you called for prints and photos?" Jake asked.

"Yes, and the coroner has been notified as well."

"Thanks Freddie. How are the kids doing?"

"They're great Jake, thanks."

"Good. When the print squad arrives, they can start with the car."

Freddie seemed puzzled, and it was obvious to Jake. "Is something troubling you?" Jake asked.

"This is a suicide. Why are we lifting prints from the car? I understand lifting prints from the gun is standard procedure, but the car isn't."

"You're right Freddie, but this guy had a lot of enemies, right?"

"Yes he did," Freddie agreed.

Jake patted him on the arm. "Thanks, Freddie."

He and Randy started toward the building.

"Jake," Freddie called out, and Jake turned around. "As far as I'm concerned, if it is a murder, whoever did it deserves a medal." Jake didn't respond, he simply nodded and walked away.

As they entered the storage room, Jake observed three officers in a semi-huddle near the entrance. The supervisor, Fran Hennington, came right over and the other two acknowledge Jake and Randy with a nod and a wave.

"Hello Fran, what have you got?" Jake asked.

"A suicide. It looks like Father Diddler took the easy way out."

Jake wasn't surprised by Fran's lack of professionalism. He had a reputation for being hard and calloused. Jake thought about the time he responded to an accident when he was in uniform. A guy was crossing the street after buying a grinder from a local pizza shop and he was hit by an SUV. It opened up his head and he was killed immediately. Fran was the first cruiser on the scene, and as the victim lay in the street with his brains spilling out, Fran picked up his sub and began eating it.

"Meatball," Fran said, before taking a bite.

"Don't you have any respect?" Jake asked.

"Well, he's not going to eat it. Why waste food? Besides, I haven't eaten yet."

The story had spread throughout the department and the joke was on Fran.

"I'd say it's the hard way out, wouldn't you?" Jake responded.

Fran reached into his pocket and pulled out a plastic bag containing a tape. "I pulled this out of his left pants pocket." He handed the clear bag to Jake. "I was looking for identification when I found it. Do you think it's a suicide message?"

Taking the tape, Jake briefly examined it and placed it in his jacket pocket. "We'll find out soon enough, thanks."

Blowing into latex gloves, Jake slipped one hand in, and then the other, as he proceeded toward the body. Randy followed suit, keeping a few paces behind his senior partner. Kneeling over the body, Jake took out his pen and lifted up the gun enough to look into the cylinder. "The chamber is empty. He only brought one bullet along," Jake said. "What if he flinched at the last second and didn't finish the job? He'd have to go back home with a missing ear to reload. That's very odd to me."

"I agree," Randy said.

"Why didn't he wear his standard black attire and white collar? Most people that take their own lives do it in the uniform that defines who they are and what they are most proud of. A soldier would typically wear his dress greens when he commits suicide. Do you know what I mean?"

Randy looked at Jake, understanding his point. "Maybe this is an unusual case. Maybe this guy was ashamed to wear his collar and decided to off himself in a sweatshirt instead."

Listening to his partner, Jake moved around the body. "That's a possibility."

Examining the body, Jake pointed with his pen. "Look here, the bullet passed through his right temple area and exited through his left cheek area. He was seated in this chair." Jake stood and walked over to the wall that was eight feet away and began studying the wall.

"Look here," Jake said, pointing his pen at a hole in the wall about two feet above the baseboard. "This is where the bullet ended up." Walking back to where the body was, Jake once again stooped down so that his head was about where LaPage's head would have been as he was seated in the chair. "If I was sitting here and I put a gun up to my head and pulled the trigger, the bullet would lodge in the wall right about here." Jake quickly walked over to the wall, pointing about three and a half feet from the floor. "In order for the bullet to end up a couple feet above the baseboard, he would have had to turn his head down, like this." Jake moved back to where the body was situated, demonstrating how his head would have been turned down in order for the bullet to resign where it had.

"So, at the last minute he turned his head down before pulling the trigger," Fran concluded.

"Maybe, or could it be that someone was standing here when they put the gun to his head and pulled the trigger?" Jake suggested.

Pulling a swab from his pocket, Jake bent down reaching below the chair. "It looks like he pissed himself." He took a culture and placed it into a small paper bag. "Why isn't there a urine stain on his pants or the chair? This chair is coming with us and going into evidence." Jake brought his hand to his chin and stood motionless. "This doesn't seem right to me," he said as he turned to Randy. "There are too many indications of foul play here."

"I think you may be reaching, partner," Randy deducted.

"I don't think so," Jake said. "Let's see what we get back from prints, photos and the lab."

"And more importantly, the tape," Randy added.

Jake and Randy brought the tape into Interview Room #2 and waited for Chief Mearald to arrive. The captain had the day off, or else he would have been there as well. Less than a minute later, the Chief entered the room and closed the door behind him.

"Anything on the gun yet?" Mearald asked, as he spun a chair around and plopped down.

"Not yet," Jake said. "They are still dusting for prints and should be wrapping that up very soon."

"Let it roll," the Chief ordered.

Jake pushed the button and the tape began to play. All three men sat without moving a muscle as LaPage's voice sounded.

This is Father Robert LaPage and this is my full confession. I am personally responsible for the sexual abuse of over forty young boys that had been placed in my trust over the past two decades. I am also responsible for the murder of Robert Anderson in 1972. I am truly sorry for all of the pain and suffering I have caused the children and their families and I am confessing to these crimes because I can't live with myself any longer. I need to be removed from society.

"Well, there you have it," Mearald said. "We have a full confession, not only for all the abused children, but the Anderson boy as well."

Jake leaned forward stretching out his back. "Why didn't he say anything about his pending death?"

"Who cares? We have his confession and we can close the case. We have a dead pedophile, and that certainly won't cause anyone to lose any sleep. I'll have a press conference scheduled and then we can move on."

"Chief, I'm not convinced that LaPage killed himself," Jake said, "Look, most people who commit suicide mention their intent to kill themselves in a letter or to someone they trust. To them, it is the most personal and sacred act they will ever commit. Also, he brought a gun with one bullet. This is also very unusual, not to mention some of the crime scene indicators. Give me some time before you release this to the public.

Mearald thought for a moment before responding. Jake thought his head would explode. "Jake, you have until tomorrow morning. By then all the prints and lab work should be completed."

"The prints will be done, but I'm not sure about the lab results," Jake said.

"Then I suggest you put a fire under their asses, Jake. You have until tomorrow morning."

"Let's play the tape again," Jake suggested. He re-wound the cassette and started the tape once again.

"Do you hear that?" Jake stopped the tape. "There's a pounding noise in the background." He continued rolling the tape. "There it is again, and again. What the hell is that noise?"

They listened again to the tape in its entirety. "During the confession there's a background noise; an inconsistent pounding of some sort, Jake said. "Can you guys make it out?" Jake looked to the two men seated with him.

"No," Randy conceded.

"It could be anything, maybe a guy swinging a hammer, or noise from a construction site next to where he taped his confession. It doesn't matter, Jake. This case is closed. Now I have work to do, and you have until tomorrow." The Chief got up and walked out without saying another word.

The next morning Jake marched directly to the Chief's office. Randy decided to sit it out and let Jake run with the ball. He was also feeling that the Chief was right and it was time to move on. Justice was served, even if it was with LaPage's own hand, he thought.

The Chief was on the phone when Jake popped his head around the corner. Mearald's demeanor clearly displayed unhappiness with the surprise visit. He waved him in and Jake took a seat.

"What have you got?" Mearald asked as he hung up the receiver.

"Well, there are several things that bother me about this case, Chief. I don't think he killed himself." Mearald turned over a frown and Jake knew he had to be very convincing in his sales pitch.

"What's bothering you, Jake?"

"There were no prints removed from LaPage's steering wheel. Not one. It was wiped clean."

The Chief stood up and walked over to his bookcase. "Who places the tips of their fingers on the wheel when they drive? I don't, I use my palms," Mearald rebutted.

"Also, the angle of the bullet was projected downward, and there was only one bullet in the gun," Jake added.

"That doesn't mean shit, Jake. So he turned his head down before pulling the trigger. Maybe he was saying a prayer in the end to avoid going to hell. As far as your one bullet theory, well, that's all it takes, Jake, one bullet."

Jake thought he had come to the meeting with a full load of ammunition, but he listened as Mearald depleted his magazine, one round at a time.

"Chief, they found a trace of polyethylene resin on his face. I think he was fastened to a chair, but not the chair tagged at the scene."

"What! Now you're suggesting that the killer switched chairs? Jake, you really need a vacation."

"Chief, the stain on the floor under the chair was LaPage's urine, and he had a urine stain on his underwear."

"So he pissed himself before pulling the trigger, or maybe after."

"There was no evidence of urine on the chair, Chief. How could he piss himself while seated and no traces of urine were found on the chair and very little on his pants?"

Mearald's ears moved; a tell-tale sign that he was deep in thought. Jake had picked up on that the second time they met. It was regarding the murder of a young woman in a convenience store robbery.

"Why would the killer bother to switch chairs, and why would he care if the guy pissed on himself?" Mearald asked.

"I've thought long and hard on this and I think the killer removed the original chair to avoid leaving any evidence that suggests anything other than a suicide. I believe he used duct tape to secure LaPage to a chair, and to muzzle him," Jake said. "This would account for the adhesive resin traces on his face, and he must have switched chairs to avoid any traces of tape on it."

"If he was fastened to a chair, then there would be evidence of duct tape resin on his clothing as well, right?" Mearald asked.

"Right," Jake belted out. "But there isn't any evidence of that because they switched his clothing as well."

"Now you think they changed his clothes?" Mearald's condescending tone irritated Jake. "This guy would have to be one clever cookie."

Jake slapped his palm against his knee. "He's brilliant," Jake said, "Except for the resin left on his face. He didn't get it all off."

"Jake, I've heard enough," Mearald said in a dismissive manner. "You have quite an imagination. The guy's conscience caught up with him, killed himself, and he left a confession. That's it in a nutshell."

"Then what about the glue on his face? It's pretty clear that his mouth was covered with tape."

"Who knows?" Mearald began pacing the floor as he spoke. "The guy was a freak. Maybe he and his boyfriend got off on some sort of twisted bondage game with duct tape. Now, I have a press conference in twenty minutes. This case is closed." His pacing ended at the entrance to his office.

Jake hesitated before rising to exit the room, allowing the agony of defeat to settle in. He walked out without saying a word. The look he gave Mearald said it all and the Chief didn't like it one bit. By the time Jake made it back to his desk he had gotten his second wind, he knew he couldn't give up, not yet. He was a fighter and he still had a fair amount of stamina left in this bout.

Bishop Reardon was in his study when the phone rang. He was finishing up paperwork before heading out for a day on the golf course. Looking at the phone, and then his watch, he figured he would let the machine pick it up and then he would determine who it was and if it was important enough to take.

At the end of his outgoing message, a long beep sounded, and then a voice came alive.

"Evan, this is Mark. If you're there, please pick up. You'll want to hear this."

Reardon figured the DA had something important to say, so he reached for the phone. "Hello Mark, what is it?"

"Put on the news. Chief Mearald is preparing to give a press conference in five minutes, but I wanted you to hear it from me first."

"Hear what?"

"Father LaPage committed suicide. He shot himself."

Grasping the receiver tight, Reardon sat upright in his chair. "What?"

"Apparently, his body was found yesterday in an abandoned warehouse with a fatal bullet wound to the head."

"My God," Reardon uttered.

"Evan, they found a tape in his pocket, confessing to sexually abusing over forty children." Corbin listened as the Bishop sighed on the other end. "There's more."

"Go on," Reardon said in an exasperated voice.

"LaPage also confessed to murdering the Anderson boy."

"My God," he said again.

"I know." The line went silent, and a few seconds later, Corbin broke the quiet with a cough. "Look at the bright side, Evan. Now this whole mess can be put to rest and the church can move on."

"Yes. What channel is the press conference on?"

"All of them. This has made national news, Evan."

"Thanks for the call Mark," he said in a subdued tone.

"Evan, do you think that we can *now* move forward with our development deal?"

"Jesus, Mark. Let me bury my priest first."

"Yes, of course," Corbin said, before the line went dead.

Corbin placed the phone down and sat back in his chair. This was the best thing that could possibly have happened. With this scandal behind them, Reardon would move forward in the land sale. Construction could begin before the winter set in. Things were looking good again, he thought, reaching for the phone to call the City Commissioner of Real Estate.

CHAPTER 34

Seated inside a diner in front of the television, Jake was gnawing on a tuna fish sandwich as Randy slurped down a bowl of turkey soup. "Can't you eat that a little quieter?" Jake asked.

"It's freaking hot, man."

"Then let it cool off, it's annoying."

Randy dropped his spoon in the bowl. "Look, just because your pissed off at the Chief, don't take it out on me."

"That son of a bitch debated every theory I put forth. It's like he doesn't care about the truth. He just wants to clear the docket and move on."

Tearing open a bag of oyster crackers, Randy began popping them in his mouth, one after the other. "Politics, man. It's all about politics. You watch, one day he'll be campaigning for mayor."

"You're probably right on target with that assumption. The scary thing is that he'll probably win. Here's the jellyfish now," Jake said, motioning toward the television.

They sat at the counter listening to Chief Mearald as they finished their lunches. Ten minutes later, Jake paid the bill and they headed for the car.

"Let's head down to the crime scene for a while."

"For what?" Randy asked.

"I have a feeling that we missed something and I can't think of a better place to think right now."

Inside the building, Jake headed right to the storage room where he took a seat on the floor, leaning up against the wall where the bullet had lodged. Randy followed suit and they both sat without speaking for a minute. Finally, Randy poked Jake's arm with his elbow. "Anything come to mind yet?"

"You know, I spent an hour the other night playing that damn tape over and over again, trying to figure out what that damn pounding noise was," Jake said.

"And what is your conclusion?"

"I don't know, but I figured we should come here and listen to see if we hear that sound from this location."

Randy exhaled and sat motionless for ten seconds. "Nope, don't hear it."

"I figure whoever killed LaPage forced the confession at gunpoint and that might have occurred right here in this room."

"Sorry to break up your party, Jake, but it's quiet as a morgue in here."

"I know. What time did the coroner estimate the time of death was?"

"Between ten and midnight," Randy said.

"Right, I think I need to come back tonight at that time and see if I hear that noise."

Randy hopped to his feet. Well, you're on your own tonight buddy. I have plans with a fine young lady."

"No problem," Jake said.

Randy reached out his hand and helped Jake to his feet. "You know, you may want to consider doing the same with Colleen tonight."

"Yeah, you're right. I need to do that, but not tonight," Jake said. "Let's get out of here."

That night Jake spent two hours sitting in the dark storage room listening for a sound similar to the one on the tape. He set his flashlight on the floor next to him with the light pointing upward, illuminating the ceiling. With his hands, he made motions above the light, creating animal figures on the ceiling, just like he did as a child. He started with an eagle and then a tarantula, and finished with his masterpiece, the barking dog. As time ticked on toward midnight, his disappointment took residence. Jake concluded that there wasn't anything more to go on and he had lost all support from the Chief. In the morning, he would be assigned another case by Captain Farris and that would consume most of his time. *If the Chief would only listen to reason, he would see how clear it is that LaPage was murdered.*

Pushing himself to his feet, Jake followed the light to the outside and he turned off the flashlight. Peering up at the night sky, the stars were magnificent, he thought. His mind drifted to Colleen and how he had fallen in love with her. Now that the case was over, he hoped he could make things right, but he had one last thing to do.

The next morning, Jake and Randy sat in Captain Farris's office while he fetched himself a cup of coffee. Jake was amazed how one man could consume so much coffee in a day without going into cardiac arrest. Farris came buzzing in with his twenty-ounce travel mug, and slid in behind his desk.

"When I heard the news of LaPage's death, and his confession in the Anderson murder, I nearly fell out of my chair with joy. That damn case was sucking up too many man hours and I have way too many unsolved cases on the docket to close out," Farris said, reaching for his crutch that was warming a small spot on his desk.

"Yeah, well I'm not convinced that LaPage is responsible for the Anderson murder," Jake said.

"I know. The Chief briefed me on your theory yesterday. It's over, Jake. I have a new case for you guys to work on." He lifted a folder from his desk and handed it to Jake.

Jake quickly opened the folder, scanning it like a speed reader. "A dead hooker," Jake said.

"I like hookers," Randy professed. "Hookers are fun." Randy saw that Jake was not amused and the Captain just frowned and continued.

"She was found in her apartment, raped and strangled with a belt. No prints, no eyewitnesses, no motive. Just a dead body and a belt. It's two days old, so you better get moving," Farris insisted. "Everything we have is in that report and you can talk to Wickman and Blakely if you have any questions. They were the initial investigators on this case. Any questions?"

Jake could see Farris was jonesing for another cup. "Just one," Jake said. "What case did you put Wickman and Blakely on?"

"They're on the Dancing case."

"The lawyer that was found shot to death? Jake asked.

"That's right. Now go and find out who killed Ms. Biggs."

"Yeah, thanks Cap."

It was apparent by Jake's tone and expression that he was agitated. He shot up and swung open the door and Randy followed him out and over to his desk. "That son of a bitch pulled his two cronies off a hooker murder and put them on the Dancing case. He should have given that case to us."

Randy nodded, understanding where Jake was coming from, believing once a detective is assigned a case, he should see it through. This type of action was a morale buster in any detective bureau.

"It is what it is," Randy said.

"Yeah, let's go," Jake said. "We have one stop to make before we go interview the neighbors of Ms. Biggs."

"Where's that?"

"To see the owner of the gun that killed LaPage, a Mr. Robert Brock."

"There's not much more I can tell you that I didn't say on the phone." Brock quietly closed the door to the real estate office where he worked, obviously attempting to keep the detectives out of the view of his co-workers. "My house was burglarized back in 1973 and they took the gun," he whispered.

Interviewing Brock while standing in a small hallway was not the best of situations, but Jake resigned himself to the fact that it was the best they could do under the circumstances.

"Were there any leads in the case, or any indication of who the perpetrators may have been?" Jake asked.

"No, nothing."

"What else was taken?" Randy asked with his pen at the ready.

"Some cash, a painting, and my wife's diamond broach." He peeked inside the door and then slowly closed it, trying to make as little noise as possible.

"What type of painting and broach?" Jake asked.

"It's all in the report. Can't you guys pull the file?"

"Yes, and we will," Jake said patiently, "but we would appreciate it if you would cooperate, *now*."

Brock's sigh was powerful enough to knock Randy over with his halitosis. "It was an original Pino and the broach was a sitting lion."

"What was the estimated value?" Randy asked, as he took a half step back.

"It was a long time ago." Brock popped his head inside the office again.

"Ballpark is fine," Jake said.

"I don't know. I would say the painting was worth around twelve or fifteen thousand and the broach, maybe five."

"The painting would be worth a lot more today," Randy added.

"Where did you buy the gun?" Jake asked.

"Carbella's. Look, it's all in the report. I have to get back in the office. My boss is in from New York."

"Alright," Jake said, wondering how much money Brock made selling commercial real estate. It was an expensive painting that was stolen, so Jake figured he made a very good living. "One last thing," Jake said.

Turning back in disappointment like a sprinter in a false start, "What?" Brock hissed.

"Is there anyone you can think of that may have been responsible for stealing your gun?"

Agitated, Brock looked toward the ceiling for a brief second and then back at Jake, "No."

Jake pulled a card from his pocket and handed it to Brock. "Call me if anything comes to mind." In a flash he was gone and the door eased shut behind him.

Two days later, Jake and Colleen sat at the kitchen table with slices of apple pie in front of them. Jake's house smelled like the salmon they just ate and he wondered how long it would be until it was back to normal. Colleen was a pretty good cook, and she could bake too. The meal was shared over few words and a mutual appreciation for peace and quiet. Colleen hadn't brought up the

Anderson case because it had created a wedge between them, and she wanted that space to be clear of all obstacles.

Jake cut a large chunk off his desert and fit it into his mouth. "I want to apologize for being so distant these last few months."

The corners of Colleen's mouth pointed up. "Apology accepted." She began eating in smaller bites.

"I was consumed with finding the boy's killer. I was only ten years older than he was when I found him, and now I'm twenty years older and I still feel like I can't get closure"

Sympathizing with Jake, Colleen reached out, gently covering his hand with hers. "It must have been very hard for you, but now it's over, thank God."

Pulling his hand away, Jake stabbed the pie and consumed another bite. "He didn't do it," he said.

"Who?" She put down her fork. "Who didn't do it?"

"LaPage. I don't think he killed the Anderson boy."

"That's not what they're saying all over the news," she said wonderingly.

"Don't believe everything you hear on the news, Colleen. They were determined to close this case, and his confession wrapped it up with a big red bow. There are too many unanswered questions, and the Chief can't be bothered to even look into them." He frowned.

"Jake, what's bothering you?" She took his hand again. "What unanswered questions?

"I believe that whoever killed LaPage made him confess to murdering Robby Anderson."

"Why?"

"Maybe because the person who killed LaPage also murdered Robby Anderson, and now, he's in the clear. Why else would he make sure LaPage confessed to the Anderson murder?" Jake asked. "If it were just about revenge for his crimes, the killer would have forced him to confess to abusing children. Why bring up a nineteen year old murder, unless he was directly impacted by it?"

"It all sounds so fantastic," she said. "Can you prove any of this?"

"No," he said like a defeated prize fighter.

She got up and moved to Jake's end of the table and slid onto his lap. "Maybe you should move on and try and put this all behind you."

Jake dismissed Colleen's suggestion without thought. "What bothers me is that no one really cares about the truth. They just want it to be done with, even if the real killer is still out there."

Colleen pulled him closer and kissed him on the cheek. "I care," she said.

He ran his fingers through her hair. "I'm the luckiest man on earth to have you."

"And you do have me, you know?"

He smiled and kissed her on the lips. "It's a beautiful night outside, let's have tea on the deck," he suggested.

The tea-pot whistled and they retired to the backyard. Jake sat next to Colleen looking up at the night sky. Clouds were migrating in, smothering the brilliant stars.

"Have you heard from your family?" he asked.

"Just my mother. I haven't spoken to my father or brother since the party."

"Have they made any effort to reconcile with you?" Jake asked.

"Are you kidding? To them it was entirely my fault."

"How can it possibly be your fault? You were in the kitchen."

"Don't you understand, Jake, they're both ignorant bigots."

"Well, I hope it works out for you all," he said thoughtfully.

At that very moment a breeze winded the chimes hanging off the deck railing, offering a nocturn into the quiet night air. The still of the night was broken in an instant. Jake's heart began beating at a faster rate; his mind raced and a chill spread throughout his entire body. With his thoughts now fixed on the pounding noise on the tape, an overwhelming feeling came over him.

"The wind," he muttered.

"What?" she asked with a confused.

"I have to go, I'll explain later." He leaned over and kissed her on the forehead and he plotted on.

Randy had just gotten out of the shower when the phone rang. He had a hard workout at the gym and was looking forward to a lazy evening in front of the TV. Randy had a feeling that he shouldn't pick up, but his curiosity got the best of him.

"Hello."

"Randy, its Jake. I need you to meet me at the factory crime scene, now."

"Now? What's going on?" His voice was less than enthusiastic.

"I'll explain when you get there, and bring a tape recorder."

Randy could hear the excitement in Jake's voice. "Okay, I'll see you in a few."

Jake sat in the same spot he always did with his back against the wall where the LaPage bullet had lodged in the wall. The wind had picked up and he sat listening to a pounding noise coming from the corner of the main factory floor. When Jake entered the building, he immediately heard a loud banging noise and it was music to his ears. With flashlight in hand, he discovered a large opening to the outside, and when a strong wind erupted, it caused a piece of sheet metal to sway back and forth, crashing against the plywood. Without a strong wind, Jake would never be able to hear the distinct crashing sound inside in the factory.

"Jake." Randy's voice echoed off the bare walls.

"In here." First Jake saw the light, and then the shadow.

"Is that what I think it is?" Randy asked as he entered the room.

"Yes it is," Jake smiled. "Do you have the tape recorder?"

"Absolutely," he responded with enthusiasm.

Randy pushed the button and the tape started to roll. They were both motionless, not making a sound. After a minute, Randy stopped the tape.

"Play it back," Jake said.

"Happy to." Randy pushed the button and they listened to the entire sequence.

Once it ended, Randy pushed the stop button and examined his partner. "It's exactly the same," he said.

"Yep," Jake replied with a grin. "And this means that LaPage's confession was taped right here. Unless he came here and taped his confession, left to get rid of the tape player, returned with the tape in his pocket, and shot himself. No, he was murdered," Jake concluded.

"You know partner, I find that highly unlikely," Randy said with a vast smile.

Jake reached out his hand and Randy ejected the tape and handed it over. "We'll see what the Chief has to say, *now*," Jake said.

"Jake, I gotta hand it to you. You were right all the time. Someone killed the son of a bitch."

"Yeah, but the question is, why did they make sure he confessed to the murder of Robby Anderson?"

"That is the million dollar question, isn't it?" Randy asked. "Let's get the hell out of here. This place gives me the willies."

"Randy." Jake reached out and shook his hand. "Good job." Jake's appreciation of Randy's dedication and performance settled nicely with Randy because positive recognition was seldom realized in the department, but if you made one significant mistake it might stay with you your whole career.

The next morning, Jake and Randy were waiting by Chief Mearald's office when he came in. The secretary listened as a verbal battle ensued behind closed doors. When the fight was over, the two detectives walked out with a clear look of defeat on their faces. Mearald had stuck to his guns, insisting that the case was closed, even though they played the tape of the banging sound, comparing it to the confessional tape.

Jake pushed the door open and stormed out, the door swung open so fast it crashed against the wall. "That son of a bitch has no integrity," he said loud enough for the Chief's secretary to hear.

"Take it easy, Jake," Randy said.

They marched down the hallway side by side, like a pair of tin soldiers. “I have the right mind to take this to the media.”

“I don’t think that’s a very good idea, if you value your career,” Randy said.

Jake thought hard. “You’re right.” He stopped in his tracks. “I’ll take it to the Bishop and let him bring it to the media,” he said in defiance.

CHAPTER 35

The living room was dimly lit with dark gray blinds covering the windows. Van Morrison's "Moon Dance" sounded at a minimal decibel though a room flooded with smoke.

Michael sat in a corner chair with a cigarette in one hand and a cup of black tea in the other. An overflowing ashtray rested on a travel magazine that he had read twice over. He needed to get away; to escape the gloom that came with the death of his brother and the reoccurring vision of LaPage's life being snuffed out by his hand.

Hearing a knock on his door, he didn't move, wishing whoever it was would go away. The knock grew louder and he remained defiant in his quest to remain alone with his miserable existence.

"Mike, it's Steve. Open the door." The banging became louder as Stephen began kicking the door with the bottom of his boot. "I know you're in there. Open the damned door!"

Michael moped his way across the room and opened up. "What?"

Stephen walked in past his friend, opened the refrigerator, and grabbed a can of Miller beer.

"Look at you," he said. Michael's hair was in shambles and he was unshaven. "You look like you haven't taken a shower in a month. What the hell is going on with you, man?"

Back in his chair, Michael took a sip of tea. "I don't feel well."

"What's the problem?" Stephen popped open his beer and tipped it back.

"I don't know. My back is killing me."

"You look like shit," Stephen said. "You're thinning out and your color isn't right. What you need is a few beers, a cheeseburger, and some pussy."

"I'm just caught up in a funk," he downplayed.

"Well, snap out of it, brother. We have a lot of partying to do."

"Yeah, well, maybe tomorrow."

"Have you been following the news?" Stephen asked. "They

bought into LaPage's confession and they believe he whacked himself out. We're in the clear."

"Yeah, I saw that."

"You don't sound too excited about it."

"That's because I feel like shit."

"Then go to the doctor and get some drugs."

"I'll give it a couple days first."

"Mike, I gotta go before I catch what you got. Feel better." A light punch on Michael's shoulder and Stephen was gone.

Three days later Stephen was in the hospital, standing over Michael as he lay in bed with an IV in his arm. "So what did the doctor say?"

"They took x-rays and found an abnormality in my right lung."

"What kind of abnormality?"

"He's not sure, so they did an MRI, and we should have the results this afternoon."

"It's those cancer sticks you keep sucking on," Stephen shook his head. "How are you feeling?"

"Tired."

"Alright, you get some sleep and I'll be back later this afternoon. By next week you'll be getting laid with a bottle of whiskey at your side, instead of this shit." He gestured toward a bottle of apple juice on the bed stand.

When Stephen returned that afternoon, the doctor was coming out of Michael's room, so he stopped him, pulling him aside. He was a young narrow guy with full dark hair and glasses. "I'm his best friend Steve. What's going on? How's he doing?"

The doctor quickly looked at Stephen, sensing his concern. "Dr. Benson," he said, shaking Stephen's hand. "We think Michael may have a tumor in his lung; we are performing an EUS in the morning."

"A tumor!" Stephen paused as the enormity settled in. "What's an EUS?"

"It's an endoscopic ultrasound and we'll do a biopsy while were in there." Stephen knew what that meant and he knew it wasn't good. "We should know more in a day or two. Check back then." He gently squeezed Stephen's shoulder and moved on.

Jake passed under the tall, iron gate that he named the Gate of Angels. Tracking the slate walkway to the front door of the Bishop's house, the door swung open as he approached, and an older woman appeared with Sister Hathaway following. "Everything will work out fine Grace," the Nun assured her.

"Thank you, Sister." She took baby steps back down the walkway, passing Jake, acknowledging him with a slight bow of her head. Jake thought about baby steps and how a person really begins taking those steps when they become old. As a toddler, we take off once we find our legs. It's when we're old that we lose our strength and balance, and resign to a slow and careful pace, like a prisoner in leg shackles.

Sister Hathaway's attention was now focused on Jake, as he approached with his hand extended. "Hello Sister, I see your roses are healthy."

"Yes, a happy bunch they are. Why are we so blessed with your visit today, Detective Waterfield?"

Her pleasant greeting was genuinely welcoming. "I thought I'd stop and take a chance that I might catch Bishop Reardon."

"I'm sorry. He has stepped out and won't return until this evening. Is there a message?"

"No, it's important that I speak with him in person."

"Then I'm afraid you'll have to catch him another time." She smiled. "Is there anything else?"

Jake hadn't expected to bump into the Sister, but there was something serene about her company that he enjoyed, and there were a few things he wanted to ask her.

"Sister, could we talk for a few minutes?"

"Sure, let's go to the garden."

Jake followed Sister Hathaway to the rear of the dwelling where a small table and three chairs were situated at the far end of the garden next to the convent building where she lived. Jake pulled a chair out for her and she humbly nodded and took the seat. He sat across from her.

"I'd like to ask you about Father LaPage." Her expression remained constant. "How well did you know him?"

"As well as I know any of the priests in our diocese. I have assisted him in some of God's work on occasion. We had food drives and conducted spiritual healing clinics together, things of that sort.

"What do you make of everything that has happened with regards to him?"

"Detective, I'll leave judgment to the Lord."

"I don't believe he killed himself," Jake said. "I think he was murdered, and possibly by the same person that killed the Anderson boy."

She touched the cross hanging off her neck, squeezing it between her fingers.

"I do, however, believe that he was guilty of molesting many young boys," Jake said, as he peered across the yard at the roses lined up, blooming in the sun. "So many boys," he added.

"If this is true, he is being judged on the other side," she said. "One can escape his conscience, but not his fate."

Jake thought about Sister Hathaway's comment and it confirmed why he enjoyed her company. Her words were always carefully chosen.

"Sister, do you have any thoughts about who is responsible for the death of Robby Anderson?"

"I try to keep thoughts like that out of my head, Detective Waterfield. Focusing on the positive things in life is a more pleasant existence, wouldn't you agree?"

"Yes, I do, Sister. Unfortunately, in my line of work it's a difficult reality. Someone has to find and remove the bad people from our streets, and that's what I do."

"I understand the choices you have made in your life and I applaud your efforts," she said with sincerity.

Jake took out a piece of paper, unfolded it, and handed it to her. "Do you recognize this button?"

Her eyebrows elevated a notch as she examined the drawing. "It looks like a sailor's button." She handed it back.

"Yes, but it's not a military button. It's been hard to trace because there's so many buttons in the world with anchors on them," he said. "We have ruled out the military."

"I can't help you," she said as she took to her feet.

"Thank you for your time, Sister. I find your company very comforting."

She smiled. "I believe the Lord has a place for you in heaven, Detective Waterfield." As he walked out of the compound, he hoped she was right, if in fact there is such a thing as Heaven. He wasn't sure he believed that any longer.

Watching Jake disappear into the street, Sister Hathaway thought about the day she learned of the murder of Robert Anderson. It was such as senseless destruction of innocent life and a horrific experience for the boy and his family. Her thoughts began to drift back to when she was a young woman of sixteen.

Life in the small town of Shuttersfield, New York was monotonous and unsatisfying. Living in a town that consisted of 337 citizens was a hard way to grow up for Patricia. The most exciting event was the annual traveling carnival that came to town every autumn.

In the back seat of Bobby Harrelson's beat up Pontiac, Patricia knew she shouldn't have let it go so far. If she rejected his advances, he might not call her again, and she would have to wait for the fall for another dose of fun. Having a boyfriend with a car, she might be able to catch a movie or an occasional dance.

Bobby wasn't ready to stop at third base. He wanted to hit a grand slam. The pinch she felt inside was uncomfortable at first, and then it began to feel pleasurable. Bobby's promises were never realized, and her life was back to where it started, except for an abrupt change two months later.

Devout Catholics, Patricia's parents were outraged and totally unreasonable regarding the circumstance that had befallen their only daughter. Her father's first reaction was to disown her and he refused to look at her for three weeks. Patricia's mother wasn't quite as stern, but her disposition was cold and distant. With little to no self esteem, Patricia wanted to curl up and die. She was all alone in the world, except for the child that grew inside her. With no one to comfort her, she survived by talking to her baby. At night she would tell stories of a happy and thriving life in the city with huge department stores and theaters where they could attend plays. There were fancy restaurants with menus four pages long and scores of gentlemen calling to escort them in their shiny new cars. One gentleman might even take them both on a picnic in the park where they would toss a ball around and have their swings pushed to the limit. Life will be an exciting adventure filled with fun, peace, and love.

The day they came to take her away, it was a cold, rainy morning. She pleaded with her father to reconsider, but he defiantly turned away, insisting he knew what was best for her and the unborn child. It was as though he was made of granite, completely devoid of regard or pity for his daughter's condition and feelings. When she reached for her mother, her arms remained empty and her cries died in the moist air, leaving a void in both her family and her heart. If it weren't for her child, she would have jumped off a cliff to end the agonizing pain that tore her up inside.

Life at the Handmaids of Mary convent was peaceful and structured. Patricia, along with the other young apprentices, spent much of the day in deep prayer. Three meals a day and a warm bed was a guarantee at the convent, however, graduating was only realized by those that excelled in their studies. Theology was much harder than she had thought it would be, but she took to it with a passion, gaining a sense of comfort in learning about Jesus and his teachings. The suffering that Jesus endured for our sins made her troubles seem minimal at best, she thought.

As her mid-section bloomed, she began finding it harder to kneel for prayer, so she began praying in a sitting position. The young ladies at the convent were taught not to be judgmental, but she could not help noticing the glares of indifference by her flat-bellied peers.

Patricia took pride in her work and she knew she was outpacing most of her classmates. As the end of her third trimester approached, a few of her classmates came to her and asked if they could join her in a study group, and she gracefully accepted. Life at the convent was becoming much more than a school for her, it was becoming a family.

Once a month she would receive a generic letter from her mother, who kept reassuring her that what they did was for her own good. She knew it was guilt rising to the surface, and she never indicated that she had adapted to the convent and found it a better home than the one her parents had provided. The resentment she carried for her parents was dissipating with each passing day. One passage kept coming to mind: "To forgive is divine."

The day her water broke, Patricia was sitting in a church pew, praying, when she felt a warm sensation rolling down her legs. A little embarrassed, she calmly rose and walked outside where she made it known to one of her friends who immediately jumped into action.

In Saint Joseph's Hospital, Patricia was content with the professionalism and concern for the health and well-being of her and her child. She was not prepared for an extended labor that dragged on for twenty hours, or the pain that accompanied it. When the baby finally surfaced, it came fast, and he jumped to life with his first cry. "It's a boy," she heard a nurse say. Reaching out so she could take her child her bosom and comfort him, her arms found no weight, her bosom found no child, and her heart sank to her stomach.

As her baby was quickly shuffled out of the room, Patricia

understood where the real pain was realized that day. The pain of the flesh was far less hurtful than the pain of the heart.

Sister Hathaway stood under the Gate of Angels with tears rolling down her face. She looked up at the angels above her, wondering where her boy was today and what kind of a man he had turned out to be. Once again, she felt a familiar pain inside, just like the one she felt the day her infant child was taken away. Wiping the tears away, she gained her composure, and turned to look at the magnificent compound that she called home.

CHAPTER 36

It was 7:03 a.m. when Jake and Randy ordered breakfast at The Rising Sun Diner. The customers were a diverse bunch of professionals and blue collar workers scrambling to get their fill before heading off for their nine-to-five workday. The overtired pair of detectives tactically sat in a corner booth with their backs against the wall with a clear view of everyone in the establishment.

Randy flipped a newspaper page. "Did you see the deal the city and the church are putting together?"

"No, I missed that." He had Jake's attention.

"It's right here. The Commissioner of Real Property for the city, Terrence Perkins, has announced the sale of the eastern quadrant of Bottle Park by the Diocese of Middleborough to the City of Middleborough for the development of custom homes. The Bishop has given a statement assuring that the new development will not affect the normal park functions or limit any access to the park from the eastern entrance."

"Let me see that." Jake took the paper and fixed his eyes on the article. "Son of a bitch," he said bitterly. Once he completed the article, he slapped the paper onto the table. "Do you know how tight Perkins and the DA are?"

"Is that a fact?" Randy said.

"Now here's a story. Corbin is in bed with the Bishop and Corbin is also in bed with Perkins. Corbin brokers a deal for the City through Perkins to buy land from the church. How much would you like to bet that the land is being bought at a very low price and sold at a premium to the construction company?"

"I'm feeling the connection here," Randy said. "It sounds like one big orgy to me."

"Yeah, and what do you think Corbin has to gain from this deal?" Jake asked.

Randy's eyes shifted to the ceiling. "Looking at the size of this deal, I would say quite a bit."

"And what do you think Bishop Reardon gains from all of this?"

"A huge favor from District Attorney Corbin," Randy said. "And maybe even some kickback of his own."

"Right, that favor may have already happened with the disappearance of an item from the evidence room and who knows how many other favors in the last two decades."

"The button," Randy said.

"Bingo!" The waitress came over with their breakfast and placed the plates down. "After breakfast, how about we take a walk in Bottle Park?"

"I could use a walk this morning," Randy concurred. "Get the circulation in my dogs flowing."

For the exception of a couple runners and a man walking his dog, the park was quiet. They parked the car at the northern entrance and started on foot toward the location where Robby's body was found nearly two decades earlier.

Jake stopped, took a deep breath, and scanned the area in quiet thought. "This is where I found him." He pointed to the ground.

The look on his face told Randy a story. Jake was haunted by the memory of the dead boy, and the unsolved murder had left a dark cloud over his head that followed him throughout most of his career.

"I know how this case has tormented you over the years. I'm sorry you had to be the one to find him like that," Randy said sincerely. "You're a good man, Jake."

Jake didn't respond, he just looked at his friend and nodded.

"What do you say we walk to the eastern side of the park," Randy suggested. "Who knows, we might find the DA operating an excavator or something," Randy said with a laugh.

Jake smiled. "Sure, let's walk over there."

"Have you gotten an appointment with the Bishop yet?" Randy asked.

"Yeah, I'm going to see him the day after tomorrow."

"Good luck with that," Randy said with a hint of sarcasm.

"Let me ask you something."

"Shoot," Randy said.

"How come you always decline to come with me when I'm heading toward a church?"

"I don't know, Jake. I guess it's because I get freaked out by the religious types. Don't get me wrong, I believe there's a higher power and I consider myself to be spiritual, but organized religion isn't my bag."

Jake stopped in his tracks. "You know, not all religious people are bad. There are some really good people in the Catholic Church. I met a nun that lives at the Bishop's compound and she is something special, almost like an angel."

"I suppose you're right," he agreed, and they continued walking. "It's just when I hear about the child abuse and corruption within the church, I get turned off by it all."

"I understand," Jake said. "There is good and bad everywhere. We just need to be able to take every individual, case by case, and determine what kind of person they are, based on how they treat other people and what do with their life."

"It looks like we have arrived at the future construction site of Reardon & Corbin developers," Randy said with a smirk.

Jake surveyed his surroundings and was in awe by the sight of a beautiful meadow with scattered wild flowers and straw grass flowing with the breeze. The landscape was lined with tall birch and oak trees that stood watch over a peaceful place that seemed uncorrupted and sacred.

"What a waste turning this into a housing development," Jake said. "This is the most beautiful part of this park."

"In my opinion, greed is the worst of all the seven deadly sins," Randy said thoughtfully.

Jake nodded in agreement and took a deep breath of clean air. "Greed," he said.

Jake stood at the front entrance to the Bishop's house anticipating the heavy mahogany door to swing open. His plan was to plant the seed that LaPage was murdered and hopefully the Bishop would bring it to the attention of the media. If this was accomplished, he would have a case showing that LaPage's confession was coerced, and the killer of Robby Anderson was still at large. Having the Bishop open this can of worms would accomplish his goal and leave him in the clear with the Chief's office, at least for the time being. Jake figured the Bishop would prefer that his Priest had been murdered; rendering the tape inadmissible and opening up the possibility that LaPage was innocent of killing the boy. With all the negative press on the diocese, the community's perception of the Church and its Clergy needed to be brought back into good graces. Jake figured the Bishop would see that this might be a means to that end.

The door opened and the Bishop's assistant asked him in. "Bishop Reardon will be with you momentarily," she said in monotone, as if she were programmed. She slowly moved across the floor like a zombie on Quaaludes and Jake followed her to the study. "You can wait in here for Bishop Reardon."

"Thank you," Jake said as he entered the room. She turned and walked in the other direction. Quickly surveying the room, Jake realized that it was nothing more than Bishop Reardon's personal shrine. With his hands clasped behind his back, he began to slowly pace the room studying who Reardon was and what he had accomplished.

His bookstand rowed all his favorite theological works and novels flanked by brass angel bookends. A small table in the corner displayed trophies from his younger days when he was an avid golfer and fisherman. Passing by the many awards nailed to the wall, he learned that Reardon had graduated from Columbia University, and went on to complete graduate school at Yale. It was apparent by the awards neatly lined up that he had dedicated most of his life to noble causes like creating battered women's shelters, last wishes for terminally ill children, cancer research fundraising, and an AIDS research foundation. Several other awards covered most of the east wall.

Jake passed behind the desk to the west side of the study and began perusing the professionally framed photographs, most of which were eight-by-tens. Standing high and centered was a photograph of Reardon and Pope John Paul at the Vatican. It was obvious this was his most prized picture. Next to it was a shot of Reardon shaking hands with President Carter. There was a photograph of the Bishop standing proud at the country club, resting on a nine iron with Jack Nicklaus smiling at his side. Moving along, he glanced at his watch wondering where the Bishop was. Stopping in front of a picture of Reardon holding up a huge striper for all to admire, Jake thought this man was quite interesting, and he was looking forward to meeting him.

Scanning the picture wall, something caught Jake's eye. He moved in for a closer look. As the picture came into focus, a tingling sensation started at the base of his skull and quickly shot down his spine, ending at his feet. Hearing his heart beat louder and faster, he closed his eyes, and then re-opened them to make sure he wasn't seeing things. A strange feeling erupted in the pit of his stomach and his mouth was suddenly parched. *It can't be.* Jake was staring into Bishop Reardon's eyes, as he stood in the photograph in front of a large yacht wearing a gray sweater with black buttons and holding a trophy in his hand. As he looked closer, it was clear that the insignia in the center of the buttons were that of an anchor. The same anchor on a button he had found so many years ago in Bottle Park next to the body of Robby Anderson.

Reaching into his pocket, Jake took out his drawing and held it next to the picture. It was an exact match. Jake couldn't believe his eyes, but it was true. The bishop was there the night Robby was killed, and he may have had something to do with the murder of his own priest. He tucked the drawing back in his pocket.

"Sergeant Waterfield." A voice startled him and he briefly tensed up before turning around to see who it was. "I apologize for the delay," Reardon said metallically. "I had an urgent matter to attend to."

"That's fine," Jake said.

"I'm Bishop Reardon. You wanted to speak with me regarding Robert LaPage?" He didn't offer his hand and Jake was comfortable with that.

"Yes." The recent discovery was making Jake's head spin and

he had to change his whole line of questioning. "Had you ever noticed anything strange about Mr. LaPage? Did he ever show any indication that he was suicidal?"

Reardon watched Jake closely and noticed that he seemed to be somewhat distracted. "I didn't notice anything unusual that might lead me to think he would have taken his own life, but with all the negative press, he certainly was not himself."

"Yes." Jake rubbed his eyes and moved around the desk thinking of what to say next. A picture kept flashing in his mind of Reardon standing over the dead boy wearing a gray sweater.

"Did he ever indicate to you that he had a gun?"

"No." Reardon stood stationary in the corner of the room with his hands folded in front of him. He didn't offer a seat to Jake, because he was hoping he wouldn't stay long. "I don't condone that kind of behavior from my priests."

"I don't suppose you would." Jake started toward the entrance. He was already thinking of how he was going to get a warrant to search Reardon's house, and how it wasn't going to go over well with the Chief and the DA. His new discovery had changed everything including his line of questioning. There wasn't much he could discuss with Reardon now. "I think that's all for now," Jake said. "Thanks for your time."

"Good day." Reardon politely responded from his location in the corner.

Once Jake was out of the house, Reardon walked to the front window and drew the curtain back, watching Jake as he quickly shuffled up the street. He was puzzled by how fast Jake's visit was and how incomplete his line of questioning had been. After Jake was out of site, Reardon went back into his study and closed the door behind him. He walked over to the place where Jake had been standing when he entered the room. Reardon found himself standing in front of one of his sailing pictures, the one where he was wearing a gray sweater. He reached out and removed the picture from the wall, contemplating which picture he would replace it with.

CHAPTER 37

Lined up over a golf ball with his putter, Mearald was in his office practicing when a knock at the door interrupted his concentration. "What!" he yelled out.

"Chief, Detectives Waterfield and Applebee are here to see you," his assistant announced in a mousy voice.

"Son of a bitch," he muttered and took the shot, missing the ball retriever completely. "I'll be right out."

Mearald's assistant moved her ear from the door and went back into the reception area where the two detectives stood impatiently waiting. "He will be with you shortly," she said, as she rolled her eyes and maneuvered behind her desk.

Less than a minute later, the door swung open. "Come in," Mearald hollered. Jake and Randy did as they were told, and it was apparent to both of them the Chief was in a bad mood. He slammed the door shut behind them. "I hope you're here to tell me you found the perp on the hooker murder and not some bullshit conspiracy theory on the Anderson case."

Randy looked at Jake and it was evident to all that he was going to do the talking. "Chief, this is not about the hooker."

"I don't want to hear anymore about the Anderson case, it's closed!" he roared.

"Just hear me out, Chief," Jake asked in an elevated tone. He took out the drawing of the button.

"Not the damned button again," Mearald said.

"I went to see the Bishop."

"You did what?" His face was ember red.

"I went to see Bishop Reardon, and while I was waiting for him, I spotted a photograph on his picture wall and he was in the picture standing in front of a yacht."

"So what?"

"Chief, he had on a gray sweater with black buttons, the same button as the drawing." He snapped the paper in his hand. "The buttons in his photograph are exactly the same as the button I found at the murder scene, the same button that disappeared from the evidence room."

Mearald rubbed his clean shaven chin, his eyes lodged on the drawing. "What do you want to do with this, Jake? You don't have a button to prove it's the same as the one in the picture. All you have is some half-ass drawing that you made up." He cracked his knuckles. "Hell, you don't even know if the button you say you found at the scene was related to the crime. Where do you think you can go from here?"

"I want to get a warrant to search his house." Jake knew this was going to go over like a fart in church.

"You what? Have you completely lost your fucking mind? Do you have any idea of the implications that would come from this?"

"Chief, I'll take my chances on that. I am just trying to uncover the truth."

"You listen to me, Jake. It's not just you that will catch hell on this. My ass will be in a sling along with yours, and I don't want my ass in a sling, Jake."

"Listen, Chief. If we find the sweater with a missing button, we can put Reardon at the scene of the murder. Fitch was there with me and he logged the button into evidence. He will testify that the missing button is the same as the one we found at the scene. Maybe we can sweat him and get a confession."

"No," Mearald said defiantly.

"Let us try, Chief," Randy pleaded.

"Look, chances are you won't find a sweater, and if you do, he isn't going to confess. We have no murder weapon and no eye witnesses that can put him at the scene on the crime. He's a very bright man and he won't just roll over based on very shaky trace evidence."

"We have to try," Jake insisted.

"The answer is no. Now get the hell out of my office and find the guy that killed the hooker." Mearald rushed to the door, pulling it open. "Get out!"

Without speaking the two men filed out.

"What are we going to do now?" Randy asked as they marched down the hall and out the front door.

"We are going to find a judge to issue us a warrant,"

"Are you crazy? You heard the Chief. It's over, Jake."

"Nothing is over!" Jake yelled. "A twelve-year-old boy had his life torn away, and in a vicious and brutal way, I might add. Who knows what the hell happened to him before that?" He grabbed Randy by the arm, stopping him. "I'm going to nail the son of a bitch, and if I lose my job in the process, so be it."

"Well, I'm not putting my career on the line for your one man crusade," Randy snapped. "I've gone through too much shit on this job over the years to throw it all away on a hunch and a missing button."

"Then just stay out of my way," Jake scorned.

"Look, Jake, I want to catch the bastard that killed the kid too." He toned down his voice. "I just want to do it right and nail him clean."

"I understand," Jake said. "I have to find out if he has a sweater with a missing button. If he does, then I'll know he was involved, and then I can take my time, and eventually I'll prove it. If you don't want to be part of this, I'll understand completely."

"When you have something solid, I'll be happy to take him down with you," Randy said.

"Understood," Jake said. He was a little disappointed, but he knew he would have done the same if he were Randy.

At the diner, Jake and Fitch sat across from each other as the waitress placed down a cup of coffee and an orange juice.

"You still don't drink coffee?" Fitch asked.

"Never touch the stuff, it makes me tired."

Fitch laughed and poured cream in his cup. "So what do you want to do?"

"I need a judge to grant a warrant to search his house." Jake tugged on his ear eliminating an itch.

"That's not going to be easy. Mearald is not supporting this, right?"

"That prick has no backbone," Jake hissed. "He's going to take my job for this, you know."

"Most judges will call the Chief's office before issuing such a writ and probably the DA as well. If those two aren't on board, you'll never get the warrant."

"There has to be a judge who wants to uncover the truth, maybe a judge with a teenage boy- or an atheist," Jake grimaced.

"I know who might help us," Fitch said.

Jake put down his juice. "Who?"

"Judge Holiday. He owes me a favor and he's retiring in a couple months, so what would he care?" Fitch said with optimism.

"What are we waiting for?" Jake was out of his seat with a five-dollar bill spread out on the table before Fitch swallowed his drink.

"Okay, let's go see a judge. Fitch got up and nudged Jake on the arm. "And by the way, don't worry about losing your job."

"Why is that?"

"When you said Mearald has no backbone, you were right on the money. He won't try to terminate you because he's afraid to. Remember when he was a captain on nights?"

"Yes." Jake's antenna was erect.

"He was accused of sexual harassment by one of the female rookies he was banging in the storage room. The scandal nearly put him under, and he almost had a nervous breakdown. Anyway, in the end, she won the lawsuit and he hid in the cracks of the department for quite a few years. I wouldn't worry too much if I were you. He's terrified of any kind of discrimination lawsuit."

While Jake was pondering what Fitch said, a loud crash abruptly snapped him out of it. A waitress dropped a plate on the floor and Jake shot a quick look to see her bending over to pick up the mess. He turned back to Fitch.

"I understand, Tom," Jake said. As they started toward the exit, Jake glanced back to see the young girl, somewhat embarrassed, picking up the little broken pieces.

Judge Anthony Holiday was in his chamber when they arrived, preparing to call it a day. His days were getting shorter as retirement approached, and he had planned it that way. Holiday was an icon in the court system. There wasn't a major case that he wasn't familiar with, even if he wasn't professionally involved himself. New judges were continually seeking his advice and he was always willing to help out.

"Good morning, Tony." Fitch shook his hand as he entered the chamber. "You know Jake Waterfield, right?"

"Yes, I have presided over many cases that Detective Waterfield brought before my bench." They also shook hands. "I'll say this, you always showed the highest degree of integrity, and that, my friend, is a commodity these days."

"Thanks, Judge. The feeling is mutual," Jake said, looking up at the large man with a full head of white hair and a long, unwavering jaw.

All three men were seated. "Now, what can I do for you?" Holiday asked. "I'm assuming it's important by the way you sounded on the phone."

"Do you remember the Anderson murder in 1972?" Fitch asked.

"Yes," Holiday said without hesitation. "It troubled me then, and continues to trouble me today."

Wrinkles on his forehead became more prominent as he spoke of the case, and it was obvious that he was troubled by the unsolved murder.

"Jake found the body in the park," Fitch said, "and I was the first detective to arrive on the scene and was ultimately assigned the case."

"Yes, I remember," Holiday said.

Jake sat still listening. Fitch had a good relationship with the judge and he figured it would serve their cause better if he let Fitch do the talking. Fitch had told Jake about an incident when the judge's wife was in a car accident and was arrested at the scene for driving under the influence of alcohol. The judge called Fitch at home and asked him for a favor, and it was granted. Fitch called the booking sergeant, had the charges dropped, and she was released after being held in protective custody for eight hours. If someone had been hurt in the accident, Fitch would have rejected the judge's pleas for leniency, but she had struck a guard rail and no other vehicles were involved.

Fitch continued on. "At the murder scene, Jake found a button with an anchor on it."

Jake took out his drawing and handed it to the judge.

"This button was logged into evidence and it has since mysteriously vanished from the evidence room," Fitch said.

Holiday's eyebrows elevated. "Vanished, you say?"

"That's right," Fitch said. "And this is an exact drawing of the button, created by Jake here." He pointed at him.

"Who do you think took it?" Holiday asked.

"We can't be sure, but Officer Jacobson was one of the few people with access to the property room. When Jake interviewed him, he seemed very edgy." Holiday looked at Jake and saw him nodding in agreement. "We all know how close Jacobson is with the DA, right?"

"Go on." Holiday placed his fist under his chin, like Rodin's statue of "The Thinker."

"Everyone thought the boy was killed by Father LaPage, right? Especially after all his victims of sexual abuse came forward." The judge was completely still and focused on Fitch. "Corbin and Bishop Reardon have this real estate deal going on, and we haven't ruled out that Reardon had the DA snatch the button to save LaPage's ass," Fitch continued, leaning forward in his chair. "We had thought Reardon did this to save LaPage's ass, but we have since learned that the button belongs to Bishop Reardon. He did it to save his own hide."

"What makes you think this?" The story was beginning to sound like a bad soap opera to Holiday.

"Jake went to see the Bishop this morning and he observed a

photograph of Reardon in his study. He was wearing a sweater with this exact same button." Fitch pointed toward the drawing.

Holiday rubbed his chin during a brief pause. "So you want me to issue a warrant to search the Bishops house?"

"Yes," Fitch said without hesitation.

The Judge stood up, walked over to his law book shelf, and ran his fingers over the green leather binders. "In any other circumstance, I would say no, but I know the two of you, and I know that you wouldn't be here unless you were sure he was involved in the murder of that poor little boy." Holiday covered his right fist with his left hand, like a martial artist preparing to bow. "I'm going to take a lot of flak for this, but I'm going to grant your warrant."

"Thank you sir," Jake said.

"We really appreciate this, Tony." Both men felt instant relief.

"I hope you're wrong about the Bishop," Holiday said. "If he was involved in this homicide our citizens' confidence in the Catholic Church will be severely compromised."

"I understand," Fitch said. He hadn't really thought too much about what Holiday said because he wanted so badly to find the killer. "I hope he's innocent as well."

Ten minutes later, they were out of the courthouse and heading toward the car. Without breaking stride, Fitch brought up the obvious. "You know, this is the end of the ride for me."

Jake could sense a hint of sadness in his voice, and he realized that for a few minutes Fitch was a cop again, doing some good. Now, he would go back to his house and garden and fall back into a monotonous life with little purpose, and one day would fall into the next month and the next year.

"I know, but I couldn't have done it without you," Jake assured him. "I really appreciate your help on this."

"It was my pleasure, Jake. How will you serve the warrant without the Chief's blessing?

"I'm just going to do it. When I surface with the picture of Reardon wearing the sweater, and possibly, the actual sweater with the missing button, the Chief will have to play ball."

"I wish you the best of luck, my friend."

"Thanks, Chief."

Fitch liked that Jake still called him Chief. Every time someone addressed him in that manner, his ego hiked up a notch. "If there's anything else I can do, call me." Fitch walked away feeling like a million bucks.

Reluctantly, Randy agreed to help serve the warrant. Jake felt his adrenalin rise as he rang the front doorbell, hoping Reardon would open the door himself, so he could deliver the warrant personally and savor the surprised look on his face. They heard the metallic clicking sound of the deadbolt as it was unlatched from the inside and the door slowly swung open. Jake and Randy were not greeted by the Bishop. Instead, they found themselves looking into the concerned eyes of Sister Hathaway.

"Detective Waterfield, to what do we owe this pleasure?" Her veil was off and she was dressed simply with a white sweater and a gray skirt. She was more physically beautiful than Jake had realized, now that he saw her head uncovered.

"Hello Sister. I'm afraid I'm not here to help you with your roses. Is Bishop Reardon at home?"

She noticed the document in Jakes hand and the look of anticipation on the detective's faces, and she knew it was trouble for the Bishop.

"Yes, I'll get him. Please come in and wait here in the foyer." She closed the door and walked to the kitchen where she found Reardon eating a sandwich. Less than a minute later, he came out, gnawing on his liverwurst sandwich.

"Detective, how can I help you?" he said through a cluttered mouth.

"Evan Reardon. I have a warrant issued by a district court judge authorizing me and Detective Applebee to search your premises." Jake handed the note to Reardon who abruptly snatched it out of his hand, briefly scanning it.

"This is outrageous," Reardon stammered. "What exactly are you looking for?"

"It's in the warrant, sir. I must ask that you take a seat in the living room and remain there until we have completed our search," Jake said robotically.

Once again Reardon studied the document. "A gray sweater, you're barging in here to look for a sweater?"

Sister Hathaway stood listening from around the corner.

"I'll need to call my lawyer," Reardon threatened.

"That's fine," Jake said. "Is there a phone in the living room?"

"No. It's in the hall," he snapped.

"Let's go then." Jake gestured with his hand and the Bishop stormed toward the phone. Randy was thinking that he might need to start looking for another job.

As Reardon made his call, both men stood with him listening as he screamed at his lawyer to get over there immediately. From the way it sounded to Jake, Reardon caught his attorney at a bad time and he was pushing back on coming right over. In the end, Reardon prevailed and hung up, slamming down the receiver.

"My lawyer is on his way over now."

"That's fine, sir. I must insist that you wait for him in the living room and that you do not leave until I say so."

"You are a pushy bastard, aren't you?" Reardon hissed.

"We appreciate your cooperation, Bishop," Jake said, surprised by his choice of words.

Reardon marched off to the living room, and Jake signaled Randy to follow him into the study. As they entered the study, Randy thought how narcissistic Reardon must be to have so many awards and trophies on display for all to see. He knew it was not uncommon for some clergy in the church to have such big egos, and this was another reason he avoided organized religion. In Randy's mind, spiritual leaders should display unwavering humility.

"It's over here," Jake said, as headed toward the picture wall.

When he moved closer to the wall he realized that something wasn't right. Suddenly Jake felt his heart drop and land in his shoe.

"Son of a bitch!" he cursed.

The picture of Reardon in front of the yacht was gone and replaced by another.

"It was right here," Jake gasped. "The son of a bitch moved it!" Jake was pointing to a photograph of Reardon tacking a sail with the wind blowing through his hair.

Jake's mind began to work overtime and a cluster of thoughts passed through his brain all at once, ending in one inevitable place. He knew he would never find the sweater. It was obvious that Reardon was on to him, because he had removed the photograph of himself wearing the gray sweater with the anchor buttons. There was no way Reardon would keep the sweater *now.* It would never be found and was most likely a pile of ashes buried in the sand. Jake looked at Randy and they both thought the same thing. Chief Mearald was going to have their asses on the chopping block.

The inventory of the rectory came up empty. Reardon was waiting with his attorney in the living room when they concluded their search.

"So how did your little fantasy work out, Detective?" Reardon asked with a smug look. Reardon's lawyer wore a grin that displayed his annoyance with the entire situation.

"I have to hand it to you, Bishop, you covered all your tracks," Jake said. "It's not over yet, though."

"Yes it is," he roared. "And we're going to have you brought up on charges for this, Mister."

Reardon looked at his attorney for confirmation. "You'll be hearing from us very soon, detective," the attorney said, just before glancing at his watch.

Jake looked at Randy. "Let's go," he muttered.

As they walked toward the front entrance, Jake glanced to his right and saw Sister Hathaway standing in the library. For a brief moment, her eyes were fixed on his and they appeared uneasy, and maybe even sad.

"You know, he never asked about the relevance of the sweater and why we were searching for it," Jake said, as they passed under the Gate of Angels. "To me, this is an admission of guilt."

"Why ask when he already knew," Randy said.

"He may have graduated from Yale, but he's not that smart," Jake concluded. "If he were, he would have asked."

"What now?" Randy asked.

"Now, we deal with the repercussions from the Chief's office, and then I'm going to find out where that sweater came from. It looked like it may have been an award for winning a race or something. In the picture, he was holding a trophy and sporting the look of a winner."

"You don't give up, do you?" Randy asked.

"No. Not until I find out who killed Robby Anderson." Jake stopped in his tracks. "Ask yourself this question. If it were your little boy that was murdered, would you want the detective on the case to give up?"

Randy didn't answer. Examining his friend, he understood his point and he knew that they were doing the right thing.

The next morning when Jake came into the office, he knew right away something was wrong. It was quieter than usual and the looks he was getting from his colleagues were concerned and distant. A few minutes later, Randy came walking in, and noticed the same thing. It made him think of a song by Steely Dan about the calm before the storm.

Before Randy could make it to his desk, Captain Farris came out of his office and stopped him. "In my office," he commanded. Randy did as ordered, and Farris signaled Jake over with a hooked index finger.

They were all seated and the door was closed. The look on Farris's face indicated that the only thing missing was war paint. "The Chief chewed my ass off this morning for nearly a half hour. If you notice that I'm sitting funny, you know why. What in the hell were you two thinking when you went to a judge behind our backs and petitioned for a warrant to search the home of the Bishop of the Diocese of Middleborough?" His voice began in a moderate tone, elevating as he spoke.

"Captain, Randy had nothing to do with getting the warrant. He wasn't even there," Jake said.

"Alright, but you served the God damned thing, didn't you?" he barked at Randy.

"Yes," Randy responded.

"Captain, I ordered him to."

"Don't hand me that bullshit, you ordered him to. I think Detective Applebee has been a cop long enough to think for himself and make sound judgment calls." Farris rubbed his temples in frustration. "The Bishop is ape shit over this, and the DA is contemplating charges of misconduct."

"Now that doesn't surprise me, the DA and Reardon are in this cover-up together," Jake concluded.

"Are you living is some sort of cartoon, Jake? Do you know everyone is laughing at you behind your back? You have this wild imagination about a conspiracy within the Church and that a bishop is involved in murder," he shouted. "You have no evidence whatsoever and you are chasing a fucking button that doesn't seem to have ever existed."

"Captain, with all due respect, you have no idea what you're talking about."

Farris cut him off. "I know this much, Jake. You're suspended from duty for ten days, effective immediately, until a hearing of the police commission. Hand over your badge and gun, now."

Farris extended his hand. Jake briefly paused, not believing what was happening. Butterflies caused an uncomfortable stir in his stomach, as he pulled his gun from the holster and unclipped his badge from his waistband and handed them over.

"The commission will determine what disciplinary action is appropriate, including termination from the department," Farris concluded.

Jake's blood began to boil, and he knew that he had better

keep his mouth shut or he might dig himself in much deeper.

"And you," Farris said pointing to Randy. "You are to report tomorrow morning to Captain Dillon in the squad. You're back in uniform, and be glad you're not on suspension as well." He shot to his feet and snatched open the door. "Now, both of you get the hell out of here."

Randy raced out and Jake remained stationary for a few seconds staring at Farris, shaking his head, and then he slowly walked out, and kept on walking.

Bishop Reardon sat in his study thinking about everything that had transpired. How could it have gone so far after all the years that had passed since the boy was found? He was relieved that the press hadn't got wind of the search warrant because that would have opened up all kinds of questions. It would be wise not to push the issue too hard and let it die a quick death, he thought. He had covered his tracks, except one. Reardon got up and went downstairs to the basement, heading directly to the workbench. In retrospect, he should have gotten rid of the monkey wrench the night he hit Robby Anderson over the head with it, but who would have thought that *he* would ever be considered a suspect? *Was I too complacent, so egotistical to think I could never be caught?* Pulling the long chain, he turned on the florescent light and reached for the wrench hanging on a nail on the workbench wall. He instantly realized that something was wrong as the wind was taken from his sail. The wrench was gone.

CHAPTER 39

Stephen hated hospitals. Ever since childhood, he remembered the distinct lingering odor of a hospital, and it reminded him of pending death. He was seven years old when he went to visit his grandfather for the last time as he lay withering away in his hospital bed.

"I'm going to die soon," his grandfather said in a faint, scratchy, voice. "Life is finite, and what you do in that limited space in time can resonate throughout the future or it can die with you."

Although he was such a young child, Stephen understood was he was saying. His grandfather was proud of him, and his appreciation for his grandson's intellect was enormous.

"You are special, Stephen," he recalled his grandfather's words. "You have a gift that comes only when the stars are favorably aligned in space, and your birth fell on that day."

Stephen reached out and took his hand, it was clammy and weak. "Why do you have to die Grandpa?"

"No reason, other than it's my time. I'm sad, Stephen," he moaned.

"Why, Grandpa?"

"Because there are so many good things I could have done with my life, but now it's too late. Don't make the same mistake I did. You have the gift of brilliance. Your mind is far superior to most boys your age. Embrace your gift and work hard to improve it. Do something meaningful with your life, something that won't die, but will live on after your ashes have perished in the soil of the earth."

"Sure, Grandpa," Stephen said, squeezing his hand one last time before leaving the room. As he waited outside for his mother to say goodbye to her father, Stephen realized that his grandfather was the most influential man in his life. He loved him so very much. His grandfather was a mechanical engineer who spent his entire career working for the same aerospace manufacturer. Stephen now understood that even though his grandfather had always felt like a mouse trapped inside a maze, his need for security and his complacency ultimately prevailed. He never roamed free to explore his unlimited possibilities.

A young nurse smiled as Stephen walked past and he returned the smile with confidence. Rounding the corner, he located room # 676 at the end of the hallway. Stopping before opening the door, Stephen thought about his life and what his grandfather had said on his deathbed. His grandfather's last wish for him had not been realized. Stephen knew that he needed to make significant changes or one day he would die with an unfulfilled life, just as his grandfather had.

Pushing the door open, Stephen made his entrance. He found Michael awake and coherent, but his head and eyes appeared heavy from drugs.

"How are you feeling, man?" Stephen walked over tapping Michel on the shoulder.

"I'm okay," he slurred.

"You look good," he lied.

"Liar, I just had a doctor slice into my lung. I look like shit."

"What did the doctor say?" Stephen asked, as he pulled up a chair.

"They removed a couple tumors and they want to start treatment."

"Chemotherapy?"

"Yeah," Michael grunted.

"How do you feel about that?"

"I'm in stage four, Steve. It has spread to both lungs and most of my upper body. All it will do is delay my death a few more months. I'm not sure if I want to go through all that."

"Hey, you have to fight this thing, Mike. Don't give up, just keep fighting."

"Can you get me the juice," he requested. Stephen held it so he could drink from the straw.

"Steve, do you think I'm paying for my sins, *now*? Michael felt the cool liquid run down his dry throat, like water over sandpaper.

"What are you talking about, Man?"

"You know, for what I've done in the past."

Stephen scratched his head. "No, I don't."

"Why did this happen to me, and why now at my age?"

"Bad luck, I suppose," Stephen said.

"It could be that, or it could be retribution."

Stephen looked around the room and then moved in closer and whispered in his ear. "What we did was prevent a child molester, and rapist, from harming anymore kids. He was the evil one, not us."

Michael looked at his friend leaning over him. "Vengeance is mine said the Lord," he whispered back.

"Yeah, well the Lord wasn't taking his vengeance, so we helped him out. Forget about all that crap and focus on getting better. I'll see you tomorrow, okay?

"Yeah, thanks for coming, Steve."

"Hey, you're my best friend since we were five years old, right?

"Blood brothers," Michael said.

"That's right, blood brothers forever." Stephen walked out of the hospital as fast as he could, not bothering to take the elevator. He found the stairs instead and raced down, pushing the exit door, which swung open to its limit crashing against the doorstop. He started walking at a fast pace and it turned into a jog and then a sprint. Stephen didn't stop going for a few miles. His only true friend was dying, and in his own way he felt lost.

The suspension hit Jake hard. During his entire career with the police department he had never been suspended. He had been reprimanded a couple times for minor infractions, but it was always verbal and never documented. Although he was suspended with pay, and many would consider it a vacation, Jake didn't look at it that way. His file would now have a dark blemish on it and he was back to square one with the investigation. The Chief had forbidden him to engage in any activities related to the Anderson case. The case of Robert Anderson was officially closed.

Four days had passed since his suspension and he was already getting antsy. His days were spent mostly jogging, reading and studying the Anderson case and his nights were spent with Colleen. Jake had an itch that he couldn't reach and it was driving him crazy. The itch was the truth about the Anderson case. He believed that his purpose for being on earth was to find the person responsible for Robby's murder and allow justice to prevail and then the Andersons could finally find peace.

The night brought a cool breeze and Colleen was well prepared with a thick wool sweater that was handmade from Donegal County, Ireland. Jake walked alongside her wearing his favorite black leather jacket, but he felt somewhat light. The gun that was usually clipped onto his belt was no longer there. Not only was his sense of pride affected by the suspension, his sense of security was also diminished.

It was Saturday night, and the North Haddam county fair was bustling with people from all over the state. They moved from one booth to the next and Jake wasn't having any luck winning a stuffed animal that was larger than Colleen's purse. He tried the ring toss, the bowling pins, and he failed at the dart throw. One throw was very questionable and he argued with the vendor, stating it was inside the red star, but he ended up with a four-inch dog.

"I'm upset that you were suspended, but I must say, I'm pretty happy that we're spending more time together," Colleen said, as she reached out and held his hand.

"Yeah, I guess there is a silver lining, isn't there?"

"What do you think will happen? Do you think you'll get fired?"

"I don't know. I doubt it will be that severe. The whole thing is political and nobody has the backbone to side with me, especially the Chief."

"I want you to know that whatever happens, I will stand by you no matter what."

He gently spun her around in mid-stride and softly kissed her on the lips. "I love you, Colleen."

"I love you back," she said.

They continued walking past the Ferris wheel and stopped for a drink of water and a diet soda.

"Let's sit over here." Jake guided her to a miniature picnic table. He took a long slug of water and placed it down. Then he leaned in and gave her a long kiss, pulling her in tight and shielding her from the north wind.

"Jake, are you going to be alright with the case?"

"What do you mean?"

"I mean, not finding closure in the Anderson case."

"I don't know." He shifted position to face her more directly. "I've been making a few calls and doing a little research since my suspension, and I found out there was a yacht race in the summer of 1970 from Portland, Maine to Newport, Rhode Island. The team that won the race was presented a trophy and a sweater. I couldn't find out what the sweater looked like, but I'd be willing to bet it was a gray sweater with black anchor buttons."

"Did you find out who won?"

"Yes, three men took the prize, and one of them was Evan Reardon."

"Well, there's proof right there, if you can determine it was the sweater with the same buttons as the one you found at the murder scene."

"I think it will be the same," Jake said, "but it's not going to be enough," he sighed. "They don't want this case open. It's all neatly bundled up and stored away, and the last thing they want is to dig it back out. Besides, we have no button. They have a taped confession and the killer is dead. What's better than that?"

"The truth," she retorted.

"Yes, the truth," he repeated. "Come on. Let's get you a stuffed animal."

A few minutes later, they arrived at a booth with large pink elephants lined up on display.

"Elephants are my favorite," she disclosed.

Jake was relieved to see that the game was right up his alley.

"Sink three baskets and win an elephant." The man behind the booth called out prior to spitting a mouthful of tobacco juice into a can. "It's as easy as taking candy from a baby."

Standing on the other side of the counter and a few feet closer to the basket, the vendor proved how easy it was and sunk a ball clean through the hoop. "Anyone can do it," he said, through a hunk of chew.

"I'll try." Colleen placed a dollar on the counter.

"The lady is feeling lucky," he said, and began placing balls in front of her.

She missed the first two and succeeded with the third.

"You made one. Why don't you take another try?" he called out like a broken record.

Jake pulled Colleen in and kissed her. "I'll give it a shot," he said to the man that was now giving him a nasty look.

"Well, put up a dollar, boy." He shifted his John Deere baseball cap upwards.

Jake was about to fire back at him when he felt Colleen's hand squeeze his elbow, so he kept quiet. After placing the money down, he picked up the first ball and fired.

"Nice shot, honey," Colleen said.

The man behind the counter frowned, mostly because she called him honey. The vendor took a couple steps back, and began straightening out some prizes. Jake sank the second shot, and the third.

"Yes!" Colleen yelled out.

Jake smiled and gave her a hug. "She'll take an elephant," he said.

The vendor turned around and looked at Jake with contempt. "That's only two, boy. You need to make three shots." He spit into the can and placed another ball down.

"He did make three," Colleen argued.

"I only saw two."

"That's because you're a moron," Jake said. "Now give up the elephant."

"I ain't giving you or your whore shit," he said, displaying his brown stained teeth.

Once again, Jake felt Colleen's hand on his arm. A wave of rage quickly built up inside and he exploded. Scooping up the over inflated basketball; Jake wound up, and drilled the ball into the vendors face. The man's hat flew off uncovering a balding head, and he fell backwards holding onto his stinging face. Quickly regaining his composure, he rebounded with a miniature bat, attacking Jake from the other side of the counter. Leaning half way over the counter, he swung the bat at Jake but missed. As he wound up for another swing, Jake moved in blocking it at the man's wrist, eluding the blow and grabbing the man by the back of the neck, slamming his face into the counter.

"Jake!" Colleen cried out.

In an instant, Jake hopped over the counter, avoiding the blood drops and tobacco chew, and the vendor fell to his knees, holding his broken nose.

"You should learn to have respect for a lady," Jake calmly advised. Reaching up, Jake snatched an elephant off the shelf and jumped back over the counter. "Let's go." He handed the stuffed animal to Colleen.

As they hurried away, Colleen thought about what had just occurred. She was upset, yet proud at the same time.

Later that evening, Colleen broke the silence as they sat on Jake's deck. "What was it that really set you off today?" she asked. "Was it that he cheated you on the game or was it the name calling?"

Jake looked her in the eye and paused before speaking. "It was that he totally disrespected me as a man."

She absorbed what he said and she took his hand, holding on tightly. That was the last time they spoke of it.

"I have something to show you," he said. "Wait here."

Darting into the house, he returned a few seconds later. Moving in deliberately, he slowly walked over without taking his eyes off hers. He got down on one knee and handed her a black velvet box. Colleen's spine began to tingle as she accepted it and slowly peeled open the lid.

"Jake, it's beautiful." She gazed down at a full carat diamond ring with a platinum setting. "Is this what I think it is?"

He blushed. "Yes it is. Will you marry me, Colleen?"

"Detective Waterfield, I would marry you right now, right here."

Jake kissed her hand and placed the ring on her finger, only to kiss it again. "You may have to wait a few weeks so I can save up."

She laughed. "Whenever you're ready," she said helping him to his feet, and in one continuous motion, he scooped her up and carried her through the threshold to the bedroom.

Fitch was right. The commission, along with the chief, decided that a ten day suspension without pay was a sufficient punishment for the offense. If it had been anyone else, Jake concluded it would have been more severe. Still, he didn't like the fact that his record was now marked with a negative action, and that could be used against him when he went for a promotion to Lieutenant.

He was seated behind his desk when the phone rang. "Sergeant Waterfield," Jake answered.

"Sergeant Waterfield?" the voice asked.

"Yes."

"This is Sister Hathaway." Her voice was shaky.

"Yes, Sister, how can I help you?"

"I called to inform you that believe I know who killed Robert Anderson."

CHAPTER 40

The station lobby was empty except for a woman cradling a toddler as she sat on the wooden bench by the front window. Jake was waiting near the door as Sister Hathaway walked in, dressed in her habit. He had never seen her dressed in all black, covered from her forehead to her ankles. She seemed so isolated to him.

Approaching her as if she were an angel, he took her hand between both of his.

"Sister, thank you for coming," he said sincerely. "Please, follow me to a private room."

Without speaking she complied, Jake escorted her to an empty squad room on the first floor that he had secured for their meeting. Jake wanted to avoid the second floor where Mearald's cronies roamed the halls looking and listening for anything they could pass on to the Chief as some sort of departmental mutiny.

Jake pulled up a chair up for her. She bowed her head in gratitude and sat down, placing her hand bag on the floor next to her. Jake took a seat directly across from the sister, anxious to hear what she had to say, but also wanting to keep the conversation calm and collected.

"It's nice to see you again, Sister." She displayed a reserved smile, that didn't amount to her usual glow. "On the phone you said that you think you know who is responsible for the death of Robert Anderson."

"Yes."

Jake took out a pocket recorder and placed it on the small table that bridged their gap. "Is it alright if I record our conversation?"

"Yes, that's fine."

"Please Sister, go ahead." Jake pushed the button and the tape started turning.

Appearing uncomfortable in her chair and sitting with perfect posture, she began. "I am ashamed that it took me so long to come forward with this, and for that, I'm truly sorry."

"That's okay, you're here now."

"I had a son of my own once, you know." A sad expression defined her face. "I was so young and foolish. The day I gave birth to my son, I lost him forever. I didn't even have a chance to hold him, and to this day, I would give anything to have had a chance to hold him tight, just once."

A tear was born and it grew until the weight carried it down her cheek. Jake produced a white handkerchief and handed it to her.

"I suppose the parents of Robert Anderson would give anything to hold their boy one more time." She gently dabbed her eyes.

"I bet they would," Jake agreed.

"I was young and new to this parish when I first noticed Father LaPage bringing boys to the Bishop's house. I really didn't think anything of it at the time." She folded her hands on her lap as if she was making a penance. "Father LaPage and the boys were received by Bishop Reardon and he would escort them to his quarters where they stayed a few hours."

"How many times did this happen?"

"I only noticed a few occasions over a period of five years or so."

"Was Robert Anderson one of the boys?"

"Yes." She pressed the cloth against her eyes one last time.

"Was it the night he went missing?"

"Yes." She handed the handkerchief back to Jake. "Thank you."

"You're welcome. Please Sister, tell me what happened." He tucked the handkerchief into his pocket.

"I was in the kitchen when Bishop Reardon received Father LaPage and the Anderson boy, and that's when I saw him." Her expression was depleted. "He smiled at me as he turned the corner and made his way toward the wing of the Bishop's quarters. I figured they were going to discuss something about his altar boy's duties, or something church related," she said. "Back then, there was no indication of any inappropriate behavior by any priests."

"I understand," Jake said sympathetically.

"I never saw him again after that night, until I saw his photograph in the newspaper."

"What makes you think you know who killed him?"

"That same night, I heard someone in the mudroom and I went to see who it was."

"What did you see, Sister?"

"Bishop Reardon was cleaning a wrench in the sink. He seemed troubled, and I noticed mud on the floor and on his shoes. I thought it was strange and I asked him what had happened."

"What did he say?" Jake asked.

"He said he had car trouble and he had to fix it by the side of the road, but that he was fine and I shouldn't worry about it."

"What did you do next?"

"I went back to my dorm."

"Sister, this is very important. What was he wearing?"

"He was wearing a sweater and black pants." She pushed herself straight to maintain her erect posture. "The day you showed me the drawing of the button, I knew."

"You knew what?" Jakes eyes widened.

"I knew that Bishop Reardon killed that poor boy. The sweater he was wearing that night had the same buttons as the drawing. Black buttons with anchors on them," she concluded.

"What time was it that you saw Bishop Reardon in the mudroom?"

"It was around nine-thirty or ten that evening."

"What time would you say it was when you saw them entering the rectory together?"

"I would say around 4:30 or 5 o'clock."

Jake was silent in thought as he massaged his face, glaring at a fly on the ceiling. Refocusing on Sister Hathaway, he resumed the conversation.

"It's not going to be enough. We can't put him at the crime scene and we have no murder weapon," he said. "All we have is a missing button and no sweater. Bishop Reardon was with the boy earlier in the day and that's all we have."

"We have more than that." She reached down, picked up her bag and unzipped it. Jake couldn't remember ever being so curious and excited with anticipation. "We have this." She slipped her hand into her bag and pulled out a monkey wrench. "This is the same wrench he was cleaning that night." She handed it to Jake.

Jake took the wrench and held it tight, shaking it three times as his wide smile lit up the room. "Are you sure this is the same wrench after all these years?"

"It's the only monkey wrench on the tool bench, and it's an old one. Yes, I'm pretty sure it's the one."

"Sister, you know what this means?" She didn't answer. "You're going to have to testify in open court to everything you told me today. Can you do that?"

"Yes," she said without hesitation.

"Excellent." Jake said.

"Sister, why did you wait to come forward, really?"

"When the news about Father LaPage broke, I thought you would catch him without me having to come forward. After we first met, I was considering telling you, but when Father LaPage was shot and he confessed, I figured it was over. The day you showed me the drawing of the button, I knew that Bishop Reardon was involved, and that's when I decided I had to divulge what I knew. Everything didn't really begin to make sense to me until recently. I know that my coming forward and testifying in court will most likely be the end of my life as a nun," she sadly proclaimed.

"Not if I have any say in the matter," Jake said. "What you are doing is good and it's the right thing to do. I thank you from the bottom of my heart, Sister."

He took her hand and she smiled. A weight had been lifted from her shoulders and she felt lighter and cleaner.

Jake escorted her out and he immediately drove to the state

lab where he asked that the wrench be put under a microscope and tested for evidence. He knew it was a long shot, but he had to try. After all the time and all the setbacks in the Anderson case, Jake was beginning to feel like he was getting some solid traction. The testimony of Sister Hathaway, along with the murder weapon would hopefully be enough to indict Bishop Reardon. One thing that still bothered Jake was that he couldn't figure out who killed Father LaPage and why.

Later that day, Jake had a conversation with Chief Mearald. It began with the Chief yelling at the top of his lungs, stating Jake had disobeyed a direct order by continuing to conduct an investigation in the Anderson case, and while he was still on suspension. Once Jake played the statement of Sister Hathaway, he calmed down, but he still insisted it wasn't enough to indict a Catholic Bishop. Jake disagreed and advised the Chief that he was going to try and get an indictment, and if Mearald interfered, he would take it to the press. Reluctantly, Mearald agreed and Jake was off to finish what he had started so many years ago.

CHAPTER 41

The greeting was cordial but somber with an underlying hint of hostility in tow. Jake figured he had just one shot at getting into the heart and mind of Reardon in order to crack him, and he had done his homework in anticipation of the meeting. Jake knew he was dealing with a very intelligent and calculated character with an ego the size of Texas, and he would win only if he could break through his emotional barrier. Bishop Reardon came packed with his lawyer, Tanner Hagen, who was bought and paid for by the Catholic Church, and they sat across the table from Jake, Captain Farris, and Drake White. Chief Mearald had bowed out of the meeting and ordered Farris to sit in, and White was the assistant district attorney sent by Corbin. The deck was obviously stacked in Reardon's favor, Jake thought. The only possible comrade he had was Farris, and he was somewhat questionable.

Having all the key players in the room gave Jake a constant flow of adrenalin that surged throughout his body. Even though it kept him alert, he knew he had to keep it under control in order to think clearly and stay focused on his agenda.

Jake rose to his feet. "I'd like to thank you gentlemen for coming to the police department this morning for this inquiry." Jake cleared his throat and took a sip of water from a glass on the table in front of him. He made sure everyone had water and a pad and pencil neatly placed in their individual space. "I'm hoping we can wrap this meeting up in two hours or less, and I appreciate your patience in this regard." By the look on everyone's face, they were hoping it would be wrapped up sooner than later, Jake thought. "I'm going to be very frank here today in my questioning of Bishop Reardon, and if anyone is insulted, I assure you it is not my intention. My intentions are very clear, and that is to find out the truth."

Jake pushed the button and activated the tape recorder that he had placed in the center of the table.

"I'd like to begin by playing a statement by Sister Patricia

Hathaway of the Diocese of Middleborough that I had taken two weeks ago." He took the pocket recorder, placed it near the other recorder, and pushed the button.

The room was still as the tape was rolling, and when it was finished, Jake pushed the stop button and quietly sat looking into the eyes of Bishop Reardon.

"So, you have a nun who lives in my compound, who saw me cleaning some tools twenty years ago," he said in a slippery manner. "And her statement that she saw a boy that looked like Robert Anderson enter the building right around that time," Reardon said with a feverishly smug look. "Is this why you dragged all of us here this morning, detective?"

Jake examined him for a moment. "Maybe you didn't hear the statement properly, should I play it again?"

"No! I heard it very well the first time, detective," he roared.

"Well, then you heard that Sister Hathaway stated that she saw you and Father LaPage escort Robert Anderson to your private quarters the night he was killed." Jake leaned forward in his chair. "To be more precise, Bishop, she saw the three of you around 5 p.m. and it was determined by the medical examiner that Robert Anderson was killed sometime between 9:00 and 11:00 that night. I would say this is very troubling to say the least," Jake said sternly. "We have you, along with a known pedophile, in the company of the victim alone in your quarters just before he is murdered and you somehow think this is inconsequential."

"Look, we had many boys come to the rectory over the years to help out with church activities, or to come for counseling if they were troubled kids. Maybe she was mistaken and thought it was Robert Anderson, when in fact it may have been another boy that looked similar to him. The truth is I have never even met Robert Anderson. We're talking nearly twenty years ago," he argued. "Can you clearly recall what a boy looked like twenty years ago at a glance?" His question was directed at Jake.

"Yes," Jake answered. "It was nearly twenty years ago that I found the dead body of Robert Anderson, and to this day, it's as clear in my mind as though it were yesterday."

"You can't compare finding a homicide victim to a casual glance by a nun twenty years ago," White blurted out.

"Maybe not, but when she saw Robert Anderson's picture in the paper a couple days later, don't you think that might stay clear in her mind?"

"I doubt it," White said.

"Okay," Jake said. "Let's talk about what Sister Hathaway saw later that evening around 10 p.m." He directed his attention back to Reardon. "She heard someone in the mudroom, and after investigating, she found you washing a monkey wrench in the sink. Sister Hathaway stated you had mud on your shoes. She also said that you appeared somewhat nervous, and when she asked you if everything was alright, you told her you had car trouble." Jake shrugged his shoulders. "Tell me Bishop, what kind of car trouble did you have that required the use of a monkey wrench?"

"How the hell do I know." he said. "It was twenty years ago."

"Alright, let me ask you this. In the past twenty years, how many times do you remember being stranded on the roadside with car trouble?"

"Well, I don't, I can't remember how many times, maybe three or four," he stumbled.

"This is all foolish and irrelevant," Hagen protested.

Jake looked at Hagan as though he was transparent, and then he refocused on Reardon. "About a month ago, I was looking at pictures in your study and I saw a picture of you standing in front of a yacht holding a trophy. You were wearing a gray sweater with black buttons that had anchors on them. The same button I found near the body of Robert Anderson in Bottle Park," Jake said. "When I returned with a search warrant, the picture was gone and replaced by another." Jake took a drawing of the button and placed it on the table in front of Reardon. "Why did you remove the picture, Bishop?"

"I don't know what you're talking about, what picture?" He squirmed in his seat.

"Have you ever owned or worn a gray sweater with buttons like the one in this drawing?" Jake asked.

"No. Not that I recall."

"Are you sure?" Jake asked again.

"Yes."

Jake glared at him. "Get on with it," Hagen demanded.

"Stand down, councilor." Jake belted out. He turned back to Reardon. "Do you remember winning a yachting race in Newport, Rhode Island in 1970?"

"I have won many yacht races in my life. I don't remember every single one."

"Let me help refresh your memory, Bishop. You, along with two other men, Richard Welker and Vincent Chavez, won first place in the coastal quest regatta in 1970. Does it ring a bell *now*, Bishop?"

"Vaguely," he muttered.

"In that race, all three winners, including you, were awarded a trophy and a gray sweater. Is it coming back to you *now*, Bishop?"

"I may have, so what?" he defiantly fired back.

"I'll ask you once more, Bishop. Did you ever own or wear a gray sweater with black anchor buttons?"

"I don't remember the buttons on every sweater I have worn in the past twenty-three years, Mr. Waterfield," he said.

Jake reached down into a large bag he kept on the floor next to him. "Maybe this will help refresh your memory, Bishop." Jake pulled out and held up a gray sweater with black buttons with anchors on them. He threw the sweater on the table in front of the Bishop, and he picked up the drawing and held it on display for everyone to see. "This is the same button I found next to the body of Robert Anderson, a button that mysteriously vanished from police evidence." Jake stood up, leaning on the table and facing Reardon like a sprinter waiting for the pop of a starter pistol. "This is the same sweater you were wearing the night Robert Anderson was killed." Jake took a piece of paper out of his bag and placed it on the table. "A sworn affidavit from Sister Hathaway stating that this is the exact type of sweater you were wearing the night she found you washing a wrench in the mudroom.

"Where did you get that sweater?" White asked.

"I got this sweater from Vincent Chavez, one of the three winners of the Regatta."

Jake reached down and brought out another piece of paper and placed it on the table. "This is a sworn affidavit from Mister Chavez, stating that Evan Reardon also received this exact same sweater for winning the Coastal Quest Regatta."

"This is absurd." Reardon proclaimed. "So you found a button in the park that is similar to a button on a sweater I won in a race twenty-two years ago. This proves nothing!"

"I'm still curious why you removed the picture from your study, Bishop," Jake said

"This is all nothing more that circumstantial evidence. This is a witch hunt here," Hagen said. "By the way, you have no button, detective, do you?"

"Well, the button was logged into evidence at the police department property room and it has since disappeared." Jake looked at Reardon. "You wouldn't know anything about that, would you Bishop?"

Reardon shook his head.

"It seems to me that we have a lot of circumstances that all point to your client," Captain Farris said in his debut statement.

"This is all bullshit," White said.

"Shut up Mr. White!" Jake said. "Everyone here knows how tight your boss is with Bishop Reardon and the reason why you're here today."

"You had better watch your tongue, detective, or you might find your ass in a sling," White threatened.

Jake dismissed his threat and began scanning the faces in the room in a moment of quiet thought and then walked toward the door. "Excuse me for one minute, gentlemen," Jake said before exiting the room. When he returned, Jake held the door open as two people walked in behind him.

"Please have a seat," he offered the two strangers. The rest of the people in the room looked surprised and curious about who these two people were and what they were doing in the room.

"Who are these people?" Hagen asked.

"Bishop Reardon, Assistant District Attorney White, Attorney Hagen, and Captain Farris." He gestured to each person with an open palm as he introduced them. "Please allow me to introduce Tim and Betty Anderson."

Reardon's jaw nearly hit the table.

"Detective Waterfield, this is unacceptable," Hagen cackled. "This is a formal and legal inquiry and these people have not been cleared to participate."

"I completely disagree, Mr. Hagen. These are the parents of Robert Anderson and they have come here to speak of their son, Robert, not to listen to any of the proceedings. These people have gone through hell over the past twenty years," Jake said. "I think they deserve the opportunity to speak about their son." Jake looked at the Anderson's drawn and sullen faces. "Tim, Betty, please."

Tim reached out and took his wife by the hand. "My son, Robby was a good boy with a heart larger than life. He had dark red hair and freckles covering most of his face, and a laugh that was contagious. Robby loved life and all the creatures that occupied a space on this earth," Tim said. "I remember one time he found an injured mouse by the side of the road. Robby took the mouse into his room and attempted to nurse it back to health by feeding it cheese and water." Tim slowly scanned the table, looking into the eyes of everyone in the room and they all engaged him, except Reardon. He kept his eyes on the pad in front of him. "Every day for over a week he would run home from school and sit by that dying mouse and talk to it. The day it died, Robby was heartbroken. He took it into the back yard and buried it under a cross he made with Popsicle sticks and Elmer's glue." His voice was soft and cracked. "My son got down onto his knees and said a prayer, and then he said goodbye. That mouse was just a rodent, but to Robby, it was one of God's creatures and he had to try and save it. Robby had named the mouse Lucky, and after the mouse died, he asked me if the name he picked was a bad choice because the mouse hadn't lived." Tim's lower lip quivered as he fought to maintain his composure. He cleared his throat and held his wife's hand tighter. "I told him that Lucky was a perfect name for the mouse because he was very lucky that you found him and became his friend." A tear found Tim's cheek and he quickly swept it away. "I told Robby, the mouse didn't die alone by the side of the road; he died in a warm place with a real friend."

Betty began to sob and Jake handed her a handkerchief. After she found her composure, she began. "My Robby was the sweetest boy any mother could ever hope for. He was just twelve years old when his life was taken away, and he would never have a chance to grow up and go to college, or fall in love and get married." Tears rolled down colliding with her frown. "Robby would never have the chance to have a family of his own and feel what it's like to have a son, and watch him grow into a man." Her voice was wavering as she continued. "Robby wanted to be a fireman when he grew up; he wanted to save lives, he used to say." She looked at her husband. "We miss him so very much."

The Andersons were lost in each other's eyes and it was apparent that's where they found their strength. Betty turned and looked into the eyes of Bishop Reardon and her husband followed suit.

"We just want to know what happened to our son."

Everyone in the room looked at Reardon and he displayed a look as clear as a summer day. It was a look of guilt.

"Thank you," Betty said. Tim nodded, and they both rose to their feet, and Jake escorted them out.

The room was quiet when Jake returned. The silence was broken by Mr. Hagen. "We are all very sympathetic to the Anderson's loss, but it changes nothing regarding the innocence of my client," he said unconvincingly.

Jake didn't bother to respond. Once again, he reached down

into his bag and pulled out a monkey wrench and held it high for all to see and then placed it on the table.

"Bishop Reardon, do you recognize this wrench?"

Reardon cleared his throat. "It looks like any wrench one might find in his tool kit," he said in a quivery tone."

Jake had not played the portion of the tape when Sister Hathaway produced the wrench, so this was a surprise to everyone.

"Bishop, this wrench was taken from your work bench by Sister Hathaway." Jake pulled out another affidavit and placed it down. "A sworn statement from Sister Hathaway stating that this wrench is the same one she saw you scrubbing the night of the murder of Robert Anderson."

"It might be," Reardon said in a squirrelly way. "I can't remember what wrench I used that long ago."

"What has this wrench got to do with anything? Hagen asked in a snotty manner. "This wrench has never been linked to the murder."

"Jake." Farris looked at him for answers.

"Bishop Reardon. Is it fair to say that this is more than likely the monkey wrench you used that night to fix your car?"

"I suppose it could be." He no longer sounded boisterous and his words lacked fire.

"I had this wrench tested at the lab, and what they determined was that it had in fact been thoroughly scrubbed," he said with ferret eyes, "but not thoroughly enough."

Jake stared at Reardon. "Trapped between the wheel that opens and closed the prongs, and the wrench, they found a tiny spatter of dried blood."

Jake leaned down to his bag and produced a report from the state forensics lab. He placed it on the table. "The blood on the wrench is an exact match with the blood type of Robert Anderson," Jake declared, "a very rare blood type. In fact, Robert Anderson's blood type is AB Negative and only 0.8 percent of the world's population has this blood type."

The room went completely still and all heads were turned toward Bishop Reardon as his face fell into his hands. Jake reached into his magical bag one last time and retrieved several eight by ten photographs of the dead body of Robert Anderson as he was found in the park. Jake placed them down, facing the Bishop.

"This is the innocent boy you killed that night in the park. Look at them!" Jake shouted. "Bishop, let's spare you and the Catholic Church the humiliation of taking this to trial. For once, do what's right, for God sake."

Reardon lifted his head up, looking down at the array of photographs on the table. His eyes grew bloodshot and his face wet.

"This inquiry is over. I need to consult with my client in private," Hagen insisted. "Let's go Bishop."

Jake extracted a Miranda warning card from his pocket and began reading it to Reardon.

"I didn't mean to kill him!" Reardon's crumbling voice sounded out.

"Evan," Hagen shouted.

"No." He addressed the room. "We played games together, sexual games," he cried. "I'm a sick man."

"Tell us what happened, Bishop," Jake said.

"Father LaPage brought him to the rectory. He had been with the boy before. We played games for a few hours and we made him do things he didn't want to do," he cried. "He threatened to expose us and I was scared."

"Evan, I advise you to not say another word," Hagen pleaded.

"Shut up, Tanner!" Reardon yelled.

"I was afraid of what would happen if he came forward and exposed what we had done, so I took him to the park for a walk to try and convince him to keep quiet about what had happened."

"Go on," Jake said.

"He wasn't playing ball, he was upset, and we began to argue and he said he was going to tell what had happened."

"What happened next?" Jake asked.

"I pulled out the wrench that I had taken from the rectory workbench and I hit him twice. I didn't mean to kill him. I just wanted him to shut up and go along with what I asked. I didn't mean to kill him," he cried.

Jake looked at the pathetic man in front of him. "God help you," he said. "I have just a few more questions, Bishop. "What happened to the button that was in the police evidence room?"

"I had District Attorney Corbin remove it from the evidence room."

"Wait a minute, Bishop!" White jumped out of his chair.

"Sit down, Councilor!" Farris yelled, and White did as he was told.

"How did the DA get to the button? He wouldn't have had access."

"Officer Jacobson took it."

"So the DA was in on this the whole time. He knew you were involved in the murder of Robert Anderson and he helped to cover it up?"

"Yes," Reardon muttered.

"But why, why would he do that?" Jake asked, already knowing the answer.

"We had a real estate deal on the sale and development of land in Bottle Park. Corbin stood to make a significant amount of money and his helping me depended on it."

"It seems to me the DA wasn't the only one trying to kill this investigation," Jake said. "Who else was involved with preventing the truth from coming out?"

Reardon looked at Farris and then back at Jake. "Chief Mearald."

CHAPTER 42

In Chiefs Mearald's office, the confession of Bishop Reardon was rolling on the tape as the Chief and Jake sat intently listening. As the confession deepened, Mearald's face changed from his usual superior, cocky expression to that of a defeated and whimpering foe. Once the tape ran its course, Jake snapped it off and sat back.

"Your ambitions of being Mayor of Middleborough are over," Jake said. "As of matter of fact, your rule as Chief of Police is over."

"Wait a minute, Jake, let's talk about this," he pleaded.

"There's nothing to talk about." Jake stood, towering over the man. "Two things are going to happen. First, you are going to reinstate Randy Applebee to detective status working on the day shift."

"Done," Mearald spurted.

"And the order is going to go out today."

"No problem."

"The second thing is: within twenty-four hours one of us is going to give a press conference. It's either going to be you tendering your resignation as Chief of Police, or it's going to be me playing this tape on live television. The choice is yours to make."

Jake picked up his tape recorder and walked out, knowing what choice Mearald was going make.

Dressed in a long white gown, Colleen was escorted down the aisle by her mother. Her father and brother were absent and both Jake and Colleen had come to terms with it. Jake figured he may have ended up tossing one of them over the buffet table and that would have ruined the day. Pastor Mead stood at the altar and Jake and his three ushers stood along-side him all sharply dressed in black tuxedos. Colleen had her three bridesmaids standing on the opposite side of the aisle downed in yellow lace dresses, all of them filled with excitement and glee for their very good friend.

"Are you nervous?" Fitch whispered in Jake's ear.

"No, I'm sure of this," Jake said.

"It's not too late to make a run for it," Randy said. "I've done it once before and I'm still alive," he chuckled.

Rick Mosko nudged Randy. "Give him a break, man."

Once they reached the end of the aisle, Mrs. Kelly removed her daughter's veil and kissed Colleen on both sides of her face. Jake moved in and stood beside her. He leaned in and whispered through her white veil.

"You are the most beautiful woman I have ever laid eyes on."

She smiled and held his arm tighter and they both proudly ascended the steps to the altar.

At the reception, Jake and Fitch stood at the bar. Jake had a club soda and Fitch a scotch on the rocks. "Here's to you and your new bride," Fitch said, raising his glass.

"Here's to Robby Anderson," Jake said, and they toasted to him.

"So I hear there's an opening for Chief of Police and District Attorney," Fitch said. "I hope both positions are filled with men of integrity."

"One can only hope," Jake added.

Fitch bit through a hunk of ice and it made a crunching sound. "It looks like the trial of Reardon is coming up soon."

"Yes, the twenty-seventh of next month," Jake answered. "It shouldn't be a very long trial since we have his full confession, and his bringing the wrench along to the park shows premeditation. He also admitted to fondling the boy post mortem."

"I may be naive here, but I still can't get over the fact that a Catholic Bishop did this."

"I know what you mean," Jake said, "but keep in mind that the majority of Catholic Priests are decent men; that do good things for people. It's only a few that spoil the good reputation of the Church. Still, I tend to remain cautiously optimistic."

Fitch nodded his head in agreement. "Jake, what you did for the Anderson family and this community is something you should be very proud of. You never gave up, even when all the odds were against you. You are one remarkable detective and I'm proud to call you my friend," he extended his arms and they embraced each other.

"Thanks, Tom. I'm not sure I could have pulled it off without you."

"So, who forced LaPage to confess before putting a bullet in his head?"

"That's the million dollar question, isn't it?" Jake said.

"What are you going to do now?"

"Now, I'm going to spend a lot of time with my new wife."

Fitch raised his glass. "I'll drink to that."

Ryan Cook had been assigned to homicide six days earlier. Excited beyond words about his promotion to detective, his mind was like a sponge; his enthusiasm unlimited. Although he was young, his deep-set eyes displayed experience and courage for his limited years. A thin scar ran along his left cheek from a childhood accident and his nose was long and pointed.

Jake sat behind the wheel as they un-wrapped the grinders they bought at a local Italian restaurant. With their car parked facing Kennedy Memorial Park, they watched the young children playing in the warm sun.

"Can I ask you something?" Ryan asked.

"Sure," Jake said.

"Some of the guys are, you know, talking about how working with you might be dangerous."

"Oh yeah," Jake said. "How so?" He bit a hunk out of his turkey sub and began chewing.

"Why is it that you've gone through two partners in less than two years?"

Jake looked at his young partner. "Let's just say there have been a series of unfortunate events."

"I can understand that." Ryan bit into his sandwich. "One more thing," he said through a full mouth. "Why do you park here almost every day to eat lunch?"

Jake looked at the young detective sitting next to him, thinking how inquisitive he was and that he might make a fine investigator. "Let's just say it calms me to watch children play." He smiled at Ryan and took another bite.

Refocusing his attention back on the children, Jake watched as a man pushed a young boy on a swing. The boy was laughing with the excitement and joy that could warm even the coldest of men's hearts. The man pushed the boy with vigor, and he laughed along, realizing the thrill he was giving the child. The man was young, tall, and good looking. As he turned, he glanced over at the two men sitting in the car, watching him from a distance. Ryan didn't notice the man as he ate his lunch, but his partner had. Jake took another bite, keeping his eyes fixed on the man dressed in black with a white collar.

Jousting on Unicycles

Jake sat at his kitchen table, a half full glass of orange juice before him. It was Sunday morning and Colleen was at church teaching Sunday school. Thumbing through the newspaper as he did every Sunday, he found himself caught up in the obituaries and reading about the death of a young man he had once interviewed.

That's strange, he thought. Michael McNulty died at the age of thirty-four. Thinking back, Jake remembered interviewing him in the case of Richard Stack, and even more clearly, he remembered his friend, Stephen Haney. Thinking about what Fitch had told him about the two boys and how they were suspects in the Anderson case, Jake now knew they were both innocent of any wrongdoing in the Bottle Park case.

Sipping his juice without taking his eyes off the article, Jake kept reading to learn that the wake was taking place the next day. Not knowing exactly why, something told him to attend the service. Maybe it was because he was never able to solve the Stack case and McNulty was one of his prime suspects. Or maybe he would run into Stephen Haney. That might be an interesting conversation to say the least. Jake tore the page out of the paper, neatly folded it into a manageable size, and tucked it into his wallet.

The line at the funeral home was small for an Irish wake. Most people in attendance were friends of Michael's parents because Michael had very few friends. The doors had just opened and people were creeping in to pay their respects. Jake was standing alone in line when three guys approached from behind, filing into line. As they moved toward the entrance, Jake listened to them reminisce about Michael McNulty and the good old days. They appeared to be about the same age as McNulty.

"He was one crazy bastard," said a stocky guy with a suit that was too small for his frame.

"Yeah, but not as crazy as Steve," Kevin, the taller of the three said.

The stocky guy socked him on the arm, "You would know that better than anyone, Kevin. Remember when we were kids and Haney and Brock jousted on unicycles?"

"Yeah," Kevin chuckled. "We were bloody nuts back then. I was Brock's coach, remember? And McNulty was Haney's coach."

"Haney ended up winning that match, caught Brock right in the balls, and knocked him face first into the ground," the stocky guy said, remembering. "Hell, I thought he killed him."

"Yeah, those were some crazy times, weren't they?" Kevin added.

As they entered the building, Jake's mind was working in overtime trying to place the name, Brock. Stopping to sign his name in the guest book, Jake handed the pen to the person behind him and kept moving into the main room. Just before he entered the receiving line, it hit him. The gun that was used in the death of father LaPage had been stolen from the real estate guy, and his name was Brock.

Jake passed through the line offering his condolences to people he had never met, and he knelt to say a prayer for a man he didn't really know. Once finished, he waited for Kevin to pass through the line. After his prayer was finished, Kevin started toward the door where he would wait outside for his two friends.

Jake approached with his badge in hand. "Hello, my name is Jake Waterfield." He discretely displayed his shield. "May I have a word with you outside for a minute?"

Kevin's mind started to race. *What did I do?* He followed Jake outside.

"Your name is Kevin, right?"

"Yeah, that's right." He couldn't think of anything that he had done wrong recently, so he decided against making a run for it.

Jake noticed his color was whitening a tad. "I was in line ahead of you and I overheard you talking about a jousting game you played with Michael McNulty when you were kids."

Kevin was confused. What the hell did a detective care about that, he wondered. "Yeah, what about it?"

"Let's just say I'm interested in jousting," Jake dodged. You said that Brock jousted against Haney, right?"

"Yeah, that's right." He was now getting cocky.

"How well do you know Brock?"

"I used to know him when we were kids. I haven't seen him in years."

"Do you remember what his father did for a living?"

"Everyone knows his father is a real estate agent, his picture is all over the paper."

"Yeah, that's right," Jake said as if he was just recollecting.

Kevin's two friends came walking over. "I gotta go," Kevin said.

"Just one more thing," Jake said, "Was Brock and Haney friends?"

"Are you kidding, they hated each other," Kevin spewed out.

"Why isn't Haney here today? He and McNulty were best friends, right?"

"He would be here if he could, but I doubt they would release him from the hospital."

"What do you mean?" Jake asked.

"Haney is on his death bed. He has pancreatic cancer."

Kevin observed that the detective had a slight change of expression. "It's funny how these two guys were best friends and spent their entire lives raising hell, and now, one is dead and the other is dying, both from cancer," Kevin said. "Maybe they both ate bad mushrooms or something. Who the hell knows?"

"Right," Jake said. "Who knows? Thanks, I appreciate it."

Jake watched Kevin and his friends' walk away discussing what Jake had wanted. He glared up at the sky and saw that the clouds were rolling in fast. Extending his arm, he looked at his watch. It was 4:33 p.m. as he started down the street.

The doors to The Angels of Mercy Hospital were on a censor and they automatically opened as Jake approached the entrance. Scanning the lobby area, he spotted the information booth and headed directly over and addressed the attendant. "Hello, I'm here to see a Mr. Stephen Haney, please."

The elderly woman behind the booth smiled and began to punch keys on her computer. Jake thought it was a good job for a senior citizen. "He's in room 618 in the east wing. Go down this long hall and take a left," she pointed. "Follow that hallway to the elevators on your right. Take it to the sixth floor."

"Thank you," Jake said and he started in the right direction. People were darting left and right as he turned the corner to the second hallway. Walking past a flower shop, he stopped and peered through the window. *Should I buy flowers for someone that may have committed murder? He is a dying man, why not?* Jake walked in and went to the counter and purchased a bouquet of mixed flowers for eighteen dollars.

It was just past five thirty when Jake reached room 618. He hoped Stephen was awake, and he figured supper time was his best opportunity. With flowers in his left hand, he pushed open the door with his right and walked in.

Stephen was alone in his room and lying awake in bed, glaring up toward the ceiling at nothing in particular. Leveling his head, he watched Jake approach with flowers in his hand. Jake scanned the room and noticed that it was flowerless and he was glad he brought them.

"I was wondering if anyone was going to bring me flowers," Stephen said in a weak voice. "It never crossed my mind that it would be a cop." He broke a smile that appeared like it may have hurt.

"Hello, Stephen. I'm glad to see that you remember me." Jake placed the flowers on the table.

"Bring them here," Stephen asked. Jake handed them over and Stephen brought them to his nose, briefly inhaling. "Anything is better than the smell in here." He handed them back.

"How are you doing, Stephen?" Jake placed the flowers down and pulled up a chair.

"The best free drugs I've ever had."

Jake didn't respond. "Well, you have a room all to yourself, no loudmouth roommate to contend with."

"Yeah, he probably would have opted out after a few hours with me anyway. What brings you to my humble abode, Detective?"

Jake pulled his chair a little closer, noticing how dried up he looked. "Yesterday I attended Michael McNulty's wake and I came to learn that you were in here, so I thought I'd stop by."

Stephen looked away and began speaking in the other direction. "I fought with them to let me go to the wake, but they wouldn't agree to let me out. I would have split from here, but I'm too weak." He turned his head back around facing Jake. "I won't ask you how he looked."

Not much worse than you, Jake thought. "I ran into a guy named Kevin Garber and he told me about a game you guys played as kids, jousting on unicycles."

Stephen smiled. "What a game that was," he said. "Not for the weak and timid." He coughed and it rolled on for a few seconds.

Jake handed him the water and he slowly drank through a straw. "Who came up with that crazy idea?" Jake asked with a grin.

"As far as I know, I invented jousting on unicycles."

"I hear you were the champ," Jake said. "Garber talked about the day you knocked Wren Brock on his ass to win the day."

"Yeah, Brock was a tough opponent, gave me a run for my money."

"That brings me to another point," Jake said. "It wasn't until today that I put two and two together," He moved in a little closer. "The gun that Father LaPage was killed with was stolen from Wren Brock's father's house back in 1973. Right about the time you and Wren were knocking each other on your asses," Jake noted. "It's common knowledge that you two despised each other, and that you might have gone the extra mile to get even with him."

Stephen's eyes appeared wider. "What's your point detective?"

"The gun that was used to murder LaPage was stolen from the Brock home," Jake said. "Also, after doing a little digging, I found out that Michael's brother Jonathan was an altar boy for father LaPage for a couple years. I also learned that he took his own life during the media frenzy on LaPage's child molestation scandal."

Stephen pointed to the water and Jake handed it to him. He drank, but didn't say anything.

"After Bishop Reardon confessed to the murder of Robby Anderson, I couldn't figure out who forced LaPage to confess to a murder he didn't commit," Jake continued. "Then it hit me, both you and Michael were prime suspects in the murder."

"It sounds like a fairy tale to me," Stephen shrugged.

"No, it was actually quite clever and you are *one* clever character," Jake complimented him. "You were able to kill two birds with one stone."

"I think you give me far too much credit, Detective." A coughing fit ensued and Jake handed him the water bottle.

"I don't think so," Jake said. "Michael took his revenge and killed LaPage because he had sexually abused his brother when he was a child. The abuse haunted Jonathan throughout his adult life, and even though he tried to sequester it, it all came back to the surface with the extensive media coverage of the other abuse victims." Jake grasped his jaw. "The bonus was the taped confession by LaPage for the murder of Robert Anderson."

"It sounds like a fabulous book, detective; fiction, of course."

"Fiction, I think not," Jake said. "Both of you were prime suspects, and you probably thought that LaPage killed the boy anyway, so you made him confess, clearing you and Michael, and at the same time, Michael sealed his revenge for the abuse of his brother." Jake smirked. "You wrapped the whole thing up very nicely and you slapped a big red bow on it."

"Have you come here to arrest me?" Stephen asked. "Do you know that I'm in stage four with pancreatic cancer?" Stephen looked out the window. "Do you know that less than ten percent of patients with cancer of the pancreas survive? I just found out six weeks ago and I have less than eight weeks to live. Isn't that a bitch?"

CPSIA information can be obtained at www.ICGtesting.com
Printed in the USA
BVOW02s1853161113

336406BV00006B/29/P